By Guess and By God

by d. h. cook

*"Blessed are the peacemakers: for they
shall be called the children of God."*
-Matthew 5:9

THIS IS A WORK OF FICTION. ALL CHARACTERS,
ORGANIZATIONS, AND EVENTS PORTRAYED IN THIS NOVEL ARE
PRODUCTS OF THE AUTHOR'S IMAGINATION OR ARE USED
FACTIOUSLY. APART FROM WELL-KNOWN HISTORICAL
FIGURES, ANY SIMILARITY TO REAL PERSONS, LIVING OR DEAD,
IS PURELY COINCIDENTAL AND NOT INTENTIONAL.

EDITED BY ROSE O'KEEFE.

COVER ART COPYRIGHT © 2012 BY LAURA CHARLES STUDIO

PRINTED IN THE UNITED STATES OF AMERICA.

FOR INFORMATION (INCLUDING SPECIAL MARKETS PURCHASES
FOR EDUCATIONAL, BUSINESS, OR SALE PROMOTION USE)
CONTACT: **WWW.NOVELISTDUANECOOK.COM**

COOK, D. H. (DUANE HAROLD), 1951-
BY GUESS AND BY GOD

LIBRARY OF CONGRESS CONTROL NUMBER: 2012919517
ISBN-10: 0615652948
ISBN-13/EAN-13: 978-0615652948
BISAC CATEGORY: FICTION / HISTORICAL

For Barb,

Merry Christmas and Happy New Year.

I hope you will enjoy my new novel, which begins with some Cork family history. Carol's grandfather raised rabbits for the US Army in Idaho and the family moved to California due to our grandmothers poor health.

May your days be filled with joy, hope, and peace.

Duane Mark

12/2012

To Patsy, My Encourager

ONE

The old farmer stormed through the door. "Get me a Gatling gun!"

Conkin looked up from the figuring he had been doing to see Jethro Buick charging toward his counter, mad as a hornet, crushing his straw hat in his closed fist. "Pardon me?"

"You heard me! Get me a Gatling gun! I told the major I wanted a gun big enough to kill a man, and he told me he'd use a..."

Conkin wrinkled his eyebrows and completed his sentence as he set down his reading glasses, "...Gatling." The major was the town's self-proclaimed Civil War veteran and expert on all things military; he was also a whole deck short of a few cards! "Now, Jethro, you've got plenty of guns."

"Yeah? Twenty-two. Shotgun. No, I need something to kill a man! NOW!"

"Do you even know..."

The farmer straightened up, "Of course." Wondering if he was pronouncing it correctly he mumbled, "Gatting, or Gatling? Something like that?"

"Yeah, something like that." Conkin shook his head. It was his own damn fault. He was the one who put the sign out: *Conkin's - Where You Can Get Anything!* It was generally true if not literally. An easy touch with every salesmen who wandered into his general store, he had listened to sales pitches a thousand times with a closing line like, "You won't regret taking three." Looking around his store he'd often thought to himself, 'I regret taking one!' Now he had stuff piled to the rafters.

He was startled back to reality when Jethro slammed his fist on the counter. "Whatsthematter! My credit's good!"

Well, it was an interesting request, even for this odd ball farmer. He scratched his chin while looking Jethro Buick in the eyes, before slowly turning to his buddies sitting at the table behind him. His associates assembled that afternoon to form a local Civilian Board. Congress was about to declare war and pass some law they were calling the Selective Service Act of 1917 to register men for military service in Europe. The State of Idaho was getting a jump on things and the town of Lewiston, as county seat of Nez Perce County, was doing its part.[1]

With a sly smile Conkin asked, "Well? What do you think, boys?"

Without a pause, they gazed at one another and played right along. "Gatling would do it."

"No doubt."

"That would be my choice!"

They looked at one another, nodding.

"Yeah, it would. You will probably want to sit on him first. Get him pinned down real good. Then take the Gatling and aim it at the middle of his torso. Crank it real hard for thirty seconds. Should get the job done."

Jethro frowned, blinked, and got a curious look on his face trying to picture a gun where one would sit on the target. It took everything Conkin had to keep from breaking up. Not knowing what a Gatling gun was, the farmer also didn't have a clue he was the butt of their joke. Nothing was going to deter him from vengeance. He was seeing red, and anger had closed his ears.

"You sure you wanta kill him? Maybe ya oughta just like--well, maybe--just maim him?"

"Yes, I'm gonna kill him. The kid got my virgin daughter in the family way. I bring him into my home and the little bastard takes advantage of my sweet, innocent Carolin."

"Carolin? How old is she?"

"Fourteen."

"Well. I can see why you are mad." His friends shifted in

---

[1] The Selective Service Act of 1917 (40 Stat. 76) was passed by the 65th United States Congress on May 18, 1917 creating the Selective Service System. All males aged 21 to 30 were required to register for 12 months of military service.

their chairs, knowing half the men in Lewiston could be the father. Carolin always was a 'friendly' girl.

Conkin rummaged through the drawers in the table of his workbench. "Hum, I don't see one? But I am sure I had one in here at one time."

His friends, once again, leaned right in. "Didn't you sell that last week?"

Conkin continued rummaging. "They are pretty popular during springtime, when love is in the air? Must be fresh out!"

"Ah, yes. So many virgin daughters gettin' in the family way this time of year, ya naturally get a run on Gatling's."[2]

"Guess I'll have to special order one for you," said Conkin as he took up his pad and pencil, moistening the pencil point with his tongue.

"How long will that take?"

His eyes nearly gave it away. He couldn't reply and ducked into an aisle to keep from breaking up. But he was back in a few seconds with a heavy wooden chest marked: .45 Government cartridges. "Well, at least I found the ammunition." He plopped the chest down on the table with a thud, stopped to eye it and rub his chin before leaving. He could his friends were ready to explode with laughter. He returned holding a Schofield Cavalry Revolver with a seven-inch barrel manufactured nearly forty years earlier. Blue with a well-worn leather holster it had last seen service in Cuba and Puerto Rico during the Spanish-American war. "Until the Gatling comes in, you can take this. Takes the same bullets. How 'bout if I let you have the revolver and a handful of cartridges, until your order comes in?"[3]

---

[2] American inventor Dr. Richard J. Gatling of Indianapolis, Indiana, designed his rapid fire, revolving battery gun in 1861. Gatling's terrifying weapon was designed to "reduce the size of armies" and "show how futile war is."
This forerunner to the modern machine gun required a single operator to 'crank' the gun, eliminating the need for triggering and hammering. Typically, six barrels revolved around a central shaft. The gun fired off gravity-feed cartridges at an astounding rate. In the Spanish-American War, during the Battle of San Juan Hill, three Gatling guns fired 18,000 rounds of .30 Army smokeless cartridges in eight and half minutes, cleared the hill top and decimated the Spanish military. (If the soldier's arms had held out for all the cranking, they could have shot nearly 23,000 rounds--almost 15 rounds, or three full turns of the six barrels, each second).

[3] The Smith & Wesson model 3 (better known as the Schofield

Jethro grunted.

"I should get about, oh, three for the revolver. But I'll tell ya what. You take the revolver and these cartridges." He reached into the chest and pulled out a handful of shells and laid them on the table. "If you change your mind..."

"I won't."

"Well, if you change your mind, or the kid does right by the girl, you can return it 'no charge' until the Gatlin gets here. Whatdoyasay?"

The farmer thought a moment, "Fair 'nough." With two swipes of his left hand, he pocketed the cartridges, picked up the revolver, turned, and stormed out.

As soon as the door shut behind him, the men broke out laughing; slamming hands on the table and and tipping chairs.

"Aren't you afraid he'll shoot the kid?"

"Nah! I figure if he shoots from a hundred yards away, the arc of them bullets will put 'em into the dirt. And if he's less than a hundred, well, with the weight of that gun, he's more likely to blow off his toenails. So the kid is pretty safe." But after thinking about it for a minute he turned somber. The merchant called over for his son, who had been watching the proceedings while sorting nails. He quickly and quietly came and stood next to his father. Conkin put his arm around his son and whispered, "Well, I guess you best go tell Romeo it's time to skedaddle. Now."

Two dozen men were already seated on hay bales in the back of the wooden wagon, drawn by two powerful draft horses.

"Whatsthename?"

"George. George Cash," he lied. He looked again, folded,

Cavalry Revolver) was a single-action, top-breaking revolver produced by Smith & Wesson. It was named after Major George W. Schofield, based on his recommendation for design modifications incorporated in the model 3. Smith & Wesson, in naming the gun after the Major, obtained significant military contracts for the revolver. It took a variety of .44 and .45 cartridges.

and returned the one dollar bill to his front pants pocket. It was all he had. George was as good a name as any--good enough for the Father of Our Country. He figured 'Cash' should be easy to remember, as long as he didn't spend this last dollar.[4]

Eddie wrote 'George Cash' in the ledger. "Welcome, George. Have a seat on the wagon." George climbed aboard. He was hungry and cold. He hadn't eaten in two days and was thinking if he was lucky he could snatch fruit while picking and maybe get supper before the sun went down. But it was early spring--he might be planting fruit trees, but he wouldn't be harvesting.

"Where ya from?" the stranger next to him asked in a low, quiet voice, without looking up.

"Lewiston." He had seen a handbill where men were needed for farm work up north. It was 180 miles to Porthill, Idaho; just the right distance away, he figured. George wrapped himself in his arms and asked the stranger back, "How 'bout you?"

"Coeur d'Alene."

George had never heard of it. The men all around them were quiet and George, figuring he was intruding on their sleep, sat back to think about what had brought him here over the last four days since Conklin's son caught up with him to warn about the pissed off farmer. He hadn't returned to the house to collect his belongings. He had walked, hitched rides on wagons, forged streams, and slept in rock caves he had stumbled upon. As long as it was light, he was on the move. Frequently he looked back, convinced that wild animals were tracking him. He would pick up rocks and toss then toward predators--both real and imagined. The last night, though exhausted by his travels, he pressed on, walking dirt roads by moonlight to get to the meeting point identified in the handbill before the 6 a.m. departure time.

The horses pulled the wagon north. The sun was beginning to shine on the pink and purple Selkirk Mountains to the left. Snow still graced the peaks. The birds were chirping

---

[4] The dollar was an 1898 "Educational Series" Silver Certificate issue. The obverse side was covered with allegorical figures representing "history instructing youth" and the reverse contained portraits of George and Martha Washington.

and George heard the swish of the Kootenai River from his right, as it twisted and turned, flowing along toward the Canadian border a few miles ahead. The soil was fertile between the river and the foothills in this northernmost section of the Idaho panhandle. There was plentiful squirreltail wild rye, needle-and-thread grass, goldenbush, and white clover. They came to the crest of a hill and George was astonished at what he saw. From this far away, the motion of the rabbits looked like a rolling sea. In a minute--for as far as the eye could see--there were thousands and thousands of Cottontail rabbits. Fences boxed in each acre.

"Here we are, boys!"

Two

George spent that first morning, as he would spend every daylight hour for the next four months, moving rabbits. Two men worked each one acre pen to prevent the rabbits from eating all the grass and clover. Each man carried either a spade or a hoe, though some never used their tool for anything but leaning.

"Why the shotguns?" Men with firearms circled the farm.
"I don't know."
George turned to another worker, "Why do those men have guns?"
"Keep hawks away."
Hawks would attack the rabbits during the day, unless deterred by guards waving their arms and an occasional blast. A little noisy deterrent went a long way. But during the night, there was little to be done to prevent owls from taking their share of the bounty. They sailed along quietly; the down of their feathers muffling their slightest sound, searching out their prey with their keen night vision. Screeching the rabbits into panic they sent their meals running in front of them, where they swooped down and talons closed around little bodies, puncturing hearts and lungs, before heading back to the nest to shred their feast.
"When you hear the shotguns, stay away from the strange meat at dinner."

It was noon before George got his meal. About an hour earlier, he had smelled the sweet smoke of an apple-wood fire.

Two

A few of the hands carried baskets down to the south end of the property and soon the smell changed to roasting rabbits and his mouth began to water. A pistol shot echoed against the foothills and the men dropped what they were doing and briskly walked toward the fire.

George began to ask, "What are they...", but stopped in mid-sentence when he figured it to be the call for dinner. They didn't have to call him twice.

The men lined up at the grills on wheel carts marked: Property of US Army. He mirrored the old man in front of him as he picked up a tin plate, fork and cup. He was served a piece of meat, bread, boiled potato, and coffee. Before leaving the cart, George, drooling, popped a whole boiled potato in his mouth and swallowed.

The old-timer asked, as he led him to a bench and table under a large tent, "New here?"

George replied, having finished his third potato before sitting down, "Yes. Got in this morning." He picked up the meat with the bread and pushed it all into his mouth.

"Well, get while the gettin's good. You'll like it here. Uncle Chet's a good man."

He slurped down coffee to clear his throat before asking, "Uncle Chet?"

"We all call him that. Chester LaVoy. Owner of the farm. He is out here every day. Right there." He pointed to a slim man near the end of the food line, who looked like any other farm hand. He was nearly bald, with kindly eyes, long fingers on big hands, and large ears. "You'll meet him. Works easy. Foods always the same--rabbit. Hawk or owl occasionally. If they find any injured or dead rabbits, that's our dinner. If the guards pick off a predator, we get that. Otherwise, just potatoes." There was a long pause. "Haven't had a slitherdown of late."

"A what?"`

The old man laughed. "A slitherdown." There was another long pause before the old-timer continued, "When you've only had a potato to eat for a few days, you might come along a new borne kit. You know, eyes not even hardly open yet. When we move the rabbits the babies get lost from their mamas. Well, they are just gonna starve to death. So, you know, you're doing both of ya a big favor, really. You'll get used to it if you have to do it. Remember--swallow, don't chew. The whimpering only lasts until they hit your stomach."

8

With that, the old-timer stood up and took his cup to get coffee, while George sat stunned.

Herding rabbits became easy, once George used his feet to encourage the rabbits to move, instead of bending down and using his hands (or as an old timer had taught, "Use your brains, instead of your back!"). The pens were a square acre, fenced with wire. Because the rabbits would gobble up nearly all vegetation before being moved to another spot, the hands made sure the land was not denuded and vegetation could grow back in a few weeks.

He got his chance to meet Chet two days later.
"What's your name, kid?"
"George Dollar...uh, George Cash."
"Whereyafrom?"
"Baltimore."
"Shit, you're a long way from home! What brings ya out this way?"
"I gotta bad habit. I like to eat."
Chester judged him to be fifteen or so. "Where are your parents?"
"I'm an orphan," he lied.
"Do you have any children of your own?" Chet said with a straight face.
"I don't think so."
"You don't know?"
"Dropped my seed everywhere I could from here back to Baltimore, but just didn't stick around to find out."
Chester laughed hardily. He liked him immediately.

When Chet was done eating, he said, "Nice to have you with us, George. A bit of advice. Keep away from the back feet. The big males will kick the snot out of ya, if you're not careful. Don't scare 'em and don't hurt 'em and they'll be happy to be your future dinner."
George laughed. He liked Chet, too, and would try to squeeze over to eat next to him every day.
"There's a war a-coming, George. Everybody with any sense knows that. They have been fighting it out in Europe already for a long time. We'll get sucked in soon enough. Just the politicians haven't figured it out. But the US Army knows--gave me a contract for rabbits. Gotta raise 'em and get

'em on the train south."

Chet invited George to his house one evening after supper. He took him into his study, closed the door, invited him to have a seat, and sprawled onto the sofa.

"George, men are as different as the sun is from the moon. Some men scamper around kicking at rabbits at every turn. They'll gouge at them with a spade just to make them whimper. Like they are mad at the little creatures. It takes all kinds of S.O.B.'s to make up the world, and there ain't one missing."

George thought back to a rumor Chet fired a worker on the spot for having carnal relations with a rabbit. Forming that picture in his mind, he thought better of it--too late; in an instant it was captured like a snapshot.

"Others are gentle, even sweet to the little creatures. They nudge rabbits and their kits along, like a shepherd."

George thought of the man he partnered with that day. "Johnny picks a rabbit up by the scuff of the neck, pets it, and whispers before carefully returning it to the ground. Musta done it fifty times today."

"They are paralyzed when you pick them up like that. Just like their mama does. I wonder if a wolf does that--pick them up by the scuff of the neck, you know, before slinging them up in the air to catch them in their jaws to crush the bones." George startled with that thought. "I try to be gentle, even when I have to kill one. You know; deformed, mangled. Some rabbits can be vicious, gnaw on a neighbor. It is a kindness to put some out of their pain. Just pick him up by the scuff, let 'em relax a bit, then crack your wrist down hard--like you're cracking a whip. Snaps their neck every time. It's a kindness to do it fast, so they don't linger."

"Can you read, George?"

"Well..." he started to lie. He could read just enough to get by if she studied and sounded out the words.

"You see all these books." He waved his hands around the room. "They contain much of the world's knowledge. I'm blessed that my mama taught me at an early age. A man who can read is never alone or without the means to find an answer. It is a skill few men have and fewer still cherish. But it is a blessing. Would you like to learn?"

"I guess."

"Stop by after supper tomorrow night and we'll get started." He did; and every night thereafter.

The large scale, open air rabbit farming was winding down as summer turned to fall. The daily visits of Army meat inspectors and veterinarians were coming to an end. Most of the hands left for greener pastures and the fall harvests from the Ohio valley in the east to California in the west. They were sorting down the final rabbits to go to slaughter from next year's breeding stock of the largest, most healthy rabbits. "Heck of a choice I am making about you", George said as he held a big male facing him. "If I throw you left, you'll be riding the big adios to Rabbit Heaven today. But if I throw you right, you'll be screwing your brains out for the next six months, while I bring you food and water. What's it gonna be?" He threw him right. The rabbit landed gently, turned, bobbed his cotton tail, and sat, looking at George. "What, too stupid to know you outta be smiling?"

George and Chet watched together as the last train to Denver pulled away. Trains in the area had been used to transport minerals from the local mines for decades, but this train was going to the slaughterhouse. The rabbits were spooked into running out of the freight cars. As the rabbits came down the ramp they were popped on the back of the head with a small baseball bat to stun them, bled, skinned, and slaughtered. The meat was cut into inch square cubes, tossed into a large cauldron with carrots and potatoes. By the time they were done cooking the stew, the meat was tough, stringy, tasteless, and ready for industrial food size cans marked: US Army Rabbit Stew. Nothing was wasted; the pelts were sold for coats and the bones used for gelatin. Not to mention, they made a lot of money on lucky rabbit's feet. Of course, they weren't all that lucky for their original owners.

"George, I like men who are gentle with the rabbits. I look for that in the men I ask to stay on through the winter. I want you to stay on. I promise the food will get better. I just got the 1918 Rabbit contract."

The few hands who stayed on were mostly old-timers who had worked for Chet since he started the farm. George was by far the youngest. The rabbits were cared for in indoor pens during the fall and winter. The old men tended the vegetable gardens, fished, and hunted. It looked to be a dull, long winter.

During the fall of 1917 George learned the truth about life in Porthill, Idaho. Months of hard work, where one never sat down, were followed by months of light work, where one rarely stood up. As Chester LaVoy had promised, he ate better. The men fished for salmon and trout along the peaceful banks of the Koonatei River. They hunted elk, moose, deer, and turkey in the foothills. Migrating geese and ducks met their fates and filled the dinner tables. The fall harvest provided plentiful vegetables. The Pacific Ocean, far to the west, continually provided a marine layer of air over the mountain peaks, which floated down and nestled into the valley. It moderated the weather, taking a bite out of the cold. Life was plentiful and comfortable. In the evening, the men sat around the fire in the large cabin they called home and told stories over coffee. No liquor was allowed; beer was only taken on special occasions. After a few months George noticed life was next to perfect in Porthill with only one thing missing.

Just before Thanksgiving, William (Will) and Marguerette, their six-year-old son, Harold (whom everyone called Billie), their fourteen-year-old daughter, Rebecca, and their Saint Bernard, Bob, returned for winter. They had followed this pattern for the last three years, as Rebecca turned out to be a distraction to the farm hands. It was nothing she did; she just happened to be beautiful, elegant, and graceful. When she rode by on her horse, without a care in the world, fifty men stopped work to watch her. Her mother felt more comfortable moving the family north to Uncle Jack's farm, where there were more women and they blended in.

Chet regretted the loss of Will, as he was a hard worker and wonderful brother; but his neighbor, Jack, gained a great worker and a bond formed between the two farms. During spring, Will moved across the border into Canada to spend time at Uncle Jack's. He was not really anybody's Uncle. His farm mirrored the LaVoy's, pressing against the US-Canada border from the north. By Thanksgiving, Will returned his family to LaVoy's farm for winter.

By tradition, all farm hands were invited into the Big

House for Thanksgiving and Christmas dinners.

"Dear Jesus, we thank you for your bounty and your blessing. Thank you that we have this time to reflect on our good fortune at being your children. Amen. Let's eat."

Will jumped up to slice the turkeys, while Chester carved off large slabs of roast venison. There were mashed potatoes, gravy, sweet potatoes, squash, corn, berry and pumpkin pies, and coffee with rich cream.

"Boys, I noticed your conversation has gone all to heck since we put this food on the table. What's got your tongue?" All laughed with full mouths.

"I think this turkey drumstick is what's got my tongue!" They grinned and kept feasting.

"Boy, that was something," moaned one man as he wiped his face with the back of his sleeve and pushed himself away from the table. "Yes, Sir, doesn't get much better than this."

"And to think we get to do it all over again in a month!"

All during dinner George couldn't keep his eyes off of Rebecca. And she couldn't keep her eyes off George. They talked quietly between themselves at the table as if they were alone.

During December, George continued coming to the Big House in the evenings for his reading lessons with Chet. But everyone noticed he was showing up far earlier than he had been. He drank coffee, always with two spoons of sugar and one of cream, and Rebecca sat next to him. No hand had ever transgressed coming to the Big House without an invitation or early for an appointment. Will was a bit surprised by the appearance of George at the kitchen table so soon after supper, but he couldn't say much if his brother permitted it--it wasn't his house, after all. Besides, he had more pressing concerns at the moment.

Rebecca's mother, Marguerette, had returned from the north with a persistent cough. Chet asked his brother about it.

"Yeah, she's had it all year. She had it when we left in the spring."

"Doesn't sound good."

"I been trying to get her to see Doc, but she keeps putting it off."

"You better press her a bit."

"Consumption! Oh, my gosh!" Chester had to sit down.[5]

"She apparently has been hiding that she has been coughing up blood for half a year," his brother replied as he sat next to him.

"Oh, Will, what can be done? My Gawd, when was she going to tell you?"

Will quietly said, "She didn't want us to worry."

"Worry? How could you not?"

"I guess she figured..." He trailed off.

Chester thought a moment, before quietly replying, "I know. Any of us may have done the same. What's Doc say?"

"He suggests we take her to Colorado or Arizona. Sanitarium."

"My gosh."

"Yes. Supposta be the best thing. Dry climate. Peaceful."

"When?"

"He wants us to go now?"

"Now? In winter? What are you gonna do for work? What about your kids?"

"I wish I knew."

It was a torturous two days, as Will talked to each child in private. The three took long walks together and visited their mother every few hours.

"Chet, we are gonna wait until after New Year's Day. We got a telegram--they found a place for her in Arizona. I wanted the kids to stay here with you, but Marguerette insists we take Harold." She couldn't think of being without her little boy.

"And leave Rebecca?"

"Yes."

"Here or at Jack's?"

"Here."

Chester was stunned. Finally he replied, "Well, of course,

---

[5] "Consumption" is the old-fashion term for tuberculosis. It describes quite well what happened to patients--they were consumed with fevers, chills, sweats, weight loss, pallor, and overpowering fatigue.

we'll do our best."

Getting Harold to go was more difficult than expected. People had not accepted when the family had not named him 'Will', after his dad. The name 'Harold' was not in either family--so they just started calling him 'Billie' and it stuck. He and his dog, Bob, were inseparable. Long hours at the sanitarium would be bad enough with a little boy in tow--a dog was out of the question, much less a dog the size of Bob.

As Christmas approached, Harold turned moody. "Son, you need to be brave. We can't take the dog. Your mother needs you with her. She may not have much time left, Son. It's decided--I don't want to hear any more about it."

Christmas was somber.

After Christmas, Chet was joking with Eddie. "I wonder if I will get him back to working!"

"Who?" frowned Eddie.

"George, of course!"

"Well, he does everything I ask him."

Chet grinned, "And if you need to ask him, you always know where to find him!"

Eddie laughed. "Were you and Tura like that one day?"

"Of course we were! I couldn't keep my mind off Tura. I wanted to spend every minute with her. Were you ever in love, Eddie?"

Eddie blushed and looked down. "Well, I guess I was, but she never paid me any mind."

"What did you do?"

He paused before he spoke. "I didn't do nothin'. I just kinda froze around her, know what I mean?"

"Where's she now?"

"Don't know. Long gone. A year or so ago, I saw her in town."

"And?"

"Well, my mouth went dry and I felt a little faint. My heart was beatin' hard. I got out a 'hello' and she smiled back and kept walking."

"I'll tell you something, Eddie. If you ever see her again, muster the nerve to stop her and tell her how you feel."

"I couldn't do that."

"Yes, you could. The worse thing that would happen is that she would walk away. And, you never know, the best thing

15

might."

George spent every spare minute with Rebecca.

"Do you ever go by Becky?"

"I hate the name, Becky. I am a Rebecca, and I'll always be a Rebecca. Do you like the name, George?"

Since he had made up his name on the spot, he hadn't given it much thought. "It's alright."

The crunch of winter's ice and snows gave way to the soggy, pitter-patter of spring rains. It was always a guessing game as to when to take the rabbits from their covered winter pens into the open-air, acre-sized pens. In many years, this one included, the explosion of kits made the decision for them. The good weather, followed by late spring rains, turned the rabbit pens into slimy mud and made caring for the rabbits hard work. In good weather and bad the rabbits needed tending. During spring thunderstorms men dawdled in the Little House or drank coffee made in large boiling pots in the food tent. A few men broke out smokes and others cards to kill the time. Unlike evenings, when smokes and card brought rest and relief, this brought no joy. It was good to be off their feet, out of danger from the lightening, and away from the risk of slipping and breaking a leg. But every minute in shelter was a minute which would have to be made up before the day was done.

On a day filled with storms and weather delays, Chet came home bone weary. Climbing the back steps to the Big House, he removed his coat, overalls, and muddy boots in a room off the kitchen. The kitchen help would recover the overalls, clean them, dry them on the wood stove, and hang them on the doorknob leading into Chet's room, by breakfast. He threw on a robe and walked through the kitchen with a simple greeting: "Evening, ladies." The ladies smiled back, already busy making his supper. Rebecca had eaten and gone to bed hours before.

Chet trudged up to his bedroom. At the landing he had thought about skipping supper and climbing into bed, but decided against it since the women were already busy with preparations. He cleaned up in the bathroom and returned to his room to dress for supper. On his dresser he noticed a letter had arrived from his brother, Will. He reached for it eagerly, but stopped as if the letter were hot. Reading it should wait until after he had eaten.

After supper, he thanked the ladies and trudged back up the stairs, turned on the lamp by his bed, and unfolded his spectacles. Maybe it was instinct that told him to wait for the privacy of his room to read the letter. Maybe it was fear.

Will's letter was of despair. Marguerette's consumption had only gotten worse in the warmer climate. The doctors had already begun, and not too subtly, preparing Will for the worst. She was down to 93 pounds. Each violent, continuous cough strangled up blood-tinged sputum and left her an ounce lighter. Chet sat in his rocking chair and wiped tears from his eyes, before he could muster the courage to finish. The note talked about Harold. 'Doctors think she is too contagious to have her son nearby.' Near the end, Chet had written, 'I don't know how I can take care of Rebecca, if Marguerette passes. What do I know about taking care of girls?'

Chet, as if he knew what was coming next, mumbled, "And what do you think I know?"

Then it came: 'I would like you to raise Rebecca. Or take her up to Jack's place to be raised, if Maggie goes.' He returned the letter to its envelope, slipped it into a dresser drawer, and crawled into bed.

Over the next month, it became obvious to Chet that Rebecca and George had fallen in love. He had daydreams of George asking him for her hand in marriage. "Preposterous! It is for her father to decide," he had rehearsed replying in his mind, even though the thought of it brought a smile to his face. Rebecca was already like a daughter to him.

The couple walked and rode together every chance they had. Spring chores absorbed most of their spare time, so they cherished what little they had. Chet had been thinking it was about time for him to be sending Rebecca north to Uncle Jack's place, when she came to his study.

"Uncle Chet, I have been thinking I want to stay here this year instead of going to Canada?"

"Why?"

"Well, it just wouldn't be the same without my whole family there. You are my family now. I don't want to be away from you."

Chet, seeing through the little white lie, grinned and gave her a squeeze. "Whatever you want is great with me, Darlin'."

The next morning after breakfast, Chet sent for George to have a second cup of coffee with him on the porch. It was bright and cool, a gift from the previous day's rainstorms. Chet began to reminisce. "Altura loved it here."

"Who?" George asked.

"My wife, Altura. Everyone 'cept me called her Tura, but her real name was Altura. Isn't that a pretty name? Just as pretty as she was. She died more than a year ago. The Good Lord took her in her sleep. That's how I want Him to take me."

He paused before he went on and his hand swept the horizon. "She loved it here. Every bit of it." It was as if he was opening George's eyes for the first time. "See those mountains?" They looked together at the purple mountains to the west. Snow glistened on the peaks. "We climbed those peaks when we were courting. Drove the wagon up as far as we could on some old mining trails. Then it took us all day to climb up and back. Shit, I thought we were gonna have to sleep out that night. Wouldabeen cold! But luckily we spotted the wagon. There is a lake there where I proposed to her and where we were married a few months later. We didn't need a preacher to link us together. We were together from the start. But we asked God to put us together in His sight and she read from Genesis in the Bible.

"She loved making pies from the apples in the orchards near the foothills. Used the wild wheat that grows by the river to make the flour for the crusts. Lot of work to make those pies, I'll tell you. She called them her Idaho Apple Pies.

"I'd fish in the river just before dusk, while she would make a fire by our favorite bend in the river. Quiet. Secluded. Just seemed to amplify the sound of the river there. Take out fresh trout or salmon. I'd clean the fish with two swipes of my knife and she would have them in the fry pan almost before they quit wiggling. After supper we'd cuddle in a blanket until the fire died and the stars began to sparkle. Did that almost every week during spring and summer for forty years.

"The Big House was her pride and joy."

"Why did you name it the Big House?" It was much smaller than the house used for all the ranch hands.

"Oh, we didn't, really. We built a house for the crew. Just to keep the two straight, one was Big and the other Little."

"What did you name the farm?"

"We never gave it a name. People just called it the old Smith place or LaVoy farm."

George thought about that while Chet looked beyond the farm to the road which matched the shape of the river; he could see Altura in his mind running up the road with a basket of apples; wildflowers poked up along the side; their dog was running with her, barking and wagging his tail. Chet and Altura spent so much time together they could anticipate each other's thoughts. He could feel her looking at him, even now. He could smell her a thousand times a day. At night he would dream they were kissing and he could taste her lips. There wasn't an hour that went by where he didn't ache to touch her, just one last time.

George broke the silence, "Why don't you name the farm Altura?"

Chet smiled. "Maybe we should."

The crew assembled in the distance to begin tending the rabbits.

George drank his last sip of coffee and started to stand.

"No, George."

"What?"

"Sit."

"But the rabbits..."

"The rabbits can do without the two of us for a bit. Altura even loved the rabbits. 'Course we didn't raise them in those early days. They were wild here and plentiful. She could watch them for hours. Only she could cook them scrawny beggars so tender and flavorful. I never could figure how she did it.

"She loved her vegetable garden and the flowers she grew around the house. I could never keep all those flower's names straight. I couldn't tell the difference between a carnation and a petunia. She would ask me to clip a few roses and bring them in to decorate the kitchen table. She would laugh and say, "Well, that was close" and place them on the table through supper. But by the next morning, there would be these big red, fragrant flowers in their place. If I asked about it, she'd say she threw out the dandelions."

George laughed.

"I don't think they were really dandelions!"

Hours later they were still talking about Altura and the farm.

"When did you begin raisin' rabbits?"

"Oh, it hasn't been that long. Couple years."

"Why rabbits?"

Chet shrugged. "When the US Army came to me, they needed someone to come in and grow rabbits. It was cheap protein. Men going to war need food. The boys love rabbit stew--hardy food, easy to prepare. In large cans, it could be easily shipped and stored. The land was fruitful with plenty of vegetation for the rabbits. The grasses and clovers were ideal, as was the terrain. They gave me a large report on the land and told me if anything went wrong, they would cover me.

"I had to explain to them that I didn't have money to start it and they said we should go to the bank together. I was a bit reluctant, but I talked to Altura and she encouraged me to see Wilfred. So, we went--me and the army man.

"We spent an hour talkin' to Wilfred Addleman at the bank. That's when the army man handed him a government check. Said it was an advance on payment, if I would just sign the contract.

"Will's eyes bugged out when he saw the check. He pulled me aside and told me I'd be crazy not to take their offer, and if I didn't, he wanted to pay me top dollar for me to manage it and he'd buy the place off Smith. Well, I didn't want to do that, so I agreed to their contract. We've been pretty flush since."

Chester stood and stretched. "I guess we better get the cooks moving or the men won't have their dinner today. Come with me." They began the long walk to the south end of the farm. "Got a disturbing letter from my brother yesterday. Marguerette is not doing well." They were quiet as they walked side by side.

"So, tell me something, George."

"Yes?"

"You getting sweet on Rebecca?"

He couldn't answer. It wasn't that he didn't already know, it was like his jaw locked when he heard the question. But his blushing gave him away.

Chet looked over at him. "Thought so."

They strolled down to the grills where the cooks had the apple-wood fires roaring and were skinning the last of the rabbits.

Chet said to George, "Well, no slitherdown today!" Chet smiled as he looked at George. "By the way, George, we've never had a slitherdown here. That old coot likes to tell that to every new man. Shit, you think any of these men wouldn't kick a rabbit to death rather than eat a live kit?"

Chet yelled over to his foreman, "Eddie!"

Eddie came running, "Yes, Sir!"

"Eddie, I want a big sign out front--"Altura Farm." Can you start it today?"

"Yes, Sir!" Eddie said, thinking 'that will be a fun project!'

One day in the late spring of 1918, Eddie got the nod from the cooks--dinner was ready. It was approaching the longest day of the year and the blazing sun was straight up in the sky. They had worked since dawn and were just sensing the stirring of a breeze. Clouds were high and puffy, giving only brief shade. Eddie walked out from under the meal tent, raised his arm into the air, and pulled the trigger on the .45 caliber Colt.

Chet was standing against a fence pole with his arms on the wire. He had taken a break to survey the land. He had men working for as far as the eye could see. He loved the land. Life was good and plentiful; the only thing missing was Tura. At the crack of the pistol he grinned and laughed. "Well, boys, you know what that means!"

The men were already walking toward the dinner wagon at the south end of the property. Those with tools dropped them exactly where they were. Watching the men come to dinner each day was like watching maple syrup streaming down a stack of hot cakes--in steady motion.

Two

The men grabbed tin plates and forks and formed a line at the cook wagons. The cooks scooped chunks of rabbit and potato as quickly as their arms would move. The line moved rapidly and the men hurried to the long tables under the tent. George had been working in the foothills all morning and was one of the last to arrive. He waited patiently, checking for Chet, but never spotted him. He tried to have dinner with Chet every day and there had been only a few times when Chet hadn't eaten or had finished before George made it in. He went through the line and took one long last look, but to no avail. Perhaps Chet had gone into town.

George sat down at the first empty spot he found, far at the end of the tables, the furthest distance from the grills. He began to dig in. Eddie was nearby just starting his dinner. "Chet gone to town?"

"I saw him a half-hour ago at the north end," Eddie replied.

He tried to eat, but his curiosity got the better of him. George went back to find Chet. Spotting him a long way off, leaning against a fence, he yelled, "CHET!"

Chet didn't move. George quickened his pace. "Chet?" he said softly as he came upon him. Still standing there, head tipped forward, George noticed his neck was bulging and his eyes were open. George slowly approached. His heart was racing as he put his hand by the side of Chet's face. He wasn't sure how to check for a pulse, especially with his neck so distorted. Chet's body slumped to the ground.

"ED-DIE!" The scream ran up the backs of startled people from one end of the farm to the other.

"I don't know."

"Why?"

"Well, look at it! The top of his head. I think someone hit him with a pickaxe."

"Who'd do that to Chet?"

"I don't know. But cover him up. I'll get the sheriff."

The men went back to work after lunch; they didn't know what else to do. It was quiet while they labored and they would all pause to look over every so often. For George, it didn't seem right to leave Chet alone with just a piece of canvas over him--so he sat, occasionally rubbing his eyes, and waited next to him for most of the afternoon.

In the late afternoon sun, the sheriff and Eddie arrived and got off their horses. The Sheriff looked Chet over from head to toe without speaking.

"Enemies?" the Sheriff asked.

"Don't know of one," Eddie responded.

"Fired anyone recently?"

"Nope. Things been good."

"Valuables missing?"

"Well, I didn't think to ask. We can check the house."

"Don't bother. I'll take care of that myself. Ride over and get Doc."

Eddie didn't return with Doc until dusk. Eddie stopped by the house for a kerosene lantern, while Doc began looking Chet over carefully. He pinched and prodded, checking his neck repeatedly. He smelled the top of his head. Then he stood up.

"Well, shit!"

"Whatdayathink?" asked Sheriff Howell.

"I don't know fer sure, but I got a hunch. Get him to my place."

"Help me up with him, boys." Eddie took the canvas and laid it flat next to Chet. George, Eddie, Sheriff Howell and Doc grabbed Chet by his shoulders and knees and hoisted the lifeless man onto the canvas. They stepped back as Doc wrapped the canvas around Chet. Then they hoisted him into Doc's wagon for the trek home.

That evening, George came to the Big House to console Rebecca. Neither could eat nor sleep. He wrapped his arms around her. They talked little; grief and disbelief seized them.

Doc worked late into the night, but his hunch was confirmed. He probed with his straight Kelly forceps through the top of Chet's head and found it flattened a bit but nearly intact at the top of the spine. It clinked as he dropped the bullet onto a glass dish.

He was sitting next to Chet when his teenage son awoke and came into the room.

"You still up, Papa?"

"Yeah. Just finished with Chet."

"And?"

"I've never seen this before myself, but I've heard of it happening. Reportedly there have been men that have survived being hit in the head by a shot in the air. Lead is soft. Can bounce off things. Guess it hit him just right to cave in his skull like that and keep going." The bullet had arched in the wind, traveled from the south end of camp to the north in 45 seconds, and couldn't have hit Chet more squarely on the top of his head if they had dropped it from a foot above.

"He was a good man."

"The best."

"At least he is with Tura now."

"Yes. They say that part is a blessing."

Doc merely smiled. "Guess I'll mount up and get Sheriff Howell."

His son saw he was exhausted. "No, Papa. It can wait. You both had a tough day. I'll fetch him at dawn. Get some sleep."

Sheriff Howell had to console Eddie when he told him it was the bullet from his gun that killed Chet. "Could have happened anytime to anybody. Just had the wrong angle and wind. You didn't mean any harm, so don't go blaming yourself. Had to have been God's will to take Chet as He did. Chet's name was on that shell."

The sheriff sent a telegram off to Will and later that morning the best carpenters on the crew made Chet's casket from an oak tree in the foothills that Chet had loved. They lined it with his dog's blanket. It had been saved from when Misty wandered away to die on her own in her old age, two years earlier. They had kept it, always hoping Misty would return; knowing full well she wouldn't.

That evening Rebecca and the kitchen ladies washed, dressed, and laid Chet out on a bed they had carried down to the parlor and over the next two days all his friends and neighbors came to pay their respects. The morning of his funeral his men were allowed to come in from the fields in small groups to say their final goodbyes.

Rebecca and George expected a telegram back from Will about his brother's death. Or that he might show up any minute. But neither happened.

Before dusk, they lowered the coffin into the ground, next to Tura, where they used to fish at the bend of the river. Reverend Douglas Jackson said some words and read a few Scriptures, before the long parade of horses, carts and carriages returned to the farms and homes of those who had been touched by Chet's life.

Three weeks after the funeral, Rebecca finally did receive a telegram from her father: YOUR MOTHER DIED THIS MORNING. LETTER TO FOLLOW.

George continued to spend his evenings in the Big House after Chet died. He held Rebecca in his arms as they talked about Chet, Tura, her mother, and how they would manage the farm.

"Why did Chet have to die that way?"

George thought a while, "I don't know."

"I mean. We didn't even get to say goodbye to him." George sighed. "It seems unfair."

"Sure does. But, at least he and Tura are together."

"How do you know that?"

"Well, it says so in the Bible somewhere. And it is just one of those things you have to take as true."

"Yeah. But a bullet in the head."

"But, you know, when I saw him propped up there on the fence, he had a big smile on his face. He loved the rabbits, and the farm, and he loved his men. They were just heading down to dinner, and he liked them all being together. We were all family to him. He loved Tura the most and needed to be with her. I am sure he didn't feel any pain. Bullet went through his brain so fast, he never knew what hit him."

Her eyes widened. "Do you think so?"

"I know so. Really no more painful a death then it had

been for Tura when she died in her sleep." She held him close.

In the early morning George kissed Rebecca on the forehead and returned to the Little House to wash up, catch a little sleep, and change his clothes. Only once did a man tease George about staying at night with Rebecca.

"I'd say Chet's death worked out pretty well for you?"

"What?"

"I mean, moving up to the Big House. Spending all night with Rebec..."

The man never saw it coming. But everyone else in the house heard his jaw crack. George flattened him with one roundhouse punch.

He addressed all the men who had run in to see the commotion, not just the one he was standing over rubbing his chin: "She needs me right now. I'm not taking advantage of her. I wouldn't. We may marry one day, until then she is safe with me. I hope you will think better of her than this fella, so I don't have to repeat my lesson." He pushed his way through the men to get out of the house.

One evening, while sitting in Chet's library, Rebecca asked the question she had been afraid to ask for too long, "Why doesn't my father love me?"

"What? He does."

"He wants to be rid of me."

"What makes you think so?"

"He hasn't even acknowledged Chet's death! He hasn't come to get me since Mother passed away."

"Well, he is probably grieving?"

"I know he is grieving! Don't you think I am? We should be grieving together, as a family--Pa, Billie, and me."

George paused before answering. "Maybe he simply doesn't know how to raise a girl on his own. He has nobody to tell him. He thinks you are better off with the women here than with him."

She snapped, "I'm better off with the kitchen ladies than with him and Harold?"

George answered slowly and carefully, "That is probably what he thinks. And if that is what he thinks, he's doing what's best in his mind."

She held him especially close that night.

George had instructed the kitchen staff to give any letters from her father to him instead of Rebecca, "if and when it appears." It was a month before the letter Will said he would send arrived. When he left the fields and entered the Big House he heard a whisper, "A letter came today, Mr. George."

"Thank you, Alice." He drew a big breath and sat down at the dining room table. The first thing he saw startled him--it was addressed to Chester LaVoy. He quickly read through the greetings and small talk, into the meat of the letter--

'I can't take her. Harold is more than a handful for me. I am sure the lady folk can do better than me. If not, why don't you see if Uncle Jack will take her off your hands? Anyway they got a bunch more women up there that could raise her. Maybe you could marry her off to their son, John.'

It went on for a few more lines about moving to California and that he would write to let them know when they got settled. It was signed, 'Little Will'.

George walked into the kitchen. "Matches?"

A few months later, he walked up to Alice. "Tomorrow?" He had a smile from ear to ear. It took her a second to figure out what he meant. When the light came on, she brightened--"Yes!"

In the early morning George kissed Rebecca on the forehead and returned to the Little House to wash up. He changed into his nicest clothes--ones the kitchen ladies had sewn for him weeks before. He came back to the Big House as the ladies were busy cooking breakfast. "Morning!"

They turned, smiled, whispered a reply, and then noticed his outfit. "Whew? Where you going?"

He grinned, but didn't reply.

Alice's eyes brightened and she stood up, wiping her hands on a dish towel. "You'll gonna need that picnic basket today, ain't ya?"

"Yes, Ma'am!"

Rebecca came down later than usual for breakfast, wearing a white dress. The kitchen ladies hugged her. "My mama wore this when she was married, and so did Tura."

"Eddie, I'll be needin' the little wagon today."

"But, how will we..." It didn't take him long to figure out there was something special going on. "Sure, George."

Two

George returned to the Big House in the wagon and Alice met him at the door with blankets, flowers, firewood, and a large picnic basket. "If you had given me some warning I would have made a peach pie! Guess you have to make do with apple."

George grinned—"Apple! My favorite."

Rebecca came onto the porch carrying the family Bible. It was heavy, bound brown leather with a matching leather strap and brass buckle to hold it closed. An image of Jesus was embossed on the front with rays of light emanating from behind.

They rode sitting close together, arm-in-arm through the fields and into the foothills. They stopped at a tree stump. "There is where Chet's tree was."

"Uh-huh. He loved it here. They made his coffin from the tree."

They continued to ride to the bend in the river where Chet and Tura spent time together and were buried. "How about here?"

"Perfect!"

They laid out the blankets and picnic lunch. Rebecca read from the passage in the Bible she had marked in Genesis 2: "Therefore shall a man leave his father and his mother, and shall cleave unto his wife: and they shall be one flesh. And they were both naked, the man and his wife, and were not ashamed."

"Well, God. I've never heard this done before or seen it myself. But if it is good enough for Tura and Chet, it is good enough for Rebecca and me. Put us together, God, as husband and wife. Just like you did for Adam and Eve, we want to be married together. So do that for us."

"Yes, this is what we both want. To be together forever as man and wife."

They undressed, without taking their eyes off each other. George had not known how beautiful Rebecca really was until she stood there before him, naked and without shame. They made love until late afternoon, and then famished, ate their picnic lunch, finishing by feeding each other large slices of apple pie.

"Well, hope Tura and Chet weren't watching."

"Did it seem odd to you marrying and making love by these tombstones?"

"No, it seemed natural."

They lit a small fire and made love again until dark. When the fire was nearly burned out, leaving just a red glow, they hitched up the wagon, put everything in the seat and laid down cuddled together in back. George yelled, "Get home, Clyde" and the horse looked back before slowly heading for the barn.

Soon after they returned from their wedding, they moved into Chet's old room. The three ladies on the kitchen crew lived in the basement of the house, with none of the other bedrooms occupied. About five o'clock one morning, as they were getting up to start their day, they heard familiar noises from upstairs.

"Oh, gosh, they're at it again!"

"Mind your manners! You just have to overlook some things when there are newlyweds in the house!"

"How can he come home from working in the field all day and keep that up all night?"

Alice blushed. "Oh, stop it!"

Claire chimed in, "And the new Mrs. Cash always has a grin on her face these days!"

Claire and June giggled, while Alice's blush turned a darker shade. "There are just some things we mustn't talk about..."

"Me and the Mister had our fun for a few weeks, but nothing like this!"

"Maybe Mr. George is better equipped for this kinda business!"

"Oh!"

"Yes, Alice, if you'd married you'd know better about these things."

"Just leave out the oil can for George with a little note about bed springs and he'll get the picture." She grinned deviously.

"Oh, don't you dare!"

"Well, I must admit I miss my old man."

"Please, ladies, we need to get breakfast started."

When Chet, Tura, and Little Will's family had lived in the Big House, the three ladies on kitchen crew had barely enough time for helping with the men's dinner each day and cleaning up afterward, in addition to gardening, cooking, and tending the household chores. Now they could spend a few idle hours talking, speculating, and teasing.

As the summer grew hotter, the farm became infested with wood ticks and deer flies.

"Gawd, they are bad this summer!"

"We handed out extra handkerchiefs, but I'm not sure it is helping."

"Everyone wants to work near the dinner wagon. Smoke seems to keep the flies down."

"That doesn't work. Men are making their own flyswatters."

"We tried leaving rabbit guts to rot. Didn't help much."

"Did you try honey water and old eggs?"

"Yep. Hasn't helped either."

"I swear the men seem to spend more time swatting then they do workin'."

"Shit! I don't know what else to try."

As George came in one evening, swatting flies and making sure the screen door was closed tight, he saw Claire had left him an official government letter addressed to Chester at his place on the dinner table. He opened it and began to read. "Hmmm." He slipped the letter into his back pocket and went upstairs to see Rebecca. After supper, he told Rebecca he had some work to do and that he would be up later.

Claire commented, "Sure is quiet upstairs tonight!"

"Maybe they wore it out!"

"More likely he broke something!"

"Stop it, you two!"

"You didn't leave the oil can out, did you?" Alice said, then joined June in a giggle.

"I said, stop it!"

George spent two hours looking over things that Chet had written and his full signature. He hadn't left a will, so George was making one up for him. He looked over the government contract completely. It was for rabbits for the full next year. He couldn't believe the numbers of rabbits they were ordering or the amount they were willing to pay.

All he knew about wills is what he had heard about in literature and seen in the local newspapers. He kept it short and simple. He got out the dictionary to look up words he wasn't sure about, such as testament and bequeath. He practiced writing to make it look like Chet's longhand. After he had done it a few times, he was satisfied. He forged Chet's name on the will and dated it, August 19, 1916. He signed his own name as witness. He identified 'Rebecca LaVoy Cash' as beneficiary. Then he forged her signature on the US Army contract and placed the contract and will in a large envelope.

Before he went upstairs he burned his practice papers in the fireplace.

Rebecca stirred as he came into the bedroom. "I've missed you," she whispered.

"I missed you, too!"

He took off his clothing and slipped into bed. She cuddled up next to him. "What were you workin' on?"

"Oh, we got some papers from the Army."

"What about?"

"How many rabbits for next year."

"Really?"

"Yes, they want us to go on with the farm."

Rebecca yawned, "That's good. I like it here."

"Me, too."

The next morning as George came down for breakfast, he handed the envelope to Alice. "Can you get to town today?"

"Yes."

Over her shoulder, Claire said, "Sure was quiet upstairs last night, Mr. George." June bit her tongue to keep from laughing and Alice glared at Claire, but George didn't seem to notice.

As they neared the time for the last deliveries of the year, rabbits began to die. It wasn't unusual for a single rabbit to die, but this was more than a random death. The dead rabbits were added to the ones being culled each day from the herd to feed the men. In a couple of weeks the numbers that were dying was increasing.

A man came down with the flu and then another. This was with a high fever, more than a few men, and for more than a few days.

The Army veterinarians were frequently on hand to inspect the rabbits and hadn't seen anything all that unusual. They began inspecting all the rabbits, finding lots of bug bites

31

in the fur around their necks.

Then a man died.

"Only four? What have you done with the others?"

"Eaten 'em."

"WHAT!"

"How were we to know?"

"My God, we don't know what this is!"

"We always eat the dead rabbits."

"What about the hides? Carcasses? Bones?"

"We burn everything."

"Are you certain the remains were completely burned?"

"Yes. I can check to see if there is anything left, but normally just an ash pile remains."

"Do it! Now! Bring anything you find right back here. Do you understand?" Eddie turned and was gone before he answered, but he certainly understood the importance.

Turning to the other veterinarians, their chief said, "We might as well get started on the four. I hope the medical team gets a break with the man who died."

The medical team had already begun. "Here is the last man to interview."

"Thank you. I'm Major Robert Brandon, M.D. Chief Medical Officer. Your name?"

"Charlie Schuster."

"Spell it."

"C-H-A-R-L-I-E-S-C-H-U-S-T-E-R"

"You bunked near Mr. Boon. Tell me what you know about him."

"Who?"

"The deceased." He looked at his paperwork. "Mr. Jon Boon."

"Oh, Jonny. Well, he come down with the fever, ya see. He had a big swollen bite he was complaining 'bout. Bug got under his hanky. Bit him on the neck. Complained about being real hot. Couldn't eat. Just lay in his rack all day. Finally the women folk started to look in on him. Maybe three weeks he lay there. No change. They fed him, but it don't do no good. It was a blessing when he finally goed."

"Anything else you remember?"

"I don't think so."

"Thank you. That has been most helpful. If you think of anything you may have forgotten, please let us know."

"I surely will."

He looked at the notes for all the men interviewed. He shook his head. He told his associate, "I hope it's not what I think it is."

"What are you thinking, Dr. Brandon?"

He sang,

"Ring Around the Rosie,
A pocket full o'posies-
Atishoo atishoo,
we all fall down."

The other doctors knew instantly what he meant.

Two doctors returned after making a full inspection of the camp. "No evidence of either rats or mice."

"Good. And nobody we interviewed mentioned bats."

"Lots of flies and ticks around. Not too many mosquitoes."

Meanwhile, the surgeon was laboring in the hot room. The external examination showed an otherwise healthy man, in his early 30's. There were the usual scratches on his hands and arms, but nothing out of the ordinary. He felt the lymph nodes and they were very swollen. He noted an enlarged orange and red bite mark on the neck.

"Scalpel!"

He removed the enlarged bite mark, followed by the swollen lymph nodes. The doctor quickly made a large, deep looping incision starting at the top of one shoulder and ending at the other, followed by a cut down the sternum to the naval. The internal examination had begun.

"All four rabbits had white spots on their livers, swollen spleens, and at least one ulcerated bite mark."

Dr. Brandon brought the doctors, veterinarians, and George together to discuss what they had learned and compare notes. After each had their say, Dr. Brandon spoke, "Initially, I was thinking bubonic plague, but I don't think so any more."

The surgeon said, "I agree. We have to run some special cultures. We can't do it here. I'll have to take them to Denver. But I suspect we are looking at Tularemia."[6]

"Tularemia?" George asked.

"Rabbit Fever."

Before he headed for the train, Dr. Brandon met with George and Eddie.

"We don't have enough evidence right now. We have to run some tests. If it comes back as Rabbit Fever we are going to have to destroy all the animals."

"What? You can't do that. You'll wipe us out."

"Sorry. There's no choice."

"But--you can't!"

"We can. And we must."

"But a lot of them rabbits are healthy."

"That may be true. We can't risk handling the animals."

"How about if we cull the bad ones?"

"I don't see how you could do that. Besides, it would put all your men at risk."

"But we..."

"Listen. I am coming back here after we get the test results. Probably ten days, two weeks. If there is one damn rabbit with so much as a tick bite, you are going to burn every last one before my eyes. Or I'll bring in the army to do it."

Life went on as usual for the next few days, except George stayed in the Big House and brooded. He sat in Chet's study and thought of Chet's words to him--"A man who can read is never alone or without the means to find an answer." But he didn't know which books could give him the answer.

---

[6] Tularemia (also known as rabbit fever) is a serious, infectious, bacterial disease. The bacterium was first isolated by G. W. McCoy of the US Public Health Service and is named after Tulare County in central California, where an outbreak had occurred.

"I don't know what to do. I'm sorry. I just don't know what to do." He curled his head onto Rebecca's heart as they sat together quietly in the study.

There was a long pause before Rebecca replied, "Why don't you go see Uncle Jack? You two will figure something out."

George loaded up Clyde and slowly rode out the following morning for the short trip to Jack's. He took with him Jack's favorite American beverage--Kentucky Bourbon Whiskey. It seemed to help his thinking.

Jack and his men were preparing their final shipment of rabbits for the year. Loaded on a barge on the Kootenai River the rabbits would be shipped for slaughter in Castlegar, British Columbia. It was hard work; especially the last shipment each year. Jack was relieved when George rode up. It wasn't uncommon to see men from the neighboring farms stop by to borrow equipment, hands, or get advice. It was a refreshing break.

"Welcome, George. What brings you to my neck of the river?"

"Hey, Jack. A problem."

"Let's get over to the house and have something to drink."

"I brought you a present!"

"From Kentucky, I hope."

"How did you guess?"

They settled in the study and Jack reached into his desk and pulled out two glasses. He opened the bourbon while George started in, "I got a big problem..."

They finished their second round of the Kentucky elixir, before George finished explaining what had gone on. Jack rubbed his grizzled chin. "We haven't seen any rabbits dying. We never seem to have a tick problem. The flies are bad where we process the apples and in the manure pile, but normal where we keep the rabbits."

Jack had brought his original breeding pair of European rabbits (Oryctolagus cuniculus) when he moved from Wales to Canada thirty years earlier. They had adapted well to the climate. Chet's original breeding pair had been Mountain Cottontail (Sylvilagus nuttallii) which he trapped himself. Between the two breeds they looked pretty much alike (except for their tails), but that is where the similarity ended. Jack's Europeans were burrowers and loved cabbage and apples. Chet's Cottontails didn't burrow, and lived on grasses and weeds. European rabbits are less susceptible to Rabbit Fever than any Sylvilagus genus rabbit (Cottontails and Brush rabbits).

"How 'bout if we trade?"

"What?"

"Trade. Yeah." His eyes glistened and got wide. "I'll move the barge to the other side of the river. You load your rabbits on." He paused as if seeing the operation in progress. "After that you take my rabbits back to your place. The hard part is going to be getting all my rabbits out of their burrows in such a small amount of time. I ain't got nearly the manpower we'd need--but you do."

"What if we get caught? What if they figure it out at the slaughterhouse?"

"Well," he said with a grin, "that's why I keep the Mounties well-supplied with hard cider."

An hour later, George rode back as quickly as Clyde could carry him. "Eddie, get the boys together."

When they all had assembled, he explained the plan of action. The men were excited by George's words--especially hearing about a cash bonus! Eddie concluded the meeting by saying, "Well, you know what that means, boys!"

They worked day and night for the next six days. They hung lanterns on every post and the kitchen crew kept them filled and made meals around the clock. By the end of the sixth day, they had transported their whole herd into Canada and transported Uncle Jack's herd back to Altura Farm.

The men walked in from the fields and dropped onto their bunks. Too tired to climb into their upper bunks, some curled up on the floor. A few didn't bother removing their muddy boots. Within fifteen minutes, the air was filled with the sound of snoring. The heaving of their chests was the only motion in the Little House, when Doctor Brandon and a dozen Army soldiers returned to observe the destruction.

"It's Rabbit Fever. You are going to need to burn them all."

"No. We've taken care of the problem."

"Now, George. Let's be reasonable."

"I am. You told me if you found even one with a tick bite when you returned we would have to burn them all."

"Yes."

"Fine. Find one."

The Doctor inspected a dozen rabbits and did not find one tick or sore. When he had gone through the herd before every other rabbit had a bite mark.

"I don't understand. Men, have a look." The soldiers began searching immediately. Nobody found a single tick or bite mark. "What did you do?"

"I told you, I solved the problem."

"I don't believe it! Bring me a half-dozen rabbits!"

One by one, he rung their necks and sliced them open. He inspected spleens and livers and didn't find a trace of the disease. He had to sit down. "How can this be?" What he hadn't noticed was that these rabbits did not have white tails.

Was it luck that kept the soldiers from finding ticks on the rabbits they inspected? No, just a little vinegar.

Jack grew cabbage (to feed the rabbits and as a cash crop) and had a large apple orchard on his farm. He sold the raw apples as well as made apple juice, apple cider, and hard cider. He kept the cider operation on the south part of the property (on the US-Canada border), where he had plentiful water from the river. He built his home on the north end where the Kootenai River makes a hairpin turn before continuing to move north. The men stampeded the rabbits through slop areas, where apple pulp combined with yeast and alcohol from the presses created a pool of naturally occurring apple cider vinegar--a natural tick repellant.

That fall, none of the cooks in the Canadian kitchens contracted Rabbit Fever and the Canadian army was well-fed.

After the army left, George paid out bonuses he had promised to the men and Jack's men for switching the two herds. Jack refused a share, "I'm sure I'll need a favor someday." It all worked well and--so far so good--each day that passed gave George greater hope he had averted disaster. As the last train to Denver pulled away, he couldn't help but think of Chet as they had watched the last train together from this spot one year earlier.

He didn't want anything to do with rabbits--or to think of them being stunned, bled, skinned, slaughtered, cooked, canned, distributed, and consumed. But there was much work to be done; first thing was to help with Uncle Jack's rabbits for their first and final boat trip.

George was weary from the hardest work of the year. The loss of Chet had drained his emotions, but he couldn't stop--there was still more to be done and it couldn't be avoided much longer--he needed to trap wild Cottontail rabbits immediately to begin the new breeding stock. His heart was heavy and he didn't want to affect the rest of the household with his troubles, so he trudged out alone, on foot, to set up rabbit traps in the foothills.

While day after day George slinked out the door, hunched over like an old man with a dour look on his face to harvest, check and reset his traps, the kitchen crew was giggling behind Rebecca's back. "When do you think she'll figure it out?"

"She finishes breakfast every morning and runs upstairs to lose breakfast."

"You'd think that might give her a clue."

"She has probably begun showing."

Rebecca already knew she was pregnant. She couldn't deny it any longer from the day the Army told George they would need to destroy the rabbits; but that didn't seem the right occasion for her to tell her husband. Then he worked day and night switching the herds for nearly a week. Exhausted, he slept every second he was home for the next few days. There was still no chance to talk. Then he was out getting Jack's final shipment off and trapping. Time was running out for her to share their good news before everyone would see for themselves.

Rebecca strolled into the kitchen. "I will be needing a picnic basket dinner tonight for two. Fried chicken. Mash potatoes. Butter. Biscuits. Ice Tea with mint. Apple pie. Thank you!"

"Some special occasion, Miss Rebecca?" Claire asked.

"Yes." She walked out toward the barn.

"Any news you want to tell us?" It was unclear whether she had not heard the question--or ignored it.

"There you are! Eddie, I would like you to prepare the little wagon for George and me."

"Right now?" Eddie said, distressed at the interruption.

"No, just before you go for supper."

Relieved he asked, "Where you going?"

"That's for me to know and George to find out!"

"What I mean is, Clyde has been working all day and..."

"Oh, it's not far and Clyde always enjoys it there."

"Alright."

"And one more thing--when you see George, send him my way."

While Eddie was delivering the wagon to the Big House--including bows and bells on Clyde's mane--George walked up with a quizzical look on his face.

"Eddie, what gives?"

Without change of expression, Eddie nodded toward the house and answered, "Rebecca would like to see you."

Wandering into the house, the aroma of fried chicken made his mouth water. He didn't stop at the kitchen and ran upstairs to find Rebecca.

"You wanted to see me?"

"Hello, Stranger!"

"What..."

"I have hardly had time to see my husband for--how long has it been?"

He gave her a hug and she hugged him back and kissed him. "Two weeks; seems like two months."

"I think we need to get to know each other again." George laughed. "You haven't been avoiding me, have you?" she asked, with a sly smile.

"Well, I have been awful busy with the..."

39

Two

"Too busy, even for me? I understand. But right now we need a little time to ourselves. So get yourself cleaned up and your clothes changed pronto." With that she slapped him on the fanny.

He was finished in no time and heard a call from the base of the stairs, "It's ready when you are!"

In addition to the picnic basket, the kitchen crew prepared a nice tablecloth with matching napkins, blankets, pillows, firewood, matches, and a pot of coffee with sugar and cream already added.

Clyde pulled up and stopped next to the graves of Chet and Tura as if he had known all along this is where they were coming. George built a small fire and laid out blankets, while Rebecca got the dinner basket out of the wagon. It was a warm day for October. A lazy breeze drifted down from the peaks to the west. Orange and brown leafs had fallen to the ground, leaving branches starkly reaching up toward the heavens. The evergreen trees foreshadowed the coming Christmas.

They cuddled before the small fire. "Are you hungry?"
"Not yet."
"Let's swim." Rebecca stood and looked around. There was only George and Clyde to see her--both of their eyes were wide open as she quickly removed her clothes. George lay back to enjoy the sight of his beautiful wife.
"Come on! Let's go!" She dashed into the lazy river as it slipped north back into Canada.
He was soon undressed and running into the water. They kissed deeply, as if they had been away from each other on a long trip and were together at last. They swam, splashed, and kissed. They did not mind the cold water.
"How's your appetite now?"
"For what?"
She laughed. "Dinner!"
"Sure."

George added more wood to the fire and Rebecca lay dinner out on one blanket. She lay naked on the other blanket, stretching it over her, and then uncovering herself and beckoned her husband to join her. They lay facing the fire, cradled in each other's arms. They were quiet, warm, and peaceful.

When she heard his stomach growl, she laughed. She propped up on one elbow to prepare a plate of chicken and biscuits for the two of them and placed it on her naked stomach. They both ate with one hand, the other intertwined, unable to break away from the other's touch.

"You are so beautiful," he whispered in her ear. "Thank you for suggesting a picnic."

"I thought we needed to have some time together. Just the two of us."

"Yes we did."

She wasn't sure how to make her announcement. He gave her a squeeze. "This is wonderful."

He reached down to grab a chicken leg. She gently took the back of his hand and brought it up to her breast. She slowly rubbed her nipple with his hand. When he started to form his fingers around her breast, she gently whispered, "No. Let me." She continued to move his hand back and forth across her breast. Her breasts were firm and full.

"We're not going to be able to use my stomach for a dinner table much longer," she whispered. "And I'll need these," she said while rubbing his fingers on her nipple, "for another purpose."

His eyes widened and his mouth fell open.

"Honey!"

"Yes, dear!"

"Do you know where your Uncle kept his business records?" For the three months since Rebecca had announced her pregnancy, George had been concerned about continuing to raise rabbits based on Chet's old contract.

"There are some things by his chair. I think there are also

some papers up in the attic."

Of course--the attic! George had been all through the farm records that Chet kept in a drawer in the china cabinet in the dining room. He hadn't thought to look for papers in the attic.

"Are you looking for something in particular?"

"Well, not really. Just interested in the Army contracts and how Chet got into the rabbit business."

George climbed to the top of the stairs and pulled down the access stairs to the attic. Rebecca wandered over, then followed him up. Now that Rebecca was showing, George wondered if she should be climbing steep steps. He guessed it would be alright, plus he liked her company.

The room was hot, with the mid-day sun beating off the cedar shingles. Their entrance stirred a layer of dust into the air where it swirled before settling down to a new resting place. He eagerly looked around the room, not knowing what he was looking for, but sensing he would know it when he saw it.

"Try that chest."

"Jackpot!"

She inspected a cane chair to make sure it would support her weight and wiped off the dust before sitting next to him. The red cedar chest was filled with christening dresses, birth certificates, cards, old rings, crushed flowers, wedding and funeral announcements from the newspaper, and romantic notes. The smell of aromatic cedar filled the room. A blue, metal box contained business papers--the deed on the farm, original agreement with the Army, and early annual contracts.

"Find what you needed?" she said, as she ran her fingers through his hair. She was thinking he was acting like a school boy, finding a treasure.

"Yes!"

She slowly looked through the mementos in the cedar chest, while he looked at the papers in the dim light. She got up and opened a shade to bring in more light.

"What a romantic Chet was!" she said as she read through love letters he'd given Tura. "I blush to even read this," she teased. George didn't respond; lost in the Army contracts. She held up her own christening dress, wondering why it would be in with her Aunt and Uncle's things instead of her parent's.

"I wonder who Chet knew?" asked George

absent-mindedly, under his breath.

"What?"

Realizing he had been heard, he asked, "I wonder who Chet knew that he would get a contract like this from the Army?"

"What do you mean?"

"Well, they basically set him up in business. Bought all the equipment he'd need and supplied him things."

"Really?"

"Yes. The farm is on a flood plain. Helped him buy the land. Indemnified him if floods put him outta business. Guaranteed him a profit--if he would simply start this rabbit farm. Told him exactly how many rabbits they'd buy. Guaranteed the price. Just running the numbers through my head, I don't see how he couldn't end up wealthy."

The Idaho newspapers did not refer to Senator William Edgar Borah as 'The Lion of Idaho' for nothing. Even though staunchly isolationist, it did not prevent him from seeking lucrative war contracts for his State. He never seemed to have been bothered by such contradictions. When President Calvin Coolidge was told of Borah's fondness for horseback riding, he replied, "It's hard to imagine Senator Borah going in the same direction as his horse."

"General, I am interested in developing a better relationship with the Army. I am not against all wars. I am not against the Army. We just don't need to get tangled up in this thing in Europe."

"Yes, Senator," replied General Albert Lee Washfield. The slogan "He kept us out of war" propelled Woodrow Wilson into the White House; strong sentiment against the war continued. Many Senators held strong reservations; but they also needed to prepare the nation for all possibilities--and they held the purse strings. It was the General's job to keep Senators happy--lucrative contracts to constituents were rewarded with handsome appropriations to the military, in war or peace.

"What do you have in mind, Senator Borah?"

"We have great agricultural potential throughout Idaho. Many natural resources. I am sure you'll see there are certain niches Idaho is well-suited to fill. Perhaps if you took a trip out to Idaho. Do you have children, General? Maybe a family vacation could be arranged, where you could experience for yourself the finer things of my State? I can help with arrangements."

The General, married with teenage boys, could see how this was going to work and it didn't sound like he was going to mind it. His travels through Idaho led him to contact his counterparts in Canada, which took him to John Easley Evans--Uncle Jack. The General had done his research well, so when he showed up at Jack's front door early one afternoon he carried a bottle. He explained the situation with openness and honesty, "Of course, I cannot contract with you directly. But there could be a finder's fee."

Jack rubbed his chin, as he sipped the bourbon. "Let me see if I got this right: you are looking for me to find a man to start a rabbit farm in Idaho? You are going to help him buy property from Old Man Smith? He needs to be a United States Citizen? And you'll do right by the both of us?"

"Yes."

The room was quiet. "I have just the man in mind." Chet had worked for him years before; now he was farming the Smith place just to the south.

When George received the 1919 contract to provide rabbits to the U. S. Army in the same quantities as 1918--made out to Rebecca LaVoy Cash--he smiled, quickly forged her signature, and returned it. The need to feed soldiers went on unabated. That night he lay in bed reflecting on his good fortune--he had escaped his past and married well; they had just made love and Rebecca slept in his arms--her belly full and round; they were excited about the new life inside her. Their house was big enough for many children to come. There was no farm equipment to replace next year; just normal maintenance. The latest payment from the Army was deposited and now with the 1919 contract in hand the farm had never been as prosperous. Next year's checks could be placed in the bank for a rainy day. With the stalemate in

Europe, this could go on forever. He drifted off thinking how good life was.

Many American businesses--large and small—prospered during the war. In fact, the Great War changed America. Britain entered the Great War as the World's dominant lender nation and ended heavily indebted to the United States. The United States entered the war as a debtor nation and ended as a lender nation well on her way to being the dominant economic superpower of the 20th century. The United States economically benefited greatly--employment, wages, and profits increased at a staggering rate. The United States economy absorbed the cost of the war quickly. No other nation on earth even came close. On the fields where the battles were waged, there was economic destruction that took years to overcome. Even neutral neighboring countries were severely impacted through trade limitations and damage to infrastructure. But America, thousands of miles away from the battlefields, prospered, and thrived--even little farms in Idaho.[7]

---

[7] To the winners go the spoils; or so it would seem. Fifty years earlier, when the shoe was on the other foot, the Germans had imposed reparations on France for its aggression during the Franco-Prussian War. After the Great War, the allies imposed severe (actually, onerous) reparations on the Germans.
Some of what went on was nearly laughable. For example, it was largely left to the Germans to police their own repayments.
During the war, Britain had borrowed heavily from the United States. After the War, the US demanded repayment. To pay the debt, Britain demanded Germany make reparations payments. So the Germans borrowed from US investors to pay the British, and Britain paid off much of their loans to the US. Then Germany defaulted on the loans when the Nazi's came to power--politically inflamed by having to pay reparations!
Of the original amount imposed only an eighth was paid; and not by the Germans, but by American investors. Historian Stephen Schuker points out that between 1921 and 1931, Germany paid 19.1 billion marks in reparations while borrowing 27 billion from the United States, which they defaulted on in 1932.

Two

The war seemed to be a hopeless stalemate. A little land would be taken; a little land given back. Men were bogged down in parallel trenches where barbed wire, mustard gas, and machine guns cut scars across France, Belgium, and Germany. The war dragged on when suddenly, half a world from Idaho, George's comfortable life was being dumped in the mire.

In Belgium's Walloon Region, Province of Liège, lay the village of Spa. Since the 14th century, it had been known for its eponymous healing mineral hot springs. It is unknown whether the German army was seeking a healing place when they placed their principal Headquarters there.

Generalquartiermeister Erich Ludendorff concluded his review by stating, "The situation has become hopeless." He had known it was hopeless for a month.

"Hopeless?" Imperial Chancellor Count Georg von Hertling replied. Bombastic and impetuous Kaiser Wilhelm II, German Emperor watched quietly. He had ignored his civilian government and allowed military commanders free reign in running the war.

"Yes. I fear a devastating breakthrough could occur within a few days; perhaps within twenty-four hours."

"What can be done?"

"We shall retreat from the battlefield in good order and I recommend you accept Wilson's demands."

"I agree," replied the Kaiser soberly.[8]

---

[8] For the three principal men who had met together that day, the next two weeks would bring cataclysmic change. Within a week, the Kaiser replaced Count von Hertling with Prince Maximilian of Baden as Chancellor to negotiate a favorable cease fire. Then he dismissed Generalquartiermeister Ludendorff. But they had misjudged President Woodrow Wilson badly--instead of a cease fire, Wilson forced the Germans to surrender and the Kaiser to abdicate his throne, fleeing to the Netherlands.
Ludendorff, in reviewing his troops for perhaps the last time, began the widely-accepted myth that the failure had been the result of the civilian government, not the military. At about the time Canadian Private George Lawrence Price fell to a sniper's bullet as the final combat death of the war, Ludendorff, in a false beard and glasses, entered his brother's home in Potsdam, on his way out of Germany.

"The Great War is over! It's over!" Rebecca shouted with joy as she entered the house.

"Thank, God!" Claire said.

Alice, June, Rebecca and Claire were dancing hand-in-hand in the kitchen a few minutes later when George came into the house. On hearing the commotion he wearily peeked in, "Hello?"

"Did you hear?"

"What?"

"The war; it's over!"

George was skeptical--he had heard the rumors before. "How do you know?"

"I was in town this afternoon. They were shooting up the place! Look." Rebecca held up the newspaper she'd picked up and George read it carefully.

"This is wonderful!" His bone weariness vanished. "I'm gonna tell the men!" He stopped by a storage shed attached to the house to grab the remaining two wooden cases of Kentucky Bourbon he saved for trips to Jack's, carrying one in each hand with the newspaper stuffed in his pants in the small of his back. When he got to the Little House he kicked in the door and stepped inside. "Well, boys, we got somethin' to celebrate. The war's over!" There was hollering and handshakes, before everyone huddled in front of George who read from the newspaper as they listened quietly. He reached into the open whiskey case, grabbed a bottle, extracted the cork with his teeth, spit it out, and raised the bottle. "Here's to those damn rabbits that won the war!" He took a big swig, before passing the bottle on. Then he reached into the two cases and passed all the bottles along to the men. "Enjoy it, boys!"

THREE

George read the newspaper while Rebecca busily opened a letter addressed to her from the United States Army. "Honey, listen to this! On November 18, 1918, the United States Congress passed the Wartime Prohibition Act, banning the sale of alcoholic beverages having an alcohol content of greater than 2.75%."

He looked over his paper. "Only our beloved Congress would pass a law with that name AFTER the war ended. And it doesn't even take effect until next June!"

She ignored what he was saying as she sat at the kitchen table reading carefully. She handed George the letter and envelope, "Does this mean what I think it does?"

"Where did you get this?" He had expressly ordered Claire to give her mail to him. He read it and his stomach turned. "The rabbit contract for 1920 has been reduced in half."

"That's quite a reduction!"

"It is."

"What does it mean we'll have to do?"

His mind was reeling. "I'm not exactly sure." It was now May 1919 and he could continue to fulfill the 1919 contract, but would have to let quite a few men go in the fall.

Rebecca came down to the kitchen before dawn. She pulled back and tied the white, taffeta curtains, then looked out over the farm. Everything was peaceful and still this spring morning. The first rays of sun had reached the mountaintops in the distance to the west. A light dusting of fog rested on the lawn, crept over the bank, and onto the river beyond her sight. She stoked the fire that had been left to dwindle during the night and added small apple-wood branches. She filled the teapot, placed it on the stove, and sat at the kitchen table. She was tired already, with a big day ahead.

The ladies in the kitchen crew had been vile with each other for the last week as they decided the midwife pecking order among themselves. As she sat, she thought of the previous evening when it had reached its peak--"I'll have the baby by myself, if you three don't quit bickering!"

"What?" It was the first they had noticed her.

"I said, 'Quit Bickering!'"

Claire jumped back as if she were being hit, "Oh, we're sorry, Miss; we want to be..."

Rebecca lifted her hand. "I know what you want. You're trying to be helpful...and you will be. But for the Land of Patsy Ann..."

"Sorry, Miss Rebecca! It's just, well, we're excited."

She had to smile at that. "When the time comes, I am sure all three of you will be helpful. And you'll be such a blessing after the birth."

It was then the pains began--they grabbed at her back unexpectedly taking her breath away. She hadn't said anything at the time. She tried to sleep as the pain grew progressively worse. There was no doubt by morning she was in labor.

Alice stumbled in a few minutes later, rubbing her eyes. It was her turn to get things going; the other two would not be up for another forty-five minutes. Startled to see Rebecca at the table she jumped as she drew her hand to her heart. "Oh, you startled me! You're up early!"

"I couldn't sleep."

"Everything alright?"

"Just a little back pain."

Alice didn't think anything of it; in her stupor, labor pains hadn't cross her mind. "Would you like some breakfast?"

Rebecca was a bit nauseous, "No, thank you. I'll just enjoy my tea."

Before the other ladies were due to begin their day, Rebecca said, "Alice?"

"Yes, Ma'am," Alice replied absent-mindedly.

"I'm in labor."

Alice gasped and a chill went up her spine. "Praise The

Lord! The blessed day is here." She was in labor alright, but would not deliver the blessed bundle until after midnight.

"He is beautiful! What are you going to name him? How about George Junior?"

"I'm not sure."

"What names have you talked 'bout?"

"We haven't."

"What?"

"Well, I know what we'd name a baby girl."

"Yes?" She was hoping Rebecca would at least give her that much.

"George told me he wanted to name our boys; and I could name our girls. I have chosen the name 'Abigail Rebecca', after Tura's sister, if we have a girl. But we'll call her Abby."

"But he has not mentioned any names?"

"No. He was insistent he get to name the boys."

"Hmmm..."

George had not left Rebecca's side all day. He tried to rest after the birth, but merely tossed and turned. Deciding sleep was a lost cause he came back downstairs. Rebecca had nodded off and Alice, unable to wait to get her hands on the newborn, scooped him up and was holding him in the kitchen when she heard George, "There's the new father! How are you?"

"Tired. Excited. Happy!"

"We tried to tell you your job was just to pace while the mid-wife delivers...but you wouldn't listen!"

George laughed. "I'll take your advice next time!"

"What's his name gonna be?" Alice looked at the sleeping infant in her arms.

George paused. "I haven't even told my wife yet..."

"Then it can just be our secret!"

George paused again. "Thomas George Cash."

"Oh, that is beautiful."

"Now, just be sure to keep this secret until I talk to Rebecca!"

"My lips are sealed!"

Rebecca pretended to be furious with George. "I have to be the last to know? Everyone else in the house knows but me? And when exactly were you going to tell me?"

"Wait...What? Tell you..."

"The name of the baby?"

"I, huh, well, guess I may have..."

"Alice? You ask Alice to keep a secret?" Unable to keep her face straight any longer she broke into a broad grin, "I love the name Thomas!"

"Thomas George Cash. Does have a nice ring to it, doesn't it?"

In the summer of 1919, Uncle Jack showed up at the door, riding an old mule, Nellie. "Got anything for a thirsty neighbor?"

George grinned. "Sure!"

"Where can we talk--in private?"

Jack got off and George took the reins to Nellie and led her to the barn where there was plentiful straw, hay, and fresh water. He came back from the barn carrying a bottle of Kentucky Bourbon and walked Jack to a table in the yard. It was warm and the afternoon colors were muted pastels. "We can start here."

"I am gonna need some help."

"With what?"

"I have been in business with some people in Vancouver."

"What kind of business?"

He whispered, "Mmmm--distribution."

For the next hour, Jack rambled about a 1916 vote in Canada where the voters said no to prohibition, which the courts overturned. George didn't know if it was the bourbon or the story that had him confused. "So to make a long story short, my associates have been producing, marketing, and distributing a certain commodity throughout British Columbia. What we've been doing ain't exactly legal."

"I gathered."

"Anyway, the war being over and no more rabbits being bought--by the way, how you doin' with your rabbits?"

"Contract has been cut in half?"

"Half? Shit, mine evaporated overnight. Zero. Anyway, that is what I have been branching off doing. My associates think we should expand. We are, shall we say, looking for an export partner?"

"I see."

"Seems your country is handing us a prime opportunity. Interested?"

George didn't give it much thought. He knew the rabbit business was good as dead. Jack never steered him wrong. "Sure."

It was approaching dusk when they shook hands on the new business venture. Both were unsteady getting up from the table. "Stay for supper, won't ya?"

"Love to. I want to see that little gal of yours."

"No, we had a baby boy."

Jack laughed, "I meant his mother."

They ate, told stories, and laughed until they cried. Jack held the baby. "What a darlin' he is! And just as pretty as his mama!"

"Oh, Uncle Jack. It is so good to see you!"

"You, too."

"So, what brought you down today?"

Jack's eyes shifted back and forth as he cautiously thought through his answer. He cleared his throat. "Well, your husband and me were talking some business."

After coffee with dessert, Jack said, "Guess I best get going."

"I'll run back with ya." George left to saddle up Nellie and Clyde. He walked them up to the house and Jack, Rebecca, and Thomas met him by the front porch. Jack kissed Thomas on the forehead, "You take care of them, little Tom!" He kissed Rebecca on the cheek, "Love ya, honey."

She hugged him and held him for a long time.

"Love you, too." Breaking her clasp, he mumbled, "Good night." The two men mounted for the short ride north.

That June, Rebecca had the ladies make a picnic lunch for her and George.

"Taking Thomas?"

"Not this time."

Alice pondered this as she prepared the chicken dinner. "She couldn't be," she said to herself. She was.

Jack met with George daily as they set up their system for exporting beverages from Canada to Idaho, Wyoming, and eastern Washington State. Jack reported, "We are set to begin a week from Saturday."

George looked at his wall calendar, "Right on schedule. November 1st."

"Yeah, it's good to get all the details worked out."

"We move at night."

"Night?"

"Yeah, they ain't got enough agents to cover the territory, but we still wanta play it safe. Hitch the wagons here. Storage is up at your place, in the barn. Bring the empty wagons and barrels back the next morning."

"How frequently are we making these trips?"

"Initially, two a week. When we get the supply line full we'll take it from there. Route one goes Bonner's Ferry, Sandpoint, Spokane."

"That should take two, maybe three days."

"Right. Route two goes Coeur d'Alene, Kellogg, Wallace, Mullan, St. Regis River. Come back up the spine or the way you come down, depending on weather."

"Four days?"

"Probably five. Remember, we're in no hurry."

"IknowIknow! No need to be in a rush--just don't get caught."

"Small shipments to start out. We'll increase size and move south as we go."

"Sounds good."

"No drinking on the wagons. Camp out. If they want to get liquored up, give them a day off up here."

"Fine. There is plenty of money to be made. Our sales people are out there now making arrangements for payments and credit to good places."

"Sounds impressive."

"Well, we've been at it up in Canada a few years already. Got a good idea of what the traffic will bear. Later, we'll add enforcement."[9]

---

[9] Prohibition began in Canada before it did in the United States. It was largely a Provincial issue, with each handling it differently. In

"Enforcement?"

"Whenever you give credit, you're gonna need enforcement."

"I see."

"We want good, reliable, dry men out there. We'll have a good thing going pretty quick."

George wasn't sure he liked this business at all. They had to carry rifles to fend off highwaymen. Enforcement was rough business. It brought in a different character than he was used to--they'd drink and get each other riled up before heading out in pairs, heavily armed and looking for trouble.

About the time of their daughter's arrival, near Christmas Day, Rebecca waddled in holding her hand to her aching back. "I got another letter."

"From whom?"

"Army." She handed it to George.

He thought, 'Shit, another letter didn't get to me first!' He hurriedly read it. "Damn!"

"What's it say?"

"Contracts been cut down again."

"What will we do?"

"More of what we have been doin'." The contract was so low, George didn't bother to sign and return it and the Army never followed up or looked for another supplier.

By January, rum-running was in full swing. With the winter, it was taking an extra day or two for round trips and the men were taking an extra day staying dry before heading back out. Shipments were leaving every day and a dozen teams covered half the state. The money was good--very good. But George was unsettled--there was a lot at risk. There were great dangers to him, the farm, and his men. As he looked over the accounting, holding his daughter, Abby, he had to smile. "Yeah, it's a lot of money, kid-o. But to me the Great War were better years."

---

places it was considered a religious issue between the Catholics and Protestants; in other places, it was enacted, but tacitly ignored. It was enacted in Canada before the Great War and gained favor during the war years in an effort to make Canada a better place for her returning soldiers. A 1919 referendum passed to continue Canadian prohibition.

George spent afternoons loading up wagons and planning for the team going out that day. By dusk, he was saying goodbye to his men before returning to the Big House to help put the kids down for the night.

Some of the old timers who had been with Chet during the rabbit years objected to what they saw.

"Hey, Shaky, what's on your mind?"

He stood opposite George at his desk, his hat in his hand. "Well, George. I've been thinking it may be time for me to be movin' on."

George was surprised and put down his pen. "Have a seat."

"It's just that, well, I am not one for living outta a wagon. Getting in and out is hard on my back, ya know."

He had heard many complaints, but this was a new one. Most of the rumbling was about the rough characters the new business was drawing in and having to carry weapons for protection. "If I could find something for you here, would you stay on?"

Shaky's eyes brightened. "Oh, yes, Sir. I like it here, I just..."

"I am going to need to have many more wagons. Would you like to work on those?"

"I'm pretty handy with a saw, but I don't know much about making wagons."

"We'll find somebody who does."

George considered gasoline-powered engines to replace the wagons. He visited Jack.

"They are not as dependable," Jack said, tipping back his glass.

"But they are faster. We'd be able to get south further, quicker."

"True. But you have to find places to buy fuel. That means traveling by day. And when you have a breakdown you will be at the mercy of whoever finds you. Lots of snoopy people will be poking through your load."

"Mmm."

In the end they decided to stick with the horse-drawn

wagons. "Before you head back, let me show you something new."

As George came out of the door Jenny pulled him aside. "Now you be gentle on Jack!" as Jenny gave him a squeeze and smiled.

"What do you mean?"

"Don't you know? Jack only drinks when you come by. No good for half a week afterward." George looked stunned as Jack came out of the house.

Jack took him back to the cider mill to show him the gin distilling operation he had set up, then they meandered along the foothills as Jack pointed out bushes, "Who would have guessed the scrubs we have against the mountains would give gin its flavor?"[10] "Junipers grow wild all around here. I've been sending men out to pick the berries. They think I'm crazy. Easy work for the old-timers."

"Are you getting enough? 'Cause we got lot of these bushes."

"Always can use more."

"I can get some of my men to pick them and bring 'em up."

"I'll buy whatever you find."

"So, how did you get started with the gin?"

"Just looking for something to branch out with. Beer and whiskey can only take you so far."

"What do your partners think of it?"

"They don't know. And I don't see any need to tell them. As soon as I am ready to start shipping, I'll cut you in."

It turned out to be a smart, but dangerous, move. His partners were already beginning to squeeze him to take a

---

[10] The flavor from Gin is derived from juniper berries (Juniperus communis), a plant commonly found in southern Canada and much of the United States.

Quinine is a white crystalline alkaloid with medicinal properties to combat malaria, fever, pain, and inflammation--quite useful in many places, but especially in the tropics. It also has a severely bitter taste even when diluted with water. Just as a 'spoon full of sugar helps the medicine go down', the strong pine flavor from the gin overshadows the bitterness of the 'tonic'-- thus the popularity of gin and tonic.

lower percentage of the take. George had his old timers doing what they had always done during the 'off season'--fishing, hunting, cleaning--and now they were picking berries, making deliveries, building wagons, cooking, and managing the living quarters for drivers and enforcement teams.

"I don't like the looks of some of these men, Pauly."

"I know what you mean, George. They come back here and get drunk."

"I want you to get rid of the worst of the lot."

"Me?"

"Yep. I am making you foreman of the drivers. I'll double your pay."

"Hell, George, I don't need money. I got everything right here."

"But, Pauly, you gotta save up for a rainy day. You never know when things will change..."

"Ah."

"...or your back could give out. Or you could decide you would rather get your own place and spend time on your front porch."

"I like the sounds of that!"

George's life turned into simple routine. He didn't need to start work until after dinner, when he would push away from the table after his third cup of coffee, thank the ladies, kiss the children and Rebecca, throw on his hat, step into the yard, and look up at the noon sun. When he wasn't working or playing with the children, he had a book in his hands. He read everything he could about the Great War--history books, poems, and novels--it didn't matter, if it was about 'the war to end all wars' George had his nose in it.

"I wonder if it is really over?" he mentioned one day to Rebecca.

"What?"

"The Great War."

"What do you mean? Of course, it is over. Our boys are home!"

"I'm not so sure. We fought and fought, but now we can't seem to settle the peace. There's such bitterness in Germany now!"

"Well, what did they expect?"

"But this peace has become mean-spirited. It is like a

spring too tightly wound."

"We have disarmed the Germans. What could they possibly do?" George didn't have an answer, but felt uneasy.

He had a restless night thinking about the Germans, but was up early doing what he loved--playing with Thomas and Abby, to let Rebecca sleep.

"You're up early."

"Morning." Thomas was on the floor by his feet and Abby was in his arms. They were playing with boxes.

"Had breakfast yet?"

"No. Been waiting for you."

"You're so sweet. Abby was hungry all night. I had to nurse her every two hours."

"Sorry. I can't help you there."

"What are you doing?"

"Nothin'"

"Bullshit!"

He grinned at Pauly.

"I told you yesterday to stay away from here."

"I'm just resting against the fence."

"Resting?"

"Admiring the view."

"You're spying!"

"Me?"

"You're spying on Mrs. Cash."

"I gotta admit she is nice to look at."

"She's out here to enjoy the sun and feed her daughter."

"I figure if she didn't want me to look at it, she wouldn't yank it out in front of me."

"What? She doesn't even know you're here."

"Maybe. Or maybe, she likes me alookin'."

"I want you out of here..."

"I'll be leaving on my rounds in a few..."

"No. I want you off this property NOW!"

"You can't do..."

"Yes I can. Mr. Cash made me foreman. You're fired!"

"Maybe I won't..."

Pauly pulled a revolver that he had hidden in the small of his back, "Maybe you will!"

With that Pauly had fired his first man. He marched him to the Little House, where the man collected his things. Pauly then cashiered him out and he was off the property within the hour, walking south, yelling over his shoulder, "I'll get you for this!"

"Good riddance!"

"What's going on?" Rebecca asked, sleepily. Her children were standing at the end of the bed in the mid-morning sun, giggling.

"A surprise! Get up, lazy bones! We're all packed, ready to go!"

When she stumbled into the kitchen a few minutes later, everyone was holding something--Alice was holding Thomas by the hand, Claire was holding a squirming, but happy, Abby, and June was holding a large picnic basket. George was leaning against the sink with a coffee mug in each hand, smiling. He handed one to her and said, "We're going on a picnic!"

They got onto the wagon and were off with Clyde leading the way.

Alice lead off, "You don't suppose she's..."

Claire slapped her hands and giggled.

June replied, "No, that's the trick when SHE takes HIM on a picnic."

The sun was lighting half the mountain to the west. It was a hazy purple with patches of puffy, white clouds clinging to the base. There was just enough breeze to fill the air with the scent of pine. Deer stopped to watch the horse and lone wagon, while twitching their tails and ears. Not sensing danger, they returned to drinking by the edge of the river.

When they arrived at their special spot, before unloading

the wagon, George said to his children, "Say hello to Uncle Chet and Aunt Tura!"

Rebecca climed in, "You would have loved them!"

George patted the kids heads, "The feeling would have been mutual!"

Rebecca laid out blankets while George unhitched Clyde, piled hay on the ground, and gave him an apple. Contented, he shook his mane and munched his breakfast. Soon he would be lying down dozing alongside his family.

"Hungry?"

Thomas quacked, "I am! I am!"

Rebecca imitated her son, "I am, too!"

George pulled out biscuits and handed two to his wife.

She broke them apart and handed one to Thomas. "Honey?"

"Yes, dear."

"No, I meant do you want some honey?"

"Yes, Honey, I'd love some honey!" George grinned. Thomas laughed at his silly parents and Abby giggled.

They lay on the blankets. Abby was trying to walk back and forth between her parents, held upright and reaching for outstretched hands. She squealed and giggled when she made it across and immediately turned around to come back the other way. Thomas was content playing with sticks and rocks. Rebecca sat watching the stream, while George dozed.

Soon Rebecca and Thomas had their shoes off and were wading in the water; Abby on her mother's hip.

"And who's the lazy bones now?"

George grinned and got off the ground. He took Thomas by the hand to show him the makeshift fishing pole he had constructed. He had brought a hook and a small, tin coffee can of earthworms. Thomas dropped his hook in the water and immediately had to see if he had caught anything. He lifted the pole until the worm was swinging in the air. Then he dropped the line back into the water.

"Catch anything, Thomas?"

"Let's see!"

"I see the worm!" George smiled, "Guess we'll have to eat the worm if you don't catch any fish!"

By noon, they were packing up and ready to head home.
"This has been fun, George; we'll have to do this again."

"Yes, we will." He lifted his wife into the back of the wagon and climbed up to kiss her. Then he climbed down and raised the children to their mother. "Alright kids, wave bye to Chet and Tura."

They did while George climbed on the back of the wagon. "Hey, Clyde, you know the drill." He didn't move. "CLYDE, HOME!" The horse pulled forward.

When Clyde came up the road onto the farm, the Cash family was cuddled together in the back, with Thomas in his mother's arms watching the workers, and Abby sound asleep on her father's chest. Clyde pulled up to the barn and stopped, then craned his head around in anticipation of being unharnessed.

Eddie came running around the corner, "George, come quick!"

"Can I take care of..."

"No, I'll do that. There has been some trouble. Go see Pauly right away."

"Little House?" he asked as he began to run. He didn't wait for the answer.

George burst in the door, searching for Pauly. Their eyes met immediately. Pauly was white as a sheet. "John's been shot!"

"Oh, my gosh, how is he? How did it happen?"

From across the room they heard John, "Don't worry. Ain't nothin'. I'll be fine."

George came to look at John's shoulder. "What happened?"

"We was ambushed outside of St. Regis. End of the route. Had one delivery left--two cases of gin. They took it. Said they were taking over our route from Kellogg and east."

"Who were you with?"

"Hoot."

"How is he?"

"Beat up, pistol whipped. Tired. He got me back on the wagon and drove straight through."

George turned to Pauly, "You getting Doc?"

"No need. We got the bullet out. Just a small chunk."

"Yeah, he winged me. Caught me square in the shoulder."

George patted John on his good arm. "You're a good man. It should heal good. Just rest up, now."

"I'll be fine."

George walked to Hoot's bunk. "How are you?"

"Alright, now."

"Sorry about this."

Hoot shrugged, "Comes with the territory."

"How did it happen?"

"They came outta nowhere. Guns drawn. We told them we didn't have no money. One of 'em said, 'We know. We're here to deliver a message. We're taking your Kellogg to St. Regis route. Don't bother to come through to get what you are owed--we'll take that, too. Don't want to see Jack's hooch over this way. Then he lifted his pistol. He was real calm-like and said, 'If we see any of your boys, this is what is gonna happen.' Then he shot. 'Now, git! Sorry about that, part of the message. Next time, my aim will be better.'" Then they picked up the two cases.

"How many were there?"

"Four."

Eddie came back from putting away Clyde and George motioned for him and Pauly to join him outside. "He 'bout killed those two horses getting back."

"Not surprised...must be eighty miles."

"I know what you are thinking, but they will be long gone before we could get down there."

"Are any teams going through there?"

"Yes, left yesterday."

"How do we get word to them?"

Nobody had an idea. "Eddie, guess you'll have to take a fast horse and catch them."

"Yes, Sir!"

George returned to the Big House muttering, "Gawd, I hate this business."

George's mind was reeling. If he did not do anything, attacks would continue and more territory taken. It was not practical to start an offensive on an unknown enemy from this far away. He stopped deliveries to part of the route. Hopefully, things would cool down.

George was troubled by the violence, though Hoot and John were recovering well. They did not appear to be afraid of going out again. "We won't get snagged a second time!" Hoot proclaimed.

John was looking to get back into the fight. "If I find the bastard that shot me, I'll even up the odds!" The men began taking target practice in the foothills. Every shot George heard was a reminder of the dangerous undertaking of rum-running. He needed to think this through a bit more.

They had been outmanned four to two. "Perhaps I should add a man to each team? Have him sit in the wagon with a shotgun."

"What fer?" The men were quite agitated about two of their friends being ambushed. They looked up to both Hoot and John for what they had been through--to a man, they were itching to get even, undermanned or not.

A week later, Abby and Thomas were with their father in the mid-morning. Thomas was playing peek-a-boo with Abby, giggling and scampering around furniture, hiding from his sister. Rebecca came from the bedroom. "Coffee?"

George stood up. "Yes, I'd love some!"

Rebecca brought coffee in from the kitchen and handed one mug to George. As she sat with her own mug, she said, "Two sugars and one cream."

"Yes, just like my family; my two sugars," he placed his hands on the children's heads, "and one cream," and patted Rebecca on the knee.

"How clever! Aren't you sweet!"

"Here. We received a letter from Harold." George handed Rebecca Harold's letter from his back pocket.

"This is the first one from Harold." She looked at the envelope, "Just like my father's letters, it's addressed to Chet."

"But never any to you." There was a long silence. "Kinda spooky, isn't it?"

"Yeah. It's like he has never acknowledged that his brother is dead...," Rebecca tilted her head and rubbed her forehead...,"or that I'm alive."

George quietly said, "I don't know what to say."

"There is nothing to say. I just have to get over it." She read the letter. "He said he had to sneak this letter to us. His aunt helped him. The others he had tried to send were ripped up by his father. Why? Says they are all well. Living in Whittier, California with my Aunt Bess. She is principal at the grammar school. He gets into a lot of trouble at school. Sits out on the front curb at the school as punishment. Father is doing leather work--made two matching pony saddles for some famous child actress. That's about it."

"How old is your brother?"

"Fifteen. No, sixteen."

He reached over and patted her arm. "We're your family now." George stood up, arched his back, sipped his coffee, and watched the children play.

Through all the disturbances George could be heard by anyone and everyone muttering under his breathe, "Gawd, I hate this business." To the east, alcohol was pouring through Whiskey Gap, Alberta, Canada into Montana and off the ridge of the Rocky Mountains into the plains. Rival bootleggers competed on price and availability. There were skirmishes as they protected territory, while venturing into neighboring stakes. Over the next four years the rich and well-prepared grew while the weak and small were pushed aside. To the west, merchants in Vancouver bootlegged down the coast of Washington through Tacoma and Seattle and down to Portland, Oregon.

"How the hell did I let you talk me into this business?"

Jack tried to cheer George up, "The advantage we have is being able to transport hooch by both land and sea. As the territory becomes saturated north and south, you watch--they'll began pushing east and west. That's where we got'em! The Mountains create a barrier of protection from the east." But he didn't add that Spokane was just to the west of their claim and forays there into their domain would become common. Law enforcement wasn't a problem. Local sheriffs all over were pointing out, "The Volstead Act is a Federal regulation; let the Feds enforce it."[11]

George spent afternoons and evenings loading the wagons and preparing the teams, followed by sleepless nights worrying about his men. He didn't know how to get out of bootlegging without taking away jobs from his friends. His only relief was time spent in the morning with his children. George grabbed Abby and swung her up on his shoulder. "You're getting too big for this!" She squealed. "How old are you now?"

"I'm four!" She giggled and hugged his head. He walked out the front door to look out over the river. Sunlight was glistening off the water. The river, 200 yards away, sang an ever-present babble. "It's no wonder Uncle Chet built the house here. He was a smart man. I never tire of that sound." He walked down off the porch, shifted Abby onto his back, leaned forward and stretched out Abby's arms. She giggled with delight, making like she was flying.

He was enjoying the sunshine, when he noticed a cloud off to his left. A concerned look came over his face. He mumbled to himself, "SHIT! That ain't a cloud! What is that?" He dropped Abby off his back. Smoke was bellowing up to the north. He stood motionless looking intently for nearly a minute. He picked up Abby, ran back into the house, and flung

---

[11] On January 16, 1919, Nebraska became the thirty-sixth state to ratify the Eighteenth Amendment to the United States Constitution. Thirteen days later, Frank Lyon Polk, Acting Secretary of State certified the ratification. He had been on the job only fifteen days, filling in for less than a month between the terms of Robert Lansing and Bainbridge Colby. But Prohibition was still not the law of the land--there was a year to wait after ratification, plenty of time to stockpile alcohol and for producers to create alternative supply chains.

When the act went into effect there were only 1,520 Federal Prohibition agents (police) assigned to enforce it nationwide. Local sheriffs and police early on saw prohibition created more problems than it was solving.

There were also various laws, based on personal use or percentage of alcohol content, which circumvented the intent of the amendment. There were creative routes around the regulations, such as a grape juice supplier who gave specific, detailed instructions on the label on how to prevent his product from fermenting.

his daughter into her mother's arms.

Startled, Rebecca cried, "What's wrong?"

He didn't answer, but ran through the house to the back door yelling, "PAULY! EDDIE!" as he exited.

Soon the three were riding as fast as their mounts would carry them. When they got to the ford, they scampered through quickly, their horses climbing the bank and pulling to a stop. The gin still was fully engulfed and the house was also on fire. "See anyone?"

Eddie pointed, "There!" The three horses exploded forward. Jack was on the ground in front of the still.

George was off his mount and running to Jack before Clyde was stopped, "JACK!"

George cradled Jack in his arms. "I tried to stop 'em, but..."

"What hurts?"

"Nothing a little bourbon wouldn't cure!" he said with a wink. "I'm alright. Just an old man. They didn't beat me up too bad."

Eddie and Pauly galloped up to the house. The ladies were running frantically to and from the well, using pots, pans, and buckets to splash water on the flames. Eddie and Pauly lent a hand and soon the house fire was out.

"They didn't have time to get a good fire started, before we saw them. Poured kerosene on branches. Lit the branches, then rode the horses over and tossed them onto the porch. The still is gone. Must have lit that first. We didn't even get a bucket of water on it."

"How many were there?"

"Four."

"Everyone alright?"

Jenny said, "Yes. We are all fine. Just a bit unsteady."

"Jack, is there a doctor up this way?"

"No. Why?"

"That leg's banged up some. Does this hurt..."

"Ohhhhh!" moaned Jack.

"You'll be fine, I don't know if it's broke, but Doc needs to take a look."

"You up for a ride in your wagon?"

"Yeah. But what about the gals? They alright?"

"You rest here and I'll go check with Eddie and Pauly."

"I aint goin' to no dance!"

Pauly had ridden out to see if he could find the men who had beaten Jack and set the place ablaze. As he trotted back to the house he saw Eddie and George talking, "They're long gone."

"It'd be quicker if we brought Jack back to our farm."

George thought a moment. "Eddie, you fetch Doc and bring him to our place. We'll take him there. But stop by and send a few men over with guns. Pauly, you stay here and guard the ladies. We'll get you some back-up pronto."

With that, Eddie rode south and George went to Jack's barn for the wagon. Jack had a matching pair of plough horses in the stalls. George rode down to the still to lift Jack onto the back. He tied Clyde's reins to the wagon and was just getting to the ford when he saw two wagons and six men barreling up from the south. He stopped to take a good look while reaching for his shotgun. A big grin came across his face when he saw they were his guys, led by John and Hoot.

After Doc tended to Jack, as he was about to leave, he pulled George outside, "What's going on here?"

"What do you mean?

"Jack wouldn't tell me what happened." George simply nodded. "Listen, what are you two into?"

"Nothing we can't handle."

"You two bootlegging?"

"Not exactly."

Doc didn't know what that meant. "Jack's left leg is broken. I didn't have any trouble setting it, but he is gonna have to be off it for a month and a half, maybe two. Can you look after him here?"

"Sure."

Doc walked down the steps before he turned for a last word with George, "Whatever you two got yourself into, you best be careful. Somebody meant business when they paid a visit to Jack." Doc climbed into his one-ton Ford Model TT truck. "I'll be back in a few days."

George watched as Doc started it up and pulled away, raising dust along the road. The hands came out to see Doc's noisy new toy. George returned to the house and the make-shift room where Jack would spend the next two months, being waited on hand-and-foot. As he peeked in, Jack grinned, looking like a cat with feathers from the pet canary on his chin, "You wouldn't happen to have anything--for medicinal purposes--would ya?"

By October, things had settled down. People were still on edge and each delivery crew now had four men--a driver, one man riding shotgun, another at the back of the wagon, and the fourth deep in--with a pistol, shotgun, and extra ammunition. It was taking its toll on George and he began dreaming of other ventures and maybe selling the farm. This rum-running was good money, but a nasty, grueling business.

"Coffee?"

"Love some." Rebecca returned with two cups. George took a sip. "Ahhh! The way I like it!"

Rebecca smiled. "The kids are having a grand time in there."

"Oh, to have that much energy!"

They both heard gun shots in the distance. "Ohh...what was that?"

"Little early for target practice, I'd say." George got up, pulled the curtain back, and looked out the window. There was some commotion down at the Little House. Grabbing his hat and walking out the back door he yelled, "I best go check!"

"They didn't hit any of us, but they blew a hole in the wagon." It was riddled with bullets and shot.

George ran his hand over the wagon where the shot had penetrated. "Where?"

"Just up the road..."

In a few minutes eight men rode south to locate the marauders and another pair rode north to alarm the guards protecting Jack's farm.

About three miles south, George pulled them to a halt. He

listened carefully. "Pauly, you and Hoot go right to the base of the foothills. Go as far south as the bridge. Then circle back along the hills and flush them back here."

"Eddie, you and me and one more man will run down by the river. If we have to chase them out, Eddie will come back and get the three men we leave here. The rest of you hide your horses, but stay lookout here. If you see anyone you don't know, shoot first and ask questions later. You are to block them up here. We'll be right on their tail."

They searched all day and Hoot and Pauly found them late in the afternoon, hiding under a large willow tree by a stream coming out of the foothills. George's men knew the spot well--the stream was fed by a favorite spring bringing ice cold water to weary feet. The horses, left to wander in the water and feed on plants, were well away from the marauders.

Hoot had a plan. He and Pauly returned to the three men that had been left to wait for the others to return--they were leading four horses by their bridles. "We got 'em. They are resting by the stream outta Willow Spring." Hoot held up the reins, "They ain't going nowhere."

Before dark, George and his other two men rode back looking disappointed. "We didn't find nothin'. No men or horses. No tracks. Nothin'."

"But we did. We got 'em cornered, Boss!"

George's eyes brightened, "Where are they?"

Tex, one of the weary marauders, continued to soak his feet in the pool at Willow Spring, wondering aloud, "Why the hell ain't Jerome back with them horses?" He looked around at the other two men and spotted Jerome's brother, "You better go find your little brother, Jackson."

"Yeah." Jackson called out as he wandered down the creek, "Jerome." He heard rustling in the bushes ahead and continued forward, calling out his brother's name.

As he came around the corner he said, "Jerome, boy am I glad to..." There were two pistols at Jerome's head and in the instant it took Jackson to realize what they were, five more were pointed at him.

George flatly asked, "Gotta gun?"

"No."

"That should even the odds a bit."

They tied Jackson's and Jerome's hands behind their

69

backs with bridles they had cut from the horses and gagged them with their own handkerchiefs. George whispered in Hoot's ear and he stepped behind the two captives. Then he quietly said to John, "You lead the way." Hoot pushed the captives forward behind John and the rest of the men huddled closely behind with their pistols and shotguns at the ready.

When the men at the pool heard a rustle, they didn't move from their restful spot under the willow. "About time!" one yelled.

John said, "That's what we thought, too!" Upon hearing a strange voice, both men jumped up and reached for their guns. "I wouldn't move, if I were you." They stopped in their tracks.

Eddie leaned over to George, "Now what are we gonna do with them?"

Rapidly, four shots rang out; two each from John and Hoot. Eddie's eyes widened and his mouth dangled open.

"Does that answer your question?"

The next morning, George stood outside his children's room and watched them sleep. His arms were crossed; his coffee cup was in his right hand, pressed against his chest. It was still early when Rebecca came out of their bedroom. She hugged him from behind. "Aren't they beautiful," he whispered.

She looked at them and smiled. "We are blessed."

"They play so hard and then sleep like angels."

"We need to bottle all that energy!"

"And you could bottle a sleep aid, too! She is out cold!"

She hugged him again and they peeked in on the two sleeping children together. "I could do this every day."

"You can." She kissed him on the cheek.

The children began to stir an hour later. Thomas got out of bed rubbing his eyes and made a beeline for the bathroom. When he was done he came back to George and raised his arms.

"You're getting too big for this." George picked him up

and kissed him on the cheek. "What are we gonna to do today?"

He immediately rubbed the kiss with a sour expression on his face.

"Rubbing that off or rubbing it in?"

Thomas yawned.

Abby woke up a few minutes later, a bit cranky. George cuddled with her while Thomas went downstairs for breakfast.

"Abby, Abby, Abby! There's my sweet dumplin'." Rebecca kissed her daughter on the stomach and Abby laughed.

"Well, I better get goin'. I need to talk to Uncle Jack." Jack was sitting in the kitchen flirting with Alice, who enjoyed the attention.

When she saw George standing at the doorway, she excused herself and returned to her duties. "Good morning!"

"Good morning, Alice!" George replied.

"She is something," replied Uncle Jack.

"When you start chasing the ladies around the kitchen, I'm taking you home to your wife!" They both laughed. "Jack, we need to talk." George closed the door.

When he opened the door a half-hour later, he said, "This has to stop!" Jack, a grim look on his face, nodded his agreement.

There was a killer frost in early November. The men were busy raking, cutting up limbs and branches, and neatly piling firewood at both Big and Little House. They were still guarding Jack's place, but George was having trouble rotating the guards back to chores on his farm. He got on Clyde one afternoon and rode north to see what was going on. A week of cold had been followed by a two week heat wave, where the temperature got into the low 80's during the day, and the sky was hazy, dry, and still.

Uncle Jack greeted George on his return, "Indian summer." He was sitting out in the shade on a kitchen chair with his leg propped up on a second chair.

"What?"

"Indian summer. Hot spell before winter."

"Yes. It is surprisingly warm."

"I was at American Falls on the Snake River when it hit 85 degrees in November. Let me think...that was 1899."

"Thermometer is reading eighty right now. It's been

staying so hot at night we've been keeping the windows open."

"Not much else you can do. Except maybe swim."

George sat down on a chair next to Jack. "How long will it last?"

"It's nearly over."

"I checked on your place. I understand why the men don't want to leave."

"Really?"

"Seems the ladies have taken a liking to having some new boys around. Guess there has been some romance in the air up that way."

Jack laughed. "I'll get the shotgun and straighten things out!"

George smiled. "They have cleaned up the farm a bit. Painted over burn marks on the house; nothing too seriously damaged. The apple press is another story. They are rebuilding your still."

"I'm thankful nobody was hurt."

"Except you."

"Well, yeah."

While George and Jack chatted, two pair of field glasses were trained on their every move. Men had been watching from the hills for the last two days. The Altura farm guards were alert and active and somebody was generally up all the time. One man said to the other, "I don't see a good way in."

"I got another idea. Let's go."

It was near two in the morning, three nights later when Eddie came out of the Little House. He hurriedly worked at his long johns; lookin' to give birth to a new river. He was a bit wobbly as he finished up, mumbling to himself, "Damn coffee!"

He looked up into the sky and saw the Milky Way. "Beautiful!" He studied the stars to get his bearings. "There she is," he said, "Sirius, the 'Dog Star.'" The air was warm. He was heading back inside when he heard a crackle of branches. He stopped and was still, determining if he was hearing someone. The crackle continued and his eyes adjusted to a glow from the other side of the house. "What the hell..."

He came around the corner to see branches stacked high against the house exploding into flame. "Shit! FIRE! FIRE!"

Men came out of the Little House in droves. Some

grabbed buckets and pails; others, shovels and spades. Two men jumped out from near the bottom of the stack of branches, coughing and covering their mouths with their handkerchiefs. Each had a kerosene can. John had grabbed his 'over and under' and had seen enough to try, convict, and condemn the men trying to escape. He pulled the gun to his shoulder and led them perfectly. He pulled the triggers one after the other and the two collapsed to the ground.

The flames were reaching to the eves. The men inched their way closer trying to pull burning branches away from the house, but the siding was roaring. They made a bucket brigade from the well to the house: Men tossed water onto the fire and white steam and black smoke danced--before the fire sprung back to life.

"Quick! Get in there and wake everyone."

The kitchen ladies were out in a few minutes, trying to stay covered in their nightgowns. Rebecca followed, carrying Thomas. George couldn't make his way past the smoke, but he kept trying--running back to the porch to suck in a breath of air, before charging back in. Rebecca moved away from the house, cradling Thomas in her arms. Finally, Jack appeared through the smoke, choking and holding Abby in his arms away from his body, looking down at her precious face. George was right behind Jack. At seeing everyone accounted for, Rebecca sighed in relief. They were getting a handle on the fire when Eddie yelled "Shit!" George and Rebecca ran over. Eddie and John had turned the two dead men over, "These two are OUR men."

Jack let out an inhuman scream, "NOOOOOOOOOOOO!" He was still looking at the four-year-old girl's precious face. She wasn't breathing.

There was no consoling Jack, Rebecca, or George--they sat on the ground crying with Abby between them. Jack kept whimpering, "Oh, Gawd, what have I done." Unable to revive her, she was dead of smoke inhalation.

Rebecca felt like taking Abby to her breast, to nurse her back to life. Though she weaned her a year earlier she expected her, at an instant, to wake from her nap and nuzzle her. But she didn't move.

George looked on, 'How could they do this to her?'

Devastated with the thought that his men could have perpetrated such an act, Eddie looked around the two dead men's belongings before meandering back to the circle of mourners, "There's wads of money in with their stuff."

"Wasn't thirty pieces of silver, was it?"

An hour before dawn, Alice, Claire, and June joined the mourners. Softly Alice said, "It's time for us to take her." There was no reply. "Thomas is back in bed." They gently picked Abby up and carried her to the kitchen.

In the pre-dawn light, George and Eddie had to prod each other to take a good look at the murder scene. It was distasteful to think two of their men--men they would call friends--could have done such a thing. Eddie whispered, "If they meant to burn the house down, they would have stacked branches to the rafters. Probably just meant to scare us." What their two friends had done was plain to see: The branches and leaves the men doused with kerosene lay just below Abby's bedroom window. Due to the warm weather the window and her bedroom door had been left open. It drew the smoke into her room and suffocated her while she slept. When the flames crept up to the windows, the curtains exploded.

Wide-eyed, absorbing every detail, George replied, "They may have just meant to scare us, but that won't bring my Abby back." She was probably already dead when Jack picked her up, cradled her, and stumped out of the room on his broken leg, gasping for air.

They put Abby on a clean blanket on the kitchen table, undressed her and folded her clothing as if to put them away. Alice warmed water on the stove. They took turns with the wash cloth wiping away soot, ash, and dirt. They used lavender soap and rinsed her body before toweling her off. The kitchen, which normally smelled of fresh-made bread, had the odor of lavender and wood smoke. They hadn't said a word to one another the whole time they cleaned her.

June asked, "This?" as she came back into the kitchen with Abby's finest Sunday clothing.

"Yes," replied Alice. They dressed her. Claire left and returned with a baby blanket and wrapped Abby as if she were chilly, with her hands and head peeking out.

"Come with me," Alice said to June. They prepared a table in the parlor to receive the body, with pillows and dried flowers.

They carried Abby's body to the parlor and gently lay her on the table, surrounded by pillows, as the first rays of the dawn sun lit the room.

"What should we do with the bodies?"

"Trash heap is what they deserve." But they prepared two plots near the foothills. Men with carpentering skills prepared two rough coffins out of spare pine planks. They were ready with the coffins by noon.

After dinner, the men assembled to walk behind the wagon carrying the two men to their final resting place. Nobody wanted to give a eulogy, but eventually Eddie was looking through the Scriptures for appropriate passages.

As the parade pulled out, Doc drove his Ford Truck onto the property and was held up a few minutes, while the somber men passed by. He was there to check on Jack's leg. Doc stepped down from the truck and paused to watch the men. Seeing where they were assembling, he spotted two mounds of dirt. He thought, 'Empty graves?' "What's going on, George?" George didn't reply. "I'm here to see Jack."

"In the house."

When he was finished with Jack, he came back to the porch where George was sitting. The men were lumbering back from the funeral. "George, know anything about the four men strung up just south of Willow Springs? Two on each side of the road. Just hanging there by their necks. Funny thing, though; their necks aren't broken. They each have been shot." George shrugged. "What happened here?" He pointed down the side of the house.

"Kitchen fire."

He looked at the siding, where the fire had been. It was near the bedrooms, on the opposite side of the house from the kitchen. He was getting pissed. He spit. "Bullshit! I have half a mind to talk to the Sheriff." George shrugged again. "What is the funeral procession for?"

"Killed a couple of weasels."

By now, Doc was fuming. He rubbed his whiskers with his hand, thinking. He went back inside the house and returned a quarter-hour later, quiet and pensive. In a low voice Doc said, "Jack told me enough. Sorry for your loss."

He walked to his truck and drove through the startled men as they jumped out of his way. He never mentioned anything to the Sheriff.

The following morning, Jack told George he needed to borrow a couple of men and three horses for a few days.

"What for?"

"I need to get to Vancouver."

"Vancouver? Hold it! We don't even know it was--"

"Yes we do. It was them. And people like them in Spokane, and in Canada. And it was me. And it was you. We all did this. And now, somebody has to bring an end to it. I figure when they find out they killed an innocent, little baby girl and six good men, they will be willing to divide up the territory and honor boundaries."

George saw the wisdom of what Jack said. Quietly he asked, "But...before we lay Abby to rest?"

Tears streamed down Jack's cheeks, but he didn't look up. "I can't watch her be put in the ground."

There was a long pause, before George could ask, "Can you travel?"

"Don't see I have a whole lot of choice."

George talked them into taking a wagon and two horses, to let Jack lay in the back.

Early in the morning, Eddie and Pauly dug into the earth next to where Tura LaVoy lay. As if he knew it was a noble task, Clyde watched as they flung dirt to the surface from six feet below. He neither flinched nor grazed. The river gurgled as it swiftly passed. A slight breeze announced relief from the sweltering heat.

"We're finished with the casket, Mum!" reported Roger to Claire. Roger had been a carpenter on a British naval vessel before misfortune sent him seeking his way 'in the colonies', as he put it.

"Bring it in."

Roger and Adam carried the wooden box into the parlor, placing it on the floor. It was maple, the wood having come from a beautiful tree in the foothills that had been split by lightening two years before, then blown over a day later. The men cut it up, dried it, and milled it the previous winters for paneling. Claire rubbed her hand on the top. "Oh, it is magnificent!" It had been sealed, coated, and polished; showing care and craftsmanship.

"Thank ye, Mum." Roger blushed.

"June! Alice! Come look!" The ladies came in from the kitchen praising Roger for his handsome creation.

"Who did the carving on the lid?" He had chiseled in Abby's given name.

"Oh, me. Wasn't nothin'", replied Roger. He beamed and blushed.

"I think this deserves a blemish of brandy, don't you ladies?" Claire stepped into the kitchen and returned with five small glasses and a bottle of brandy. "We save this for cookin' when we need it and for celebratin' when we don't!" The men laughed while Claire poured the drinks. It was the first anyone had laughed since the tragedy. "To great workmanship!"

"And to Abigail Rebecca Cash. May our loss, be heaven's gain!"

"Here! Here!" They sloshed the brandy down their throats, warming them immediately.

"Now help us with her body." Roger and Adam lifted the top and placed it on edge on the floor. The casket was unlined.

"Blankets and all, Mum?"

"Yes, but just one of the pillows." Roger carefully took one pillow and placed it at the head of the casket and pressed down on the middle. He and Adam lifted Abby's stiff body and gently laid her in the box. Alice looked at her, then stepped forward to make final adjustments. Claire placed dried flowers in her left hand and June lifted her stiff right hand and slipped the girl's tiny Bible underneath. They stepped back to look.

"She looks so peaceful. Like a sleepin' angel!"

The men lifted the coffin off the floor and onto the table. They left the lid off so her family could see her at peace and rest.

Later that morning, Clyde and the small wagon waited by the main door to the house. George, Rebecca, and Thomas said their final goodbyes. George helped his wife onboard, then took hold of his son's hand and walked back to the house. Roger slipped into the house with a hammer and nails. "Now, Mum?"

"Yes." When he was done, he stood and looked at the finished work. June slipped over to him and gave him a kiss on the cheek. He blushed.

Eddie, Pauly, Roger, and George grasped the wooden handles to lift the coffin. They walked it out the door, down the steps, and slid it onto the wagon, as the men assembled to walk behind the wagon down to the burial site. The kitchen ladies removed their aprons and dried their hands, as they slipped behind the men for the funeral procession.

The air was noticeably cooler--the hot spell broken. They marched slowly. George parked the wagon twenty yards from the grave and the men formed two rows facing each other, from the back of the wagon to the grave. They passed the casket along with dignity. Eddie placed two ropes on the ground next to the hole and they placed the casket on top.

The ladies assembled near the head of the casket. George stepped forward. "Lord, I am not sure why you have chosen to take our daughter to yourself, but you have. So take good care of her and love her like we do. Tell her we are looking forward to seeing her in heaven someday. Help her mama as she grieves our loss. Amen."

With few words said, men grasped the two ropes on each side of the casket, and as if playing tug-of-war, pulled tight to lift the casket into the air. They positioned it over the hole and moved toward the center to lower the box into the ground. Collecting a shovel from the wagon, George shoved it into the pile of dirt and threw some on the casket. He called his son over to help with the next shovelful, and then passed the shovel along to the waiting men--each taking a turn with the grim task. When finished, Roger took a wooden cross he had made and crammed it into the soft soil. He'd forgotten to bring his hammer, so he slammed it into the ground using the back of the shovel.

"Clyde!" The horse looked back. "Let's go home!" He started for the barn.

The day had been long and hard. Neighbors and friends expressed their love and support, but at times all Rebecca and George wanted to do was run away, to be alone, and hope to wake up from this horrible dream. They were finally alone after they trudged upstairs to bed late that evening.

"You alright?"

"Sure," Rebecca said in an unconvincing tone. "How about you?"

"I made it through."

"What you said was nice."

"Thank you. Hard day."

"The hardest." He hugged his wife. "Why did she have to die?" He didn't answer, because there was none.

While the funeral was finishing, Jack was getting off the barge. It was the halfway point in their trip to Vancouver. He had been in a great deal of pain the whole way--grimacing and fighting through the ache. They rolled the wagon off the barge, then led the two horses off, and harnessed them. Soon, Jack was again in the back of the wagon and the two men with him headed out. Jack wished he had something for the pain, but needed to be sober for the task ahead.

"No, we're not selling you our territory!" snapped Jack to his business partners. He took a long draw on his cigar.

"But be reasonable..." started his second partner, Allan Edmondson.

The third partner, Jacques Péppin, reached his hand over to gently stop him. "We have all lost enough good men. Now an innocent girl is dead because of us. I think we can work out a deal here. You take from the south end of the Bitterroot and go north to the border..."

"I need all the way to Challis."

Péppin thought a moment. It was giving up a lot of territory, but not many towns. "Alright, but we need free passage to camp and travel from Coeur d'Alene down to..."

"Hell, no, you can come in at Weiser." They all looked at the map. Yes, that would be a way of getting to Caldwell and the Treasure Valley.

"You drive a hard bargain, but I think we can make that work."

"One more thing. I'll protect competitors from coming at you and you'll do the same for me." It seemed reasonable, so they agreed. What the Vancouver men hadn't realized was that there was no real threat to them from the east, while there was a large threat to Jack from Spokane. It was a lopsided agreement that would cost them more in labor than they knew and cost Jack nothing. They shook hands on the 'cooperative arrangement' and Jack opened the bottle he had been saving for the occasion. While his partners had not directly been involved in attacking Jack's and George's farms, they hadn't protected them either. They had marauded others' territories, which had encouraged them to do the same. Perhaps what Jack started could lead to other, similar agreements to bring peace to the Pacific Northwest.

Some days, Rebecca broke down crying. "It just comes over me, like a wave from the ocean."

"I know. I can spot one of her old toys and it's as if..." George couldn't finish.

"How do you think Thomas is dealing with it?"

"He seems quiet. Asks a lot of questions about what happens when you die."

"He told me he wants to be buried next to his sister."

"Really? What did you say?"

"I told him he has a long life ahead of him, but if that is

what he wants we will honor it and if he changes his mind in the future, that's fine, too."

"We don't really know when it is our time."

"That's right. You can never tell. One minute a man's working and the next he's collapsed in the dust."

"Do you believe what you said at the funeral?"

The question caught him off guard. He wasn't sure what he had said. "Which part?"

"You know, about God taking care of Abby for us, until we come to see her."

"Yes, that is what I believe. God loves His children and wants us to be with Him in His paradise."

"I believe that as well." There was a long pause. "I have to, now."

The first Thanksgiving was the hardest. Rebecca almost refused to come to dinner, "How am I supposta thank God for taking away our daughter!" Next came Abby's birthday. There was a hole inside Christmas you could run a wagon through. Then the first anniversary of her death. Things seemed to get better after the first year. Thomas would bring up Abby's death occasionally. He missed his playmate and friend. Rebecca was sad, but held no grudge. She knew the men would not have intentionally killed her child. They didn't know she was asleep just above them. She believed the fire was only meant to scare them, as Eddie said, not to kill anyone. Anyway, they got their due.

By early winter it was clear the truce with Jack's business partners in Vancouver was working out well. There were few conflicts now. Everyone still carried rifles and expected an assault now and again. Usually it was just people trying to get free liquor. Beer and whiskey was now available in Canada and there was a steady supply of buyers just across the border. Jack's gin distilling operation was back in full force. With winter, there were fewer teams being sent, which gave George more time to think. And with more time to think, George would show up on Jack's doorstep to talk things out.

"If it wasn't for this business, we would not have been attacked." Jack just let him talk it out. He thought to himself, 'that may be true--but what's done is done'.

George looked at the glass he had been nursing, "This is

pretty good stuff."

"Not as good as bourbon, but it will get you by in a pinch," replied Jack.

"No, I mean it. Tastes pretty good."

"That's because I distill it. The other way to make it is to use grain alcohol and add ground up juniper berries and whatnot."

"Is that good?"

"Mine's better; the other is way cheaper."

"Could we sell more of the cheaper stuff?"

"Don't know. Seems we are doing pretty good with what we got." George could tell Jack didn't want to change things, so he let it drop.

In early March, 1929, Rebecca stopped by the kitchen and asked June to make a picnic lunch for her and George.

"Thomas, too?"

"Not this time."

June looked out the window. It was cold and crispy out. There was a hint of rain. They all were looking forward to sunny days ahead, but this was no day for a picnic. As Rebecca walked away, June's eyes followed her. Then it clicked. "Claire! Alice! I know something you don't know!"

Two days later, George burst through the door. "The bank was robbed!"

"Our bank?" said Rebecca.

"Yes. Porthill Bank."

"How?"

"Busted in at night. Took everything from the safe."

"Did we lose much?"

"A few hundred. Most of our money is safe."

When he had started in the rum-running business, George asked Jack's advice on where to keep his money.

"Where have you got it now?"

"At the house."

Jack's eyes lit up. "Does anyone know it is there?"

"Probably."

"Then you better get it out soon. You're asking to be robbed. Your own men will do it or let word leak out."

"Who of our men would do it?"

"The enforcement men."

George hadn't thought about them, 'They probably would'.

Jack told George, "I keep a small amount at the local bank and transfer most to a bigger bank in Vancouver, where I do a good deal of my business. You'll probably want to take over what you have in the house and open an account at Porthill. Then have them transfer funds to a national bank--like one in New York City--like all us big tycoons do!" Jack laughed. Later that day, George--escorted by two enforcement teams--made a considerable deposit at Porthill Bank and had accounts set up in New York.

The banker whispered, "Swiss, too?"[12]

George did not know what that meant, but whispered, "Yes." It turned out to be one of the smartest moves he made. Over time, he added a Canadian bank in Vancouver.

The morning broke bright and crisp. George was drinking coffee in the kitchen when he saw a rider coming in at a fast gallop from the north. He didn't recognize the man, so he walked outside.

"Mr. Cash?"

"Yes."

"I have a message for you."

"What is it?"

"Jack is dead. Funeral is today at 10 sharp."

"What? Today? How did he die? When did he die?"

"I can't answer that." With that final word he rode off as

---

[12] Swiss Parliament passed the Banking Law of 1934, which codified 'secrecy'-- which had been their banks tradition since the Middles Ages. It criminalized violations and mandated administration, such as bank supervision, in keeping with the secrecy tradition.

quickly as he had come.

In a fog, George put on his Sunday best and rode to Jack's farm, arriving at half past nine. He took off his hat as he approached the wagon with the coffin on the back, stared at it for a moment, before walking up to Jack's wife. "Jenny, how did it happen?"

Her eyes searched the ground. "Heart attack."

"I didn't know he was sick."

"He wasn't."

"When did he die?"

"Last night." She seemed more preoccupied than grief stricken. Maybe it was just her way of dealing with the shock.

It seemed odd to George that the funeral was so soon. He rode behind the cortège of three other friends and the widow. They had chosen an odd place to bury Jack. The funeral was brief; with Wiley Owens reading two totally unrelated passages of Scripture as if he were in a hurry. George scratched his head wondering what the words had to do with death. The funeral was solemn and respectful, but nobody seemed all that sad. George chalked it up to surprise and the suddenness of death. They returned to the house, but there was no meal or time given over for grieving together. The three friends hardly said a word to one another, jumped on their horses or wagons and left. Uncle Jack's wife, Jenny, didn't say a word and quickly returned to the house, leaving George sitting alone on his horse hardly knowing what to think.

When the horses and buggies were out of sight he said to Clyde, "Let's go!" Just then, he saw eight men riding in at full gallop on brown thoroughbreds. He stopped the horse, "Whoa!" They were wearing scarlet tunics, midnight blue breeches with yellow-gold strapping, light-brown, wide, felt, flat-brimmed Stetson hats with Montana creases, Sam Browne belts with shoulder cross straps, and white sidearm lanyards. Their attire was unmistakable. "What the heck would Mounties be..." He waited to see what was going on.

He figured that they had come late to the funeral, so he started right in as they pulled to a stop, "You missed the..."

The lead horseman either had not heard him or ignored him, interrupted with, "We have papers to arrest John Easley Evans and to seize his farm and assets. Where is he?"

"Dead."

When they roused Jenny out of the house, she claimed she wasn't Jack's wife. Things were getting more strange by the minute. After talking to George at length, the Mounties let him go.

"Home, Clyde!" he said to his horse. Sadly, he put Clyde away, then wandered over to look in on the store of whiskey he kept for Jack's visits. He closed the door, hurting from the loss of his dear friend.

A month later he got a picture postcard--"Arrived in Alabama safe and sound. Jenny." It was postmarked Mobile, Alabama.

"Mobile?" Strange, he thought. He didn't know she had family there. He flipped the card over and back. Then he saw something he passed off as a printer's mark, trademark symbol, or the like, at the bottom of the postcard. It was small, very neat print: UJ2 inside of a circle. He broke into laughter as he recognized the handwriting--it belonged to Uncle Jack. Unwittingly, he had played his role perfectly.

With Jack thought dead, the Cash family received an unexpected visitor. The stranger stepped out of a taxi one afternoon while George was playing catch with Thomas. Rebecca was nearby, darning socks and drinking lemonade. The man turned to the driver, "You'll need to wait."

"Your nickel, Mac."

He walked up to the Cash family. "You are George Cash, I presume."

"Yes. This is my wife, Rebecca, and son, Thomas," said George as he removed this glove and reached out his hand. They shook. "Pleasure."

"I was an associate of Jack Evans. I understand you were in business with him?"

"Yes, I am...," then he corrected himself, "...was." It was obvious the stranger believed he was dead. "And your name?"

"Jacques Péppin. May I have a word with you?"

"Of course." With that, the two men walked into the

house. "Will this do?"

"Could you close the door?"

"Certainly."

"I'll make this brief as possible. Jack's death has left a large void in our operation." With that statement a three-hour conversation began, while the taxi driver napped near the river.

Jack had done George a big favor in the week leading up to his 'death'; he moved his inventory to Altura Farm, so when the Mounties confiscated liquor at his place they got little. Of course, they destroyed the distillery. In their discussions, George said he needed a replacement.

Péppin replied, "That will be no problem."

"And none of that bathtub stuff."

"That will be a little more difficult." Over time, a suitable replacement was found. Little changed in the day-to-day operation, but George reflected it was 'not like the good old days'.

FOUR

As the due date approached, Rebecca asked about names if the baby was a boy.

"Abraham."

She winced, "What?"

"We are going to name him 'Abraham George Cash' if we have another boy."

"But, that's not a very pretty name."

"Pretty?"

"Yes. It doesn't go with anything. I don't have the name Abraham in my family. Was it in yours?" He groaned. "I don't like the name. Can't we pick another?"

"It is Abraham if we have a boy. What have you chosen for a girl?"

"Wait. Can't we discuss this?"

"No. I name the boys: You name the girls. What name have you chosen for a girl?" She tried several times to bring up the subject again, but to no avail.

That evening, Rebecca assailed George with a litany of dreadful girl's names.
"Matilda...Beatrice...Oleander...Hogarth...Helclare...Jessenia."

But her ploy didn't work. "Whatever name you choose is fine with me."

She hoped he would object and she would then be free to do the same with the name, Abraham. When he didn't bite, she turned over, exclaiming, "Oh, you're impossible!"

"What did I do?"

FOUR

The baby came struggling into the world on September 29, 1929.

"It may be breach," Alice whispered to Claire.

"Mr. George, I think you better bring the Doctor." George rode as quickly as Clyde could carry him to Doc's office in Porthill. They returned in Doc's truck with Clyde tied to the rear, working hard to keep up. Doc sprang into the house. Forty-five minutes later there was a cry heard throughout the house, followed by a second--"It's a boy!" Once Rebecca laid eyes on the baby and heard his first cry, memories of his difficult delivery evaporated and she no longer hated the name, Abraham.

"I am not sure why he was so damn stubborn about coming out. Must have known something we don't know," Doc commented .

"He's wonderful!"

"Yep, all the parts are there and seem to be working fine. I want you to get a good rest. He is mighty beautiful!" said Doc with a smile as he backed away from the bed and turned to leave the room. Doc stopped off at the kitchen where he had dropped his coat on his hurried arrival. "Hello, ladies! It's a boy. And he's beautiful."

"What caused the difficulties? Breech?"

"Oh, heavens no--he was just being stubborn. Little bastard--excuse me, ladies--little dickens has a mind of his own."

The Stock Market collapse in late October 1929 had a rolling effect on the economy. Investors were initially hurt. This led to withdrawing capital needed to keep businesses growing, which led to business protectionism, retraction, and job loss. No part of the nation was left untouched. Sheriffs and police chiefs across Idaho were not exempt from the economic downturn and looked for new ways of making ends meet.

"Whoa." The sheriff, shotgun in hand, stepped out of the dark to stop the wagon. His deputy aimed his small pistol at the driver.

"What gives here?"

"Name is Sheriff Dawson. What are you carrying?"

"Just some..."

"Don't bother lying. I already know."

"What's on your mind?"

"The Prohis been asking my help."

"Who? Pro-his?"

"Prohibition Agents."[13]

"Ah. So?"

"Well, I don't see much reason to help those bastards out. It is a Federal law they're worried about and doesn't do much for us here. They don't pay my salary."

The driver could see where this conversation was going. "We don't have any money..."

"I know. Your payment people collect that. We'll get that soon enough. But since the Feds don't pay my salary, maybe they can help me out in some other way, like better firearms and ammunition, if I help them. Of course, I reckon there are other ways of helping out an old country sheriff, don't you?"

The driver thought, 'Here it comes!' but said, "How much?"

"Twenty a month."

"I'll ask the boss."

"Good. You do that. Quick." He began to walk away. "Oh, and one other thing. Just in case your boss doesn't think I am serious, I have a message for him."

"What is it?" Sheriff Dawson turned to his deputy and nodded. The Deputy shot the driver in the leg.

By the time the relief driver pulled into Altura Farm his injured partner had lost a lot of blood and was unconscious. Having driven all night and day, they hadn't appreciated the glorious spring day around them. They laid out the injured man at the Small House and one man ran to find George.

---

[13] The Prohibition Unit of the IRS was a federal law enforcement agency formed to enforce the Volstead Act in 1920. What it had to do with collecting revenue, nobody knows--which is probably why it was ineffective. In 1927, it became an independent entity within the Department of the Treasury, changing its name to the Bureau of Prohibition. It was still slow in gaining traction. By this time, in Chicago--a hotbed for prohibition-related offenses--there were around 300 agents to cover a population of over 3 million people. In 1930, it was transferred to the Justice Department. It was briefly absorbed into the Federal Bureau of Investigation, where it was managed as a separate, autonomous agency, until J. Edgar Hoover could unload the hot potato--liquor enforcement was tainted of corruption from top to bottom. It was not until the later years of Prohibition that enforcement became somewhat effective.

"Who did this?"

"Sheriff Dawson and his deputy out in Idaho County. Wants twenty dollars a month." It was the day George knew was coming and dreaded. It would snowball from there.

"You'll have to get Doc to take the bullet out."

"I'll go get him."

George thought to himself, 'Dammit! This is twice now! What the hell is this world comin' to? Whatever happened to talking things out?'

Soon every sheriff and police chief in Northern Idaho had his hand out to George. It was becoming a nasty business. When the lesser police chiefs started roughing up his people, George had enough.

"Grangeville?"

"Yes, Grangeville."

"You gotta be shitting me!"

"No, I'm not."

"How much do we sell there?"

"Not much. If it's not rodeo time we don't take in as much as he is asking."

"You've got to tell him he needs to be more reasonable."

"We did, but he said if you can't get through Grangeville, there is no taking liquor to more profitable areas."

George thought a moment. It was true. "We can't afford it. Do you think he'll get violent?"

"I don't think so. He doesn't have a deputy, so it's just him."

"Alrighty then, this is what we are a-gonna do..."

The next time his men rode through the area, the Grangeville Police Chief stopped their wagon. He wasn't even armed.

"Well?"

"He says he'll give ya ten a month."

"That's not good enough."

"It's gonna have to do."

"And if I don't take it?"

"You won't have your job for long. Or your life. You choose."

The pattern repeated throughout the territory.

Sometimes when it came to the negotiation, the police or sheriff accepted. Other times liquor was confiscated or destroyed. Occasionally his men were arrested--which was more a nuisance than anything.

"Why do they have to arrest the men?"

"They figure they can press you harder."

"We plead guilty and, hell, the fine is less than what they want us to pay them."

"I know, but the damn lawyers are expensive."

"Yeah, have to bring someone up from Boise. Well, guess you better wire Boswell."

George couldn't bring himself to use violence, unless forced. "You meet violence with violence. Otherwise, they think you are sissy. They'll continue to push you around. But if a man will be reasonable, you keep talking." He didn't order his men to kill anybody, but made sure they heard that lawmen were being killed around the country, so they could pass it along.

"You heard what happened in Wisconsin, didn't ya?"

"You mean about the agents who were killed?"

"Yeah."

"You're not threatening me, are ya?"

"Would we do that? I am just making sure you understand the situation. I have heard it said 'it is better to leave no witnesses', have you?"

The message was clearly received. "Alright, ten a month."

After years of high revenues and higher costs, George yearned for the good old days of the Great War and the rabbits. He was still making a great deal of money and his overhead was low, but he hated injuries to his men, threats he had to make, and violence on all sides. There had to be a better way.

In the spring of 1931, George received an unexpected visitor. He had been playing with the children in the middle of the morning on the front porch. Wild baby rabbits ran through the vegetation next to the porch and George would reach down between the pickets to snatch them by the neck and pull them through to the deck to the delighted squeals of his children. He held them until they calmed and allowed his children to pet them before placing them back in the flower bed.

When a taxi pulled to the front door, George stood to see who had arrived. "Mr. Péppin, nice to see you again."

Péppin tossed a wad of dollar bills to the taxi driver, told him to return in one hour, and turned around to shake George's hand. "Nice to see you, too."

"Can I get you a lemonade?"

"Something stronger, if you don't mind."

"I suspect we can scrounge up something." The two men walked into the parlor and George closed the door. He extracted a bottle and two glasses. "Bourbon?"

"Please."

"Don't have much use for this stuff, now that Jack is gone."

"Well, yes. And that's what brings me here." The Vancouver partners still didn't know Jack was alive and well in Alabama. They talked for about an hour.

"So, you see, the decline of the economy has put us in a pinch. Jack was a silent financial backer for us. When we needed money, we would wire him the amount. The usual terms were thirty percent profit in sixty days. He would wire funds into our numbered Swiss bank account. We would wire him the original amount plus thirty percent back to his account sixty days later."

"What if you didn't have the money to wire back?"

"We always had it."

They went on to talk about the code words that were telegraphed--'decades' or 'centennial'.

"What do you mean?"

"The payment terms and bank accounts we used were always the same. So that part was easy. We would send him a telegram that might say, "HIGH SCHOOL CLASS REUNION. THIRD DECADE. COMING? and he might send back a telegram saying, "YES I AM." But normally he would just start the funds transfer of thirty thousand Canadian dollars through the bank. For you, we would be asking in United States Dollars."

"So far, I am interested."

"Good. If we sent a telegram saying, 'VANCOUVER BICENTENNIAL CELEBRATION NEXT YEAR. PLAN TO ATTEND' how much would you send?"

"Two hundred thousand US Dollars."

"Right! Are you in?"

"Well, I'm not sure."

"Think about it. Here is the bank information." He handed him a small card. "Keep that in a safe place. I'll set-up a test. It will be for ten thousand dollars. If you decide you want to play with us, do the transfer. If not, send me a telegram telling me. In code, of course."

"Fine. What was the largest amount Uncle Jack ever sent?"

"Two hundred fifty thousand."

George's eyes lit up. "Whew?"

"Would there be a problem, if we ask for that much?"

"No. Not at all." He didn't sound convincing, even to himself.

"Like I said, think about it. And you can expect a telegram from us within the week."

"Fine. By the way, what are you using the money for? Rum-running?"

"You don't want to know--and you didn't ask." He stood up, shook George's hand again, and returned to the taxi.

In early September 1933, George relaxed over breakfast with his wife and two sons. As usual there was a book in his hand. Thomas, who had turned fourteen that July, also read while spooning oatmeal. Abraham, fidgeting and singing to himself, left his oatmeal untouched.

"It is hard to believe our big boy is going to have a birthday in a few days."

"What, dear?" said George as he put down his book and returned to the newspaper he had been reading earlier.

"Abraham will be four on the seventh."

"Boy, time does fly!" His attention went back to the paper. He was looking for a particular article in the *Porthill Gazette*.

"What should we do? Have a cake? Have a picnic?"

"Both!" mumbled George, barely paying attention to his wife.

She sat drinking her tea.

"Well, it looks like common sense may be upon us."

"What do you mean, George?"

"I was reading here in the *Gazette* about Franklin Roosevelt--you know, the fellow running for President--related to Teddy Roosevelt."

"Yes?"

"Quotes from a campaign speech. Wants to repeal Prohibition."

"Really?"

"Yes, listen to this: *The attempt to impose the practice of virtue by mandate of the fundamental law produced an attitude of intolerance to other forms of restraint and a denial even of the basis of authority. The violation of fundamental principles set in motion a chain of consequences that no one not politically blind could fail to see; and all the time a steady flow of profits, resulting from the exactions of a newly created industry, was running into the pockets of racketeers...lucrative, vicious and corrupting in its influence on the enforcement agencies of Government.*"[14]

"Roosevelt sounds serious."

"I suspect he is."

"What will you do after Prohibition?"

"I'm not sure. But I'll find something. I'll be happy to be out of it. Until then, I hope the police will pay attention and stop bothering my people."

"That would be nice."

"Yes. I have never liked this business one bit. Sneaking around. Never knowing what we are going to face next. Too much violence. I'll be happy to be rid of it."

"Why didn't you get out, if you disliked it so much?"

George shrugged and muttered, "Hard to say."

Shortly after becoming President, Franklin D. Roosevelt signed the Cullen-Harrison Act authorizing sale of low alcohol content beer and wine.[15]

---

[14] Campaign Address on Prohibition given at Sea Girt, New Jersey on August 27, 1932. Later that year the Democratic platform included a plank for the repeal of Prohibition. Franklin Roosevelt promised repeal of federal laws on Prohibition, in favor of state-driven laws.

[15] The Cullen–Harrison Act, named for two Democrats and enacted on March 21, 1933, legalized the sale of beer with an alcohol

That November, George and Rebecca were reading the newspaper together and drinking coffee.

"Rebecca, did you see here the state legislature voted for the Twenty-first amendment."

"Whats that mean?"

"It's the amendment to eliminate Prohibition."[16]

"Does that mean we don't have it any longer?"

"No. We are the twenty-seventh state to vote yes on the repeal. There has to be thirty-six states for it to pass."[17]

With the end of Prohibition, it was time for George to shut down his rum-running operations and let people go.

---

content of 3.2% (by weight) and similarly low alcohol content wines. It was thought too low to be intoxicating. Each state had to have legislation allowing low alcohol beverages in their state.

[16] The amendment was fully ratified on December 5, 1933. Some states continued Prohibition within their jurisdictions-- 38% of Americans lived in areas with Prohibition after passage of the Twenty-first Amendment. By 1966, all states had repealed their state-wide Prohibition laws, with Mississippi being last.

[17] Article V of the United States Constitution begins, "The Congress, whenever two thirds of both Houses shall deem it necessary, shall propose Amendments to this Constitution, or, on the Application of the Legislatures of two thirds of the several States, shall call a Convention for proposing Amendments, which, in either Case, shall be valid to all Intents and Purposes, as Part of this Constitution, when ratified by the Legislatures of three fourths thereof, or by Conventions in three fourths thereof, as the one or the other Mode of Ratification may be proposed by the Congress...."

The framers of the Constitution recognized it needed a method of bypassing the state legislatures in the ratification process. The people retained great power in this provision--expressly bypassing their own State Legislators to make the highest law of the land.

It has only been used one time--for ratification of the twenty-first amendment to repeal the eighteenth amendment. The convention method of ratification approximates a 'one-state, one-vote' national referendum.

There is no involvement by the President of the United States concerning Constitutional Amendments. He neither signs the legislation nor does he have the power to veto.

Some of the old timers stayed on to tend the farm and gardens, for their room and board. June and Claire, seeing they weren't needed any longer, found work in Porthill. George gave each an extra months pay as a bonus. Only Alice stayed.

George received fewer telegrams from Vancouver, when Jacques Péppin came to his door, ashen and tired, with a nasty cough.

"Welcome, my old friend."

"It's been a long time," Péppin gasped.

"Yes, it has."

"I need to have a word with you," he coughed.

"Please, plan on staying with us tonight."

"Thank you. I will." Péppin paid the taxi driver and let him go.

They settled in the parlor and George closed the door. "Drink?"

"Please." George pulled out the last of the bourbon. "Did I tell you Jack is still alive?"

"What? No! I was at his funeral." He tried to act surprised.

"But did you see his body?"

George acted like he was thinking about that for a moment. "That old fox."

"Yes. He knew the Mounties were coming for him. He had set aside enough money to disappear."

"That sneaky bastard!"

"Ended up on the gulf."

"In Mexico?"

"No. Alabama."

"Really?"

"Yes. We had done some business with a stranger there after he left here. Then the bastard let us know it was him. Came as quite a shock--and a good laugh. When he had left, we were on good terms with him. We picked up right where we left off. He bought a big, fast schooner, named it the 'Porthill'--of all things. Brought liquor in from the Bahamas, into Miami, and up the gulf to Mobile. He was an expert at running through Government Cut to avoid the Feds. While others were cracking their hulls on reefs and stranding themselves on sandbars, Jack would shoot through like a pirate."

"What is Government Cut?"

"A passageway that the Government cut to aid access to Miami harbor from the Atlantic. Jack would run through it at full speed, dodging other boats, and leaving the Coast Guard behind. Heck, they'd station boats on the other side and he still evaded them. Then he would disappear. Next day he would be dining on steak and crab in Tampa Bay." Péppin's trip was not about old times. "We are going to have to make some adjustments to our arrangement."

George had been expecting this. "What kind?"

"It's taking longer to set up things with new customers. We are having more expenses and taking on higher risks."

"But higher risks should mean higher rewards."

"Well, either that, or you are priced out of the market. We need to cut to one-and-a-quarter in return and one hundred twenty days to pay."

George thought it was going to be worse. "I'll have to sleep on it."

They ate dinner with Rebecca and the boys, and then drank late into the evening. Péppin opened up as the liquor pried loose his tongue. "I've been sick. Coughing a lot. They tell me it's cancer."

"I'm sorry to hear that." He was not surprised.

"Well, I guess it comes with good living. Too many fine cigars."

"Is there treatment?"

"No."

"Nothing they can do?"

"Nothing they have thought of yet."

"What are you going to do?"

"I'm breaking in my son to take over the business. I'll bring him through next time I travel. I usually try to get out of Vancouver twice a year."

"What is his name?"

"Jean-Michel. He just graduated from the university."

"Does he know about your cancer?"

"Yes, he was the one who insisted I see a doctor. I'm proud of him. He will take good care of my wife."

The evening grew quiet. Soon George asked Alice to make up a bed for Mr. Péppin.

The following morning they had a nice breakfast in the

dining room. George called for a taxi.

"I've decided I can live with the new terms."

"Good. I promise I will bring Jean-Michel around in about six months." He never did; he was dead in four. "Until then, things in Spain look promising." George had no idea what he meant.

They heard the 1914 Buick B 25 5-Passenger Touring Car rumbling up the dirt road before they saw the taxi out the window. Highly-polished, canary yellow, with an orange canvas rag top and orange wheels, it slid to a stop in the morning sun where the brass radiator ornament shined in their window. George carried Péppin's suitcase and placed it in the seat next to the driver.

Péppin reached his hand out to George, "Sorry we had to reduce your rate. Since the stock market crash, every world economy has struggled." With that, he removed his hat and stepped into the car.

What Jean-Michel had said was mostly true--nearly every major world economy was struggling. The one major exception was Germany. The impact of the Great War on Germany had been severe. Beginning in 1922, they faced hyperinflation and soaring unemployment (30%). They were being forced to pay war reparations at a staggering level and for a long time.[18]

---

[18] Money was only part of the impact--they were forced to confess sole guilt and responsibility over having caused the war. While it was certainly true there was guilt on their part, nothing is ever that simple. Economics professor at University of Warwick Mark Harrison said "These reparations were as important politically as economically." It was offensive to German national pride that they should be called on the carpet by her sister nations. The German people sought to cast off their oppressors and promote national pride. It all played into the hands of an aggressive politician from a minority political party. In fewer than ten years, the National Socialist German Workers' Party went from a handful of representatives in parliament to over a hundred. They put together a coalition of parties and gained power on January 30, 1933. Their leader--Adolph Hitler--rapidly gained control of the coalition.
The yearly payment amount was renegotiated and reduced in 1924 and again in 1929. The total amount was cut by more than half. It was still an economic drain. Final payment was made on October 4, 2010, the twentieth anniversary of German reunification.

In the mid-30's, Germany's Führer restored economic prosperity and ended massive unemployment the same way the United States would during World War II--with heavy military spending and by suppressing labor unions and strikes. Germany discontinued making war reparation payments.[19]

Rudolf Hess ended a speech by throwing his right arm in the air, saying "The Party is Hitler. But Hitler is Germany, just as Germany is Hitler. Hitler! Sieg Heil!" Hitler and the Nazi Party became inseparable.[20] The world went about appeasing Hitler. They listened to his lies, complemented him on his reasonableness, reported back to their home countries that all was well--and Hitler did whatever he pleased. The United States continued friendly relations with Germany, aghast at what they were seeing take place in Europe, while bickering internally about what, if any, role to play.

For George, July 17, 1936 was a Godsend. The floodgates opened and contracts were flying in from Vancouver. It didn't take long to figure out he was helping supply the Spanish Civil War. The three-sided conflict had been brewing for two years, so much was already in place with George and his business

---

[19] On August 2, 1934, Hitler was named Führer (Leader) of the German state and people. In June 1941, Hitler declared himself the "Germanic Führer" (Germanischer Führer) which the Nazi's described as the "Nordic-Germanic master race"--expanding to include Norwegians, Danes, Swedes, Icelanders, Finns, Dutch, and Faroese people.

[20] On Wednesday, September 5, 1934, during the opening of the Nazi Party's annual national convention (commonly called the 1934 Nuremberg Rally).

Sieg means Victory. Heil mean Hail. "Hail victory!" The saying was stolen from the Italians and the salute originated in ancient Rome. Nazi members would greet their leaders with a rigid, outstretched right arm--and the leader responded by raising his own right hand, frequently crooked at the elbow, in acceptance.

partners--transportation, teams, supply chain, ports--when hostilities erupted. The claims of non-intervention by the French and British meant support for all three sides of the conflict went underground for weapons and materials.

"Another telegram, George."

"Thank you, Alice."

After transferring millions of dollars, George was beginning to question the stability of his arrangements. The latest telegram read, "AFTER TWO AND A HALF CENTURIES, MUSEUM QUALITY DIAMONDS FOUND. He sent a telegram to Vancouver in response: BEFORE YOU BUY DIAMONDS, SEND JM.

Jean-Michel was not in the country. He was in Mexico City meeting with His Excellency Lázaro Cárdenas, President of Mexico and head of the National Revolutionary Party. President Cárdenas actively pursued assisting the Republican government in the Spanish Civil War, but his efforts were thwarted by the Roosevelt administration. Cárdenas went underground and began placing large orders with Jean-Michel Péppin. Weapons were supplied by American and Canadian manufacturers, shipped through Alabama, and off-loaded in Morocco before being delivered wherever most needed in Spain.

"Señor Presidente, we will be able to supply your order within ninety-days, upon receipt of either gold bullion or funds deposited to our Swiss bank account."

"The Swiss bank account will be acceptable. I will have our Minister of Finance make arrangements this afternoon."

"It will be the same..."

The President raised his right hand, indicating 'Stop!' "I will leave you with my staff to carry out the details." He turned to his aid, "Please attend to Mr. Péppin and see him out." He turned back to Jean-Michel, "Jean-Michel, always a pleasure." Their mutually beneficial arrangement would continue into 1940, with Jean-Michel bringing refugees to Mexico and supplying rations to massive refugee camps. The next leg of his trip took Jean-Michel to Buenos Aires.[21]

---

[21] Mexico furnished $2,000,000 to the Spanish Republicans effort in aid and material assistance. This included 20,000 rifles and 20 million cartridges.

Argentina had been a favorite migration destination for Germans since the 1870's. A wave of immigration and investment during the last quarter of the nineteenth century brought prosperity and prominence, and had turned Argentina into one of the ten richest countries by 1929. Technically neutral, it would be an important food source for the Allies during World War II while maintaining a strong alliance with Germany as the dominate player in European politics.

"It is good to see you again, Señor Presidente."

"Thank you." President Agustín Pedro Justo welcomed his guest and made small talk before turning him over to Alberto Hueyo, who had important economic positions in and out of the government for the last decade, including Treasury Secretary and head of the corrupt electric utility, CHADE.

"Our friends in Germany have asked our assistance and suggested we contact you."

"Very good. What have they told you about our business?"

"A great deal. It is imperative that our dealings not reach American ears."

"That is our specialty."

"We would like to export weapons and materials from Argentinian businesses and purchase items for delivery. Both of these can be arranged through you?"

"It is likely we can get whatever you require and certainly shipping from Argentina to Europe will not be a problem."

"It is essential our brothers in the Nationalist Party get what they need, or the Republicans will overrun them!"

"Deliveries can go through A Coruña, our secure seaport in Northwestern Spain. German U-boats will provide protection." Hueyo smiled.

That evening, over an excellent bottle of German Spätburgunder wine, Jean-Michel raised his glass--"To the Spanish Civil War!" Patrons at the bar ignored him. In the previous seventy-two hours, he had made extremely profitable deals with the Mexicans to supply the Republicans and the Argentinians to supply the Nationalist. He thought to himself, 'If you call supplying an army wonderful, what do you call supplying all three sides of a war?'[22]

---

[22] Germany furnished $215,000,000 to the Spanish Nationalist

FOUR

The following morning they worked out final details. "I would like to ask my Military Aide to join us," said President Justo.

"Certainly."

"Jean-Michel Péppin, I'd like you to meet Colonel Juan Domingo Perón." The men shook hands. "He would like to hear about your transport arrangements."

"Certainly. We have a large fleet of ships...everything from schooners to modern freighters. Generally they are smaller in size than you might expect--to deflect suspicions. We have multilingual crews that carry three sets of papers."

"Three?"

"Yes. Each identifies different ports of call and destinations. The captains and crews are more intelligent and better paid than others. They are adept at changing the identifications of ships to different nationalities on the fly."

"Impressive!"

"They have been well-trained by professional acting coaches."

"Oh?"

"They have no national interests of their own. Their interest is only in the currency of their choice. We weed out any that express a potential conflict of interest."

"Have you had to weed out many?"

Jean-Michel shrugged. "Enough."

"Aren't you concerned that creates a security leak."

"No. We let them off the boat. Apparently not many have been great swimmers." Perón grinned. "And they have all been guaranteed full salaries for any times they land in prison for their activities with us."

"Have they ever been caught?"

"We have had cargos confiscated, but the crews have never been detained more than one day."

"Impressive. I'm amazed!"

"You should be--for what I am going to charge you!"

For the next three years, Jack's ships rendezvoused with

---

effort in aid, material assistance, direct military personal, tanks, weapons, and U-boats. As many as fifty-six thousand Nationalist soldiers (infantry, artillery, aerial and naval forces) were trained by German detachments.

supply ships coming from Canada, the United States, and Mexico. They traveled down the eastern coast of South America, calling on ports as needed, ending in Buenos Aires. After a few day's rest and relaxation they followed the southern Atlantic trade winds across to Africa and up the western coast to the Mediterranean. They carried contraband for two of the three sides of the Spanish Civil War, sometimes on the same ships.

A secretary interrupted the meeting. "Excuse me. I have a telegram for Mr. Péppin," she said, walking in and handed the paper to Jean-Michel.

"Thank you."

He read it: STALLED FLY TO GEORGE QUICKLY. He frowned.

"A problem?"

"No. Just urgent business back in the States."

Before he left, Perón handed him a slip of paper. It read in one column: Rabbits, Alcohol, Tobacco, Coffee, Chocolate and a second column was a list of numbers. "Thank you." 'Ah, the test--but most unusual items', he thought to himself. Jean-Michel sent three telegrams before returning to a private airport, on property that is now part of Ministro Pistarini International Airport. His private Boeing 247 was fueled and awaiting departure. There were four people on board the 10-passenger plane when he got on; a pilot, co-pilot, chef/steward, and himself. He loved this plane. It was pure luxury. He lay back with a smile, remembering the call he had placed to get the plane four months before.[23]

"Hello?"

"Clairmont L. Egtvedt, please?"

---

[23] The Boeing 247 is considered the first modern airliner. It had all-aluminum construction, a fully cantilevered wing, retractable landing gear, control surface trim tabs, autopilot, and sophisticated deicing boots.

"He is not here right now, may I take a message?"

"Yes, he is there. On the golf course. Ninth hole. You may get him! NOW! IMMEDIATELY! This is an emergency! I'll hold."

The operator tracked down Clairmont Egtvedt, Chairman of the Board, Chief Executive Officer, and Acting President of Boeing Airplane Company just coming off the ninth hole.

A secretary led Egtvedt off the course to a desk in the clubhouse. He picked up the phone. He was wearing a bright yellow golf shirt with matching sweater, beige plus fours, argyle socks, Kelly green silk necktie, and smoking a Panatela. *"Hello?"*

"Mr. Egtvedt?"

"Speaking."

"Mr. Egtvedt, you don't know me. My name is Jean-Michel Péppin. I am a business man. I saw your model 247 at the World's Fair and want to purchase one."

Egtvedt slammed his hand on the desk, sending ashes everywhere. *"Damn it! I thought this was an emergency! Damn you! You got me off the golf course on a Saturday, because you think you can order a friggin' plane from me. Damn it! That is what we have sales departments for. Call them on Monday. Good day."* He started to slam down the phone.

"I can see you right now through that open door. I am in the locker room."

That got his attention. He pulled the phone back to his ear, while looking up to spot Jean-Michel.

"I know you are selling this plane for $65,000 a unit. Do you see the four armed guards behind me? There is two hundred thousand dollars in gold bullion here right now--a few bars here in the locker room, the balance in an armored car out front." He scrunched his neck down to hold the phone while he used both arms to lift a 44 pound (20 kilogram) bar of gold so Egtvedt could see it. He positioned it precisely to reflect light from the room into his eyes. He put down the bar and grabbed the phone. "I would like to order one plane. And be put at the top of the delivery schedule. I know this transaction would have to go through you eventually, and I thought we could just sidestep your middlemen and their sales commissions. I will deliver the gold to whomever you would like to assay it. Sixty-five grand for the plane; one hundred thirty-five as a bonus--it does not matter to me if it goes to you or your company. I hope we can conclude our agreement quickly so you can get back onto the links. I will work out the details with your staff people on Monday."

With a range of 745 miles and top speed of 200 miles per hour, they made multiple stops to refuel, including Panama, Mexico City, Havana, and Miami, before picking up a passenger in Mobile, Alabama and starting out across the country. Péppin slept most of the way to Mobile and talked to Jack most of the way from there to Idaho.

In the late afternoon, Jack burst through the front door of the Big House at Altura Farm without knocking, "I brought my own this time!" He was carrying two bottles of bourbon.
Rebecca laughed and jumped up from her supper to greet him. "Oh, Jack, how nice to see you! You look wonderful!"
"LIAR!"
She laughed again, "Oh, the same old Jack."
"Boys, I don't suppose you remember Uncle Jack."
Neither of them did, but Thomas had heard many stories about him.
Jean-Michel came through the door, carrying their two suitcases. "Hello!"
"Hello! Welcome, Jean-Michel!"
"Boys, you remember Mr. Péppin, don't you?"
Thomas nodded his head, and Abraham watched.
Uncle Jack came up to Thomas and put his hand on his head, "Last time I saw you, you had just hatched!" He held out his hand to Abraham and they shook. "You are getting big! Quite a nice grip ya got there."
"Honey, you remember Jean-Michel don't you?"
Rebecca said, "Of course. Welcome! Make yourself at home. We weren't expecting you until later tonight. Let me get some plates."
They didn't object.

After pushing back from the table, Jack smiled. "That was a wonderful supper. We came on Jean-Michel's new plane and the accommodations ain't great. I thought they weren't gonna feed us at all. "
Jean-Michel sneered and shook his head. Jack had eaten a steady stream of lobster, shrimp, and Porterhouse steaks

along the way.

"Before we start talkin' business, I have one request."

"A glass of bourbon?"

"Okay. Two requests." He laughed. "I'd love to see my old place."

The three horses left the stable and headed north. Jean-Michel struggling to keep up confessed, "I'm a little rusty." Riding slow and easy in the late afternoon sun, they forded the river and climbed the banks. Birds were beginning their evening migrations from the water to the foothills. As the men pulled up to where the gin mill had been they silently looked at what had been destroyed. There was no equipment left. "Mounties pretty well took care of this operation, didn't they?"

"Yes, they did." They rode through the fallow fields and the untended apple orchards. "Shame nobody is taking care of the place."

"They wouldn't let us. Mounties come through once a month and chase vagrants off. They lock everything up and board up the place, but the people are back soon."

Jack rode over and pulled an apple from the tree. He bit into it. "Gosh that is good." They rode to the house. The sun was setting and they would have to return quickly to be back before dark. Jack pulled off a board that was across the door and ripped off a faded paper sign telling people to stay out. He pushed open the unlocked door and walked in. Everything was there, but the furniture had been pressed against the walls. A cat wandered over and rubbed his face on Jack's boot. Jack picked him up. "I don't think I know you. But thanks for the welcome home!" He looked around the house as Jean-Michel and George wandered into the living room, inspecting spider webs and dust piles.

Jack strolled next to the fireplace. Well, they didn't get one thing." He set down the cat.

"What's that?"

Jack reared back with his right shoulder and arm, then punched his fist through the wall. At first George thought he had done it in anger, but Jack laughed. There was a void in the wall where lath was missing and a thin layer of plaster had been placed over the hole. He reached in and extracted a bottle. He read the label: "Jacob Spears Bourbon Whiskey, Stone Castle, Clay-Kiser Road, Bourbon County, Paris,

Kentucky, 160 barrel-proof, aged twenty-five years before bottling." Jack smiled, "Let's get back to your place before it gets dark. Now that I have this, I should be able to concentrate."

     As the horses strolled back to Altura Farm the sun dipped below the mountains to the west and it quickly went from dusk to dark. The farm was calm and peaceful. The hands were finishing their chores, putting away tools, putting on their coats, cleaning up, and lighting lanterns. Bugs were starting to come out and wildlife was carefully strolling in from the foothills. Deer came up to the house to gnaw on bushes and munch on clover. George was thinking how he would love to be fishing right now with the kids on a picnic by the river.

     "I never tire of the peace here," said Jack.

     "Me either," George replied. "I can't imagine not being here." Jean-Michel and Jack looked at each other, but did not say a word. "Will you ever come back, Jack?"

     "There's still a bounty on my head, I'm guessin'. Mounties are persistent, ya know."

     "You believe that 'Always get their man' crap!"

     Uncle Jack frowned. "Yes."

     "Why couldn't you stay here in Idaho?"

     "Wouldn't matter where I was. They would figure a way to drag me across the border and arrest me."

     "I suppose so."

     They rode up to the house and one of the hands took the three reins and walked the animals down to the barn, while George led the men into the house.

     Rebecca met them before they went into the study. "Did you have a nice visit to your place, Jack?"

     "Yes--brought back lots of good memories."

     "How is Jenny? Does she like Alabama?" Jack stiffened and couldn't answer. Tears welled up in his eyes. "Oh, I'm sorry." Jack still couldn't speak. Rebecca did not know what else to say. "Well, I'll let you gentlemen tend to your business."

They all nodded and the tension left the room. "We're still on for lunch tomorrow, George." she said coyly, batting her eyes before closing the door.

"What's tomorrow?"

Jean-Michel, Jack, and George made themselves comfortable. Jack studied the label of the bourbon bottle before setting it on the floor, "Were gonna save you for later, little lady!" He grabbed one of the two bottles he had brought in earlier and pulled off the cork, "Before you get too comfortable, we need three glasses."

Jean-Michel began, "George you are a bit of an enigma to me. Where did you say you were from?"

"I didn't say," snapped George. Jack laughed.

"Well, then, where are you from?"

"East."

Jack laughed again, "See! You'll never get some things out of him."

Jean-Michel continued, "Well, where you are from does not really matter. We just need to know if your past can become known. Could catch up with you. You know, something that could be used against you."

"Why?"

Jean-Michel rolled his eyes over at Jack. "Let's just say, it could be a great benefit to be--unknown."

"There are farts in the wind better known than this guy. He is Melchizedek," replied Jack.

"Who?" asked Jean-Michel.

"Melchizedek. From the Bible. No Father. No Mother. No beginning and no end. Lives forever. Nobody knows shit about him until he shows up and gets a tenth of the booty! That's George."

Jean-Michel stared at George. Thinking. "We had our people look at your banking. You are nearly invisible." George cautiously nodded. "How many bank accounts do you have?" George squirmed in his chair. "Look, George, I am going to make you an offer that is going to make you a potentate. You are going to have wealth beyond your imagination. I need to know if you can be trusted."

"I have five bank accounts."

"We only found two."

"Five--Porthill Bank, National City Bank, Chase National Bank, Swiss National Bank, and Toronto Bank."

"Very good."

"The Porthill Bank is for the farm. The others," he squirmed, "are for--investments."

Uncle Jack roared, "Investments! That's rich!"

"What have you done with the interest gained on your 'investments'?"

"Nothing."

"Nothing?"

"They sit in my accounts. Except for the Porthill Bank, which we use to run the farm."

"There has been no mingling of the accounts?"

"None."

"How about the farm? What mortgage do you have on it?"

"No mortgage."

"None? How do you run a farm without borrowing against it each year?"

"Been paid off through the U. S. Army."

Alarm bells went off in Jean-Michel's head. "United States Army?"

"Yes, they set Chet up in business during the war."

"Chet?"

"My wife's uncle. He had no family, so he left the farm to her."

"Are you on the deed?"

"No."

"How about any previous mortgages?"

"No."

"Never borrowed money against the farm in your name?"

"I wouldn't know how to start doing that."

Jean-Michel grinned. "George, we want you to have fewer accounts--Porthill Bank for your farm and Union Bank of Switzerland for investments, as you say. We will open that account for you, transfer the money, and close the others." George looked at him wearily. "That's, of course, if we all agree to move the business in your direction. George do you know what we have been doing?"

"I got an idea. Spanish Civil War?"

"Good! Yes, that is where we started. When there is a war, people need things. Usually basic items--food, water--"

"Bourbon!" Jean-Michel and George grinned. Some things are predictable.

"What Jack means is that there are also luxury items that people will pay a premium to get. Can you imagine how good a steak would taste right now, if you were just getting out of jail and hadn't had one in six months?" George could smell the aroma in his mind and his mouth began to water. "Sometimes the things people want are in the possession of the enemy. Sometimes the roads have been destroyed. In any event, when there is a war, people need things. People on both sides of the battle lines."

Jack added, "So if you are not too squeamish about selling to all parties, you can make a bundle." George understood.

"Right now in America, you are neutral," said Jean-Michel, "but it will not remain that way long."

George nodded.

"Nobody really wants to go to war. Oh, some look at what Hitler is doing and want to box his ears. But others just want to wait it out. Not get involved. There will be a cost in American lives when you get drawn in." George kept nodding. "Roosevelt has chosen sides already. He has put his toes in with the Brits. It is just a matter of time--accidently or intentionally--until somebody gets a bloody nose and America will be sucked in."

About midnight, they all needed to pee and stretch their legs, so they wandered out behind the barn to take care of business. The moon was bright and the air clear. Stars shimmered across the length of the horizon. A large fireball streaked across the sky. "Ooh! Aah!" After they returned, Jack opened the second bottle and refilled their glasses.

"George, why are you in this business?"

"Whatdoyamean?"

"Why are you doing this?"

He looked straight ahead and his eyes blinked. "I really don't know."

Jack said, "I'll tell you why I am. I don't need much. Dry place to sleep. Food couple times a day. A little refreshment." He raised his glass and took a large swig. "I loved running the farm. Damn rabbits were a good business. Liquor was good. Well, pretty good. When Prohibition stopped, I could have grown apples. Maybe made some hooch. But I wouldn't have squat, if something went wrong. If the apple trees got a disease or we had a drought, I would be back where I started. I'm too old for that." He took another swallow. "I look at all those poor bastards on the breadlines. Nothing they did caused all the problems. Yet they can't feed themselves. Turned into beggars, just like that." He tried to snap his fingers, but with all the bourbon, they wouldn't and he looked at them quizzically. "Anyway. Where was I? Oh, yeah--I'm too old to beg and too set in my ways to trust anyone else to care for me. I've got my goose eggs in the nest. Which is why I am quitting now."

George was shocked. "What?"

"Yes, that is why we are here. I am leaving the business. Gonna disappear. Found a place overlooking the Mediterranean Sea. Gonna find me a young Spanish girl to keep me warm at night and siesta with me beneath a tree all afternoon. Whenever I need anything, I'll take one of the gold bullion bars I have buried beneath the house. Figure I got enough there already for a million years."

It was getting light outside. The sky was clear and gray. Birds were chirping. Someone was in the kitchen preparing breakfast. Men were stirring in the Little House. George and Jean-Michel refused Jack's offer of more bourbon. He was just about to open the bottle he had hidden away and thought about all those years. "I guess I can wait."

"George, I am still not convinced you are 'all in' with us here. Jack is leaving and recommended you take his place. You would need to spend a good bit of time away coordinating operations. How old are you?"

"Thirty-eight."

"You have a wife and need to be thinking about your kids. You have a nice tidy operation here. But if I bring someone else in to replace Jack, they are gonna want to bring in their own investors, and you'll be cut out."

"Why?"

"It's just the way it is. People work with those they trust. Especially in higher risk things. If they don't know you from Adam, they are not gonna want to put their neck on the line doing business with you. George, you already have enough money--small countries would be jealous. You are going to have the chance to turn it into a lot more, I expect. Half the world is at war already and the powder keg is ready to blow. That means a lot of opportunity to sell high in a lot of places. We are in good stead with the Nazis. They benefited enough from our operating in Spain to look the other way when we were dealing with others."

Jack continued, "My boats have been baffling the British for years. We sneak by them pretty good. When we do get caught, the counterfeit paperwork we provide always does the trick. We have converted them to Panamanian registry--all twenty-six ships."

George's eyes lit up, "You have twenty-six ships?"

Jack grinned, "Yep."

Alice knocked on the door, "Breakfast, gentlemen?"

It had been a long night and the steak and eggs were a welcome relief. They looked tired and enjoyed the hot coffee. Their red eyes hurt and they yawned as they chewed. As they ate at the kitchen table, Alice began getting down a picnic basket from storage. She blew flour dust off the top, mumbling, "This hasn't seen much use of late."

After breakfast, the men returned to their discussion, bringing with them their coffee cups and a full pot.

"You can see, George, we are at a critical juncture. Jack is retiring. The world is falling apart. Many places are at war today and all hell is going to break loose. There is going to be a critical need for our services. You are the most logical one to take it on. You know the most. You have the most invested moneywise, and the most to make by doing this. If you are not in, we are going to find another man. But we need you all in or all out. And we don't have much time for you to decide." He nodded to Jack. "Jack will stay on to train you and for a transition. But he wants to get on with his life. So what is it gonna be?"

Jean-Michel was hopeful he would accept--so he wouldn't have to kill George.

By one in the afternoon, George had accepted and there were grins all around. Jack opened his last bottle of bourbon and poured healthy servings. "To war!"

It seemed like such an absurd thing to salute, both Jean-Michel and George laughed and raised their glasses and repeated in unison, "To war!"

On hearing the commotion, Rebecca opened the door.

"Are you going to be ready to go soon?" George looked at her quizzically. "Picnic? Remember? Alice has lunch for you gentlemen prepared and waiting at the table outside. George promised me a picnic today."

Then it hit him. Under his breath, George said, "Oh, my gosh, she's pregnant!"

Clyde pulled up to the river snorting and pawing the dirt. This was one of his favorite places and he looked forward to being off his restraints where he could drink, wade in the water, eat grass, roll on his back, and take a leisurely nap. George guessed at Rebecca's pregnancy, but in hindsight he should have seen it earlier. He had been preoccupied with his business and Jack coming. Now he helped her down from the wagon, carried the picnic basket and blankets to the water's edge, freed Clyde, and gave him an apple. The rest of the afternoon was for her.

"So when did you figure it out?"

"Figure what out?"

"That I was expecting, silly!" She rubbed her stomach.

"Well, I don't know."

She smiled, "Don't give me that! You didn't know until today, did you? You haven't paid any attention to me for weeks."

"I'm sorry. I know I have been preoccupied. After all, Thomas is twenty and Abe, ten. It wasn't something I thought could happen. When did you know?"

"Oh, I suspected a month ago, but had to wait to see."

"Is it different this time?"

"No. It's another boy."

"What? You can tell!"

"I can."

"You sound pretty certain."

"I am; I'm not even going to bother thinking of girl's names!" George laughed. Soon their shoes and socks were off and they sat side-by-side, with one arm around the other, and their feet in the water. Clyde had finished scratching his back and was lying on his side, occasionally twitching his tail.

"Lunch?"

"Yes, I could eat."

"Did you three ever knock off last night?"

"No, we talked all night and through until noon."

"Lots of big things to talk about?"

"Yes. Jack is going to quit the business. He is going to train me to take over."

"Is that what you want to do?"

"I guess."

"What about the farm?"

"Well, Eddie seems to be managing fine. There is a drawback; I am going to have to be gone more."

Rebecca frowned. "How much more?"

"Initially a lot. Jack and I will be training together. He has built up a fleet of ships with the export business. Jean-Michel and me are gonna buy him out, over time--one ship per month."

"Are you sure you want to be doing this?"

"Yes," he said halfheartedly.

"You know, we have done pretty well with the farm."

In the late afternoon, Clyde stretched and snorted. "Good boy! Did you have a nice nap? I sure did." While George got the wagon ready, Rebecca sat by the water.

"I miss the children."

"Do they know you have been blessed?"

"Yes. I have put their hands on my stomach and told them about our new son." Clyde walked home in the twilight.

George and Rebecca looked in on the boys in their beds and had a late supper. Rebecca went up to bed, while George sat up and thought about the new agreement he had made.

Her question haunted him--"Are you sure you want to do this?" He tossed and turned that night and the little sleep he did get gave him no rest. It seemed the whole world was struggling. People were out of work and had been for an extended time. For many, they were lucky if they had anything to eat, much less enough. With the hard times came political instability. People were angry and having crazy thoughts on what needed to change. Socialist, Communist, and Fascist factions everywhere were pointing to the failure of Capitalism.

The American Dream--a decade of extravagance, followed by a decade of worldwide depression--seemed to be a rudderless ship, drifting into the rocks.

George knew he never wanted to return to his earlier life. Yesterday, there was never enough to eat. Hunger had gnawed at his belly like fingers clawing at him from the inside. Father would beat him for no reason--just because he was there, just because he was another mouth to feed. Oh, that was it, wasn't it? Every morsel in the son's mouth was one less in the father's. His father medicated his pain with cheap drink and then it would start. Drink made it all easier. His father reaching over to grab him. Or chasing him around the room, when he tried to escape. Funny--his father's fists to his belly really did take away the gnawing from the inside.

That all changed when he changed his name. Today he was living a dream--beautiful wife, wonderful children, work that protected him from his yesterday--from the breadlines, the poverty of his youth, the rage. He was building a hedge against his past. Hard work wasn't enough. How many hard working men were standing on breadlines? Jack was right--the farm could disappear with drought or disease. The answer was in wealth. Jean-Michel told him he would make him a potentate. His sons would never have to face what he had. Yes, he would go with Jack.

"Well, I am off." George kissed Rebecca. The day he had been dreading had arrived. John picked up George's bags and winced. He had had trouble with his shoulder ever since he had been ambushed. George felt obligated to continue to employ him. John dropped the bag in the back of the wagon, while Clyde turned his head to watch.

"Mobile, here I come!"

Jack suggested to George that he take the train route he always did: On the Canadian National Railways (CNR) out of Vancouver that made a large rainbow shaped route into Toronto and Niagara Falls, on the New York Central Railroad's 20th Century Limited to Chicago. It was longer, but every inch was beautiful.

George wasn't sure how much he was going to like the train trip, so he decided on the shortest route: Great Northern Railway 'Empire Builder' from Sandpoint, Idaho to Chicago. Either route would take the Illinois Central Railroad's 'City of

New Orleans' to Louisiana. Jack arranged one of his boats to take him from Port of New Orleans to Port of Mobile.

George enjoyed the train rides immensely as he slept, ate, and read military history and novels the whole week. The next month was going to be grueling.

The training George received was most unusual. There was a depth to their operations he had not appreciated.

Jean-Michel, who was responsible for sales, was busy making contacts throughout Europe, Africa, and South America and offering services in importing goods into war-torn areas. If you couldn't get something, you called Jean-Michel. Somewhere in the world what was needed was for sale. It was just a matter of time. For those apprehensive about selling off a favored item, violence or blackmail usually loosened their grip.

Jack was responsible for operations. He had been working his way toward having thirty boats in their fleet over the last eight years--one for every day of the month. Jean-Michel had little trouble filling each ship, which were relatively small and fast, the better to evade the British blockade. Jack handled scheduling, maintenance, loading and unloading in Alabama (and coordination at other ports of call), documentation (e.g., illegal documents), and language training. He put together intelligent crews, training them about their missions and requiring instruction in language, geography, history, and economics. Even while sailing they were expected to attend classes when not on duty or sleeping. Crews consisted of uncles, cousins, and brothers. They knew they were signing on for a long-term position. Besides being paid well, they were expected not to drink (except at specific times and places). Payments went directly to their families back home, except for a small stipend for personal goods (usually tobacco).

George trained in Mobile before joining Jack for their first cruise together. Havana was the first stop, then ports in

Mexico and South America, across the Atlantic to Cape Agulhas and up to Morocco.[24]

Jack disappeared for a three day layover in the Mediterranean Sea, before the ship returned across the Atlantic to the Port of Mobile. Over the next nine months, the cycle was repeated, except twice when George returned to Rebecca for a week.

Jack had been swimming in the warm, azure blue waters and now was lying naked on a large towel in a secluded cove. The beach was just down the bluffs from his house. His workcrew started construction of his home by building a stand-alone, wooden cabaña where Jack could stay when he came on his visits. The single-room structure had a large window overlooking the beach and a thatched roof.

"Buenos días!"

"Buenos días!" he said, with his eyes still closed.

"Disfrutando del sol?" Not knowing what she had said, he smiled. "If you are going to live here, you need to learn Spanish."

With that, he opened his eyes. She stood next to him with a towel around her waist, bare breasted in the morning sun. He scanned her from top to bottom. Flowing raven hair. Large brown eyes. Long, graceful neck, smooth, full breasts. She had graceful hips and long legs.

"I could teach you Spanish." He didn't know what to say. Self-consciously, he reached over to cover himself with the towel, but without lifting his weight, it was too small to cover him. Seeing what he was doing, she snickered, stepped on his towel, and said, "If you don't mind, I don't."

He laughed. He looked at her. "How old are you?"

"Seventeen. How old are you?"

He coughed nervously. "Sixty-four. Old enough to be your grandfather. What is your name?"

"Natania." She was beautiful, with small features and bright eyes. He couldn't keep his eyes off her breasts and thin

---

[24] Cape Agulhas (Portuguese for "Cape of Needles") is a rocky headland in Western Cape, South Africa--geographic southern tip of Africa and official dividing point between the Atlantic and Indian oceans. That Cape of Good Hope is the dividing point is a misconception, off by 90 miles.

waist. Jack felt himself becoming aroused about the same time she did. "Oh, Señor Jack, YOU ARE happy to meet me!" He thought, how did she know my name? As he self-consciously looked away.

As if reading his mind, she said, "My brother is your foreman and has told me about you."

She dropped her towel, squatted while reaching down to align his erect penis, and slowly slid on top of him. "But he didn't tell me everything about you."

After making love, she told about herself. She told Jack about her three brothers. They had all gone to the church school and she had done well, until the war. She told about her Basque mother and Jewish father who had been killed before her eyes in the first days of the war. Her brothers scattered. She had come southeast to the coast and survived by living in deserted huts near Barcelona and by cooking for others. She began working at a small restaurant just for food, where she ran into her brother.

"What will you do now that the war is over?"

"I would like to live here. Work. Fall in love. Raise a family?"

"Why did you make love to me?"

She brushed away her hair. "I don't know. The boys don't know what they are doing. But men like you make the best lovers."

He invited her up to his home. She made him dinner and Jack opened a bottle of bourbon. She grabbed it from him with a sly grin and took it outside. She came back a few seconds later naked, still holding the bottle. Softly she said to him. "My brother tells me you drink too much. You can't have both. Will it be bourbon," she pushed the bottle forward, "or me," then she pushed her breasts forward. He chose wisely.

The following day he told her that tomorrow he needed to leave, but she should stay until he returned.

"Yes, I will take care of your cabaña. And I will make sure the builders do a good job on your house. And then we will see."

With that, he rode the circuit of the high seas. She was never far from his thoughts. When he hit Morocco, he could hardly wait to be with her, for he was certain she would keep her promise to be there in the cabaña with candles burning in the window.

When he came inside, a bottle of wine was open and baskets of fruit were everywhere. Though it was nearly three in the morning, she was naked in bed waiting for him with the sheets up to her waist and her breasts fully exposed. Rose petals covered the bed. Candles were ablaze along the windows.

"Sabía que esta noche sería la noche."

Following Jack's excursion, the crew was back together one hour before the designated sailing time. George had stayed on the ship the whole time, wondering whether this stop had been a good idea. The cook couldn't leave the boat with George still aboard, so he was grumpy and let George know it by slamming pots and pans and swearing. George missed Rebecca and the boys desperately and he knew he had signed on to do this trip repeatedly until he had learned the ropes. There was no other option.

"Jack, where do you go when we hit Morocco?"

A sailor, who had overheard George's question, jumped in and grabbed Jack by the shoulders, "And why do you always come back with a smile?"

Jack laughed while the sailor grinned and patted him on the shoulders. "I've been building a house north of Barcelona."

"But that's not why he grins!"

"I have met a señorita."

The Spanish Civil War officially had ended the previous spring (1939) though factions continued to fight on for years. Barcelona had been bombed, but the land Jack selected for his home was firmly in Republican control and had been throughout the conflict. He had received the land in trade for smuggling the previous owners out of Spain to America.

After a few passages, George went back to the Port of New Orleans, to travel by train to Idaho for a week. The first time back, Rebecca was glad to see him, but progressively her anger at his being gone so much got to her. Her brooding, resentfulness, and verbal lashing out grew as she grew larger.

In contrast, Jack's return visits to his home in Spain were joyous. Jack and Natania made love all night. She fed Jack and played with him. They were rarely a step away from one another, except for about once a day when she walked or bicycled to the market to get fresh bread, milk, fish, and fruits.

She updated him on the progress on the house. "I told my brother he could find better tiles for the entry and made him rip the old ones out. Look at the new ones---aren't they beautiful? And they didn't cost any more."

"They are wonderful! As beautiful as you!" He was never jealous of the virile young men who worked around the house all day where the beautiful, young woman was princess. They strutted like peacocks in front of her, but she ignored them all. "Why aren't you attracted to the younger men?"

"Jack, you are all I need. Even if we never lived in the big house, the cabaña would be fine with me. The boys around here don't interest me. But you are a real man. You have lived a full life and have the scars for it. You appreciate me as if I were a delicate, young flower to be unfolded, smelled, and tasted. They would take me for a few seconds of pleasure and discard me. They will never appreciate the fullness of the life you live."

George was packing for his return to Mobile, when Rebecca's water broke. He attended to her, but continued to pack as her pains increased.

"You bastard, you pack and get out!"

"I'm staying!"

"Why? You don't love me anymore."

"Of course I love you!"

"Your job is more important than I am!"

"Oh, no. Not more important. Just more--immediate--right now."

"Get out!" He slipped out of the room.

Alice pulled him aside. "It is the pain speaking!"

Alexander was born six hours later. Rebecca had calmed down and held George's hand as the baby lay on her chest. "He is beautiful, isn't he?"

"Yes he is."

She felt tired and asked to be alone. With that, he kissed his wife goodbye, left their bedroom, picked up his suitcase, and walked out the door, calling for John to bring the wagon.

"Well, he finally returns!"
"Sorry I am late. Rebecca gave birth to a son. I named him Alexander."
"Congratulations! How are things?"
"Alright," he said without conviction.

Upon arriving in Spain, Jack walked off the boat for the last time. He had selected to take a five-masted schooner he had renamed 'The Natania', built in Gloucester, Massachusetts ten years before. The ship made brief stops in Caracas, São Paulo, Buenos Aires, Rio de Janeiro, and Porto Alegre before sailing across the Atlantic. Jack was impatient with his crew as the trip, for him, seemed to drag on. But in the evenings he would speak of his new home.
"They are nearly done with my castle by the sea."
"Where is it?"
"I have named it 'Catalunya Castillo de Jacques'. It is near Costa Brava, Spain on the Mediterranean overlooking the Balearic Sea, north of Barcelona.
"Can we see it?"
"Yes. From the water. You may not come inside. That is for my woman and me alone. But you may see it from the sea." They all nodded. "It has dry, warm summers that seem to go on almost all year. The spring is filled with flowers and gentle breezes. There is little fall or winter, mostly just a rainy season that cleans and polishes the cliffs."
As they sailed past Barcelona, Jack went down to shave, clean-up, and dress. He came back on deck in a white peasant shirt, white cotton pants, moccasins, and a black pair of binoculars. He pointed out his castle on the cliffs from a great distance, then pulled the binoculars to his eyes. All the crew could see was the reflection of the windows in the sunrise. As they got closer, they could make out the orange and cream color slabs of rock in the building, red tile roof, large windows, and the dark cliff face below the house. The house sat on a rugged cliff with sandy inlets on both sides. Almond groves, cork oaks, olive trees, and pines filled the green, rolling hillsides behind the house. Natania had recently planted a small vineyard immediately behind the house as a surprise.

FOUR

Jack kept looking through his binoculars until he saw what he hoped to see: Natania in a white dress, repeatedly looking through the brass telescope on the terrace, then waving with both arms outstretched, her long black hair flowing behind her.

When they were a safe distance from shore, they lowered the skiff and four sailors descended the rope ladder. Jack shook hands and hugged his friends, leaving behind the life he had known. His final hug was for George, but he could no longer speak. He handed George the binoculars and climbed down to the skiff.

They rowed the boat to the shore, while Jack removed his moccasins and rolled up his pant legs. Stepping into the surf, he quickly walked out of the water, turned and waved, and then quickened his pace on the narrow, winding pathway up to the house. Natania waited for him at the top.

They feasted, and laughed, and made love as if they were teenagers. They roamed around the house and rested and drank dark, red wine. It was a three-day celebration.

She rolled off of Jack and bounced next to him on the bed.

"Not bad for an old man."

He tickled her, "Who you callin' old?"

She laughed with delight, and he kissed her breasts. She snuggled next to him and they rested, intertwined.

"I am going to have to go to the market today."

"No! Stay here with me."

"I have to. We're out of food."

"So."

She poked him with an index finger. "I want you to keep up your strength!"

"Oh! In that case!"

She laughed as she got out of bed. He sat up and looked out at the islands in the distance and the blue of the sea. "It is so beautiful here."

She put on her blouse and buttoned it. Pulling it up with one hand, she expose her stomach in the mirror, and rubbed it with the other as she twisted back and forth from her waist. She thought to herself, he hasn't noticed yet, smiling.

"Come back soon," he said as he stood naked by the door nearest the cliff.

"I will." She smiled, turned, and walked briskly to her

bicycle. The morning sun was getting high, as he slowly walked to the hammock. It lay in the shade of a tall tree overlooking the water. He lay down to admire the Balearic Sea as he drifted off the sleep.

There was no malice in his heart as he watched her leave from the nearby cliff. He was merely cleaning up: Making sure what Jack knew was not shared with others, especially the Nazis. He went about his business with coolness. He liked Jack, so he would make it as quick and painless as possible. He had been a good business partner. There was no reason to believe he would talk to others; but there was always that risk. He had been successful in business by eliminating risks. Others would have not thought to bother with this detail, but Jean-Michel was not like others. He thought to himself, crew members were never permitted to leave, why should Jack?

He approached Jack from behind. Jack was sound asleep; tired from three days of lovemaking. He noticed the soft smile on his face, as he pushed the rope slowly and quietly under the back of Jack's neck through a small space between his neck and the pillow. As it came out the other side, he slowly pulled it until the length of rope on each side was equal. He worked carefully to make sure the rope didn't touch Jack's skin. Crossing the ends above, Jack's mouth dropped open and he began to snore. Jean-Michel paused to let Jack relax; then he pulled the rope tight across Jack's throat with all the force he could muster.

Jack's eyes sprung open, while Jean-Michel pressed his chest against Jack's to keep his arms trapped and the hammock from twisting. The struggle lasted two minutes. The last things Jack sensed was the smell of Jean-Michel's breath as his vision went black. His last thought: you son of a bitch!

FIVE

A note landed on Jean-Michel's desk the next week in Mobile, Alabama. His secretary didn't know how it had gotten there. It read, "We need to meet. The Oysters tonight at eleven. Come alone, Brüno."

Jean-Michel had been cultivating a relationship with Brüno for some time. He had transported materials for him during the Spanish Civil War and found him easy to work with and prompt in paying. He suspected he was a Nazi spy. They had met at The Oysters a dozen times for hour long meetings, slurping down copious quantities of oysters and champagne. Brüno always picked up the tab. On previous occasions, Brüno had called his secretary to arrange the meeting.

The Oysters was a cocktail lounge where tuxedos and evening dress were required. They had a dinner floor show of singers and big bands at ten and a second show at midnight. Eleven was the quiet time, when mild music was played for the lovers and where businessmen would make deals. Once Brüno reported "Their specialty is an exotic breed of fresh oyster, served raw and reputed to be an aphrodisiac."

When Jean-Michel walked in at eleven sharp, looking stunning in his tuxedo, Brüno was already there with a companion.

"Always on time," Brüno said as he jumped up from his seat to shake his hand. "Allow me to introduce to you, Fritz Wiedemann."[25]

---

[25] Fritz Wiedemann was personal adjutant to Adolf Hitler, having served with him in World War I. In January 1939, Wiedemann was

Wiedemann was built like a boxer with chiseled features, raven-black hair combed straight back, and an elegantly-tailored tuxedo. After small talk, Brüno spoke about Wiedemann's role, background, and qualifications, while Wiedemann sat quietly sizing up Jean-Michel.

"Enough. Let's get down to business, shall we?" Wiedemann broke in.

"Of course."

"How much do you know about Wolframite?"

"It's an important mineral."

"Very!"[26]

"We have been watching your operations since the Spanish Civil War. You have an uncanny ability to avoid the British navy in the South Atlantic and Mediterranean. We know you traded with all three sides of the Spanish conflict, including us, without interference. Very clever. You seem to have no ideology--you will trade with Socialist, Communists, Capitalist, Facists..."

"Yes we do. Our ideology is cash."

Wiedemann laughed. "We know you still trade with all parties, including our enemies. We are willing to look aside to this arrangement, if you would be willing to transport Wolframite for us. We have been mining and stockpiling ore in Bolivia."

"I see..." The waiter showed up with another bottle of champagne and a plate piled high with oysters. Jean-Michel went on, "...and you need my help transporting the ore."

"Yes."

"I think we can meet your needs." He pulled out a Cuban cigar, unwrapped and licked it, and a book of matches from The Oysters. After lighting the cigar, he reached into his side coat pocket, unscrewed his fountain pen, wrote a figure on the inside of the match book, and tossed it to Wiedemann in such

---

appointed Consul General to the United States in San Francisco. He traveled extensively in the United States in support of Nazi activities, such as the German-American Business League.

[26] Wolframite, an iron manganese tungsten ore mineral, is found in granite and derives its name from German "wolf rahm" (translated "wolf soot" or "wolf cream"). It is also commonly known as Tungsten. During WWII, wolframite mines were strategic assets for both sides. The metal is used in lighting, industrial tools, munitions, and armor piercing ammunitions and projectiles.

a way that he had to grab it out of the air to prevent it from hitting him in the face.

Wiedemann looked at the figure and gasped, "A ton?"

Jean-Michel screwed the top back on the pen and placed it in his coat pocket as he answered, "Yes, a ton."

"This seems like a..."

"If you could do it without me, you would."

Wiedemann sized him up again. "Agreed."

They shook hands.

Brüno said, "I will contact you with dates and shipment tonnage." The floor show was about to begin so the three men headed toward the door as Brüno threw down hundred dollar bills on the table as if they were telephone call-back slips.

Brüno again contacted Jean-Michel. Over black caviar, oysters, and champagne at The Oysters, he was most direct. "Can you find us industrial diamonds?"

"Of course. I have been expecting your call." He handed him a matchbook he pulled from his vest pocket. He had already written in the price. "Here is my rate."

"I'm afraid to look at what this is going to cost us."

"You should be. Industrial diamonds are in short supply. The British hold all the largest mines and control the ports for most others--even yours."

The British were smothering trade with naval blockades and strategic measures. The only supply the Germans could count on were mines in Portugal. Jean-Michel knew the day was coming when the Germans would need diamonds and had come up with two solutions. One was too daring, even for his tastes--he decided not to move them out of eastern Canada directly to Germany. Instead, he had made contacts in the British Protectorate of Sierra Leone. It was as if he were taunting the British.

Strictly speaking, by common law a Protectorate exists only with permission of those being protected. The British unilaterally acquired the Sierra Leone territory. There were rich mines throughout the land, with open mining immediately south of Koidu-Sefad. Jean-Michel paid locals to collect diamonds from the open mines and surrounding terrain. The diamonds were transported overland through territories held by the enemies of Sierra Leona, on a circuitous route before arriving from the south at Casablanca.

A projectile crossed the bow of the vessel as it moved north along the West African coast. An officer held a megaphone to his mouth, "HALT AND PREPARE TO BE BOARDED."

"What is the meaning of firing upon my ship?" the captain demanded, speaking in proper English.

The captain of the British warship was taken back. "You are suspected of smuggling diamonds. Let me see your papers."

"Certainly. But this is preposterous! We aren't smuggling anything. This is rubbish!"

The crew spoke with their guests in a friendly manner, in as formal English as one might find in Parliament. The guards uneasily let down their rifles. The crew offered the marines English cigarettes, scotch and gin, which further confused them. There must be some mistake they thought; how could these chaps be our enemies?

The captain returned with papers, documenting the Panamanian registry, titled to Péppin and Cash Company. They were all in order, but could be forgeries (which they were, but of the finest quality). The British captain observed his men leisurely enjoying their guest's cigarettes and tossing back whiskey. "SEARCH!," he bellowed. British sailors flooded into the holds, while the Panamanian captain objected, "I dare say, this is most irregular. I demand you consult with your superiors before continuing on with this unlawful search."

The search was entirely lawful, the ship being in Sierra Leone territorial waters. The men found absolutely no contraband. The British captain ordered the ship into the port of Freetown, where the crew would be searched and interrogated, while the ship was unloaded onto the dock and searched inch-by-inch. The sailors spoke impeccable English during their interrogations and calmly proclaimed their personal innocence and that of their ship. Not one illegal good was found, only common items--fruits, vegetables, farm tools in wooden cases, and clothing. The captain scratched his head, while he watched the Panamanian captain's animated demands for an apology and asking how quickly they could be underway.

"I don't know how you did it!"
"Did what? We did nothing."
With nothing to go on, the British Captain could detain them no longer. He released them without apology. Three days later, American and British intelligence would report the ship unloading crates of industrial diamonds onto Vichy-French Nazi vessels in the port of Casablanca, Morocco. The maneuver was of particular interest to the Americans.

Nazi sailors had walked single file onto the ship in port. They walked off a few minutes later carrying a single case of diamonds each. What the British and American spies did not see is that each sailor was walking onto the ship with thirty pounds of diamonds under their clothing, before being placed in the wooden cases, and the full cases of diamonds carried off. The ruse was intended to baffle the British and American spies and it worked exceptionally well.

In addition to landing spies in occupied territories, Jean-Michel and George were asked to assist in building aid to Great Britain. Over the past six months they had been pressured to let them know what materials were being supplied to the Nazis, but always refused.
"Admiral McCorley on line 1."
Admiral McCorley, how have you been?"
"I have been well, Jean-Michel. How about you?"
"Can't complain. What's on your mind?"
"There is something we would like to discuss with you."
"Bob, were not going to rehash old things, are we?"
"No. We have something new for you. We want to bring a team of scientists to study your methods. What works, what

doesn't work, and why."

"You want to study our methods? Why?"

"We are building up aid to Great Britain. We have been crafting a route through the Netherlands."

"Why don't you hire us to do it?"

"We see this as a large scale operation. The Navy wants a crack at it as part of their expanded presence in the Atlantic."

"Go on."

"Frankly, I think FDR wouldn't mind if the Nazis took some pot shots at us to justify the next level."[27]

"So, why do you want our help?"

"You have been able to evade every..."

"No we haven't. We don't evade anybody. We have partnered with all sides. In assuring your goods are handled, one must assure to us they will overlook our other business interests." The Admiral didn't have a response, but he did press on with Jean-Michel until he agreed to allow a team to come down. For a price. They made arrangements for a small team to come to Mobile two weeks later.

"Get me, Rear Admiral Robert Allen McCorley!"

There was a substantial delay.

"McCorley."

"You bastard! You weasel!"

"What?"

"Péppin here. We caught your boys red-handed. I wouldn't give you information, so you sent those so-called scientists here to steal it."

"Now, wait a minute--"

"No. I am not waiting. Your scientists have already confessed."

"Okay, Okay. It wasn't my idea."

"I don't give a shit whose idea it was. You put my business and the life of each of my crews at risk."

"I know, but--"

"But nothing. I am going to double my prices for all my services, effective immediately."

---

[27] In his personal diary on May 23, 1941, Secretary of War Henry Lewis Stimson, worried "because the President shows evidence of waiting for the accidental shot of some irresponsible captain on either side to be the occasion of his going to war."

"Okay, okay, let's not get carried away."

"You can expect a few dozen shipments delivered to your home, starting next week."

"What are you talking about?"

"1877 Chestnut Ave, Buena Vista, Virginia?"

"What? How did you get my home address?"

"Your spies gave it to me."

"Why would you need my address?"

"Shipments. Body parts." Jean-Michel slammed down the phone. He planned to keep the spies imprisoned through the balance of the war, if necessary.

Jean-Michel called a few days later to discuss with McCorley his terms of release.

Chief of Naval Operations Admiral Harold Rainsford "Betty" Stark came to a major conclusion. It was not based on abstract ideology or political posturing. It was simple math. In December 1940 he predicted Britain might not be able to hold out for more than six months in its war against Nazi Germany. Britain was losing warships at an annualized rate of 7.3 million gross tons against an ability to build at 1.25 million gross tons for all purposes--military and merchant. A nation island would quickly be strangled at that level of disparity.

The United States quietly entered war that spring, though it wouldn't declare war until December. On March 11, 1941, nine months before the attack on Pearl Harbor, Franklin Delano Roosevelt signed Public Law 77-11, An Act to Further Promote the Defense of the United States, committing $50.1 billion in material and equipment to assist belligerent nations.[28]

---

[28] The legislation was more commonly known as "Lend-Lease." The intent was to lend or lease equipment to favorable governments. It was done on a 'cash on the barrel head' basis--when payment was done at all. Franklin D. Roosevelt came up with a practical example to describe it to the American people when asked at a press

"What could they want?" wondered Jean-Michel Péppin to his secretary in response to the letter asking to meet with him. "Go ahead and schedule it with them, but find out what it is about." Even though he was assured the meeting was not about their men he held, he was worried it was a trap and insisted they come to him. The meeting was held in Jean-Michel's office the following week with two mid-level Navy Officers. There were casual greetings all around before they got down to business. Rear Admiral James Beaumont Owens said, "Let's be frank, we know what you have been doing."

Jean-Michel's brow furrowed, "What?"

"I said, we know what you have been doing."

"What the hell does that mean?"

Rear Admiral Robert Allen McCorley came to his defense, "What Admiral Owens is saying, is that we have observed your operations."

"And?"

"We just wanted you to know that we are aware of what you are capable--"

"Are you threatening me?" He reached toward the phone and pressed a buzzer.

"Oh, no. Don't get us wrong, we admire what you have been able to do and we need your help."

"Yes, Sir," came over the intercom.

"Never mind, Janet."

"I'm sorry we got off on the wrong foot."

"Let's start again. I was about to have you escorted out.

---

conference, "What do I do in such a crisis? I don't say, 'Neighbor, my garden hose cost me $15; you have to pay me $15 for it'. I don't want $15--I want my garden hose back after the fire is over."

At the same time, the United States seized 600,000 tons of Axis-owned and Danish-owned ships in American ports and soon turned them over to the British.

Secretary of War Henry Lewis Stimson called Lend-Lease a "limited alliance with a warring democracy"; but in wars you intend to win, nothing can ever be limited. Hitler and Roosevelt both quickly drew lines in the ocean. Nazi Germany extended their war zone to the 38th meridian west. Roosevelt approved Western Hemisphere Defense Plan No. 2, declaring the Western Hemisphere extended from longitude 26th meridian west in the Atlantic to the International Date Line in the Pacific (overlapping the German plan by including Iceland, a large portion of Greenland, and the Azores). The Monroe Doctrine was alive and well.

FIVE

What brings you gentlemen here?"

Over the next hour, the two Navy officers described what they had seen. They also described how Jean-Michel could help them.

"This is so different from what we have been doing, I am going to need to bring my partner in on it."

"That would be fine."

Jean-Michel thought for a moment, "There will be some additional things I require that will need to be discussed at the highest levels of the Navy or perhaps the Executive branch." The officers looked at each other. They had heard Jean-Michel was a tough negotiator. They agreed to meet in Washington in one week. Even meeting with the Navy was risky for Jean-Michel--if the Nazi's found out they would seize their ships and crews for a perceived betrayal.

A week later, on the ride to Washington, Jean-Michel described to George the Navy's plan to land espionage agents in the Azores, Morocco, and Western Mediterranean. In the future, their own submarines would carry the load, but with losses heavy in the North Atlantic this was a safer route in the short term.

"We should be able to train them as our own crew members, in order for them to blend in. Our standard crew complement is four officers and seven sailors. We can bump up to eight."

"What about equipment?"

"That could get dangerous."

"I agree. We need to minimize what they take."

"Alright."

"What if we get caught?"

"That puts our whole business at risk."

"Make sure the Navy understands that."

"Right."

"Everyone is getting nervous and trigger happy."

"Yeah, the number of stoppages has tripled over the last six months."

"It is a wonder nobody has gotten killed."

"Realistically, it is just a matter of time. More gun waving. More searches. More angry talks."

"Fortunately, our captains have been well-trained. They don't carry firearms. They don't resist."

"Yes. Remind me to thank Jack for training them so well, next time I see him."

"Bien sûr!" responded Jean-Michel as he looked away.

"We have to continue to remind everyone that we are doing a service for them and they are only hurting themselves when they delay one of our ships," warned George.

"Yes, we will continue to stress that," replied Jean-Michel.

"What are we going to charge the Navy for doing this?"

"Well, it is going to depend on some of the conditions we run into today. This is a once in a lifetime opportunity and it is not going to last long."

"What if they pull out?"

"They won't. We have them over a barrel. I am going to ask an exemption from prosecution for future and past deeds--"

"Without admitting guilt?"

"Of course. And exemption from the draft for all crew members and our families."

"We can't turn over a list of names."

"Right. We will have to handle it through our contacts as draft notices come in." Jean-Michel chugged his last swallow as his Boeing 247 touched down at Anacostia Naval Air Station.

Jean-Michel thought of the arrangement that he had made to kill the men he held if this meeting was a trap and he and George were detained, or worse. George knew nothing about them.

Over the next two days, Jean-Michel and George held meetings during the day with the Navy and spent evenings with the acting Secretary of the Navy William Franklin "Frank" Knox.

"Are my boys treating you alright?"

"Yes, Sir."

"Oh, hell. Don't sir me! Call me Frank. I'm an old reporter and businessman, you know." He was more than reporter and publisher-businessman; he had been the Republican nominee for vice-president under Alf Landon. "We can't go into this war blind. We need to use every resource at our disposal, and develop some we don't have."

George looked at Jean-Michel, but both men remained silent.

"I agree to your price and terms. I am gonna have to twist arms to get all of it. But FDR will be sympathetic. Did you know he was Assistant Secretary of the Navy during Wilson?"

They didn't.

"Yes, he was a good man in that position. Very thoughtful. Did you know he created the Naval Reserve?"

Neither did.

"Before we go to dinner, I need to get something for my stomach. Indigestion has been bad all day," said Jean-Michel, rubbing his stomach and his left shoulder.

"Hey, and over dinner you have got to tell me something--how the hell did you get those diamonds past us?"

The trees were beginning to change—leaves on whole branches of the maples turning from green to dull reds and yellows before they dried up, lost their grip on their limbs, and fluttered to the ground. The season of colors, Rebecca's favorite, had at last arrived. Having picked up since noon, the wind was swirling leaves in the air. Gusts crashed into the house, but Alexander didn't move. Rebecca stood over his bed and smiled--he could sleep through anything. Rebecca wandered down from the house toward the river in the beautiful afternoon sun. The wind streamed north along the river, when she noticed smoke coming from Jack's old place. She made a mental note to see what was going on during her next afternoon ride.

For the last year, she could count on one hand the weeks George had come back for a visit and have fingers left over. She wasn't angry with him, she told herself. But with a 11-year-old and a toddler, trying to be mother and father was taking its toll. She began riding horseback through the foothills alone in the afternoons, while Abraham was at school and Alexander down for his nap. For the last week she'd been distracted, impatiently waiting to take her ride each day.

As she rode up, she saw him chopping wood and stacking

it against the house. He was tall, with a chiseled chest, large arms, and piercing blue eyes. He wore midnight blue breeches with yellow leg stripes, a Sam Browne belt, oxblood riding boots, and brown gloves up to the elbow with leather gauntlets. She was startled by how handsome he was, but overcame her shyness as she got closer: "Hello!"

"Hello to you." Self-consciously he stopped to towel off his sweat and put on his faded red work shirt. He pulled off his right glove as he walked toward her. She felt faint as he arrived by her horse and reached up his hand. She could smell his hot, delicious sweat. "I'm Bent. Clement Peter Bentshure."

She recovered enough to get out her name, "Rebecca Cash. Did you know Jack?"

He laughed. Even his laugh was handsome. "Everyone knows Jack. He is legendary. But no, I have never met the man. Do you?"

"Yes. I was raised on the farm on the other side of the river." She pointed south. "We used to spend summers up here when I was a girl."

He eyed her from top to bottom, and was pleased with what he saw. "I have been patrolling Jack's place for the last year as part of my rounds. I feel like I have known Jack all my life and have stayed at his place many times. It is a shame how it's run down. I just resigned from the Royal Canadian Mounted Police and taking time off."

"Why did you patrol here?"

"We thought his burial may have been a ruse. We came back here and dug up the empty coffin. We've been riding by in case he returns. Do you know where he is?"

"Other side of the world, I suspect."

He laughed again. "I bet he is."

Rebecca rode home, but couldn't keep her mind off Bent.

"Can you help me make a pie?"

"A pie? You have never made a pie before; what's the occasion?

"New neighbors. I thought it would be nice to take a pie."

"Yes, it would."

The following morning, she took a long bath and did her hair. She was nervous as Abraham left for school, and distracted and inattentive to Alexander. After lunch, she rode off to Jack's farm with a picnic basket holding a fresh peach pie.

"Boy, she sure took out of here today. Where is she going, all dolled up?"

"Taking a pie up to a family that has moved into Jack's farm." Eddie was suspicious and he gave Alice a concerned look. "It is like she can't wait to ride."

"I was up to Jack's yesterday. There is no family there. Just a Mountie living there. Nice enough guy, I guess. Rugged. Tall. Well-mannered."

"I wonder what she is doing there."

He gave a half smile and thought to himself, probably mounting the Mountie.

He was once again chopping wood where she rode up. Barechested and sweaty, he stopped to wipe off his hands. "Rebecca! What a pleasant surprise. To what do I owe this kindly visit?"

"I made a present to welcome you."

He helped her off her horse and lingered holding her waist after she placed her feet on the ground. She noticed, but tried not to react. Her heart was racing. "It's in my basket." She grabbed the basket and opened one of the lids for him to peek in. He placed his right hand gently on her left hip as he leaned around to see. "Let's have some! Where can I find a knife?"

He led her to the kitchen. She quickly placed the pie on the table. Spotting the knife on the counter, she ran over, grabbed it, and turned around. Bent was inches from her and she startled at him being so close, dropped the knife, and reached out to steady herself, grabbing him by his strong biceps. Her eyes stared into his hairy, sweaty chest before she scanned up to his eyes. They made love in the afternoon sun. Their lovemaking each day thereafter was wild, rigorous, and unrestrained.

She lay nestled in his strong arms. "You are quite a work stoppage."

"You don't seem to be complaining."

He laughed. "I am never going to get enough wood cut with these breaks each afternoon."

"I guess I will just have to keep you warm all winter." She rolled over on top of him.

"I need you to help me make a cake."

"It is your birthday tomorrow; I was planning on making you one."

"I need another."

Alice thought this might be the opportunity to raise a difficult subject. "Rebecca, this is difficult for me to bring up..."

Rebecca stiffened. "Then don't."

"Rebecca, there has been a lot of talk--"

"STOP!"

"You are a married woman and--"

"SHUT UP!"

"I know it has been hard with George being gone so much."

Rebecca slapped her across the face. They stood face-to-face staring at each other. There was a long pause before Rebecca said flatly, "You can help me make a cake. Or you can pack your bags." Alice wiped her hands on her apron and tried not to reach up to her face. They did not speak one word while they stood side-by-side making two birthday cakes.

That evening, George unexpectedly walked through the door. "SURPRISE!" He took Rebecca in his arms to kiss her passionately. She flinched. "Are you alright?"

"I just wasn't expecting you."

"I couldn't miss your fortieth birthday." She looked sad, but he didn't see it. "Where are the boys?"

She pointed upstairs, but looked behind George. "Didn't you bring Thomas?"

"No. He is training with Jean-Michel and watching the fort while I'm away. And I can't stay long."

At bedtime, George rolled over in bed to kiss his wife. It had been a long time since they had been together. Without saying a word, she rebuked his advances. "What's wrong?"

"I guess I'm tired."

"Did you miss me?" She remained lying on her side facing away. "Are you mad at me?"

She really had to think about her answer. "No," she lied. Seeing his advances rebuked he lay back and stared at the ceiling, while Rebecca faked sleep.

The next day was Rebecca's birthday. George asked Alice

to make a special birthday dinner. They spent the afternoon with the boys, fishing along the river. The evenings were growing cold as the daylight hours shrunk each day. As they rode back to the house, Rebecca looked north to see if she could see smoke from the fireplace across the border.

After supper, George was teasing the boys at the dinner table. Alice brought in two birthday cakes, while Rebecca gave her an angry look. "Look, two birthday cakes!" The boys cheered. "Why two cakes?"

Alice looked up to see Rebecca, with her mouth open. "Ask your wife."

The week vacation went by quickly for George and the boys and was interminable for Rebecca. George was sad and frustrated that his advances with Rebecca had been rebuffed all week.

"What time is your train?"

"It comes through late. We'll have to leave for Sandpoint at six tonight."

After an early supper, George, Rebecca, and the boys were playing on the parlor floor when the Grandfather clock struck six.

George kissed Abraham and Alexander. "I have to be going, boys." He stood up and walked over to Rebecca. "I will try to get back here soon. I hope you will quickly get over your anger with me. It has been a long time since we--"

"Goodbye, George." She pecked him on the cheek.

They walked out to see John had harnessed Clyde to the wagon and had George's bags in back. John helped George up onto the small surrey wagon. George threw kisses to the boys and Rebecca as they rode away.

"Boys, go see Alice for more dessert!" They ran into the house. Rebecca turned and strode purposely to the barn. Less than a minute later, she rode bareback at full speed out of the barn, heading north.

When 353 Japanese aircraft from six aircraft carriers savaged the United States Pacific Naval Fleet at Pearl Harbor, the Japanese public reaction was surprise, shock, disbelief, apprehension, and distress--identical to the Americans.[29] Immediately, FDR had a free hand "with perfect assurance that the country was solidly behind him. Never has the United States been so united." The next day, he asked Congress for a Declaration of War. The vote was unanimous, with one Congresswoman merely voting 'Present'.[30] America was thrust into the war with Germany that George was so sure was coming.

For the week following the attack Rebecca did not ride up to see Bent. Each day, he spent a full morning working, ate lunch, cleaned up, and idly awaited Rebecca's return. When

---

[29] In America, the shock quickly turned to anger. One motorist in San Francisco found out about the Japanese bombing as he pulled into a service station. "Just now down the street, I almost hit a Jap on a motorcycle--guess I should have run over him," he said.
"Up to today I wondered whether we were another France--too soft. But now we'll see if Americans can fight in the old way--I know Maine people can," one man noted.
In 1942, former Japanese Ambassador to the United States Saburō Kurusu talked about the "historical inevitability of the war of Greater East Asia."
The history of American-Japanese relations had not been good for nearly a century and had gotten progressively worse. In the mid-nineteenth century American imposed "Unequal Treaties" on Asian nations, forcing them into disadvantageous economic relationships. Many European countries followed suit.
Racial prejudice ran high.
[30] Montana's Congresswoman Jeannette Pickering Rankin, a lifelong pacifist, voted against the entry of the United States into both World Wars. She said "she wanted to show that a good democracy does not always vote unanimously for war." She also said "As a woman, I can't go to war and I refuse to send anyone else."
President Roosevelt's administrative assistant at the time, Jonathan Daniels, noted FDR's subsequent reflection on Pearl Harbor, "The blow was heavier than he had hoped it would necessarily be" ... "But the risks paid off; even the loss was worth the price."

she didn't arrive, he was disappointed. Perhaps one of the boys was sick. Or maybe George had returned. While clearing twigs and leaves from around the house, he looked south to Altura Farm, hoping to see her on the horizon.

Rebecca rode slowly up with Alexander in the saddle in front of her. She handed Alexander down to Bent--it was the first time she'd brought him. "I'm sorry I have not come by--I have been so distraught."

"What is it?"

"About the bombing."

He looked startled, "Bombing?"

"Pearl Harbor. Haven't you heard?"

"No." He had neither radio nor newspaper. The only news he received was what Rebecca passed along or on the rare times he went to Porthill.

"The Japanese bombed us in Pearl Harbor, Hawaii."

Bent didn't point out he was not an 'us'--he was Canadian. "I hadn't heard!"

"Sneak attack. A week ago Sunday."

Bent tried to take all this in and remember where Hawaii was located. "Come in the house." He made tea and heard the details--planes, submarines, surprise attack, Pacific fleet nearly wiped out, and thousands dead.

"What if their planes are flying here?"

He thought that highly unlikely, but didn't want to offend her. "That would be horrible."

"I heard they may attack through Seattle or Vancouver."

Bent thought a minute before he answered, "We just can't let ourselves get carried away. We are going to hear a lot of rumors--they cannot be trusted. We have to remain calm."

"The President spoke to Congress. They have declared war, Bent." He didn't say anything. "Now they'll take my sons from us!"

"Yes, they may draft them now." He thought to himself--I, too, may have to go.

"Oh, Bent, what will happen to us?" He didn't have any answers. She pulled on his strong arms, bringing his hands to her back. "Bent, I'm so afraid." He held her as Alexander played by their feet.

In Mobile's finest nightclub, Jean-Michel and George had a late dinner. Somber and reflective, George sipped his wine. He wore a black business suit with vest, white-shirt and broad tie. Jean-Michel was jovial. The yellow silk ascot in his open shirt contrasted with his burnt amber suit. Well-tailored and trim, he read the menu by slipping a monocle over his right eye, and then quickly tucked it into his vest. He had begun losing vision since an early age, but was too vain to wear glasses.

"I believe I will order champagne!"

"You seem to be in a good mood."

"Why not!"

"Your country has just declared war, if for no other reason."

"George, don't you understand? This is going to make us rich!"

"We already are rich." George had spent the afternoon fretting about whether their business was right in selling to the Nazis.

Jean-Michel laughed. "Very rich!"

During dinner, George push away from the table and turned his chair to squarely face Jean-Michel. "It is treasonous not to support the war effort now. We obviously must not support our enemies. They are making bombs and bullets to kill our boys!"

"Nothing changes." He took of bite of his bloody steak.

"I'm not so sure."

Firmly, Jean-Michel replied, "Nothing changes. Nothing."

They ate dinner and as he finished, Jean-Michel slid back his chair and lit a cigar. "Why are you so apprehensive?"

"We are at war."

"True. But we are helping the war effort."

"And hurting as well."

Jean-Michel grinned. "We are doing what everyone else is doing."

"What do you mean?"

Jean-Michel puffed on his cigar, as he thought of a way to

explain it. "George, have you ever thought how a free market nation fights a war?"

"What do you mean?"

"In a free market, things get bought and sold. For the United States to fight a war, they have to buy everything they need. That is different from other countries, where the government either already controls, or will just take over, the strategic resources."

"Strategic resources?"

"Yes. If the Nazis need steel to make tanks, what do they do? They take over the steel mills and make the tanks. But what does America do? It buys the steel from Bethlehem Steel, or US Steel. Or has the manufacturers buy it for them. Bethlehem and the manufacturers make a lot of money that way."

Jean-Michel took another long drag on his cigar. "You know Henry Ford is an anti-Semite?"

George had seen some of Ford's pamphlets at a dealership. "Yes. He hates Jews. It's common knowledge. So what? Lots of people hate Jews."

"The Nazis also hate the Jews. What if Ford was a Nazi. What if he wouldn't sell to America for war purposes. Or jacked up the price. What if he takes all his money and ramps up production in Europe to sell automobiles and trucks to the Germans?"[31]

"Preposterous!"

"Why? Who could stop him? Now suppose our side made a deal with Henry that said he could continue to sell in the German market as long as he continued to sell to our side, too?"

"Why would our side do that?

"Because you know we CAN'T stop the Nazis from getting the cars! They would just take over what Ford had in Europe.

---

[31] In July 1938, the German consul at Cleveland gave Henry Ford the award of the Grand Cross of the German Eagle, the highest medal Nazi Germany could bestow on a foreigner. According to historian Steven Watts, Hitler 'revered' Ford, saying--"I shall do my best to put his theories into practice in Germany," and modeled the Volkswagen--'The People's Car'--on the Model T. Henry Ford is the only American mentioned in Mein Kampf. Hitler regarded Ford as his 'inspiration' in explaining why he kept a life-size portrait of Henry Ford next to his desk.

All those plants they could get their hands on would just go on without skipping a beat making cars and trucks for the Nazis. Just Henry wouldn't be making the money anymore."[32]

"True."

"You can bet everyone is getting in line to get a waiver to the T-W-E-A."

"T-W-E-A?"

"The Trading with the Enemy Act. General Motors, General Electric, Ford, DuPont, Dow Chemical, Standard Oil, US Steel, Alcoa, IBM will all get waivers. Every bank in the US will get a waiver, starting with National City and Chase National. We're getting one, too. Just run off to the Treasury and get the 'Morgenthau scrawl'.[33]

"Really?"

"Piece of cake. I'm trading a handful of spies we are holding for Hank's signature, our recognition as essential war work, and exemption for the draft for our workers, and your

---

[32] By 1932, one of every three cars in the world was a Ford. Henry Ford had subsidiaries in Australia, Britain, Argentina, Brazil, Canada, India, South Africa, Mexico, and all nations in Continental Europe.
According to American intelligence reports, GM and Ford subsidiaries built nearly 90 percent of the armored 'mule' 3-ton half-trucks and more than 70 percent of the Reich's medium and heavy-duty trucks--"the backbone of the German Army transportation system."

[33] The Trading with the Enemy Act of 1917 (TWEA) is a United States federal law, 12 U.S.C. § 95a, restricting trade with countries hostile to the United States. The President could restrict (or permit) any trade in times of war.
Within a week of Pearl Harbor, FDR had signed Executive Order 8389 giving "general license" to the Secretary of the Treasury (Henry Morgenthau, Jr.) to administer the program.
The State Department unofficially assumed authority as well. For a period, they dutifully went to the Treasury for permission. Nevertheless, and probably for political reasons only, The State Department assumed it knew best--as the 'feet of the street' purveyor of economic interests wherever they were stationed--when waivers or general licenses should be given. As a result, they often gave cover to companies asking permission under the act.
There were also situations during World War II where, unable to gain permission from either the Treasury or State Departments, US companies went ahead with violating the law, while the administration ignored the practice.

sons." George's mouth dropped. Jean-Michel took a long drag on his cigar, before rolling out an enormous smoke ring. "Yes, I have an embarrassed Admiral doing my bidding right now."

Steady rains in the mountains east of Porthill started before Thanksgiving and turned to snow by Christmas. Thomas, now twenty-three, came home from Mobile for the holidays and the three boys enjoyed time together.

"How do you like your job?"

Thomas did not want to disclose too much to his mother about the work he was doing for his father. "It is good work. Long hours, but good pay. Nice people. But work is work. I'm happy to have a break."

He enjoyed hugging and mock wrestling with his three-year-old brother, Alexander, and playing catch in the house with Abraham. With ten years between each boy, Thomas was a man, Abraham was just entering his teen years, and Alexander was a toddler. They looked alike and enjoyed each other. They were free to be boys this Christmas and Thomas could show things to Abraham that amazed him--magic tricks he had learned, sleight of hand with cards, chemistry he'd learned in college, and pranks he had done in his dorm. Abraham idolized his older brother. They enjoyed making snowmen and having snowball fights. Thomas was particularly attentive and protective of Alexander.

The rain and snow turned the roads into mud. A mudslide covered the main road to the south and blocked traffic. The Sheriff came to Altura Farm asking help in clearing the road and three men went down for a few days.

"Sheriff, we're not as flush with men as we used to be," said Eddie.

"Any help you can give would be appreciated."

The endless battle between weather and man continued for weeks into the new year. Thomas missed his train out of Sandpoint because of snow and mudslides and returned to the farm to wait it out. After a blistering telegram from his father he left for Vancouver to take the circle route north through Niagara Falls.

Snow melting on the mountains and continuous heavy rains brought the river to the tops of its banks. The surging, raging river bit away soil from the banks and golden prairie grasses that held the soil on the banks were sucked one by one out of the ground and swept north. Water splashed over the banks repeatedly, further thinning the banks. The men from Altura Farm filled and stacked cloth potato bags along the shore, until it was obvious they would lose the battle. They scampered to the foothills while volunteers rode to the Big House to alert Rebecca, Alice, and the boys.

"No, leave everything! We must go!" Rebecca ordered the boys, "Just bring your coats and boots!"

They jumped on the backs of the men's horses and rode toward the foothills. One man stopped at the barn to open the corrals and stalls where the farm animals stood. They looked at him, contentedly chewing the dried corn stalks, as he tried to spook them out. Deciding he couldn't wait any longer he rode hard toward the hills.

Their collection point was a hill called Carol's Stand, where maple trees stood in the shape of a heart around a pond of sweet water, fed by a nearby spring. They made shelters best they could with limbs, canvas, and rope. In the twilight, volunteers went back to the Big House for food. They found ham and potatoes to tide them over for a few days. Alice cooked supper over the fire they could barely keep lit. They huddled under the canvas structures, attempting to keep warm, unable to stay dry, and tried to sleep.

In a single position in their beds for long periods, men and rivers both need to change positions from time to time. As a man bends and tosses in his sleep, the Kootenai River bent and tossed that winter. Mud, silt, water, trees, logs, and lumber clogged, backed up, and gouged a new channel through existing levees and banks into the middle of Altura Farm and filled much of Porthill with muddy water. Brown-gray mud pressed and formed a new wall. The low land of Altura farm, once protected by the raised river bank, became the low point in the river. Flooding water pushed debris out of its path like a paper boat down a stream. The buildings of the farm bobbed, creaked and crashed; Altura Farm was no more.

When the Army convinced Chet to start raising rabbits they hadn't given him the Army Corp of Engineer's full report.[34] The Corp examined the contour of the land upstream where the Kootenai River lazily switched back and forth from the border through the lowland fields as far as Bonner's Ferry, 27 miles south. They studied the Kootenai Dominion Park and Beaverfoot Range in Canada. They studied the river near Rexford and Libby in Montana. A dam was needed to prevent flooding in the basin--until then, massive floods three or four times a century should be expected. They published their report, causing land prices from Bonner's Ferry to the border to plummet.

Chet studied the maps, 'Those crazy fools! That's too hundred miles away, on the other side of the mountains, and the river is goin' in the opposite direction! Besides, my contract says the army will make it right by me'. He looked out at the river from his study and saw the sturdy, wide banks of the levee. Chet bought at rock bottom, amused by the how easily people could be spooked.[35]

After two days nobody could understand what they were seeing. The farm was devastated beyond recognition. They looked at the destruction from Carol's Stand and some climbed the maples to get a better look.

"What are those bushes doing there?"

"Those aren't bushes, they are the tops of the apple trees!"

"Can't be."

"What's that stone structure?" He pointed to the chimney of the Big House.

"I don't know. What are we gonna do now?"

"We can head south along the foothills. We'll get to some

---

[34] In 1975, a joint Canadian-American project built the Libby Dam near Libby, Montana. It created a 90-mile long reservoir, Lake Koocanusa.

[35] The Flood Control Act of 1936, Public Law 74-738, (FCA 1936) was an act of the United States Congress authorized civil engineering projects such as dams, levees, dikes, and other flood control measures through the United States Army Corps of Engineers and other Federal agencies.

village somewhere. We're sure not going back to Altura!"

That afternoon the men left, walking south along the foothills. A few stopped to say farewell. "Miss Rebecca, it's been nice knowing you. But we are gonna be going south," said Eddie.

"Can you take Alice with you?"

"Of course. We can also take you and the boys, if you'd like, but we really don't know what we are gonna find."

"No. This is our home. We'll stay here."

"But, Ma'am, the house is under water. There is no home to go to."

"We'll be fine, Eddie." He looked at her quizzically, before turning to leave. She had seen something nobody else had been looking for--smoke from Bent's chimney.

The telegram George received read--ALTURA FLOODED. DESTROYED. FAMILY AT JACKS. It was unsigned.

George interrupted Thomas as he and Jean-Michel went over plans and schedules, "We must go! Altura is flooded."

Thomas and Jean-Michel simply looked at each other. Jean-Michel broke the silence, "Everyone okay?"

"I think so."

George and Thomas took the first train out of Mobile to Chicago. "I think we better take the Canada train to Vancouver. We can hire a wagon or barge from there." Thomas spent daylight hours watching for majestic western moose, migratory woodland caribou, and elk they encountered along the tracks. One late afternoon at the base of the Rockies, the train stopped for a large, elderly bull moose with an antler span of nearly six feet, as he grazed on fireweed plant which poked up between the rails.

As the train climbed the Canadian Rockies, Thomas dropped down from his berth.

"Still can't sleep?" his father asked.

"I hope everyone is alright."

"I am sure they are," he said with as much confidence as he could muster. George pulled out the telegram. "It says the family is at Jack's. I think they would have said something if anyone was injured." He thought, but did not say, 'or was dead'.

"Who sent the telegram?"

"Came from Porthill."

"Mother? Sheriff?"

George shrugged. "Probably."

"What will we do?"

"We'll bring everyone to Mobile until we can assess the damage after the waters subside."

"That could be summer."

"Or later."

George made plans for when the train pulled into Vancouver in the early morning--pay cash for a horse, carriage and boat to take them to Idaho. They arrived more than a week later at Balfour Bay, British Colombia, where they stayed at the Canadian Pacific Hotel overnight before hiring a private boat to take them through to Kootenai Lake where the Kootenai River bulges.

Over venison steaks Thomas said, "It's sure nice to be on dry land. I took a hot bath. Felt good. Are we all set for tomorrow?"

"I hired a boat."

"What about the horse and buggy?"

"We'll bring them along. Not sure we are going to be able to use them, from what I hear."

"Really?"

"The damage is more extensive than even I imagined." Thomas nodded. "I'll be happy to see them safe."

They left at mid-afternoon the following day to travel by boat the 50 miles south to Jack's Farm. It was late at night when they arrived, so they stayed on the boat and awaited dawn. When smoke bellowed from the chimney George and Thomas walked up to the house and knocked.

Bent swung open the door and answered sleepily, "Hello." He was wearing faded red long johns.

"I'm George Cash."

From the bedroom, Rebecca called, "Who is it, Honey?"

Bent opened the door and let the two men in. The house had changed since George had last been there. The furniture was still the same, but pictures on the walls and makeshift curtains were different. There was a bearskin rug on the floor. He scanned the room to see Abraham sleeping on a couch, with his brother next to him on the floor. George was relieved at the sight of Thomas bending down to touch Abraham's hair and stroke Alexander's back. Neither stirred. From where George was standing he could see into the bedroom as Rebecca's naked body twisted out of the sheets next to where Bent had been. It was easy to see what the sleeping arrangements had been.

"Coffee?"

"Yes," responded George, in shock over what he had just seen.

As George, Thomas, and Bent ate breakfast, Rebecca came from the bedroom. She ran over to hug Thomas.

"Oh, Mother, it's wonderful to see you. We were so worried."

"I love you!"

She leaned over to hug George, but got a cool response, which she shrugged off.

"Eggs? Toast?" asked Bent.

"Please!"

Alexander got up from his bed and ran to his mother to hug and cuddle.

"Say 'hi' to your father! He just came in this morning with Tommy!" He was too shy to say hello. Soon he got down from his mother's lap to cuddle up with Bent and eat toast off his plate.

"Is everything alright, George?" asked Rebecca.

"We'll talk about it later. Right now, we need to have a look at the farm. Do you want to come with us or pack?"

"There is nothing to pack. I'll come with you."

The boat traveled down river toward Porthill. They couldn't recognize landmarks, other than details in the foothills, and continued south. Arriving at the top of a tree, they looked under the water to see how tall it was, but it was too muddy and dark. Something looked like concrete slabs. If it had been clearer they would have recognized the burial place of Chet, Tura, and Abby.

They turned north and saw tangled, floating debris even this many days after the flood. Books from Chet's library that hadn't waterlogged lined the new river bank.

"Look! Over there. What is it?"

The boat took them to an outcropping tangled with branches. They drifted alongside. "What is it?"

It was minutes before George said, "It's the chimney of the Big House." The wooden structure had detached from the stone chimney and floated away with all their belongings and memories. "Let's go."

They came upon the carcass of a horse. The poor thing had drowned, bloated, its rotting body exploded and deflated, and was now covered with flies and maggots. Recognizing the pattern on the horse George leaned over the railing and vomited. They were feasting on what was left of Old Clyde.

"Go over to Porthill," George instructed the captain as he wiped his mouth.

They docked and the family disembarked. George handed Rebecca cash, "Get whatever you need. We'll be leaving for Mobile as soon as we get back to Jack's." She took the money, but hesitated before going to the shops while George purposefully walked to the Telegraph Office.

"Well, I don't rightly know who sent it," said the telegraph agent as he rubbed his lips with his fingers.

"Do you have records?"

"Yes."

"I'll make it worth your while." He handed him a crisp one-hundred dollar bill.

The clerk pocketed the bill while saying, "You don't have to do that." He looked through the records in the back for a half-hour before returning to the desk with a box. "It's gotta be in this one." He scratched through the papers until he found what he was looking for. "It was sent by a Mister Bentsnyder, no...a Mister Bent Shires...hell, I can't hardly read the writing...looks like a Mister Bent Sure, I think. Do you know who that might be?"

"Yes."

When they arrived back at Bent's house Rebecca showed off her purchases.

"I'd like to leave soon."

"Alright," was Rebecca's hesitant reply. She seemed to delay--making excuses to keep from going. Bent finally walked her into the bedroom and closed the door. Rebecca came out minutes later and announced she was ready, wiping tears from her eyes. George shook Bent's hand, thanked him for his hospitality, and escorted his wife and three sons to the boat, while Bent stood on the porch watching her go. Bent told her she had to go. He lied that he was being called up into the service. She couldn't stay. She wasn't welcome there any longer. She had to leave--NOW! Tears streamed from his eyes as he watched the ship disappear on the horizon.

After a few days, when he figured the risk of running into the family had passed, Bent followed their route to Vancouver. He enlisted in the Canadian Army and was attached to the 1st Canadian Division. In July 1943, he died from a single sniper's bullet to the heart in Calabria, Italy during the assault landing on Sicily. The bullet went through a leather case. When they inspected his body, they found it contained three items--a poem which Abraham had written, a snippet of Alexander's fine, curly, blond baby hair, and his only photograph of Rebecca--now unrecognizable from a large hole and covered in Bent's blood.

SIX

Rear Admiral Robert Allen McCorley called Jean-Michel, "It has all been arranged."

"Great! Send me the documents."

"What documents?"

"Whatever I need to prove the Government has made these promises to me and George, which I can stick away in a safe deposit box, and that will hold up in court."

"I'll have to get back to you."

"As soon as I get the documents, and they are to my satisfaction, I'll let your spies go."

"Couldn't you let them go now? On good faith?"

"What good faith did you show in spying on me?"

A week later the documents arrived in the mail, marked 'personal'. They contained the signatures of Chief of Naval Operations Fleet Admiral Ernest Joseph King, Secretary of the Navy William Franklin Knox, Secretary of the Treasury Henry Morgenthau, Jr., and lawyers from the executive branch. Each document had been certified for authenticity. Jean-Michel smiled as he fingered the pages and carefully reviewed each one. He made photographs of the documents before taking them personally to the bank for placement in his safe deposit box. When he returned to the office he made a telephone call and had the spies released. He had hidden them in an apartment in Washington, D.C., less than one mile from Admiral McCorley's office in the Munitions Building at Constitution Avenue on The National Mall (Potomac Park). Each walked to their own home that evening--none could remember exactly where the apartment was where they had been held.[36]

The next week Jean-Michel received another call from McCorley.

"Thanks for letting our guys out."

"No problem. I never wanted them."

"I have another special job for you. Very unusual."

"Do I need to bring George in on this from the beginning? He had a little flooding at his home and isn't back yet."

"I think we can get together and get the ball rolling. Where would you like to meet?"

Since he had given him the choice, Jean-Michel didn't feel they were in danger this time. "I'll come to Washington. Set up my landing for Thursday afternoon at Anacostia."

"We're stealing ball bearings."

"We can't make our own?"

"Swedes make the best."

"Again, we can't make our own?"

"Not as good as they can."

"And you want me to steal them?"

"No. We'll take care of stealing them. We want you to transport them. We plan to get our hands on them in South America."

"Alright. How do we get started?"

"I want you to fly to London. Talk to Sir George Binney. He pulled off getting five steamships full of ball bearings last year from the Swedes."[37]

Two hours after the meeting ended Jean-Michel was aboard a naval seaplane with Admiral's markings headed for

---

[36] The Munitions Building was constructed by the Navy's Bureau of Yards and Docks during the Great War. While it was intended to be a temporary structure, it had been constructed using concrete. It was sufficiently solid to be used until the 1960's, though its usefulness was supplanted by construction of The Pentagon during World War II. The building was demolished in 1970 and the space turned into Constitution Gardens. It was near where the Vietnam Veterans Memorial was placed in 1982.

[37] Operation Rubble (January 1941) was a British blockade-running operation, that delivered 18,600 metric tons of materiel, mostly ball bearings. Binney was Attaché to Stockholm representing the UK Ministry of Supply (Iron and Steel Control) and directed the blockade running from one of the steamships.

Six

London.

Sven Wingqvist's Swedish patent No. 25406 for multi-row, self-aligning radial ball bearings changed the mechanical world. Granted on June 6, 1907 in Sweden and simultaneously in ten other countries, it was an instant success. Five years later manufacturing was taking place in 32 countries. By World War II they were colossal, operating under the name SKF AB. Four thousand ball bearings on average were needed per Focke-Wulf plane. Similar numbers were needed for the Flying Fortresses. Planes, trains, trucks, ships all relied on ball bearings, as did radar, bombsights, generators, ventilation systems, mining and manufacturing equipment, and communications devices. SKF controlled every stage of the raw material mining and supply, manufacturing, and distribution processes. The war rolled along on SKF ball bearings.[38]

---

[38] The company Wingqvist founded had a simple name--Svenska Kullagerfabriken AB (Swedish for Swedish Ball Bearing Factory AB). Today it is known as SKF.

They controlled 80% of the ball bearings manufactured in Europe and had monopolies around the world. Their largest plant, in Philadelphia, supplied the Nazis with ball bearings throughout the war. Even as US workers threatened to walk off the production lines, management swore none were going to the Germans, and the supply continued. SKF Philadelphia had been granted a general license under The Trading with The Enemies Act to supply internationally.

Profit was SKF's sole concern. On paper, they made it appear they were a US Company, when in reality the Treasury Department knew they were Swedish.

The Nazis and Allied countries negotiated with SKF for allotments of ball bearings. There was no combatant country on either side of the conflict that didn't rely on SKF. Complaints about supplies led to SKF blackmailing the complainers with threats of disclosing to the public the negotiations, even complaints when SKF supply to the Nazis exceeded the agreed to amount. Dashing playboy Sven Gustaf Wingqvist, founder and Chief Executive Officer of SKF, was a good friend of Hermann Wilhelm Göring.

The Federal Bureau of Investigation collected information concerning shipments for South American subsidiaries of international corporations--Siemens, Diesel, ASEA, Electrolux, and ITT.

By the time the Cash family got to Vancouver the younger
boys were restless. Thomas had his hands full. George sold
back the horse and wagon, which they had been unable to use,
to the original owner at a considerable loss. They boarded the
train and occupied three adjoining compartments in a sleeper
car. The three boys were having an adventure investigating the
railcars, while George and Rebecca settled in.

George was quite blunt with his comments, "You seemed
to have had a cozy arrangement at Jack's." Rebecca bristled.
"Do you want to talk about it?"

"Not particularly."

"Do you love me?" The question caught her off guard, and
she did not know how to answer. "Listen, I know how hard it
has been."

"Do you?"

"I have been gone a great deal and have left you to fend
for yourself."

Assertively she answered, "Yes, you did."

"I did not mean to leave you for such long periods. I am
sorry."

She started to thaw. "I am sorry, too." She paused,
"I...I...have been unfaithf..."

"I know you have and I understand." Neither said
anything for a long time as the railcar bumped and slid
through a turn. "Do you love me?"

"I was hurt. Badly. But I still do have feelings for you."

"Well, that's a start."

"Do you love Bent, or was he just--convenient?"

"I don't know." She didn't know if she was lying to save
his feelings, or not.

There was another pause. "Did you know it was Bent who
telegraphed me to tell me where you were?" He handed her the
telegram and she read it.

"How did you know it was Bent?"

"Do you remember when we stopped for you to shop in
Porthill? I stopped by the Telegraph Office."

"Ahhh." She looked down at her hands thinking about
what Bent had said to her when he forced her to go with
George. "Bent and I have been...had been...meeting regularly.

We had a...a strong magnetism...from the moment we met."

George nodded. "Mostly physical?"

Rebecca hugged George tightly, "Like my father, you deserted me." It was as if her words and hug seared him; guilt and shame burned him to his core--the sting was overwhelming. Wrapped in each other's arms, they cried.

Upon arriving in Mobile, George had his family stay at the luxury hotel suite he shared with Jack and Jean-Michel. When Rebecca grew tired of hotel food, George rented quarters on Florence Place for the following month. It was modest, but Rebecca fell in love with its azaleas, weeping willows, and pine trees with moss. With three bedrooms and two bathrooms on a small lot, it was quite a contrast from Idaho. There were neighbors and noises they had never experienced. George only intended this for the month or so it would take him to find or begin building a new home. He really wanted to live in Spanish Fork where Jack kept a small boat to get from one facility to another and two cars--one at his home and another where he landed the boat in Mobile.

While George was intent on getting his wife out to look at houses, she dragged her feet. George and Thomas came home from work one evening and the dining room was set for two. George didn't even notice as he went to take his shower. Rebecca whispered in Thomas's ear. Though he was tired he collected his brothers and a small suitcase his mother had packed. Rebecca called a taxi to take the boys to the hotel. It was Friday evening and Rebecca had dinner in the oven. She had purchased a cookbook and was experimenting with a pot roast. For a woman who always had hired people to prepare meals, it was an adventure.

When George came from his shower he was surprised to see they were alone. Rebecca was charming all evening. They played music on the phonograph, drank wine, and danced to romantic music. She ended the evening in a graceful negligee. They made love through the night as they hadn't made love in years. He thought part of it was making up for "her indiscretions", as he called them. That may have been part of it. But she had another plan on her mind. The following morning they lay in bed, listening to the birds singing.

"George, I love it here."

"I'm glad you love Mobile. I was worried you wouldn't like it."

"No, I didn't mean Mobile." He looked at her quizzically. "I mean this house. Buy this house for us."

He thought of all the reasons this house would not work--it was too small, too far from work, old, in need of repairs--but he simply said, "Yes." She may have duped him, but there was another reason to stay--Thomas had fallen head-over-heals in love with the girl next door.

Penny McConnell had just turned eighteen. She was a tall blond, with long legs and a trim figure. The day they moved into the house on Florence Place she arrived at the front door carrying a pie. When Thomas opened the door, he saw nothing but the girl's big eyes and freckles.

"Welcome to the neighborhood." She handed him the pie. "My name is Penny." He stood there with the pie, unable to speak. "What is your name?"

"Thom-ass"

He was either shy or she had caught him off-guard. "Thom-ass what?"

He continued to stare. "Thomas Cash."

"Glad to meet you. Welcome to the neighborhood." When he didn't say anything, she thought to herself--'he's cute!'--but said, "I'll be seeing ya. Hope we can talk sometime." She batted her eyelashes, smiled at him, and turned to leave. When she got a few steps away she turned to take one more glimpse and saw he was still standing at the open door, both hands holding the pie, with a far off look in his eyes and a large grin. She turned and began to run, grinning to herself.

Only half the shipments were destined for the Nazis, but they didn't know that.

"Im Bereich," announced the Kriegsmarine.

Now that the ship was within range and the torpedoes in position, the Captain could take his U-Boat up for a look, "Sehrohrtiefe!"

"Jawohl, Herr Hauptmann!" He brought the submarine

to periscope depth.

The Captain waited for the periscope to slide into position, thinking through a checklist of details to observe. As he looked, he thought, 'Well, no war flag. Just a small steamer. Ah, a merchant vessel'. He called out "Nicht Kriegsflagge. Dampfer. Kaufmann."

He thought of the list in his shirt pocket. He pulled out his cigarettes, then the paper. He looked back into the periscope, then again at the numbers on the list—they matched! He relaxed and smiled. "Schauen Sie in das Sehrohr." He handed over the periscope to his protégé. After his assistant had taken a look, the captain handed him the list, and ordered, "Oberfläche!"

The U-boat began to surface. "Fernglas!" He was handed his field glasses.

As the submarine broke the surface, the Captain called, "Maschinenpistole!" and a sailor parted in front of him with his MP40 submachine gun.

The Captain stood with his assistant smoking cigarettes in the open air. There was a breeze at the southern opening to the Mediterranean Sea. He was teaching his protégé all the tricks. He pointed out it was safer to pass the ships on the list. No harm would come to a Captain personally for passing a ship, but a severe reprimand would happen for holding one up. Wondering if the order came from Military Intelligence his assistant asked "Militärnachrichtendienst?"

The Captain let out a roar of laughter. He knew there was no military reason not to blow the little merchant steamers out of the water. It was just political, or more likely some underhanded financial deal that procured safe passage. He replied with a derogatory term for the Nazi leadership: "Goldfasan!"

The men who heard it laughed in reply and smiling, the captain threw his cigarette into the ocean and descended the stairs. Soon the hatch was sealed.

"Tauchen!"

"Jawohl, Herr Hauptmann!" The ship began to submerge.

"Schleichfahrt!" She silently followed the small steamer through the mouth of the Mediterranean.

Jack managed operations at various locations near Mobile--Chickasaw, Spanish Fort, Weeks Bay, Goat Island, East Fowl River, and Mon Louis. He made his home in Spanish Fort, traveling between sites by boat and car. Jean-Michel lived in a mansion he built for himself in Mon Louis. While George had been training he had lived at Jack's. George and Thomas stayed in barracks they built for the crews north of Mon Louis.

The three jointly maintained a suite at a luxury hotel in Mobile near the train station. It was convenient for conducting business, when preparing to travel, and for entertaining. Late nights at the theatre, orchestra, and dinner had often ended there with sexual liaisons for Jack or Jean-Michel.

Major work on ships took place outside the United States, generally in Brazil. Minor work and retrofitting was done in Mobile, as was training and scheduling. Jack mostly bought freighters of roughly 5,000 tons, as they were plentiful, easy to finance, and versatile. They were small enough to avoid notice when sailing alone and easy to identify. A good part of the success of their operations was making sure their ships were easy to spot. Expertise and skilled labor was available at naval stations, shipyards, and docks nearby. He also bought a few schooners, as much for their grace and beauty as for their maneuverability.

Jean-Michel provided information on ships to the Nazis, for example, suggesting the cargo had been personally ordered by Rudolf Hess and telling them they needed to be protected. They would let the ships pass unharmed. He played the same game with both Allied and Axis powers. Each side knew part of the cost of getting their materials was to look the other way at just the right times.

As the War progressed, communications became more difficult and, as a result, there were more boarding of ships and searches.

"Admiral, I must protest," said Jean-Michel loudly over the telephone. George and Jean-Michel had private offices, but often left their doors open to aid in air circulation against the Mobile heat and humidity. Thomas's desk was in the main

room and he could see into his father's office. Overhearing just one side of the conversation, Thomas would guess which side of the war Jean-Michel was speaking with. He pulled a five dollar bill from his pocket and waved it in the air to get his father's attention. *"I'm thinking American Navy!"*

"This can't happen again."

George grinned at his son and mouthed, "I'll take that bet!" Reaching into his vest, he pulled out his money clip, slipped out a crisp, fresh five dollar bill, and slapped it down on the edge of his desk.

"No. Absolutely not."

A few minutes later they heard, *"If this ever happens again, I will be forced to go directly to the Führer!"* Thomas's face went from a smile to a frown, as he looked over to his father. George returned his five dollar bill to his vest, "Keep it! I knew he was making the call."

Jean-Michel came out of his office fuming. "Bastards!"

George came out also, "Close call this time?"

"Yes. A couple of minor injuries. Could have been a hell-of-a-lot worse!"

"Anything else we can do to keep our guys safe?"

Jean-Michel sighed, "No. We have thought of just about everything."

"How did the Captain handle it?"

"Exceptionally well. He didn't panic. Played it by the script, down to the last line. Shuffled the right papers in front of the Germans."

"Good."

"Yes. I'm gonna give him a bonus."

"Great idea."

"But it is just a matter of time. Somebody is going do some shooting."

"Jean-Michel, I've got something that has been bothering me."

"Yes, Thomas?"

"How the heck can you get telephone calls into Germany just like you are telephoning a neighbor?"

"What do you mean?"

"For gosh sake, we are at war with these people. How can you get your calls through?"

"Thomas, you have a lot to learn," Jean-Michel accentuated with his faint French accent.

George smiled and said over his shoulder as he returned

to his office. "It's great to have friends at ITT! Jean-Michel's telephone service is better than the White House."

"Yes, and I pay more for it!"

There were a flood of requests early in the war, but as the tide turned the requests changed and became more sporadic. Unauthorized halting of ships continued and calls became more frequent.

Noticing antacids, George asked Jean-Michel, "What are those you are taking? Having trouble?"

"They are for my stomach. I was diagnosed with a peptic ulcer. My stomach is all in a knot these days. Just expecting one of our ships to get sunk."

"Sleeping Ok?

"Sleep?"

"That is what I expected you'd say."

His stomach may have also been in knots from the arguments with George, which had been increasing.

"Legitimate war industries?"

"You know what I mean, Jean-Michel!"

"Yes, George. You mean more orthodox war materials and equipment than we have traditionally supplied."

"There ya go!"

"Yes, we could go there, but I think I have something much better."

"Let me hear it!"

"Refugees."

"Come on, everyone is trying to do that."

"Yes, but we have an additional asset that is difficult for others to produce." He pulled out a box of antacids and popped two in his mouth.

"You still havin' trouble?"

"Yeah. Doctor has me drinking cream and eating soft boiled eggs. Then I am taking this calcium crap all day. Doesn't help much. Anyway, I figure we can take people out at southern France, northern Spain and bring them to an Island somewhere, maybe Cuba. Then run a shuttle into Mobile, Miami, or New Orleans."

George smiled and teased Jean-Michel, "You softie. Gonna do some good deeds, helping people escape Europe?"

"Good deeds, bullshit! Cash up front and lots of it!" George's smile disappeared.

"My back is killing me," exclaimed Jean-Michel.

"What did you do?" asked George.

"Nothing."

The phone rang and Jean-Michel answered. He turned white. "When?...Where?...George, get on the line."

"*...it was definitely a Nazi sub. Far as we can tell, they followed them out of the mouth of the Mediterranean. Right up the coast...*"

Jean-Michel rubbed his legs, while fumbling for more pills. "Thanks, Jim. I'll be in touch."

George, shaken, walked into Jean-Michel's office with Thomas on his heels. "Could A Coruña muster a rescue?"

"There is nothing to rescue. Split the freighter in half with the first torpedo. Second one hit an instant later and blew up the crew's quarters. Both halves went to the bottom within minutes."

"Shit."

"What were they carrying?"

"Empty. They had just delivered a full load of Wolf Cream to the Krauts. We had specifically sent them up the coast for protection BY Nazi subs. And one of theirs blows it away."

"What will you do?"

He was reeling with all the things he had to do, most of it unpleasant. But the first would not be. "I am going to start with a call to the Germans. There will be one less Nazi U-boat Captain in a few hours."

Jean-Michel experienced fatigue, nausea, and vomiting for the next week. He thought it was tied to the stress of informing families of their loss and working with insurance companies. Then he didn't show up for work, nor did he call in.

George rummaged through Jean-Michel's desk to find his spare house key. He wasn't particularly alarmed--Jean-Michel seemed to be in good health, other than the stomach problems. He was still traveling a great deal and loved what he did. Still he never took a sick day off and always let George know when he would be gone.

He turned the key in the door and entered. A cat immediately ran into the room and rubbed against George's leg. "Jean-Michel? Jean-Michel?" There was no answer. He checked a few closed doors, but most rooms were empty. He came to a room where light spilled into the hallway under the door and knocked, "Jean-Michel?" He swung the door open and cautiously walked in. He stared down thinking, 'At least he died quietly'.

After calling the police, he sat waiting in the living room. "How did you know Mr. Péppin?"

"He was my business partner."

"How long have you known him?"

"Maybe ten years. I worked with his father before that."

"Does his father live nearby?"

"No. He is dead. Gone for years."

"Had Péppin been in ill health?"

"Nothing serious. Stomach was acting up."

"Did he ever mention heart problems?"

"No."

"What did his father die of?"

"Cancer."

"Does he have any family?"

"Not that I know of." He didn't have an idea what had happened to his mother or whether he had siblings.

"Well, at least he died peacefully--in his sleep. That's the way I wanna go. Where can we reach you?"

When the coroner opened him up, Jean-Michel's stomach looked like a war had gone on, with three-quarter inch pock marks. It contained stomach acid, blood, cream, and a handful of partially dissolved antacids. The blood tests were conclusive. He had never seen elevated calcium levels in the blood that high. The coroner thought, 'Bloodstream filled with liquid chalk' as he typed in, Severe Hypercalcaemia. What a way to go!

George made funeral arrangements for Jean-Michel and gave away his cat. He didn't find a will and there was no address book in the house. Every phone number in Jean-Michel's desk was business related. There was no memorial service and not even George attended the burial. There is still no headstone where he is interred. George moved his son into Jean-Michel's office to answer the phone. Orders kept being called in and Thomas had learned enough to keep boats floating and materials flowing.

With Jean-Michel gone, George's stomach began giving him problems, but he thought it was more rooted in what had happened to Jean-Michel than a medical issue. He told himself he would begin taking vacations, leave work on time, ease back a bit, get reconnected with Rebecca, and spend more time with his sons. "Screw it! We're going home!"

He had hardly noticed some changes that were taking place right under his nose.
"Where is Thomas going?"
"Bible study. Next door at Penny's."
"Bible study?"
"Yes, he seems to be enjoying it."
"Really?"
"Yes. And spending time with Penny."
"Penny?"
"Yes. Haven't you noticed anything?"
"Like what?"
"Well, like he never eats dessert with us anymore?"
"I thought..."
"You thought what? No dessert? This is Thomas..."
He had to agree--he had never seen Thomas pass up dessert. George was amazed at what he hadn't observed.
"He zips out of here after supper while you go read your books."
"I hadn't noticed."
"Hadn't noticed? How could you not?"
"Well, I've been busy. How long has this been going on?"
"Six months."
"SIX MONTHS!"
"At least."
"Well--"
"And I think they are getting serious."
"Penny?"
"Yeah. You know the girl next door. Body like Myrna Loy. Legs like Betty Grable. Voice like Jeanette MacDonald. More wholesome than Shirley Temple. You can't miss her! She lives

next door! Your son can't keep his eyes off her!"

With Alexander and Abraham put to bed for the night and Thomas next door visiting, Rebecca decided she needed to give George an eye test. She bathed, put on his favorite perfume, applied lipstick and make-up, and donned her bathrobe. George was sitting in the study in his favorite overstuffed chair, his feet up on an ottoman, reading a book, and sipping on single malt scotch. She quietly slipped into the room and stood at his feet. She let the robe fall to the floor. He didn't move.

"George?"

"Un-huh."

"You aren't very observant these days, are you?"

"What?" He finally looked up and his eyes got big.

A few months later, Thomas was riding to the office with his father. "I have decided to ask Penny to marry me."

George's heart skipped a beat. "That's wonderful! Congratulations. She is a beautiful young lady. Have you spoken to her father?"

"Tonight."

"No, I don't think so, Son."

It had taken all his nerve to get this far, and now to have Penny's father say no was just too unexpected. His mouth began to form words, but the air had left him. Thomas visibly deflated as if he were a balloon.

"We like you a lot, Thomas. You're a great kid. But both of you are too young."

"I'm twenty, Sir, and I have a great job."

"I'm sure you do. But Penny is nineteen. Come talk to me in a few years. In the meantime, you are welcome in our home. It is just too soon." It wasn't Thomas's age that bothered her father; he wasn't sure about his religious faith.

Thomas was back at their home nearly every night, as he

had been for months. Penny and Thomas alternated in whose house they celebrated each holiday and, in short order, the families began to merge holiday celebrations and informal occasions. At a barbeque the following weekend Peter spoke to his neighbor, "George, I gotta tell you, it hurt to tell your son he couldn't marry Penny."

"Yeah, but he'll get over it."

"Do you agree with my decision?"

"Sure. Waiting won't kill them. He just finished his accounting degree work at State. My business is going fine. It's not going to kill them to wait." Inside, he wanted his son to be happy and marrying now was fine with him. But he also didn't want to contradict his new friend and neighbor.

"I was hoping you would agree. Penny is our first daughter and, well, we think it is best to wait." It sounded to George that Peter wasn't convinced he had made the right decision.

A week later, after dinner, while Penny and Thomas flirted and her parents made small talk, her father asked, "Penny, would you like to invite Thomas to join us going to Church this Sunday?"

"Oh, Daddy, he's right here, why don't you invite him yourself?" He was sitting on the couch next to Penny, while her father was in his easy chair reading and her mother in a hardbacked chair, knitting.

"Penny, he's your friend."

Thomas said, "I'd like that."

They spent evenings on the front porch talking about news from the war in Europe. Penny wore long shorts that accentuated her well-toned legs, and in the cool of the evening, she scrunched her legs up and stretched her sweat shirt over them, while they swung on a bench that hung from the porch rafters.

Thomas didn't tell Penny much about his work. By day, he might be figuring how to supply diamonds to the Nazis for their war machine industrial saws; by night, he was courting the all-American girl next door. It was easy for him to put his duplicity out of his mind when he heard it was all justified to get spies into war-torn Europe and Africa. All she knew is that it was supplying materials for the war.

She worked, as all her siblings did, in her father's grocery store on Old Shell Road. They were a hard-working family, committed to the store and their church.

Prosperity began to ripple through Mobile as Gulf Shipbuilding Corporation hired 15,000 workers and ramped up to three shifts, supplying vessels initially to the Royal Navy, and later to the United States Maritime Commission and United States Navy. Employees lived in company-provided housing, but money soon leaked throughout Mobile. On the heels of the depression, it was flooding into the area like a warm, welcome gulf stream.

"Busy today!" noted Penny as she pushed her hair back from her face.

"You bet ya! Lots of families coming in," replied her father with a big grin.

"What's happening?"

"Gulf's filling out their graveyard shift."

"So soon?"

"Happens every time. When they ramp up, people need more cooking utensils and cleaning items than they brought with them. And two weeks later, when they get handed that first pay envelope and are feeling flush they add hamburger or an occasional steak to their bread, milk, and potatoes."

"What else changes?"

"Your Mom and me take more trips to the bank! And this time, it's for making DEPOSITS!" Penny laughed at her father![39]

Every evening ended with the same ritual.

"Penny, it's time for bed."

"Oh, Mother!"

"Yeah, Honey, give Tommy his nighty-night kiss, boot him out, and hit the hay," her father said in a high falsetto.

"Daddy, please!"

Peter laughed.

All of their social activities in the evenings revolved around church events and Sundays were given over to worship and sailing. Penny had picked up her love of sailing from her father. "Would you like me to teach you to sail?"

---

[39] Between 1940 and 1943, 89,000 people moved to Mobile, Alabama as wartime employment exploded at Alabama Drydock and Shipbuilding Company, Gulf Shipbuilding Corporation, and Brookley Army Air Field.

"Yes!"

"Okay, after church on Sunday we always have a picnic lunch and Daddy takes out the boats."

"What do I need to bring?"

"Daddy says there are only two things you need for sailing--a strong back and a weak mind!" Thomas smiled, but didn't get the joke. "He says a boat owner needs two thing--lots of cash, and a hole in the water to throw it into!" Thomas laughed to be polite, but did not understand this joke either. "Have you got tennis shoes?"

"Sure."

"Wear those and bring a swim suit and towel. We leave straight from Church. We eat, sail, nap, and then get back to church for evening worship at six."

"Sounds fun."

Sailing, for Thomas, was going to be just another way of staying around Penny; until he tried it out. The boat glided across the water, propelling spray and wind into his face and within minutes he was smitten.

"That is amazing! How can you make it go in a opposite direction from the wind?"

"You'll have to ask Daddy."

"How far over can we lean the boat?"

Penny laughed. "I am not sure, but pretty far!"

"Let's try it!"

In the evenings Thomas asked Peter how it all worked and he was only too pleased to share his love of sailing with the young man. The following Sunday Thomas would try out whatever he learned from Peter.

The war was ever-present--creeping into conversations at unexpected times. Penny heard stories at the store about German spies in the Gulf of Mexico. She heard about neighborhood boys enlisting. There were already rumors of a draft. There were many more people being employed every day at the shipyards.

Thomas noticed changes being made--new schedules, different bank transactions, and negotiations with suppliers being held in multiple languages. In the evenings, Thomas and Penny shared what they each heard during the day. They would then allow the discussion to drift to more joyful subjects. Despite wanting to be oblivious to the war going on in Europe, they were continually drawn in.

The Cash family began attending church with Penny's every Sunday. They had never attended church in the past and were pleasantly surprised by the warm, encouraging people they met. When invited by the McConnell's, or when Thomas insisted, they socialized more. George came back into Peter's study, "The girls want us to take them to the Peony Pageant this weekend."

Peter snarled, "Peony Pageant?"

"Yes."

"Oh, noooooo!"

"What?"

"Do you know what peonies are?"

"Some kinda flower?"

"Yeah, they are those bushes with the ridiculously large flowers. Mobile Peony Society tries to grow them here. They are particularly poorly suited for Mobile's climate and soil, so they don't get as big as they do in other places. If they can keep them alive at all. This society--I don't know why they call it a society--puts on a weeklong event to look at the sickly plants and the old matrons give each other advise for keeping them going."

"That's it?"

"No, they have tea and cookies. You can buy crappy snack food. Listen to bad, local bands. It's held at a city park where the things are planted. No booze or beer. About two acres, I'd say. Everybody goes to it, so there is never any place to park. I consider it a 'decker'."

"A what?"

"A decker. A place a husband should go once a decade, to remind himself why he should never go there!"

George was looking over company records one afternoon, "It is interesting to look at what we have shipped."

"What do you mean, Pop?" Thomas asked.

"I have been looking over our records since 1938.

Interesting patterns."

"Let me see." He looked at the ledgers, dates, and quantities.

"Look here. In early forty, look at the spike in iron ore we were shipping."

"Yes."

"Look at it fall off here in spring."

"Yes. Like it dropped off the table."

"As soon as the Nazis had secured Denmark and Norway--"

"That meant they had their pipeline of iron ore out of Sweden."

"Where were we taking the ore?"

"France. Unloaded both on the Atlantic and Mediterranean."

"They were using us to stockpile iron ore in the event Sweden didn't pan out."

"But look at Wolf cream! Shipments from South America."

"Yes, they needed lots of tungsten. Everyone did."

"We were supplying that throughout the Mediterranean Sea for them. Italy, Africa, Spain, France."

"They couldn't get enough."

"Look at the numbers of diamonds we shipped!"

"Amazing isn't it."

"We pulled some good ones on the Brits!"

"Look at the peaks in machine parts and electronics."

"Yeah, ITT couldn't make that stuff quick enough. They were flooding it into Brazil and Argentina and we were transporting it all to Europe."

"Did I ever tell you the Japs asked us to supply tankers for petroleum in the South Pacific before Pearl Harbor?"

"No, why?"

"They couldn't build them fast enough."

"Huh."

"We only had a few anyway."

"Why?"

"The Nazis were filling up their boats directly from the Standard Oil tankers. Our guys saw it all the time. Standard had a good part of their refining business in South America. They had large contracts to sell to the Germans from before the war."

"Jean-Michel told me that."

"We are still not prepared to handle much petroleum. Too flammable! One stray bullet or off target warning shot and we could lose cargo and crew in an instant."

"What do the Germans ask for most these days?"

"Petroleum. We still say 'no' almost all the time. The only exception is aviation fuel, which we will sometimes handle. The next is food, then rubber. Diamonds are way down."

"Who is our next largest customer?"

"Americans and Brits are about the same. They use us for stuff they don't want to get caught red-handed with!"

"How about the Russians?"

"We never did much business with them. They would steal you blind, if they could. Never played by the rules well."

"The rules?"

"Yes. The main rule was that in order to get what you wanted you had to turn a blind eye to whatever else we were transporting and to whom? Russians would board us while we were unloading their stuff to rifle through our other shipments."

"What did you do?"

"We would charge them for anything they took at a premium price, plus we would say 'no' when they were most desperate to get something through. They would remember the lesson for a while, but forget again. We started requiring payment up front--that hurt them--then full shipload only."

"Who were the best to deal with?"

"Brits and Americans. Germans were pretty good. But not as good as Brits and Americans."

"Yeah?"

"They wouldn't bat an eye at our deals with the Nazis."

"Really?"

"They were both honorable in their dealings with us."

"What are we making the most money with now?"

"Smuggling refugees."

"Where?"

"The Confederate States of America!"

She slipped her purse onto her arm and leaned over to say in a conspirator's whisper, "Did you hear about Johnny Tinelli?"

"No," said Penny as she handed Mrs. Owens her bag of groceries at the end of the checkout aisle.

"Drafted! Off to the army in a few days." She stood while proudly beaming and placed the bag in the crook of her arm.

"Really? So soon! Why, Mrs. Tinelli didn't say a word when she was in here."

"Well, you know Jean. She would be stoic about these things." The possessor and purveyor of all the community's gossip had done her work. She straighten her flowered dress and straw hat and flew to the door like a bee having spread his pollen.

After Mrs. Owens left, Peter threw his arms around Penny. "Honey, do you remember what I told you?"

"About what?"

"Rumors. Don't spread them. Until you hear it from the horse's mouth, we shouldn't talk."

Penny gave her father a sly smile. "But, Daddy, did you just call Mrs. Tinelli a horse?" Peter smiled back. He knew Penny had learned the lesson. Rumors could be most hurtful and a merchant who participated in them was at risk of ruining his reputation. What was heard was not to be passed along or confirmed. What was heard could be acknowledged ('No, I hadn't heard that'), but that is where it ended.[40]

---

[40] Between the World Wars, a Joint Army-Navy Selective Service Committee worked behind the scenes to keep the United States ready to draft men for military service. By 1926, they had the majority of the process designed of what would become The Selective Training and Service Act of 1940 (Burke-Wadsworth Act, 54 Stat. 885). It was passed by Congress and signed into law two days later on September 19, 1940. The following month, the draft began. The necessary training programs, facilities, and equipment to make the draft effective were not yet in place or fully funded. The following summer, Congress doubled the commitment of draftees from one to two years. Upon entering World War II, all men between 18 and 65 were required to register. The draft began in the

When the full force of the draft began to be felt by late spring the following year, men began disappearing in large numbers. The newspapers reported the first loss of a neighbor's son to the war (a training accident) and a blanket of sadness fell over Mobile. Families were rushing into Mobile to fill the void as men left for a war that had not yet been declared. When men were in short supply women easily plug into vacancies in war factories.

War correspondents introduced facts about the war that expanded peoples understanding of the battles shortly after they occurred, even when exact locations were not given. Even small details in far away Europe permeated conversations across Mobile. At their weekly Bible study, Penny and her girlfriend's discussion strayed toward stories of the war.

"Did you hear the Nazis are splitting up France three ways?"

"What do you mean?"

"There is going to be a German section, an Italian section, and an independent 'free-zone.'"

"Why?"

"Girls, let's get back to our study of Esther!"

The following morning Penny was reading the newspaper while she ate breakfast. "Daddy, what is a 'Rump State'?"

He replied absent-mindedly, "Oh, we sell that at the store. It is the top round steak, you know the...

"Daddy, "Rump State, not steak. S. T. A. T. E.!"

"Oh, yes. Let me think. Well, it is the remnant of a government." He thought of a Biblical example before he continued. "Do you remember when Nebuchadnezzar conquered Judah and Jerusalem, and took the Jews into exile in Babylon?"

"Yes."

"He left a remnant of Jews to tend the fields and orchards and a bare bones staff to administer the area. That would have been a 'rump state'; the left overs of a previous government."

United States in October 1940; immediately, announcements in newspapers and bulletins at the post office told men between 18 and 45 to fill out their selective service registrations. By the end of 1940, over 40,000 men had been called up to active service.

"The newspaper is calling the French 'Free-State' a rump state."

"I suspect that is true. Leave some of the French government in place to collect taxes, keep the people in line, and help the Nazis--while not sending in troops to actually occupy the land."

"Why wouldn't they want to occupy the land?"

"No need. They can control the area with fewer soldiers. That frees the Nazis up to use the soldiers elsewhere."

"Like here?" Her father did not know how to answer her. He reached over to squeeze her hand.

There was a change at church. People who only attended at Easter and Christmas began filling the pews. The stress and strain of the war on the community caused many to seek relief or reassurance--some in the bottle and some at the altar.

Advance men for a well-respected regional evangelist called on the pastors of Mobile to come together to support a faith campaign.

"Jimmy will come and help you deliver the people of Mobile into the Lord's Hands, but you must help."

"What must we do?"

"You need to provide lumber and laborers to build a glorious Tabernacle!"

"We've got plenty of canvas from when he came through last time."

"No canvas tents! No more circus tents! You build a monument to the Lord's glory, or Jimmy will not join with you!"

"How big?"

"Seating for ten thousand!"

Advance men kept returning until the local pastors caught the vision.

"Jimmy wants a wooden structure. A wooden structure won't blow away in the wind. Events are less likely to get cancelled. It speaks of the Lord's provision to the audience.

They're more generous when they see the expense the local churches have gone to in bringing Preacher Jimmy to town." The advance man didn't mention it also protected his free-will offerings, and his take was greater. And all that lumber--donated or bought at cost--could be resold for a healthy profit.

The advance men talked of promotion and partnership. Soon, Jimmy McManus Victory's staff of thirty paid employees (mostly family members) was in town. The fairgrounds had been rented at a bargain price. There was ample transportation with church buses volunteered to pick up devotees and plentiful parking.

The Evangelist's last name was actually, 'Victor', which he legally changed, adding the 'Y' by saying, "That is 'Y' I was born; to show God's victory!"

People appreciated his homespun stories of families and neighbors ("People just like you--") who were led to faith ("running down the hopeless path, UNTIL--"). He was sincere in every word he spoke, if not entirely honest in every detail.

He held up an Oreo cookie, saying, "Do you know what this is?" Most people didn't know this 'shtick', so the audience grew quiet. "This is a cookie, baked at the National Biscuit Company of East Hanover, New Jersey." He cleared his throat and stepped up to the microphone to be heard on radios throughout the south. "Some of you have an outside of black, like this cookie. Full of sin you are! You know yourself who you are. I was like you once."

He opened the cookie up. "But look here on the inside. God wants to make you white as snow, like the crème on the inside of this cookie!" He scrapped the filling off with his teeth and threw down the black cookies onto the platform and crushed them under his feet, while he grabbed his Bible from the lectern. "He made it easy, all I had to do was ask--and He crushed my sin under His feet!"

He returned to the microphone, "In Isaiah 1:18, God told us, 'Come now, and let us reason together, saith the LORD: though your sins be as scarlet, they shall be as white as snow; though they be red like crimson, they shall be as wool.'"

He wiped his mouth with a handkerchief, nestled back to the microphone, and spoke softly, "Men are going away to Europe--your neighbors--or you. Men will die in this war who have not yet accepted the Lord into their hearts. How sad it is,

175

when it is so easy. They are making their own decision; will they be in heaven or will they choose hell? Where will you be?"

Victory called the packed house to come forward in faith. The audience was filled with 'church goers' and their neighbors, coming night after night, for weeks on end. In the third week, Thomas could not stand it any longer. He found himself wandering down the aisle, as if in a daze. He was hardly conscious of his movement. All he knew that night is that he didn't want to be lost to hell and wanted the Lord's sweet crème in his life. Penny looked on with a broad smile and her father reached over to touch her hand. George and Rebecca looked at each other and tears streamed down Rebecca's cheeks.

Thomas waited until Penny's 22nd birthday on May 4, 1942, to talk to her father again about marriage. He didn't need to worry this time, but did anyway. He stewed for days ahead about the right time and place for talking with Peter. He mentioned none of this to Penny, or anyone else, for fear it would jinx things.

The evening was warm, a prelude to the summer that was fast approaching. The grass was lush and green and flowers were in full bloom. The tree branches linked arms to complete the canopy along both sides of the street. The oak tree in their front lawn reached one hundred feet and Peter had recently hung a bench swing from a large branch.

Dinner that evening was Penny's favorite--roast beef, mashed potatoes with sweet butter, buttermilk biscuits, and okra. There was birthday cake in the dining room and presents in the living room. The Cash family had been invited. Thomas had a special gift for Penny, but waited until he had spoken with her father before he gave it to her.

They enjoyed coffee and small talk, when Thomas leaned over to Peter, "Sir, may I speak with you?"

"Of course." He sat there attentively. He suspected what Thomas wanted to talk to him about and wasn't about to make it easy.

"In private, Sir."

"Oh, yes. Let's take our coffee out to the deck." Peter refilled his coffee cup while Thomas stood fidgeting by the front door. "Please excuse us." He made a big show of going out to speak with Thomas in private without having said much.

"Mr. McConnell, we spoke of this once before."

Peter gave him a quizzical look. "Please. Call me Peter."

"Yes, Sir. You know I have a good job."

"Yes, are you looking for work? I could use another hand around the store."

"No, Sir. I am doing quite well."

"Well, what is it then?"

"Well, Sir..."

"Peter. Please."

"Peter, I would like to ask for your daughter's hand in marriage."

"Well, I wondered if you ever were going to ask!"

"What?"

"Yes, I was mentioning to Penny's mother the other day that if you didn't get around to asking we were going to have to cut off access to our dinner table soon. Can't waste food on a lost cause." Now it was time for Thomas's quizzical look. "Only kidding, Tom. We would be honored to have you join our family. We are pleased and happy to add our blessing. It's just that--" He paused for Thomas to take the bait.

"Sir?"

He sighed. "I am not quite sure Penny will say yes." He couldn't contain his smile.

Thomas grinned. "I guess I'll just have to ask her myself!"

Peter grabbed Thomas's coffee cup and returned to the house, "I'll send her out. Why don't you go down to the swing? Good luck!"

They set their wedding for September 5, 1942. Thomas would have preferred it to be earlier, but the McConnell and Clark families (Penny's mother's family), large and sprinkled throughout the South, could not be summoned together on short notice. Labor Day weekend gave everyone extra travel time, though Peter's business would suffer by being closed for the long holiday weekend.

The sanctuary of Springhill Christian Church in Mobile was filled with Penny's favorite flower, abbey road masterwort. Their vibrant pinks and purples were a perfect offset to the dazzling white bouquet Penny carried of alba plena camellia. Her sisters served as bridesmaids and Thomas's brothers were his groomsmen. There were two strikingly beautiful women in the wedding--Penny and Rebecca.

The wedding was simple, with a violinist and harpist providing the music. Reverend Robert Fetter, who had baptized the bride as a girl, beamed at being able to officiate. A reception followed in the packed Fellowship Hall. The happy couple left on the late afternoon train through Chicago to Niagara Falls. They were oblivious that the train was filled with men reporting for military service across the United States.

As soon as Thomas and Penny Cash arrived in Chicago in the early morning, they checked into their hotel across the street. The following morning, Labor Day, they walked arm-in-arm through Chicago Union Station's Great Hall, enjoying the 110 foot atrium and barrel-vaulted skylight. They ate breakfast in an adjoining restaurant.

"I have been thinking about something for a long time?"

"House? Children? I can't wait."

"How much do you like Mobile?"

"I love Mobile." A frown developed on her face.

"Could you live elsewhere for a while?"

She looked startled, but then composed herself. "I could live anywhere, as long as it is with you."

"Could you live here in Chicago?"

She frowned and furled her eyebrows. "I have never thought of living in a big city. But I guess I could."

"I have been thinking of bringing us here. Actually, not right here--little ways west, Wheaton."

"Wheaton?" She only knew of one thing about Wheaton,

Illinois and she could feel her excitement welling up, but didn't want to appear too thrilled in case he was leading down another path.

"Yes, there is a Graduate School there--"

She screamed, "Yes!" and kissed him after he rushed to get out the words, "Seminary. Biblical and Theological Studies." She had an unspoken dream of being the wife of a pastor.

On their way back from their honeymoon, they took a side trip to Wheaton College. They met with a member of the admissions staff who talked to them at length. He saw in Thomas a well-rounded young man, but new in his faith. He learned about Thomas's accounting degree and ended their time together promising to see what he could do. After considerable prayer about the matter, he decided to offer Thomas one of the few remaining openings for the spring semester. In January 1943, Thomas began a two-year program leading to a Master of Arts Degree in Theology.

Abraham had lived in the shadow of his older brother. Once Thomas married and moved away, it was his turn to shine. At twelve, he tended to his studies and had broad interests. His teachers had passed him through second grade, because he seemed bored. They also tried to talk his parents into letting him skip fourth grade, but George said, "No. He needs to be close to kids his own age." When he once again began exceeding his fellow students, teachers gave him extra work to keep him entertained and he absorbed it like a sponge.

He had been quite disturbed when the Japanese attacked Pearl Harbor.

"Dad, do you think they will bomb Alabama next?"

"No, Son, I don't think so."

"How about your boats?"

George gave him a squeeze. "No. Go get your world globe?"

He was back in a few minutes with a globe that spun on an axis of brass, attached to a solid wood base. "Here it is!"

George couldn't resist giving the globe a hardy spin, and it wobbled a bit while it rotated and as it slowed down it squeaked. George laughed, "Just like our own world, a little wobbly and squeaky these days." Abraham scooted back on the couch next to his father, pushed his glasses up on his nose, and put his hands on George's right arm attentively. "Do you know where the United States is?"

Abraham spun the globe and poked at Kansas. "Sure. We're right here."

"Great! So where is Alabama?"

He found the Gulf of Mexico, then came up to Louisiana. He scooted his finger over Mississippi and came to rest on a little notch of water that came in from the gulf. "We live right here, in this notch of water on the southwest corner of Alabama."

"Excellent! Now find me Japan."

He spun the globe and had a little more difficulty finding it, but he started reading the large print until he located Tokyo. George had him find Pearl Harbor. It took him a while, but he finally squeaked in a cheery voice, "Here!"

"Very good. So as you can see, the Japanese are still far away from us." Abraham pondered what his father had said.

"Where are the Germans?" He showed him Germany, as well as some of the surrounding nations Abraham had heard about in the news: Sweden, Denmark, Holland, England, Ireland, France, and Italy. "Where do your boats go?" George showed him the places his boats traveled in a generalized route down to South America, Africa, Spain, and back. "Will the German's attack us soon?"

"No. Not soon. Probably never." He didn't say anything about sightings of boats in the Atlantic, off the east coast, or in the Gulf of Mexico, but the German U-boats were certainly around.

"Where do the Jews live?"

The question took George by surprise. "Well, Jews live everywhere."

"Am I a Jew?"

George laughed. "No, you are an American and you are a Christian."

"Some boys at school called me a Jew."

"What did you say?"

"I just said, 'Oh, Okay.'"

"Did they threaten you--or tease you?"

"No. They said Jews are the cause of all the problems."

"Did they hurt you?"

"No, they said I had to be a Jew, because I have a Jew name, Abraham. Do I have a Jew name?"

George smiled. "Well, there is an Abraham in the Bible and he was the Father of the Jews. But you are named after Abraham Lincoln. He was not a Jew."

"Oh."

"And Jews are not the cause of all the problems. People always have to blame something else, when it is usually they themselves, or just circumstances nobody can control."

As a teen, Abraham's life revolved around three things--boy scouts, baseball, and school.

"Dad, I have decided what I want to do for my Eagle Scout project. I want to catalog all the public and private Civil War memorials and monuments in Mobile."

George's brow furrowed, "What?"

"Catalog Civil War memorials and monuments."

"Can you do that? I mean--they allow that for an Eagle Scout project? I thought you did things like clean parks and make benches for the elderly."

"Well, I could do those things. But I thought this would be of more value."

"How big a project will this be?"

"I'm not sure. The public stuff is probably pretty easy. But the private things may be more difficult to find."

"I imagine so. How did you even think of this?"

"Mr. O'Brien was polishing the sundial in his backyard. It is made of stone and brass. It has an inscription on it about the Civil War."

"How would you find out about the private things?"

"My history teacher thought maybe we could put a notice in the newspaper."

A week later an advertisement appeared in the *Mobile Press-Register* asking for private Civil War memorials and monuments for battles that took place in Mobile. Over the next three weeks there were more than 400 replies, but most were about soldiers from Mobile, rather than for battles that took place there. Of the remaining roughly one hundred, most were like Mr. O'Brien's sundial, marking places where known battles had occurred or troop encampment sites. A few marked the places where their family's loved ones had died. About two dozen marked places on people's property where Confederate soldiers had fallen. Some had the names of soldiers, their home towns, and the dispositions of the bodies. In the south, dead Confederate soldiers were commonly returned to their families or buried in local cemeteries near where battles occurred. Sometimes soldiers were temporarily buried to be reinterred later. There were few known locations outside of public cemeteries where the bodies of soldiers remained.

A hotel owner called to say he had a file of documents from the previous owner, related to two brothers, which said they were buried in his backyard. Abraham was intrigued by the story and catalogued this just like all the other private monuments. For his project he provided a detailed list of memorials. But he kept coming back to the story of the two brothers, which he couldn't get out of his head.

"Dad, could you help me?"

"Sure."

"I have been looking through the Thompson brothers stuff again. One place it says the two brothers were buried together--'double down' they called it, but in another place it says the younger brother, Randall, was buried at Confederate Rest at Magnolia. But I cannot find where the older brother, Richard, is buried. I was wondering if I could go see Mr. Vanderpool. Just to see what other information he might have."

"Who?"

"Mr. Vanderpool, the owner of the hotel."

Three nights later, George and Abraham met Mr. Clarence Vanderpool at his hotel on Government Street.

"I can't find this number." George pointed to the slip of paper. "It should be right here."

"There it is!"

"Where?"

"Right through those trees."

"This can't be it!"

"Why?"

"Because it is supposta be a hotel."

"It's gotta be it."

"Well, it is the next number on the block."

"Follow the path."

"Okay." George pulled onto a driveway and in his headlights he could see that it was more grass and weeds than concrete. He pushed through with branches and bushes scrapping both sides of the car, and pulled to a stop at the front porch. "Whoa!"

The brick house was two stories tall, with balconies, dormers, a cupola, and bay windows that hadn't seen paint since the First World War. Looking carefully at the house, George recognized the Doric, Greek revival style. In the moonlight, he could see there were three fireplace chimneys and nearly all the windows were stained-glass. The porch creaked as George and Abraham stepped onto it and George looked for a door bell. There was no porch light.

"There!" Abraham said, pointing at two red wires coming out of the brickwork. George stepped forward, grabbed the wires by the insulation, and pushed them together. Nothing. George looked at the door, saw the tarnished green brass doorknocker, and knocked.

A man in overalls with a wrinkled face opened the door.

"Welcome! You must be my cubby scout, Mr. Abraham Cash?"

"Huh, well, I am Abraham Cash. But I am an Eagle Scout, or rather will be soon."

"Of course. And you must be Master Cash's father?"

"Yes."

"Please excuse me, but I'll be ready to open soon." He led them into a small room, which looked more like a coat closet than an entry.

"Open?"

"Yes, the hotel will be opening directly."

"Oh."

"I expect by next summer, or maybe the summer after that. They all seem to run together."

"How long have you lived here?"

"Well, let me think, I bought the property in '31. Let me have your coats." He hung them up. "I have been working to get the inside ready ever since." He swung the door in from the coat room and their jaws dropped. It was as decrepit on the outside as it was opulent inside. The hand-carved oak staircase dominated the foyer, with 'heart of pine' flooring, solid-gold candelabras, and elegant stained-glass windows.

"It was built in 1843. Actually, before that if you consider the original log cabin." He walked into the next room and you could see a wall of rustic pine, lacquered and well-polished. "I know you are probably wondering about the upkeep on the outside. Early on I had been advised that my taxes would not go up until I fixed the outside of the house, so I have concentrated on the inside. Let me show you around. Let's start upstairs." There were brass electric switch plates, antique tables and lamps everywhere, gold leaf wallpaper, and elegant rugs. "Ten foot ceilings. The house was wired for electrical and telephone only when I bought it. Gas was put in after the turn of the century. The bedframes are all original, from 1843, as are the wood floors."

"This is beautiful."

"Thank you. I do hope the hotel will be a success when I open."

"I'm sure it will be."

"There are six bedrooms upstairs, each with its own bathroom. Two more bedrooms downstairs. Smaller. Of course, the bathrooms are not original."

They returned downstairs and Vanderpool escorted them to his study. There were large game animal trophies hanging on the walls--antelope, elk, moose, and a grizzly bear stood on the floor and reached to the 10-foot ceiling. Seeing Abraham was intrigued by the stuffed bear, Vanderpool said, "If Gertrude were any taller, I would need to tip her over."

"Gertrude was one big girl, Mr. Vanderpool," noticed George.

"I'm not Mr. Vanderpool. That was my father. I'm Clarence."

"And I'm George."

"So, what can I do for you fellas?"

Abraham said, "I'd like to look through the file you said you had."

"Sure. I only mailed to you a few copies from the file. There is plenty more." He turned his chair around to face a bookcase and grabbed a rosewood box on the lowest shelf. "Just bring this back when you are done. Take good care of it.

There is some valuable information in there."

"Where did you get the file?"

"The previous owner--a descendent of the original--made me promise to keep it with the house and to give it to the next buyer, with the provision that the next do the same. Had it written into the purchase contract. That way the file never separates from the house, except to be temporarily loaned out."

"Thank you so much. We will take good care of it."

"I know you will."

"Well, we shouldn't take up any more of your valuable time."

"Oh, but don't you want to see the graveyard?" Abraham's eyes grew large. "It will be dark back there." He reached into his desk and pulled out a flashlight.

The moon was blocked by large trees at the back of the house. Vanderpool led them out through the back porch and walked out into the yard to a metal bulb. It looked like a brass spittoon turned upside down and pressed down into a concrete square. "There it is! The civil war monument. Right dead center in the middle of the family cemetery. Look." He pointed at four identical tombstones. They were not that easy to see by flashlight. "Originally, I thought they marked directions."

"Directions?"

"Cardinal points--North, East, South, West. But they don't."

"What were they?"

"The four grandparents of the first master of the house. Each buried at the corner of the cemetery to make a twenty-five foot square. With the civil war monument in the center. Rest of the family members are buried randomly within the square, from around 1843 until 1929."

When George came down for breakfast the next morning, Rebecca was loaded for bear. "Why did you let him stay up so late on a school night?"

"Let him? I told him fifteen more minutes and went to bed."

"Well, he didn't! It is going to be impossible to get him up this morning!"

Abraham sprung in the kitchen, "Hi Mama! Hi, Pop!"

"Well! How late did you stay up?"

"I kinda lost track of time."

"I guess so. It was almost four when I saw your light."

When Abraham came home that afternoon, he was
earlier than usual.

"Didn't you have baseball practice?"

"Yes. I just came straight home afterward."

"Why?"

"Because I think I figured something out last night."

"Oh."

"Yeah. When will Dad be home?"

Abraham was impatient as he watched his father driving
up the road. "Dad, I gotta show you what I found!"

"Well, let me get out of the car!"

"I found something in the files."

"Great!"

They looked through the materials together, took a break
for dinner, and returned to the files. "I'll call Mr. Vanderpool
in the morning and see if we can see him on Saturday."

Abraham laid the documents on the floor of Vanderpool's
study to show him everything he had found. He went from
document-to-document and point-to-point. "I don't think
both brothers are buried in your back yard."

"Uh-huh."

"I think Randall was maybe temporarily buried here and
then moved to the Confederate Rest in Magnolia Cemetery."

"See where it says 'Double Down' here?"

"Yes."

"I think that is 'Richard' and somebody else."

Vanderpool stood up and scratched his chin. It turned
out Mr. Vanderpool was as eccentric as his face was craggy. He
scooped up the papers, quickly returned them to the case and
placed the case on the bottom shelf, while George and
Abraham watched in stunned silence. "Come!" He showed
them to the door. Abraham was almost in tears, wondering
what they had done wrong. "Come back four weeks from
today, nine o'clock sharp." He lightly pushed George and
Abraham out the door. "That day I shall open my hotel!" He
slammed the door in their startled faces.

When they drove up, they hardly recognized the place.

The trees had been trimmed, flowers had been planted everywhere, and the lawn was manicured. All exterior woodwork had been replaced or repainted. There was a new roof. The driveway had new concrete. There were two new signs out front: 'Vanderpool Manor' and 'Vacancy'. A white canvas banner read 'Grand Opening' and another, 'New Owner'.

They found Mr. Vanderpool in the backyard with two newspaper reporters.

"Gentlemen! Thank you for joining us for the Grand Opening!"

George shook his hand.

"Abraham, thank you for giving me the push I needed to get the hotel done." Abraham didn't know what to say. "Are you ready to get started?" He handed him a shovel.

"Started?"

"Yes, we are going to dig up old Richard Thompson and see who he is buried with."

Vanderpool dug like a man possessed. When he waned, he handed the shovel to George. When George needed a rest, Abraham climbed into the hole. When they got down to eight feet under, it became clear there was no coffin. Abraham felt dejected. Vanderpool was tired. The newspaper reporters made excuses and wandered away, but George kept digging. The words 'double down' kept rolling off his tongue. At about ten feet down, he thought he hit a rock. He scraped it with the shovel and then with his hand. It was flat, metal, and man-made. "We've got something here." They dug for another hour before they had the dirt fully pulled away from the coffin.

Vanderpool had invited the Chair of the University of Alabama Anthropology Department to his grand opening and got a curt reply, "When you find the coffin, call me. Not before." When it was apparent they had discovered a casket, Vanderpool instead called a local high school science teacher to see if he wanted to join them. "I'll be there in fifteen minutes." The teacher really did not expect much--perhaps the poorly preserved body of a civil war soldier. There could be other artifacts; probably nothing particularly interesting. Still, you didn't get to dig up a civil war burial site often.

When he walked up, Abraham looked surprise. "Mr. Dodd, what are you doing here?"

"Hello, Abraham." He had him as a student the previous spring semester. "I didn't know you were interested in anthropology!" Abraham explained about his Eagle Scout project.

"Well, let's get started. I'd like to jump down into the site." Abraham pointed over to the wooden ladder they were using. "I'll start with some photographs." He reached into his large case and removed a 4x5 inch "Pre-Anniversary" Speed Graphic camera with a five-inch reflector flash attached. As soon as he was down, he shot five photos, carefully adjusting the focus each time. "Throw me down a rag." They did. A few minutes later, he said, "Do you have a small gardening trowel?"

"Yes," replied Vanderpool. After locating it, he tossed it into the pit with a cheery, "Hereyago!"

Dodd busied himself for a few minutes. "Better come down here. You're not going to believe this." The three climbed down the ladder in single file fashion. "Mr. Vanderpool, are you sure this is a Confederate soldier buried here?"

"Well, we can't really be sure of anything."

"Abraham, notice anything unusual here?"

"The bottom is beveled."

"Very good. Look further."

"The bottom piece looks bowed."

"Right! One more thing."

"The bottom piece is larger, it extends past the, oh my gosh..."

"Ah, you have figured it out, too!"

"What is it, Son?"

"The coffin--it's upside down!"

The four looked at the coffin carefully. "Why would they bury it upside down?"

"That is why I was wondering if it could be a Yankee soldier they buried here. Guess we are not going to know until we open it up. But that creates a dilemma--do we tear through the back of the coffin, or do we bring the coffin up to the surface to turn it over?" They did not have the equipment to do either, just screwdrivers and a crowbar.

They spent the next two hours finding someone who could help them bring the coffin to the surface. A local farmer had two draft horses, ropes, and some strapping. A friend of his had a metal frame they could use. They jerry-rigged pulleys and by suppertime were ready to go. The newspaper reporters were back, as was half the neighborhood. The farmer apologized to Vanderpool. "Sorry, but this is gonna tear up your yard a bit."

"No problem. Best advertising I could possibly buy for my new hotel."

The draft horses made it look easy and the men guided the coffin onto the platform and then maneuvered the strapping until the coffin was right side up for the first time in more than eighty years. A policeman showed up and asked what the trouble was.

"Nothing, Officer."

"Why the big crowd?"

"Just neighbors stopping by to see the coffin we are bringing up."

"What?" The officer leaned up against the steps to the porch, where a reporter was asking Abraham questions and scratching on a notepad. Vanderpool paid the farmer and thanked him.

"Well, I guess we are gonna have to knock off for the night. Getting too dark here and I'm getting hungry." He went into his garage and returned with a heavy canvas to cover the coffin. "Everybody, be back here at nine o'clock sharp tomorrow morning!" The neighbors left immediately, followed by the policeman and reporters, leaving George, Abraham, and Vanderpool.

George said, "Guess we better be getting home to supper."

"I haven't got anything for you to eat, but why don't you stay here tonight for my grand opening."

"I have a better idea. Come with us to have dinner, and then we'll all come back for the night." Vanderpool looked reluctant to leave the coffin, but agreed.

Six

Abraham was awake before the sun was up. He heard birds chirping long before the first rays beamed over the ridge to the east. He had been given a room by himself, while George and Rebecca were next door. Rebecca had been impressed with the hotel and all the antiques. At about seven she went downstairs and fixed breakfast. The smell of bacon waffled through the house and Vanderpool came downstairs grinning, "What a treat! I haven't had bacon and eggs in an age. Haven't gotten around to hiring a cook for my hotel. Want a job?" Rebecca smiled back.

They were drinking coffee around the dining room table when the front doorbell rang. It was Mr. Dodd. "Hi everyone! I couldn't sleep last night."

Abraham said, "Me neither!"

George replied, "I couldn't because I am so sore from all that digging."

Soon one of the newspaper reporters was back and the backyard was filling up with neighbors. Vanderpool commented, "I wished I had told everyone to be back at seven instead of nine."

At nine o'clock sharp Mr. Dodd removed the canvas from the coffin. He had brought more tools to remove the cover and was taking photographs at every step. "Well, that is a surprise. Look, screws." The men proceeded to detach the top by removing eighteen screws that held the beveled, solid oak coffin top. "Pretty nice coffin, I'd say. Solid oak." With the screws removed the top still wouldn't budge until Dodd pounded on it with a rubber mallet. They lifted the top and set it aside.

The body was surprisingly well-preserved but askew from turning the coffin over. It was male, late teens. Long, black hair, sparse whiskers, with his hands in front wearing white and brown gloves. He was wearing a tuxedo, white cotton shirt, black bow tie, and no shoes. There were dead leaves on his lapel and a book. On closer inspection, the book turned out to be a Bible. There was an envelope in his jacket, which Dodd slipped into his case to look at later. They poked and prodded at the corpse, stopping frequently so the reporters and Dodd could scribble notes concerning their findings and take more photographs.

"Oh, my gosh."

"What is it?"

"Help me turn him on his side." They did. "Look here, Abraham."

"Ohhh. His head..."

"Yes. The head is caved in."

"Murdered?"

"Well, killed anyway. I suspected as much when I saw the gloves."

"The gloves?"

"Yes. Let's move him onto his back." They settled him back down. "The gloves are cotton. But notice the darker portions. They have faded considerably, but I believe it is blood."

"Blood?"

"Yes. They dipped his gloved fingers in blood. Probably his own. The white cotton gloves are a sign of either innocence or forgiveness. But the man was not innocent. There was blood on his hands, so they dipped his fingers in blood before they buried his body, as a sign of guilt. Over time, the blood has gone from red to brown. Well, that does it for the physical evidence. Let's have a look at the envelope."

The neighbors had long since left and they adjourned to the porch to have a drink of lemonade and look over the envelope. "Mr. Vanderpool, do you have a letter opener?"

The opener was made of highly-polished gold and Dodd carefully pushed the blade in to break the seal. He used the blade of the opener to fold open the letter and pressed it flat onto the surface of the table. It was two pages of flourishing hand script. The ink was mostly faded, but Dodd read aloud what he could make out.

"To Whom It May Concern,

Here lies the body of Richard Leslie Thompson of Birmingham, Alabama.

Died in the year of Our Lord 1865 on the 6th of June.

Confederate Traitor - ran away with his injured brother from Red Fort during the battle of Spanish Fort, by rowboat.

Came to our home seeking medical assistance for his brother, Randall. Busted leg and bullets in his back. We should have figured the bullets in the back was them running away, but we didn't.

I can't make out this next line.

191

We *something something* him back to health. Just before he left his brother decided to take advantage of our hospitality by taking the virginity of our daughter, Emma.

We made him marry her.

And we made him dig his own grave--double down--twice as close to hell as the normal man.

When he was close to done digging, I, John Henry McClary, drove a pickaxe into his skull from behind.

He squealed like a pig and I'm might...*I can't make out the end of the sentence*.

I alone am his judge, jury, and executioner. None other is accountable before the Lord for what my hand has done.

I am the Lord's instrument in bringing about justice, and if He has a problem with that I will take full responsibility at His judgment seat.

May God have mercy on me.

We buried him upside down as a sign of dishonor and to get him pointed in the right direction.

J. H. M., Mobile, Confederate State of Alabama."

When the front page article about digging up a confederate soldier hit the newsstands, at the first rays of dawn the following morning, Vanderpool found himself in his robe on his doorstep with the Sheriff and Coroner.

"What are you doing digging up a body?"

"We didn't know rightly what was there!"

"Yes, but you knew you were digging in a family plot."

"True."

Sheriff Johnston intervened. "Well, let's not get too excited here. Where is the body?" Vanderpool led the men to the shed, where he had placed the casket until he got somebody to rebury it. "We need the body, since there is evidence of a murder."

"Go right ahead."

"Is there anything that has been removed from the casket."

"An envelope that contained a letter."

"Where are they?"

"I have the envelope. Mr. Dodd has the letter."

"Dodd?"

"High School science teacher. Amateur anthropologist."

"My men will be here in a few minutes to take away the coffin for a thorough investigation."

"What will happen to the body?"

"We'll see if we can find next-of-kin. If we can't, do you want him back?"

"I don't think so. Where will he go if you can't find next of kin?"

"I am not sure right now."

"His brother, Randall Thompson, is buried at Magnolia Cemetery, Confederate Rest. It would be nice if you could lay him out near his brother."

The Coroner nodded. "I'm sure with all the publicity; somebody will want to pay for that."

On Monday, Abraham pitched for his high school baseball team. The crowd was three times normal size and strangers came up to shake Abraham's hand and ask him about the Confederate soldier. They called him 'gravedigger' from the stands and the opposing team, spooked by it all, lost six-to-one.

Abraham was getting calls from every civic and church group in the county to come talk about his Eagle Scout project. He was doing well with all the attention and began to relax as a public speaker. He was invited to attend a Rotary dinner as guest speaker, but a local politician horned in on the dais.

Longtime Democrat Congressman Frank William Boykin, Sr. was doing everything he could to get his face in front of the public as he campaigned in a special election. He had served in Congress as Alabama's 1st congressional district representative since 1935. He had exactly one asset--seniority. He could steer millions of federal dollars to his district, but he also frustrated his party's leadership by failing at the most simple task--missing, by far, more roll call votes than any other member of the state's congressional delegation. Uneducated, he was poorly suited to lead. Surprisingly, he had successful run lumber and turpentine businesses. When he ran for congress to fill an open position he had to pay fourteen years' worth of poll taxes just to vote for himself.[41]

After Abraham gave his talk, while the Rotary meeting droned on, the Congressman leaned over. "Hey, kid. Nice talk. What's your name again?"

"Abraham Cash."

"Is that your mom over there?"

"Yes." She brought him and waited to take him home, beaming with pride in her son.

Boykin smiled at Rebecca, while he wiggled his pinky ring, thinking, 'Classy Dame'! "So, how are your grades, kid?"

"Very good. I am graduating with honors."

"Honors? I'm impressed."

"Thank you."

"Where are you going to college?"

"I haven't decided yet."

"Ever think about West Point?"

Richard L. Thompson was finally laid in the tender Alabama soil of Confederate Rest, Magnolia Cemetery, Mobile, Alabama, next to his brother. A contingent of southern civil war actors and musicians volunteered to pay homage to a man who's history and dishonor they never knew. The newspapers made up heroic deeds and acts of daring for the two brothers, ignoring bullets in the back and a pickax to the brain. Richard lost his life preserving southern freedoms and protecting the cherished mothers and sisters of the Confederacy. Unable to find a real Confederate flag, they laid over the coffin the battle flag of the Army of Tennessee--the 'Dixie' flag. Once the south rose again, their names would be recalled in the the pantheon

---

[41] Boykin finished a distant third in his bid for the United States Senate in 1946. He won fourteen elections to the House of Representatives, serving from 1935 to 1963. He chaired the House Patents Committee from 1943 to 1947. He was married for nearly 56 years and openly bragged about his numerous affairs.

After the 1960 Census, Alabama lost one Congressional seat. All nine incumbents ran against each other in a statewide election, where the eight survivors became 'at-large' congressman (representing the state, not a specific district) and the last-place finisher was dropped. Boykin finished dead last--100,000 votes behind the eighth place finisher. He didn't even win Mobile.

But his troubles were not over. The following July he was convicted of conspiracy and conflict-of-interest for getting mail fraud charges dismissed by the Justice Department against two Maryland bankers, J. Kenneth Edlin and William L. Robinson.

of heros.

The following fall, Abraham Cash ended up in "The Long Gray Line" on the scenic west bank, high ground overlooking the Hudson River, fifty miles north of New York City, thanks to Boykin's Congressional nomination.

SEVEN

Abraham found an empty bench seat on the train, threw down a small bag, and scooted next to the window. Rebecca leaned against George as they searched through the windows from the platform. Spotting them Abraham waved, but they did not pick up his motion. Alexander, unable to spot his older brother, began to cry.

"Lower your window!" Startled, not sure what had been said, he craned his head. "The latch is at the top. Unlatch it and lower your window." He instantly obeyed and his parents caught sight of him. "There he is!" Rebecca pointed to the opening window near the back of the third railcar. They couldn't hear each other over the noises, but yelled and waved nonetheless. They only heard the conductor yelling, "All aboard" and the engineer bringing the steam up in the powerful locomotive engine. There was a long toot on the horn as the engineer looked for final passengers. The conductor lifted a stool and stood on the train's lowest step assuring himself everyone alongside was safe.

Panic set in for a second; Abraham scrambled to find his bag. Opening it he grabbed the envelope and pulled open the letter. It is here; safe; this is really happening. He looked carefully at the signature--Lieutenant General Maxwell Davenport Taylor, Class of 1922, Superintendent, United States Military Academy. His mother frantically blew kisses as the train jerked and rumbled forward. In seconds they were gone.

He sat back to reread the letter. It contained instructions

on what to bring (practically nothing), how to get from the train station to the Academy, and where to present this letter upon arriving. Out the window, fields were ripe with cotton. Green pods had exploded like giant popcorn kernels. Rows extended for as far as his eyes could see. Occasionally the train ran by fields loaded with trucks, wagons, and hundreds of negro field hands bent over to tend the plants. This last week of June, Abraham felt the Alabama morning sun already hot on his arm. He thought, what a hellish, dreadful way to live--up early, being bossed around, obeying orders all day, out in all types of weather--I could never live like that.

As the train clacked on a bridge, half awake and half asleep, he thought of the Mobile River flowing beneath him diagonally from east to west and north to south across Alabama. A drop of water falling south of Birmingham meanders across the State knocking topsoil, sand, and silt into the delta near his home and out to the Gulf of Mexico.

Startled awake, he looked into his bag and pulled out a book. He inspected the beaten, battered binding and edges and ran his fingers across gold, raised letters--*Adventures of Huckleberry Finn*. He read and took frequent naps. The landscape flew by. Cotton fields gave way to meadows of Bluegrass. Groves of spruce and pine gave off their fragrance, combating the odor of burning coal from the locomotive. He saw wild stands of sunflowers and cultivated wheat fields, patches of gourds and green pumpkins. Dairy farms and beef cattle gave off their own stench and Abraham didn't mind the overpowering smell of the coal train. As the day wore on they ran through frequent towns until they pulled into Union Station in downtown Chicago.

He hopped down from the train, leaving Huck Finn behind on the seat. He had read it from cover to cover more times than he could count. Abraham walked from the station to find a place to eat. Coming upon a diner half filled with families, he thought 'this might do the trick'. He held onto his bag tightly--having been warned to keep his money in front pockets and a lock grip on his wallet whenever he was in the big city. He opened the door and stood, half in and half out, deciding his next steps.

"Born in a barn, Son?"

He looked up and saw a waitress standing with her pencil at the ready to take an order. She nodded, "Don't mind him. Take a seat at the counter if you are alone."

He stepped to the well-worn, plastic-laminate counter, and sat on a red, simulated-leather bar stool. He wrapped the handle to the bag around his ankle, so he wouldn't forget it. Picking up the menu he perused it like he ordered out every day.

"Thespecialsroastbeef!"

"Huh?"

"The special is roast beef."

"Oh."

"Comes with coffee and apple pie for dessert. Buck thirty-five."

"Okay. I'll take it." He had been too excited to eat breakfast and hadn't had lunch on the train. She stood looking at him for a few seconds to answer two questions in her mind. The first was, what are the chances this kid has a buck-fifty on him? She figured he had come down from the train station and there was a good chance whoever sent him made sure he had enough to get a meal. The second question was, at a buck-thirty-five, this kid doesn't even know we are robbing him, does he? Satisfied with both questions, she turned toward the cook and called in the order.

Abraham sat alone, while customers jostled behind him. He ate quickly and slurped down the coffee.

"More coffee?"

He wondered if he would be charged extra, but decided he could afford it. "Sure!"

As she poured, she asked, "Where you off to, kid?"

"I've been accepted to West Point."

"Where's that?"

"New York."

"What are you gonna do there?"

He realized she didn't know what West Point was. "I have been accepted to the United States Military Academy. I'll be studying for a career in the army. Probably take a degree in engineering. I am particularly good at math."

She smiled and cracked her gum. "Just trying to make conversation, Hon', I didn't need your life history." She moved on to the next customer.

The train east would not leave until eight the following morning. He sat down at an uncomfortable bench, made his bag into a pillow, and fell asleep. He woke with a start--he had drooled on himself and needed to pee. He jumped up and--almost forgetting his bag--grabbed it and ran to the Men's Room. When he returned his seat was taken and the station was beginning to fill. He looked for a clock. Six-thirty--another hour and forty minutes to wait.

The ride took all day. He was bored and nervous--or maybe just excited. The trip seemed to take forever. He read the letter again--as he had a thousand times--get off the train at Poughkeepsie, where a vehicle would provide transportation to the Academy. As the train pulled into the station, he stood up, collected his bag, and walked to the back of the car. Stepping off the train he noticed two other young men getting off, looking as lost as he felt.

"Over here plebes!" He spotted the man who had spoken and raised his hand to his chest and looked at him quizzically.

"If you're looking to get to West Point, I'm your ride."

The three young men assembled in front of the cadet, quickly shaking hands and introducing themselves to each other.

"I'm Abraham Cash." He stretched out his hand to the driver.

"I don't care who or what you are. Shit, they get stupider every year. You are now a Plebeian. Plebe for short. In the grand order of things, you are the lowest level of animal that maggots bother to eat. Given the choice between you and the south end of a north-bound skunk a vulture will go for the skunk every time. Follow me."[42]

He walked briskly to the car. "Get in."

"Can I put my suitcase in the back?" one boy asked.

"Was your letter different than everyone else's? Didn't it say to bring the minimum?"

"Yes."

"Yes, Sir, to you!"

"Yes, Sir!"

"Son, I am going to do you a big favor and save you a lot of embarrassment. Get in."

He unlocked and opened the trunk, which blocked the

---

[42] Plebeians were not the lowest order in the Roman Empire. There were slaves and capite censi (literally, "those counted by head") who were citizens who owned no land, but could own other property. Plebeians could become extremely wealthy and successful.

view of his three passengers. Picking up the suitcase, he tossed it into the closest trash can. Brushing off his hands, he returned to the car and closed the trunk.

"Thank you, Sir."

"You are welcome, Plebe. Now shut up, all three of you."

As they pulled to the front gate, the driver stopped his car, received and returned a sharp salute and drove in.

"Here is where you get out, ladies."

"What about my suitcase."

"Have you got your letter?"

"Yes."

"Yes, what?"

"Yes, Sir!"

"That's all you'll need, Son." The driver was a cadet yearling (or sophomore); one year older than the boys he had transported.

"Rest up, ladies. R-day tomorrow."

Every fall, R-day begins cadet basic training (CBT) --the Beast-- at the United States Military Academy in West Point. The strenuous transition away from civilian to military life had begun for Abraham and he loved every minute of it. The academics were ideally suited for him; small classes, daily assignments, ownership of one's success, and collaboration.

His first trouble at the Academy came with the fall leaves. When he was to be at attention, his eyes and mind wandered to the surrounding maple trees that exploded with color.

"Cadet Cash, what are you looking at!"

"I'm sorry, Sir. I have never seen anything like that, Sir!"

"Like what, Cash?"

"The leaves on the maple trees, Sir!"

"What about the leaves?"

"Sir, I have never seen trees like that. With all the colors."

"Where are you from, Cash?"

"Mobile, Alabama, Sir!"

"Perhaps you will get your fill of looking at the damn trees when 'walking the area' for twenty hours!"

"Yes, Sir! Thank you, Sir!"

The next two weekends he performed his punishment tour, walking off the hours of retribution he had been awarded, in his dress gray uniform, carrying a rifle, walking back and forth through the cadet barracks courtyard, with never a glimpse of a maple tree. For long hours he deliberately and precisely marched, as he watched the gray ground squirrels scampering between the trees in a last ditch effort to store away nuts, seeds, and pine cones which had dropped onto the courtyard.

He was teased for being from the South. He was teased for being so serious. He was also teased for his first reaction to the snow.

"What is it, Cash?"

"I was noticing the Parade Grounds look like an Alabama cotton field in September, Sir!"

"Cadet, that is the most stupid thing I have ever heard."

"Yes, Sir! Thank you, Sir!"

This caught him another twenty hours of punishment, but he didn't seem to mind as it snowed the whole time. The squirrels only peeked out curiously from the snug holes in the trees watching the man in dress gray walk back and forth. In a few weeks he was well on his way to becoming a 'Century Man'.

Cadet Abraham Cash saw things in black-and white terms. He memorized his Bugle Notes--the lengthy collection of myths, legends, traditions, facts, songs, and even poems, about everything military. He studied the myths as if his life might depend on it. He especially took to heart the Cadet Honor Code introduced to the Cadets during his first year, "A cadet will not lie, cheat, or steal." He believed if he worked hard and honestly, he would be a success.[43]

---

[43] The phrase, "...or tolerate those who do" was added following the 1976 West Point cheating scandal where originally 117 "cow" cadets (3rd year students; juniors) were accused of cheating on an Electrical Engineering exam. An additional 138 were added later. The sheer numbers rocked the Academy's ability to deal with the scandal, and ended with investigations at the highest levels of the military and in Congress.

Cadet Cash was not furloughed to spend his summers at home. He spent them at Camp Buckner learning (and later teaching) field craft and tactical military skills. After his second summer, he became a "cow" cadet (3rd year student or junior). Colonel Maxwell Jackson "Mack Jack" Nichols volunteered to mentor Abraham after the first three classes in an introductory course of military tactics under him. Mack Jack considered mentoring a full-time responsibility, including taking Abraham after chapel on Sunday. Each Sunday afternoon included a large dinner (usually chicken or pot roast with all the sides), a three-hour forced nap ("man was made to rest on the Sabbath"), a game of flag football with the neighbor kids, an advanced discussion on military strategy and tactics ("my advanced degree"), supper, dishes ("I'll wash, you dry, my daughter will put away"), card (canasta was the colonel's favorite) or board games, and dessert.

Nichols liked that Cash asked bizarre questions in class, reaching far beyond the typical introductory student. Questions came out of nowhere and were frequently carried over to Sunday.

"Why did Lee violate his own rules so frequently?"

"Since generals from both the North and South were educated here at West Point, weren't they stuck with the same thinking? Why was it that the Civil War came down to brute force for a Northern victory?"

"Why didn't Lee just let the North dig in at Gettysburg and then make an end run to the south straight to Washington, instead of insisting on making three days of disadvantaged assaults?"

"Why was the United States so ill equipped at the start of World War II? Why did we learn so little from our experience in the First World War?"

"Why didn't the Allies land troops closer to Rome, send one column north to Rome and the other south to Anzio?"

By the fall semester, when Abraham had become a "firstie" (4th year or senior) things began to change at the Nichols.

"That was a delicious dinner, Dear."

"Thank you, Mack." The Colonel began to pick up the dinner plates. "Honey, would you come to the porch with me? Bring your pipe."

"What? But the dishes!"

"Mel and Abraham, I'm sure, will be happy to take care of them."

"But--"

She grabbed his hand as she stood. She drew him to his easy chair, where his pipe stand and tobacco were kept, grabbed his pipe and matches while peeking back at the dining room, and continued to lead him to the front porch. "Now, isn't this better?"

They sat on the double swing. "Well, I, I guess."

"Honey, did you notice your daughter in church today?"

"Yes."

"Anything unusual?"

"Not that I can think of."

"How about last week?"

He thought for a second. "Nothing that comes to mind. What are you driving at?"

"Melbourne did not sit between us."

"So."

"She sat between you and Abraham."

"Yes."

"Did you notice anything at lunch?"

"Let me think. The biscuits were particularly tasty."

"Nothing else?"

"No."

"And during nap time did you notice anything?"

"In blue blazes, Ellen, how am I to notice things while I sleep?"

She sighed. "Abraham didn't go up to the guest bedroom as usual."

"So."

"Mel didn't go to her room either."

Colonel Nichols looked over to the screen door. "How long does it take to wash four dishes? I want to play canasta!"

"Did Mel play football with you today?"

"What? No! We play too rough. She never plays with us! Just the neighbor boys."

"But she did stand out there while you played?"

"Well, yes. Blazes, Woman, why all the questions?"

"Has she ever done that before?"

"Done what before?"

"Stood out there while you played football!"

"Heck, how am I supposed to remember?" He thought for

a few seconds. "I guess not before last Sunday."

There was a pause as Ellen thought how to tell her husband. "Does the army pay you to be watchful and observant?"

"What?"

"For your job, are you required to notice things?"

"Huh? What are you--"

"They have fallen in love, Dear!"

The pipe drooped from the Colonel's mouth.

Fathers are always surprised when their first daughters fall in love. They never see it coming. Melbourne Dawn Nichols had been born October 15, 1930 while Lieutenant and Mrs. Nichols were stationed at Fort Bragg, North Carolina. They had been married for exactly nine months and fifteen days, honeymooning in Australia. Only her parents knew where and when she had been conceived.

During Abraham's final year at the United States Military Academy, Mack Jack and Ellen stressed the importance of appreciating the social, as well as academics and athletics, of West Point.

"The Ring Dance is coming up," teased Ellen, "anyone special you're planning to take?"

"Yes, I know--"

Ellen reached over and grabbed Abraham's arm. "Just to let you know, I happen to be free that evening, I am sure my husband will not mind."

"Yeah. You need to quit studying maneuvers and start studying, well, maneuvers!"

"I've already asked Mel, but I--" There was a long pause. "I'm going to need some help."

They looked at him with a puzzled expression. "You don't need any money, do you, Son?"

"No, Sir. It's just that--" There was another pause.

"What the hell is it around here! Spit it out!"

"I don't know how to dance."

"What?"

"No, I mean, I don't know how to dance the kind of dances they will be doing at the ball."

After Abraham's confession, Mel said she could use some help, too. So the next four Sunday afternoons, after nap time, were given over to dance instruction. The Colonel teaching his daughter and Ellen teaching Abraham, in adjoining rooms, listening to the same records on the phonograph.

Their first dance together was at the Ring Dance.

"Hey, I think we are doing pretty well."

"Yes, my parents were good instructors."

"You look so beautiful!"

"And you are so handsome. Let me see your ring?" She examined the ornate casting. "It's beautiful." She read: "1950 USMA" on top, and flipped it to one side "Country. Honor. Duty." She placed it back on his finger, hugged him, and whispered in his ear slowly, in her most seductive voice: "Oh My God, Sir! What a Beautiful Ring! What a crass mass of brass and glass! What a bold mold of rolled gold! What a cool jewel you got from your school! See how it sparkles and shines? It must have cost you a fortune! May I touch it? May I touch it please, Sir?"

The Goat-Engineer game came next. Being in the upper half of his class, Abraham was an Engineer; being fast and agile, he was a running back. They beat the Goats by six points which would shortly test the prophecy that 'if the Goats win, Army will win that year's Army-Navy game and if the Engineers win, the reverse will take place'. Three weeks later, Navy beat Army at the annual Army-Navy Game held at Philadelphia Municipal Stadium, 14-2. Coach Earl "Red" Blaik led the Black Knights to second in the AP Poll with an 8-1 season, but by losing to Navy the biggest prize of the year escaped him.

By Christmas, rumors of moving up graduation were everywhere.

"Sir, how does that work if they move up a graduating class? Because of the stuff going on in Korea."

"They won't. I'm still praying they will get things settled down there. Hopefully it won't come to an armed conflict."

"How sure are you, Colonel?"

"About graduation? Very. No, if they were moving up a class, we would be getting ready now."

"Alright. But what if they did?"

"If I remember right, during World War II the first year they did it mid-year. After that, they graduated men after their third year."

"That would have been rough."

"Yes. They are taking men back through to pick up on what they missed. Most got their final exams under fire--literally."

As isolated as West Point could be, Korea was the subject in every classroom and dining hall.

Baseball games started in the spring and Abraham excelled on the mound. Professional scouts dropped by to see him pitch, regardless of his military commitment, but Abraham didn't give professional baseball a second thought. Mel attended every game.

On Easter Sunday the family relaxed, enjoying a roast lamb together, but Abraham was fidgety.

"Could I have a word with you, Sir?"

"Certainly. Let me get my pipe." In a loud voice he said, "Ladies, we will be on the front porch."

"Sir, I have been thinking very hard."

"Yes, Son." The Colonel lit his pipe.

"Well, you know Mel and I have gotten to know each other over the last two years?"

The Colonel couldn't help it: He gave Abraham a stern look, "And I already know what you are going to ask." He took a long draw on his pipe. "I believe it would be alright if you want to ask her out for a date. She would probably say yes, so you should go right ahead."

"That isn't it, Sir."

"What? What the hell is it then?"

"I would like Mel's hand in marriage."

He got a far off look in his eyes and took a long drag on his pipe. "Oh! I don't know. Low pay. Never in charge. Filling out forms in order to get forms to fill out! You'll be sent all over the country, dragging her along, sprinkling brats all over the countryside. Military marriages are tough." But he couldn't keep his straight face and they both laughed. "Abraham, we would be honored. But I think it would be wise to give it some time. Things are heating up in Korea. A good number of graduates will be sent shortly. You might want to wait until after your first tour for the wedding."

"I see."

"But, you'll still have my blessings, unless you do one thing."

"What is that?"

"Elope. I want to march my only daughter down the aisle."

A few weeks later, Mack Jack asked Abraham, "Are your parents coming up for graduation?"

"I have written to them with the dates."

"Good. We would love to have them stay with us."

Abraham's eyes shifted to Mel. "I asked them to come and stay through the following weekend. We have been talking about going ahead with the wedding the following Saturday." He wasn't sure how the Colonel was going to react.

"Wonderful!"

Abraham sighed in relief.

"Where?"

"Either Main chapel or the Old Chapel."

"Go for Main; Old is too close to the cemetery. You better reserve it tomorrow. Also, make an appointment with the Superintendent."

"Superintendent?"

"Yes. You're not getting married without his permission!"

George and Rebecca had not seen Abraham since Christmas when they stepped off the train in New York. They marvelled at his mannerism and speech. He had grown taller and filled out during his four years away.

Graduation was held on June 6, 1950. The following day Abraham received his commission as a 2nd lieutenant and orders to prepare to leave by the end of the month for Tokyo, on his way to Korea.

"Dad, could I see you and the Colonel." He looked at Ellen and Mel, then returned his eyes to the men, "In private."

Both men, who had been drinking scotches in the dining room and telling stories about Abraham, stepped onto the front porch. "I received my commission this morning--2nd lieutenant."

"Congratulations!"

"Well done! I'm proud of you."

"Thank you, Father."

"You've done well here."

"Yes he has. Far better than I did. Low fifties is quite an accomplishment."

"I have some other news as well. No traditional graduation furloughs are being given this year. I'll be leaving for Tokyo by the end of the month. Then Korea."

"Or you could be on MacArthur's staff." The colonel looked at the papers. There was not a hint that he was there for the occupation of Japan. "You'll like working for Mac. He was quite a left fielder when he was here. Maybe he'll put you on his baseball team. I'm sure he's got one started." The Colonel handed the paper to George. "Mac is a good man. Army through and through. He can be stern. Demanding. He is fair. He's got an ego, but what successful General doesn't? He'll take credit for everything, but everyone knows he develops good people and who does the lion's share of the work. Doesn't leave much time for a honeymoon. Thayers may be the best you can do."[44]

Bag pipes accompanied the massive pipe organ playing Mendelssohn's "Wedding March" in C major, Opus 61, signaling the bride's father to walk his daughter down the aisle. Colonel Maxwell Jackson Nichols insisted he escort his daughter the entire 210 foot long, narrow nave. Historic and current battle banners and flags hung from the massive

---

[44] The Thayers Hotel is at the end of the United States Military Academy post on the banks of the Hudson River, overlooking the parade grounds, and has hosted five presidents, numerous distinguished generals, and families of prominent cadets. It was named for superintendent of the Academy, Colonel and Brevet Brigadier General Sylvanus Thayer (1785 - 1872). Thayer is recognized as 'the Father of West Point'.

ceiling.

The bride wore a white, French antique floral lace wedding gown over a tulle underskirt with silk lining. The floral fitted lace mid-waist bodice emphasized Melbourne's waist. The skirt was fully flared with a slight train cascade lace. The see-through floral lace sleeves and scalloped, boat-neckline had hand beaded opalescent sequins in a floral pattern. The gown was simple, sparkling, and glamorous. She wore a wisp of a veil, so her face was uncovered. Her smile was radiant.

The Cadet Chapel at the United States Military Academy, which seats over 800, was less than a quarter full. Abraham stood before the ornately carved alter with the minister, best man, and four groomsmen. He wore full dress uniform; dark-blue coat and trousers with polished gold buttons and yellow piping, white dress shirt with wingtip collar, black bow tie, blue and gold ceremonial belt, and white gloves.[45]

"Who gives this woman to be married to this man?"

"I d-o." Unexpectedly, his voice cracked and, embarrassed, Mack Jack coughed, handed his daughter off to the groom, and sat next to his wife. There were tears on his cheeks, which he didn't wipe away. Rebecca and George, touched by Colonel Nichols's tears, squeezed each other's hands and teared up themselves.

"Welcome. We are gathered here today in the sight of God, to witness and celebrate the union of Abraham George Cash and Melbourne Dawn Nichols in Holy..."

After exchanging vows and wedding rings, Reverend Shipp pronounced them 'man and wife' and they proceeded

---

[45] The United States Military Academy Cadet Chapel was designed by Bertram Grosvenor Goodhue (1869 - 1924) of the Boston architectural firm of Cram, Goodhue and Ferguson. Winning the project in 1902 was the major milestone in the firm's history. The chapel is gothic revival architecture, with a cross-shape, soaring arches and buttresses, ornate stone carvings, and large, intricate, stained glass windows depicting Biblical scenes. The dark gray biotite granite gneiss was locally quarried.
It contains the largest chapel pipe organ in the world, with over 23,500 individual pipes, and growing. Originally it had a few hundred pipes, but has steadily increased as graduating classes have frequently donated more.

down the aisle to the sounds of the enormous organ reverberating throughout the stone-walled room. They stepped out of the massive granite structure, which sits on a cliff at the highest point of the post, and listened to the bells from the 135 foot bell tower. As the bridesmaids and groomsmen left the chapel, they waited for the assembled guests to collect at the entrance, before Mr. and Mrs. Abraham Cash walked beneath a cavalry saber arch held in place by the groomsmen.[46]

The reception was in the Officer's Club. It included dinner, drinks, and dancing, and lasted well into the night. One groomsman tried his best FDR imitation as he ribbed Abraham, "Tonight, Saturday, June 10th, 1950, a night that will live in infamy, the graceful and beautiful Melbourne Dawn Nichols Cash was suddenly and deliberately attacked by the hideous and lecherous 2nd Lieutenant Abraham George Cash!"

The bridal suite at The Thayers Hotel, overlooking the parade grounds of the Academy, sufficed for the wedding night, or more accurately, the day following the wedding. They got to bed shortly after 4 a.m., but sleep was the last thing on Abraham's mind.

Melbourne returned from the bathroom in an elegant robe. She stood at the end of the bed where Abraham lay under a single sheet, propped up against two pillows. "I am sorry, but with graduation and all, I just didn't have time to find a nice nightgown. A negligée provides the right mood. I am so sorry--you must be disappointed." She dropped the robe; all she was wearing was a smile. He wasn't disappointed at all.

They spent three days at The Thayers, before traveling to New York City for three more. The next week was spent at a cabin in the Catskills the Colonel had borrowed. As the week came to a close, the 'elephant in the room' loomed larger and larger.

---

[46] Model 1913 Cavalry Saber was the last saber used by the United States Cavalry. George Smith Patton, Jr. (1885 - 1945), at the time a United States Army Lieutenant, designed the Model 1913 for 'cut and thrust'; it has a two-edged, forged steel, chisel-pointed blade, is thirty-eight inches long, and weighs two pounds. It has a large, basket hilt. Blood-letting grooves run down the sides.

"Only a few more days."

"Don't remind me."

"When we get back on Saturday, we will stay at Daddy's. Now I am married, I am not sure I want to stay there much longer."

"Really?"

"I'm thinking of renting a room."

"I am surprised."

"I know. We should have talked about this before. It's just that--if I stay there it will feel awkward when you return from your tour. A year is a long time."

"True. But..."

"I know. It isn't very practical."

"Maybe you should return to your parents' home and take a little time finding a place for us."

There was a long pause, as she thought about her response. "Abraham?"

"Yes?"

"I'm afraid."

He hugged her. "We can face this together."

"What if you don't--" She couldn't end her question and began to cry.

He understood where she was going. "I will come home. I'll be back in no time."

Lieutenant-General Walton Harris "Johnnie" Walker did not like what he saw. His soldiers were being rushed out of training, only a third of the officers had seen combat, and the Army was selling off equipment for scrap at an alarming rate. General Douglas MacArthur had recently been named Commander-in-Chief of the United Nations Command (UNCOM) by the Joint Chiefs of Staff, while remaining Supreme Commander of the Allied Powers (SCAP) in Japan and Commander of the United States Army Forces Far East (USAFFE). He demanded his Eighth Army be whipped into combat-worthy condition.

Walker complained, "But, Mac, it is going to take some time--"

"Get the whip out, Johnnie!"

"I don't have the place to do it or any weapons."

"You'll figure it out."

"And we need better training--Academy, O. C. S., and Basic! All the way through."

"I agree. I've talked to the Chiefs already. We're getting our first group out of The Military Academy in a few days."

"Great! Now I'm getting to babysit toddlers from the Point, too!"

"Johnnie!"

"When will we get some relief on equipment? I'm talking basic weaponry here--machine guns, mortars, howitzers, launchers, ammunition. And don't get me started on amphibians!"

Abraham arrived in Japan with three other newly commissioned 2nd lieutenants during the first week of July. They spent two weeks getting physically and mentally acclimated before being dispatched to the front.

"Cash and Caminetti, we're sending you two to the far right flank. Eighth army, 1st Cavalry Division, 5th Cavalry Regiment, 1st Battalion, Company G. It's a mortar company. You will be observers. Assess battle readiness and combat equipment utilization. Pick up your gear. You'll leave from Itazuke Air Base at 0600!"

They each picked up an M1 Rifle, 120 rounds of ammunition, and two days of C-rations.

"Hey, Sarge, can we get rid of these yet?" He pointed to a stack of helmets with a sign which read: HOLD.

"Yeah."

"Here are your M-1 helmets. Sign here."

"Thanks, Corporal.

"You're all set."

Seven M-1 helmets had been sitting in the supply depot since May awaiting 'approval to distribute'. They were prototypes from the Sharon Steel Corporation of Sharon, Pennsylvania in Mercer County, near the Ohio border.

"Yeah, the next five guys are the winners of the remaining helmets."

"What's wrong with 'em?"

"Nothin'."

"Well, why'd we have 'em?"

"You know, some Congressman has a company in his district that needs business. You know, fancier metal, stronger stuff..."

"Payola!"

"You got it! So they slip us prototypes. We're supposta track how well they work."

"How do we do that?"

"We don't in this case. This one was 'Dead on Arrival'! Got the note yesterday."

"Yeah? Why?"

"You know how much steel goes into a helmet?"

"No."

"Twelve cents! You think the Army is gonna spend thirteen cents when they can get it for twelve."

Sharon Steel Corporation prototypes were a slightly different alloy from the twenty million Hadfield steel M-1 helmets that had been stamped out by Sharon and Carnegie-Illinois for McCord Radiator and Manufacturing Company of Detroit, Michigan for supply to the United States Army.[47]

The Douglas Aircraft Company C-54 Skymaster lifted off from Itazuke Air Base near the city of Fukuoka in southern Japan for the 335 mile trip to Seoul, South Korea.

"This is your Captain speaking. Well, boys, we'll be at your vacation destination in two hours. Keep those belts tight. We'll be over water for half the trip. You can see Navy ships down there. We shouldn't need them today. Then we'll be entering the war zone. This old bucket has been humming along pretty good, so going down is the least of your worries

---

[47] In 1816, a German researcher found adding large amounts of manganese to iron increased steels hardness without affecting malleability or strength. Sixty-six years later, Sir Robert Abbott Hadfield, 1st Baronet, Fellow of the Royal Society (1858 - 1940) discovered manganese steel. Hadfield steel was the first alloy from carbon steel (also known as "Mangalloy", a combining from the words manganese and alloy).

right now. I want to wish you all the best of luck. Hopefully
we'll get out of this damn war as quickly as we're gettin' in.
Good luck, boys!"

Cash and Caminetti looked at each other and shrugged.
There were close to two dozen other men on the flight, the
cabin packed with gear.

As they got off the Skymaster they heard, "Over here! I'm
your ride, Lieutenants."

They walked over to the jeep carrying their equipment.

"You're Caminetti and Cash, right?"

"Yes."

"I'm Hastings. Is that all your crap?"

"Uh, yes."

"Okay. Drop it in the back and jump in."

He lit a cigar and drove at breakneck speed to the far end
of the landing field to a Bell H-13B Sioux three-seat helicopter
with a full bubble canopy, open sides, exposed welded-tube
tail boom, saddle fuel tanks, and skid landing gear.

Caminetti recognized the problem immediately. "Where
are we gonna put all this?"

"What we can't rope outside goes in your lap."

"What?"

"You heard me."

"But..."

"If you gotta take a piss now's the time. Ain't no WACS up
this way, so you can whip'er-out right here and take care of
business." They looked at him incredulously. "Listen. It will
take us 'a buck and three-quarters' to get there. If you can hold
it that long, fine. If not, you can deal with wet pants. I ain't
putting this baby down so you can take a leak."

It was difficult to get the flow started under these
conditions, but Hastings didn't mind the delay. He had a cigar
to finish. When they were done, Hastings strapped what he
could onto the welded-tube frame. "Get in. Hold that junk on
your lap."

They climbed in, while Hasting started the two
thirty-seven foot main rotors.

"How far did you say we are goin?'"

"Camp Carroll? Out by Waegwan? One-three-five clicks
as the crow flies. Half-a-tank o'gas."

"We practiced on better crap than this two years ago at Camp Buckner."

"You got that right. Four obsolete M9A1 Bazooka rocket launchers, two M20 75mm recoilless rifles, two M2 4.2 inch mortars, and four M2 60mm mortars. That's a quarter of the equipment we're gonna need."

"Yeah, and twice as many men." Their first few hours at the base of a hill near the Naktong River had not been encouraging.

"This is all?"

The platoon leader nodded.

Abraham shook his head, thinking 'How could they deploy these men with so little?'

"Intelligence picked up heavy North Korean concentrations across the river and up a-ways."

"How far?"

"Seven clicks."

The platoon leader looked through his binoculars. "They need us to stay here. There are reports of action up there."

"Yeah. We'll snuggle up here in this foxhole. I can hear small weapons fire."

"They're calling in an air strike for dawn. Gonna hit a bridge and underwater tunnel."

"What time is it?"

"Oh-Oh-Thirty."

"Hey, what is the date?"

"August 15."

"Two days 'til I turn nineteen!"

The corporal slammed down the field phone and turned to the Captain as they lay side-by-side in the shallow fox hole."They're sending sixty South Korean Army reinforcements over."

"How soon?"

"Don't know."

"Shit! Well, call headquarters and find out!"

"Here's the situation, Lieutenants. We have a fifteen-mile front which runs north to south protecting Taegu. That's where headquarters is set up. The river and mountains give us some protection. This hill is a two-mile long oval."

"How many troops?"

"Two Korean divisions, plus we have three regiments."

Caminetti did some quick math. "That should do. Thirty thousand men."

Abraham corrected him. "Fewer. Twenty-five. Twenty. Our regiments are nowhere near normal force."

"Good point."

They didn't know five North Korean divisions (up to 75,000 soldiers) were within ten miles of their position.

The sentinel whispered, "Company to the south!"

"Roger."

"Must be our reinforcements."

"Yeah. Confirm with Charlie Company."

"This is Golf. Where are you?"

"Is that the reinforcements between us?"

"They can't confirm."

"Alright, we'll hang tight."

"Charlie has been ordered back across the river."

"Why?"

"I'm not sure. Get ahold of headquarters, find out what they want us to do."

"Henry Company on the radio. Says they're moving south and the Koreans will be up to reinforce us shortly."

"Roger," replied the platoon leader over the radio.

"No. We're blocked on the south side of the hill, better than half way up. Until those reinforcements get here, we're stuck."

"We have good defenses here, Sir. The men are dug in."

"Look! Bombers are coming in! Fireworks starting."

"Poor bastards catching that crap."

"Glad they're on our side."

"Foxtrot is moving south."

"Damn. We're gonna be by ourselves."

"If this pesky small arms stuff keeps up, we'll have to move, too."

"Where? The mountains are blocked."

"Is that our reinforcements?"

"Gotta be. They must be pinned down, too. Can't get up here yet."

"Our other option is to retreat toward the city?"

"That gives us the best cover."

"When?"

"Looks to be about noon now. We can't wait until dark."

"Can we set up mortars?"

"Negative. Not with that sniper fire."

"Tell the men to hunker down."

"Roger."

"Hey, look over there. US tanks coming this way."

"Where are those ROK tanks?"

"Stalled at the base of the hill."

"Shit."

"Get the men ready to move."

"Okay, I'll pass the word."

"No. Hold it. Here come our reinforcements."

"Really?"

"They said about fifty, right?"

"Sixty!"

"Even better."

"Okay, boys, relax. They will be up here in a few minutes to relieve us."

"Hold your fire, men!"

"Boy, are we glad to--What the fuck?" North Korean soldiers came to the foxholes without firing a single shot. Until they got close enough to see red stars on their helmets, they didn't know it wasn't their South Korean replacements.

The platoon leader assessed the situation. It was hopeless. There was only one choice. He had been drilled over and over that a live prisoner was better than a dead soldier. Outnumbered and outgunned there was only one thing to do.

The enemy leader tried to remember English phrases he had been taught. "Hangs zup!" The enemy soldier motioned with his gun.

"Men, lay down your weapons and surrender."

"You lee der?"

"I am the platoon leader"

"Hangs zup!"

"Hands up, men!"

"You sir rend dear!"

217

"Yes, we surrender."

"Geez uz yer we pons."

"Men, lay down your weapons."

North Korean soldiers picked up pistols and rifles from each man. They collected rocket launchers, recoilless rifles, and mortars and piled them up. They carefully examined each prisoner, taking away watches, wallets, and rings.

A soldier walked up to Abraham and pantomimed stretching his hands forward. Abraham complied. The North Korean soldier removed his helmet and gave his friends a silly grin. He was thin with a big smile, small eyes, close cropped hair, and large misshapen ears. The soldier slipped Abraham's West Point ring from his right hand and carefully examined it before dropping it into his helmet. He beamed to his fellow soldiers. Then he slipped Abraham's shiny wedding band from his left hand. He quickly looked at it and broke into a wide grin.

The platoon leader nodded for Corporal Day to come over to him. He slowly moved closer. "Stay by me." Day spoke a little Japanese, and his leader thought he might pick up what was going on.

More than thirty mortar men were marched down the hill to a small orchard. They wired the men's hands behind their backs, rummaged through their belongings, removing remaining valuables and shoes.

"What did he say, Day?"

"He said we will be treated well, if we behave."

"Where are they taking us?"

"Prisoner of War Camp in Seoul."

"Seoul! That can't be right! They don't possess Seoul."

"I think he plans to, Sir."

That night, North Korean troops from the 3rd Division took over guarding the prisoners. In an orchard, they removed the wires and give them water, fruit, and cigarettes, before rewiring their wrists. The men complained the wires were too tight and some of the soldiers loosen them slightly. The following morning they were clustered closer together. There was no more water or food.

Day whispered, "If you dig in the sand, you may be able to get water."

"How the hell are we gonna do that with our hands wired again?"

"When you get thirsty enough you'll figure it out."

The second night they were marched around to the other side of the hill and at dawn, back to the orchard to hide again. The movement loosened the wire shackles. The guards became concerned and roughed up prisoners.

A guard raised his pistol to the eyes of one of the prisoners and the man instinctively raised his now loose hands to his face. "No!" *Bang!* The noise echoed through the mountains as the guard fell over dead, shot by his commander for threatening a prisoner.

The American Forces, led by Baker Company with a 700-man battalion, advanced on the North Korean position. Soon artillery began a relentless barrage on the hill that lasted into the night. The Americans were fought to a standstill, before retreating when sniper fire was taking men as they rested under cover. The North Korean commander was furious!

"Day, what did he say?"

"Something about paying for this."

"What? What did we do?"

"He is furious so many of his men have died. He is going to shoot some of our men."

"What?"

"You!" The barrel of the rifle was pointed directly at Abraham's face. "You!" He next pointed at a soldier who looked to be sixteen. "You!" He pointed to a man they called 'Arbuckle'--who had an uncanny resemblance to Fatty Arbuckle. He swung around to point out two other men. One of the men broke down crying, pleading for his life. "Come!"

A soldier removed the wires from their wrists and led the five American soldiers to the far side of the hill with another soldier trailing them. "Here!" He pushed them tightly together. The trailing soldier pulled up his PPSh-41 Soviet submachine gun. At a rate of 900 rounds per minute, it didn't take but a second to mow the five Americans down.

The following day, their comrades were lined up in a trench on the hill to meet a similar fate--the Hill 303

219

SEVEN

Massacre.[48]

It's so dark. This isn't what I expected heaven to be like. Where am I? Why can't I move? I can't feel my hands. What is that pressure on my wrists? Abraham fell back to sleep.

Before dawn, he began to see light, but couldn't make out any features. "Hello!" Nobody heard his weak voice. *Oh, my head hurts so bad!* His face was turned to the side and all the ground he could see was too close for his eyes to focus. He realized his hands were pressing into his chest. *That's why they are numb! I can't move. Why?* He fell asleep again.

"Help me!" he screamed; it came out as a whisper. *I am so thirsty! Where am I?* Something was pressing into his back. *What is that?* He tried to move; wiggling took all his energy. *I am so tired.* Sleep came easily.

I'm outdoors. My face is in the mud. No, really dirt. If it was mud, I could drink. Where am I? He began to wiggle under the load on his back. *I think I am moving! Maybe I can free a hand? Which one should I try to move? Right one. I think it is closest to the edge of my body. Is there anything broken? I don't know. What's on my head? Get it off, it's hurting.* He nearly got his right arm free. *Let me try to rock it.*

---

[48] The Hill 303 Massacre took place on August 17, 1950 on a hill near Waegwan, South Korea. North Korean troops held American prisoners and tried to move them out of the battle. Around 1400 on August 17, the hill was hit with napalm, bombs, rockets, mortars, tank fire, and machine guns. Because the American counterattack was so heavy, the North Koreans were forced to retreat. So they would not be slowed, an officer ordered the forty-one remaining prisoners be shot. It was the first of 1,800 reported war crimes committed by Communist forces during the conflict. Four men lived through the ordeal. The Hill 303 Massacre had been preceded a few days earlier by the marching off of a handful of American prisoners, presumably for execution. The identity and fate of those men is unknown.

"There!" He rocked his body and wiggled his arm enough that he thought he might be able to get himself free soon. He rested.

He dreamed he was the relief pitcher. The manager was handing him the ball. *Who is this man? What is his name? I know him.*

"Son, you are gonna need to suck it up and pitch these last three innings." *I looked over and it was just me and a catcher in the fenced warm-up area.* "We've got a one run lead, but I got nobody else in the bullpen." He spit chewing tobacco juice on the ground. "It's up to you, Kid. I'm counting on ya. You've done it before, you can do it now. Whatdoyasay?"

He rested and collected his strength. He kept fading in and out. "I can do it, Coach!" *What is his name?*

Abraham slowly slipped his body from what was trapping him. He stood. He couldn't remove his helmet--it wouldn't budge. His head hurt, his thirst overwhelming--like he had eaten sandpaper and his tongue and throat were sticking. He looked down. "Shit, are you alright, Pal?"

The body did not respond to his push, nor speak. It was covered with blood, mostly dry, but with large saturated, sticky spots. That's when he noticed the other three men. *Who are these guys? Why are they here? Where am I?* A pair of broken glasses were on the ground. *"Who do those belong to?"* He could hear rumbling and wondered what it was. He looked around. *Hey, look--a river!*

His thirst was overwhelming and he yearned for water. He began to slowly walk, feeling pain throughout his body. *Stay focused,* he told himself. *Walk to the water.* He crossed in front of men with rifles. *Focus on the water. What are they doing here? They don't look like hunters. They look like soldiers. Why are they here?*

More than one soldier raised his rifle and pointed it at Abraham's chest, before startling, "No! He's American. Don't shoot. Where is he going?"

He steadily stumbled toward the river. Maybe it was the roar of the river that drew him in that direction; perhaps it was the smell of which he wasn't even conscious. He couldn't get down to it. *Damn. There is a bridge, maybe from the other side I can get there.* He walked across the bridge. *Oh, look there, here comes a car. Funny convertible. Hey, that's a*

Jeep. What is that doing here?

"You okay, Buddy?"

"Water."

"Sure. What happened to you?" He unscrewed the top of the canteen and handed it to Abraham, who drank it ravenously.

"I said, what happened?"

"Don't know."

The driver took back his canteen. He noticed the man was covered with dried blood.

"Sit down." He patted the seat. Abraham slowly climbed in.

"Water."

The driver handed him back the canteen. "What's your name?" Abraham gave him a blank stare. The jeep driver drove to the far end of the bridge and called in help on his radio.

His second time traveling in a Bell H-13 Helicopter, it carried MASH markings on the side, medical evacuation panniers (one on each skid), and an acrylic patient shield.

"I can't get the shield to lock."

"Why?"

"We can't get his helmet off!"

"What?"

"Yeah, it is like it's clamped onto his scull!"

"Shit!"

"Well. I don't know what to tell ya. Strap him down as much as you can and block the shield with cloth so it isn't banging him in the head. He doesn't have far to go."

Abraham fell asleep in the pannier and was jostled awake after the twenty-minute trip by soldiers preparing to carry him away.

"I don't know what to do next, Colonel."

"What do ya mean?"

"The helmet. We tried soap, axle grease, ropes. I'm afraid we'll bust his neck or scull if we put any more pressure on it." Three bullets had ricocheted off the helmet, just above the rim. The blasts had contorted the composite steel like a bear trap onto his head, but nothing penetrated the shell. "Damnest thing I ever saw. I do have an idea, though." He ran to the closest phone.

"You want me to what?"
"See if you can help get this soldier's helmet off!"
"Billy, are you shittin' me? If I get over there and..."
"No, Chris, this is legit."
"Okay, mix me a martini and I'll be there in fifteen."
"It's in the shaker."

"Well, I'll be damned."
"Ain't that the strangest thing you ever saw." He looked it over carefully for thirty minutes before asking for a dozen tongue depressors. He carefully jammed the tongue depressors between Abraham's scull and the helmet. "Have you got some chalk?"
"Somewhere here, we must."
He carefully marked two opposing points on the helmet. "Now I need your phone."

"You can fix me a second martini while we wait."
"So, what's going on?"
"I have two specialty hydraulic jacks in Seoul. They are gonna get those, some pipes, and a few other items, and drive them over."
"How big?"
"Small, fit in a toolbox."
"Heavy?"
"Nah.
"Tell'm we're sending a helicopter."
"I'll call; you stir."

When the helicopter arrived, Colonel Christopher Callum ran out to receive the requested tools. He examined them as he strode into the operating room and came back out in a few minutes carrying the helmet. "Amazing what you can do with the right tools." He handed the helmet to the assembled doctors, who looked and passed it around. "It jerry-rigged pretty good. Didn't have to flex the steel much before it slipped right off his head."
"Who is the soldier?"
"They don't know. Haven't found his dog tags."
"Well, whoever the hell he is; he is one lucky son-of-a-bitch."

They found his dog tags later when they got off his clothes. Chris was just finishing his third martini when Billy returned. "2nd lieutenant Cash. Abraham George Cash is his name."

"How is he gonna be?"

"Hard to tell. Could have severe brain injuries, mild concussion, or anything in between."

"Chris, that was great work. Here. You deserve this." He handed him the helmet as a souvenir.

"Good God! What are they doing?" exclaimed Major General Bryant Edward Moore, Superintendent of the United States Military Academy at West Point, as he stood up from his chair while reading the dispatch that had been dropped on his desk a few minutes before. He thought of his own daughters and what their reactions would be if this was happening to one of them. "Higgins! Get in here! Now!"

Higgins came running. "Hig, read this! Why don't they think? They are sending a bicycle courier with this right now to Nichols' daughter!"

"My gosh!"

"Take somebody to Colonel Nichols's class to relieve him and send him to be with her immediately!"

"Yes, Sir!"

The doorbell rang. Mel was home alone, doing laundry. She vaguely heard the doorbell. Her blue jeans were rolled up to mid-calf, she wore a wrinkled white blouse, bedroom slippers, and a large bandana. The day was sunny and warm. She was carrying a basket taking laundry out to the line, when she heard the doorbell ring a second time and a muffled yell, "Telegram!" She dropped the basket and came to the front door, expecting a friend playing a joke. They never received telegrams. She opened the door and squinted against the mid-afternoon sun.

"Melbourne Cash?"

She still wasn't used to her new name. "Yes?"

"Telegram, Ma'am."

He reached out with an envelope and she took it as the courier spun around and was gone in an instant. 'What the heck could this be?' she wondered as she tore it open. She scanned the tan Western Union form.

GOVT - WUX WEST POINT NY 1028A
MRS MELBOURNE CASH
4 HICKORY ST HIGHLAND FALLS NY

Her heart began pounding and she felt lightheaded.

= REGRET TO INFORM YOU YOUR HUSBAND 2ND LT ABRAHAM CASH
"Oh Gawd"
SUSTAINED SEVERE HEAD INJURY IN ACTION IN KOREA PERIOD YOU
"Dear God, NO!"
WILL BE ADVISED AS REPORTS OF CONDITION ARE RECEIVED:

She could feel her legs buckling, darkness and stars came to her eyes.
= WITSELL THE ADJUTANT GENERAL

The Colonel came running in the back door. She was on the floor, the telegram fluttering in her fingers

Over the next six months Abraham was moved from field hospitals to military hospitals in Korea, Japan, Hawaii, California, and Maryland, before Mel saw him again.

Inside the South Korean Hospital tent a doctor held up the head X-ray, "I have never seen anything like this!"

"Like what?" the MASH surgeon asked.

"I'm a pediatrician. We see infants and young children trauma cases with widening of scull sutures. But look--every suture is open!" He pointed out the openings to his associate.

"Jesus! Why is this x-ray so white?"

"That is the other thing. It is not a flawed x-ray. His whole scull is microfractured--they are everywhere! Ever take a marble and heat it up, then drop it into very cold water? That's what this looks like."

"Yes. And look here." He took him to the head of the bed and used both hands to point out marks on Abraham's head. "Two relatively small depression fractures on opposing sides of the scull."

"Is this the guy they had to pry the helmet off?"

"They didn't pry it off. This happened in the shooting."

"Think he'll live?"

"Hard to tell. Probably not. We'll give him as much relief as we can."

Abraham had bleeding from his ears and nose, with bruises everywhere on his head, but especially dark around the eyes and ears.

"And they said they found this guy walking?" As he cut through the skin.

"Yeah."

"Unbelievable! Damn. Look at this dura?"

"Shit." It was embedded with thousands of slivers of bone. "What do we do?"

"Close him up. If we go any further, his scull is gonna crumble in our hands."

"How can he survive?"

"He can't."

"I wonder if he will ever regain consciousness."

"Yeah. Been two weeks."

"His scull is so unstable we don't dare move him."

"I doubt he'll ever regain consciousness."

"Be a blessing if he doesn't." The other doctor could not disagree.

A few days later Abraham began having convulsions.

"Is this the end?"

"Probably. Scull is so fragile he is likely to bleed to death from convulsion-induced brain hemorrhages."

"Should we tie him down?"

The doctor thought for quite a while before answering. "It would be merciful not to. Just let the convulsions take him."

"Standard medical procedure is to immobilize him."

The surgeon mumbled, "Yes, I know." Against their better judgments they strapped him down tightly.

"Is he dead?"

"No. I think he is waking up!"

"What? Impossible!"

The doctor thought, 'Oh gawd, what have I done? God forgive me! I have kept him alive, but he will be a vegetable!'

Slowly he began to awaken for longer periods. The few minute long stretches of consciousness were filled with panicked looks, confusion, vomiting, and collapse. The doctor was not trying to be funny, when he wrote: 'Four-month mark. Blurred vision, balance problems, drowsiness, dramatic changes in pupil size, slurred speech, neck stiffness. Big improvement!' It was unusual to retain a man at a field hospital for so long, but they didn't dare move him. The doctor indicated on the chart it was time to evacuate him to Japan.

Abraham made steady progress for the next two months in Japan, after which he was moved to Hawaii.

"We can't do any more for him here."

"What do you suggest?"

"He is going to have headaches--probably forever."

"No telling what memory he will have when this is done."

"What about rehabilitation?"

"I'm not sure what anyone can do."

"Agreed."

"So, what the hell do we do with him?"

"There is only one thing we can do." He scribbled on the chart: WRAMC. He was sending him off to Walter Reed Army Medical Center.

His parents and wife arrived in Washington, D.C. the day before Abraham did.

"Thanks for coming."

"You are welcome. When can we see Abraham?"

"Hopefully tomorrow." Mel looked disappointed. "He is not here yet."

"But the telegram said--" She held up the telegram.

"I know what the telegram said. I wanted you here ahead of his arrival. To prepare you. He has been making remarkable progress. He has come a long way."

"And?"

"He still has a long way to go. This could also be as far as he ever gets. I need to prepare you for the shock you will experience tomorrow. He may not even--may never--recognize you."

Melbourne stared at the Doctor, while George slumped and Rebecca stiffened. George broke the silence, by quietly asking, "Is there anything we can do?" The doctor had no answers.

The three were sleepless in two adjoining rooms on the sixth floor at the Willard Hotel. Occasionally, George could hear his daughter-in-law nervously coughing, then getting up and running to the bathroom to vomit.

At four-thirty, George got up to order breakfast. "Yes, that is what I said. Next door to my room...I don't care if the kitchen isn't open yet. Get somebody to it!" He slammed down the phone.

Forty minutes later, he heard knocking on Mel's door and he walked to the man standing next to the food cart, handed him a twenty, saying "I'll take it from here."

"Wow, Mister! Thanks!" George could hear Mel running around her room. He knocked. "Just a minute!" He didn't reply. She greeted him with a harried look, which turned into a broad smile.

"Thought you could use some breakfast." She let him in and he gave her a hug. She hung on, as if for dear life. He whispered, "We'll get through this." They held each other while the food cooled.

The newly-installed sign read, "Lieutenant Abraham Cash." He didn't arrive in his room until mid-afternoon. They had been waiting since nine that morning in a sitting room on the first floor. A nurse escorted them to the doctor's office.

"Please be seated. You will be seeing him shortly. We sedated him during his train ride and he is coming around now. The bandages around his head have been removed, but you will see some distortion." All three were afraid to ask what that meant. "You will not be able to see him for long. He will likely be drowsy and fall in and out of sleep. It is just the medication, I assure you. In the next days and weeks you will see a marked improvement." His tone wasn't convincing. "I hope you'll see him daily, but visits need to be brief."

"Alright."

"He will not be able to eat until tomorrow. Perhaps you can come at meal time? Well, I guess this is the time you have been waiting for." He stood and escorted them to a semi-private room. The man in the next bed was awake and acknowledged their arrival.

Abraham's eyes were closed and he startled to the new noise in the room. He slowly opened his eyes and instantly recognized Rebecca. He started to form words, but the effort was beyond him. He stared at his mother. His head was lopsided, but she hoped her reaction did not come across. She smiled and he tried to smile back, but his eyes grew heavy with the effort and he blinked slowly instead.

"Darling, you look so good. We are so happy to see you. Your father and I arrived from Alabama yesterday." She turned to her husband and he followed her eyes. He recognized his father and mustered a better smile this time, but didn't speak. His eyes continued to scan the room. Melbourne and Abraham's eyes met, and her heart leapt! He looked at her softly and formed his words slowly, "A-nd who arh you, Miss?"

Mel visited him twice every day. She talked to him and held his hands. She showed him pictures from their wedding album. "Do you remember this?"

He didn't want to tell her no, so he simply said, "I'm trying."

She fought back tears by biting her lip and replied, "I know you are."

"Do you remember the chapel?"

"West Point?"

"Right! Do you remember the minister who married us?"

"No."

"That's alright. Neither do I!" She laughed. "It hasn't even been a year yet." She pointed out people in the pictures from the wedding and he struggled to remember. She closed the book.

"Do you remember our honeymoon?" He did not reply.

"We went to New York City. Look--this is the cabin we stayed at in the Catskills." She opened the album to show him. He gave her a blank stare, which answered the question she had not asked. "I'll bet you remember The Thayers!" She dropped the book, took his hands and cupped them around her breasts. He pulled his hands away, confused and embarrassed.

That afternoon, two doctors came in while Mel sat next to her husband. They checked his progress and made notes. Once they left the room, one doctor said, "Remarkable. He remembers things learned at West Point, but he can't remember her."

"And how could you forget her?"

Mel worked with Abraham day and night for the next four months.

"Mrs. Cash, when you are done there I'd like to see you in my office." A few minutes later she walked into the doctor's office and sat in his guest chair.

"Mrs. Cash. I think it is time for Abraham to go home."

Mel frowned. "We don't have a home."

"Where have you been staying?"

"At the Willard. I've kept a small room."

"I see. Perhaps you could take him to his parents?" She shrugged. "What I mean is, you are doing a great job with his rehabilitation--better than we could. He is coming along well. The next step is to return him to a familiar environment."

"He hasn't had a familiar environment in five or six years. He was at West Point, in dorms. Then Korea. He has spent the last year in hospitals."

"Well. I don't know what to tell you. I suggest you rent a house where you and he can live as husband and wife."

"He still doesn't remember ever being married to me." She couldn't hold back her tears from streaming down her cheeks.

The doctor swallowed hard and handed her a tissue. "I'm sorry. He needs to be with you, now, if you ever expect to have a marriage with him."

"What?" She was startled by his comment.

"He is at a vulnerable place right now. He is beginning to reform interests. You need to be one of those interests, if I may be blunt."

She rented a house in Washington, D.C. that afternoon. It was small, single-level, and quiet. He wasn't experiencing balance problems any longer, but she was concerned he might fall. Their first night together, he lay looking at the ceiling.

"Can't sleep?" She snuggled up next to him. She was nervous. 'Give him time,' she thought. She fell asleep as he stiffly lay trying not to disturb her. The next night was no better, nor the next. After a week both were looking weary and haggard. She visited his doctor to explain the situation as best she could.

"I see. Well, Mrs. Cash. I think you need to talk to Nurse Bedford. Give me a few minutes to speak with her. I'll send her in."

Nurse Bedford came in shortly. She was course and crude by nature, swearing like a sailor to the delight of the sailors. Making seductive remarks to the joy of men who might never be rehabilitated to enable normal relations again. But she could also be gentle. She'd been married over thirty years and the years had not been kind--overweight, smoked too much. Sitting in the doctor's chair she leaned forward and reached out her hands to Mel. "Honey. I'm afraid you are going to have to take matters into your own hands."

Melbourne stopped by the department store on the way home. She fixed a wonderful dinner, with all his favorite foods. Instead of their usual regiment of rehabilitation exercises in the evening, she put a record on the player. She sat next to him on the davenport. He was curious about the changes tonight. She kept reaching over to touch him. She spoke quietly. When he grew tired, she took him by the hand and walked him to their bed.

"Lay back and relax. I'll be right back." She left the nightstand light on, but he reached over to turn it off. "No." He stopped. "Lay down. I won't be long." She returned a few minutes with her hair and teeth brushed, wearing a new nightgown. "Do you like this?"

He hadn't given it a thought. "Yes, it's pretty."

"Dear, there are some things a husband and wife--" She stopped and dropped her nightgown on the floor. He looked at her curiously. Returning to the bed she began to unbutton his pajama top. He reached up. "I'll do that." She pushed his hands down gently. She slid her hands onto his chest. He was still and weary. She slowly, carefully worked her way down his body, allowing him time to relax before methodically moving to the next level. Periodically she took his hands and placed them to her breasts. She pressed his fingers against her erect nipples. When she reached his pajama bottoms, she pulled them down as he looked on curiously. She kissed and straddled him. She kept kissing him and rubbing her breasts against his chest. She began to notice his reaction. "You see, you have equipment made for me," she reached down and stroked his penis, "and I have equipment made for you." The lessons continued every night for a week, until he began to initiate the process.

During the day, she continued rebuilding his memory, through recall and reinforcement. It was an arduous process, with many starts and stops.

She received an answer she didn't want to hear to a series of her questions and she called her father.

"Nichols here."

"Daddy, I need to talk."

"Now is a good time. Don't have a class for forty-five minutes. Mel, how are you? How is Abraham doing today?"

"We're both fine, Daddy."

"Good."

"Daddy, he wants to resume his army career."

There was a long pause, before Mack Jack asked, "You had been expecting that, hadn't you?"

"No. Yes! Oh, I don't know!"

"Mel, I have been expecting this from the day he came home."

"Really?"

"Yes. Mel, it is the only thing he knows. He has to do it." She couldn't speak. "Dear, it doesn't mean it will be permanent. Nor does it mean the Army will let him. But he must try. He has to get back up on the horse."

The Army physicians cleared him medically. They watched his physical, mental, and emotional progress carefully. Colonel Nichols thought he had a great idea and called friends. Soon orders arrived for 1st Lieutenant Abraham George Cash. He had been promoted during his convalescence and was ordered to be an instructor for Basic Training at Fort

Sill, Oklahoma.

The physical rigors of basic training were good for Abraham. Laura came along in 1953 and Juliann a year later.

George and Rebecca asked their children to return to their home each year for Christmas beginning in 1955. Each had come a few times, but not on a consistent basis. They visited one another, but family hadn't been together since Abraham's West Point graduation in 1950.

Penny was six months pregnant. "I thought ministers always had lots of kids! What's taken you so long?"

"Hasn't been for lack of trying!"

"Must lack 'know-how!'" smirked George. "I told you everything you needed. Guess I should have shown you!"

"George!" scolded Rebecca.

"Okay, okay. Just look at those two lovely girls Abraham and Mel have blessed us with!"

"Yeah. Bullets only hit him in the head. Missed all his vital organs." Everyone laughed.

"Just remember boys what you promised."

Melbourne leaned over to Abraham, smiling, "Do you remember what you promised?"

"No."

"George, what did he promise?"

"He didn't tell you?"

"No."

George looked her in the eyes, "Each of my boys has promised me that if they have sons, I get to name them." Mel looked stunned, thinking 'What an odd request!'

Penny gave birth to Andrew Cash on March 14, 1956. He had curly, brown hair and was long and lanky from the start--and stayed that way his entire life. Later that year, Thomas changed his family's last name from Cash to Buck. He had been advised that Cash was not a good name for preachers and evangelists.

"Your name reminds people that preachers always have

their hand out! You need to change it, or you're not gonna go far." He asked his father what he should do.

"It kinda makes sense to me." Cash had been the name George had selected, but while he had gotten used to it, he wasn't that attached to it.

"Do you have any suggestions?"

He thought of reverting back to his birth name, but decided against it as it would raise questions about why he had changed it in the first place. "No."

Over the next few weeks, Thomas came up with 'Buck'--"You know. Kind of a play on the Cash theme. Rugged. Short and to the point. Even Penny likes it."

"Good."

In the spring of 1957, Mel suggested to Abraham. "How about if we take a trip to Idaho soon?"

"Idaho?"

"Yeah. I have been hearing stories from your mother. She was telling me about how she used to pack a picnic lunch for George, just the two of them, take the wagon and horse to a favorite spot."

"You? You?"

"Yes!"

They began thinking up girls names.

"If we have a boy, we are going to name him, right?" Abraham looked away. "I mean, he's not going to hold you to your promise, is he?" He shrugged. "At least let me have veto power."

"He has always picked good names, hasn't he?"

"That's beside the point."

"Come on! Indulge the old man his quirks!" He poked her in the arm.

"Yeah! We may live to regret it!"

Later that spring, Penny announced she was also pregnant. The family teased about a race between Penny and Mel to see who would deliver first. Penny won by two days, giving birth to their daughter, Dorothea. They called her Dodie.

Two weeks before Thanksgiving in 1957, Melbourne Dawn gave birth to a boy. His grandfather named him:

Ulysses.

EIGHT

As George and Rebecca's youngest son, Alexander, was about to graduate from high school, he grew moody and reserved. Usually fun-loving and always the family jokester, he now withdrew. Colleges recruited him to play baseball, as did professional major league scouts, but he was undecided. There were too many good options before him. He was unsure which path to take or even how to choose. The whole family had seen him struggle and tried to get him to talk about how he felt, but he wouldn't. They waited until he was ready.

"Dad, can we talk."

"Sure," mumbled George, without looking up from his book.

"Could we take a drive?"

George took off his reading glasses and looked at him. "I'll get my keys."

George let Alexander drive and they spoke little as they headed south to the Gulf of Mexico and turned west. Finally he pulled up to a secluded cliff overlooking the water and turned off the engine. He turned in his seat toward his father. "Dad, I don't want to go into the family business with you."

The comment caught George off guard. He hadn't even considered asking Alexander to do so. "That's fine."

"I really hate what you did during the War!" George remained quiet. He wondered how much he knew and where he came upon the information. "How could you sell to the Nazis?" He asked it not in an accusatory way, but inquisitively.

George looked down, wanting to tell the truth. In his

mind, he said to Andrew, 'I've asked myself that question a million times. I follow the path of least resistance. Done it all my life. Anything that took me away from hunger and my father's beatings was better than the life I had. Duplicity in trading with the enemy was easy. I learned to profit on the backs of dead American soldiers'.

Instead it came out as if it were a good, even noble, calling. "There are certain things that can be done by playing both sides. During the war we delivered American spies all over Europe, Africa, and the Mediterranean." Alexander's eyes grew wide. "At the start of the war, it was something our government couldn't do. But we could."

"I never heard that. But you also sold the enemy guns and bomb materials."

"We never sold guns. I can't say I am proud of what I did. But it was necessary," he lied.

"I heard you supplied materials that killed American Soldiers."

"We sold materials to make bombs and munitions. We sold coal, tungsten, and diamonds for industrial equipment. All that is true." He then stretched the truth, "It was the only way to get spies, equipment, and materials into belligerent areas that would help our side."

"Did the government know what you were doing?"

"Yes, of course. They even gave us papers that sanctioned our work." Alexander hugged his father tightly.

As he rode back, George was angry with himself over the half-truths he had told. He didn't have a better explanation to give him, that wouldn't alienate his son. He couldn't bring himself to tell his son the truth. George asked, "What do you think about taking a trip to Europe?" It was something he had wanted to do for some time. "A father-son adventure." Alexander liked that thought, if for no other reason than to escape the immediate decision he faced.

George said, "I would like to see Europe, before it all gets rebuilt. While the scars still remain. Do you know what I mean?" Part of it was to see the damage he had done.

"Yes."

"I hope we will have peace. But I doubt that's possible. We've got the Russians still to deal with. I don't think it is going to go smoothly."

"Will you continue in your business?"

"I'm not sure what I am going to do." George continued to transport goods on a small scale, but had given up smuggling after the war.

As he planned the trip, George wished he had paid better attention to where Jack's Castle was located. He knew it was near Costa Brava, Spain. Looking on the map he found London, Southhampton, Cherbourg, Paris and Barcelona. He scribbled a quick note about Pyrénées-Orientales.

In October 1957, they sailed on the last remaining schooner from Jack's fleet for New York City. Alexander enjoyed the sailing, as well as layovers in Miami and Myrtle Beach. George regaled Alexander with accounts of Jack steering Government Cut in Miami Bay as if he were a pirate. Later that month they left for Southampton on the RMS Queen Mary.

London had normal weather for that time of year--cloudy and rainy. They spent a week seeing the city. George was introspective as they walked through war-ravaged areas that were being turned into parks.

"Dad, why are you so quiet?"

"Just sad to see the damage." He thought to himself, 'How much of this did I cause?'

"Which were worse, the German bombers or the missiles?"

"I am sure both were terrifying."

"Looking at the holes here, it sure looks like the bombs were effective during the Blitz."

"What you are looking at are the empty spaces where whole neighborhoods once lived."

"Wow!"

"But even as the raids were going on, the British reported production of weapons and war materials rose steadily. So I am not sure how effective they were. They certainly terrorized people."[49]

"Do you believe all that stuff about the British being stoic during the attacks?"

"Not really. I believe they were brave in what they faced.

---

[49] Luftwaffe dropped 41,000 tons of bombs during the Blitz.

They didn't run away in large numbers or revolt against their government. They didn't surrender. But I think they probably reacted as you or I would--scared and worn down by it."[50]

"I suppose so."

"The V-1's would have given me the creeps."

"Why?"

"They were launched from ramps across the channel in France pointed to London. They were just bombs that looked like small planes. They buzzed as they flew. Put enough gas in them so they would run out over their target and rain down on their victims. Boom! Whole blocks disappeared."[51]

After England, George and Alexander traveled to Cherbourg, where they walked quietly through graveyards on the bluffs above Normandy's beaches. American soldiers had been laid to rest in long rows of white crosses and stars of David. They walked through broken concrete bunkers where the Germans placed machine guns against beach landings. The following day they looked at crumbled concrete launch sites near Pas-de-Calais.

They spent the next week in Paris, enjoying food--especially the salmon, breads, cheeses, and wines. The City of Lights had been spared much of the damage that wrecked the rest of Europe. They enjoyed music and the

---

[50] The myth of stoicism, intended to reinforce calm during the storm, was an organized effort on the part of the British government. Anti-social, divisive behaviors, and lowering morale were driven by lack of sleep, insufficient bomb shelters, and inefficient warning systems.

[51] In June 1944, Londoners started hearing strange noises they believed to be burning aircraft arching across the sky. It was the first vengeance weapon, code named by British Intelligence "Diver" in retaliation for the D-Day assault. They were essentially cruise missiles; launched with minimal guidance after takeoff. Hitler ordered concrete launching bunkers built in Pas-de-Calais (Northern France) under the codename "Cherry Stone." Hidden in forests they were easily spotted and bombed. Nazis designed mobile ramps.

Their pulse jet engines ran on gasoline (saving aviation fuel) and made a distinctive sound. Pulsing fifty times a second, they buzzed. They became known as Doodlebugs; a common term for insects. They resembled dragonflies. More than one hundred V-1s were fired at southeastern England daily during the peak; 9,521 in total. 6,184 Londoners were killed and 17,981 injured.

theater. During the days they walked the streets, marveling at the architecture and history

George and Alexander took the train from Gare de Lyon and spent a week in Lyon relaxing, feasting on local delights--Rosette Lyonnaise, Saucisson de Lyon, and Cardoon au Gratin. The only dish Alexander turned his nose up to was Gras Double (tripe with onions). They enjoyed theatres, museums, and talking. At the end of the week they found themselves sitting at the base of an equestrian statue of Louis XIV in Place Bellecour. George asked, "Have you been thinking about your future?"

"Yes."

"And what do you think?"

"I love baseball, but I don't want to play it professionally. There can't be any money in that!"

"I guess Babe Ruth did alright for himself."

"Sure, but he is the exception. Made more than the President!"

"Yes. His home run record will stand forever."

"Dad, I am more convinced than ever not to join you in the business, but I feel like an opportunity will come along soon."

"College?"

"Yes, I want to do that."

"Good enough. I am glad you want to go to college."

"You have given yourself a college education, with all the reading you do!"

"I'm not so sure. Yes, I read a lot. It keeps the mind active. But the more history I read, the more I find we don't learn from it."

"I have a good feeling this trip will help me decide what I want to do with my life."

"Wonderful! I'm glad." He also thought, 'I wish I knew what I wanted to do with mine!'

They didn't rush through the next leg of their trip, but

getting to see Jack was constantly on George's mind. As they headed across the border into Spain, George told his son about his plans.

"I'd like to hire a boat to take us along the coast."

"Very good, Mr. Cash." After brief negotiations, they settled on a price and the Captain assembled his crew. They sailed within a half mile of the shore.

George had only seen Jack's place from the water, and he wasn't convinced he would be able to identify it after this many years. The first thing he noticed was the polished cliff. He tried to make out a path leading to the top, but couldn't spot it. He looked carefully at the orange and cream slabs of rock that comprised the buildings walls and the red tile roof.

"Could you slow the boat?"

"I can."

He still wasn't sure it was Jack's. "Turn and take us away from the cliff, then head straight in toward that house." He pointed to the massive home on the cliff. From further out, he could see almond and olive groves, a rolling hillside and mature vineyards behind the house. He hesitated. "No, this must be it." George told his son to get ready. "I want you to row us into that cove. You may drop us off."

"When would you like us to pick you up?"

He took another look at the place, to convince himself. "I don't. You are free to go."

They trudged up the hillside path, each carrying a suitcase. They were met at the top of the hill by a prematurely white-haired lady. She was slim, tan and wore a light-weight, off-white cape which partially covered her Capri pants and white peasant blouse. She was barefoot and wore solid silver earrings and a matching long necklace. George couldn't figure out how old she was--thirty or seventy.

She stood staring at the two men as they finished their assent, when a heavily armed guard leveled his rifle at the men. Before he could speak, she raised her right hand to her brother and quietly said, in English, "It is fine! These are friends, I am sure."

He glared at the two, then lowered his rifle. "I'll be nearby if you need me."

"Won't you come in?" With that she lead them into the house and offered them dark, red wine. "It's from my own vineyard."

"Thank you. But, I am not sure we are at the right place."
She paused. Quietly and slowly she said, "You are."
"Have we met before?"
"No." He started to speak, but she raised her hand to cut him off. "I have been expecting you."
George remained quiet and his eyes widened. "I am not sure you understand; I am a married man and--"
"Your bedrooms are up the stairs and to the left. Welcome to Catalunya Castillo de Jacques. Rest and clean up. Dinner is in two hours." She walked outside.

🐈 🐈 🐈 🐈 🐈 🐈

As Alexander entered his bedroom, he kicked off his tennis shoes and tossed his small, brown suitcase on the floor where it tipped on its side. Fully dressed he flopped onto the bed and slept like a rock from the instant his head hit the pillow. Someone knocked on the bedroom doors in the upstairs hall before seven, "Dinner is in five minutes." He had drooled on the pillow and his mind was in a haze, 'Five minutes' and 'I could eat' and 'where am I?' His father had come to his room, looked over the small desk, the knickknacks, and the paintings on the wall. He was nervous and anxious to see Jack, whenever he would return. The lady of the house was pleasant enough, but she seemed to be melancholy and distant. She didn't even introduce herself, he thought. He felt he was forced to oblige her request and spend his time waiting in the bedroom. She disappeared so quickly; obviously not ready to answer questions. He had looked out the window and the view was glorious--vineyards, old trees, sweeping hills, cliffs, the azure sea, whitecaps, and seagulls. Time passed slowly as he sat on the bed, until the rap on his door interrupted his trance. He washed his face in the adjoining bathroom and patted it dry with the fluffy, coral-color, cotton towel.

He was met by a slim, middle-aged man wearing dark slacks, white-shirt, bow tie and a short coat. "Dinner will be on the terrace. Señora is waiting there for you." A black-and-white cat came up to George and rubbed against his leg. "That is Sweetie."

The terrace was a glass-enclosed sun-room, with olivewood plank floors, and pots with grapevines climbing up the window casings. There were translucent curtains that flowed in the breeze of the open windows. A glass-topped, white, wrought-iron table was in the center of the room, with place settings for four, and white wicker chairs with yellow cushions.

"Welcome, George. I'm Natania. Sit here next to me." She pointed to a chair. He extended his hand to shake hers, and she held it there for him to kiss. He obliged her nervously, and pulled out his chair to sit. She pointed to a photo album at his place. "This is how I knew who you were."

He lifted it to the light. It was open to a picture of him and Jack, from when he was first married. He grinned and looked at other pictures in the album. "These are wonderful. I don't remember seeing these before."

"Jack didn't have many, but he loved them." Alexander walked into the terrace. "And is this your son?"

"Yes. Alexander this is--I'm sorry, forgive me--I have forgotten your name already."

"Natania. Natania Evans."

"Natania, this is my son, Alexander Cash."

"So pleased to meet you. You look like your father."

"Will Uncle Jack be joining us?"

"Only in spirit. He died long ago."

"Oh--" George gasped.

"I'm sorry. It must come as quite a shock."

"Yes. It has been a long while. I shouldn't have assumed--" his voice petered out. Coming to himself he said, "I am so sorry for your loss."

"Thank you. I will take you to his grave site in the morning. It was a spot he particularly loved. He had a hammock and he used to lay there looking at the sea for hours at a time. It was so peaceful for him." She drifted off, thinking of the times she had fallen asleep in his arms. Only a few days, but precious.

Alexander tried to ease them back from the awkward moment, "I love your home."

"Yes, it is beautiful, isn't it? Jack picked just the right place. But I miss him."

"Of course. It must get lonely here."

"No, I have my daughter to keep me company."

"How did Jack die?"

"Oh, here she is now! I would like you to meet Jacqueline."

The men stood and turned to watch Jacqueline glide into the room. Both their mouths dropped open, but for different reasons. She had her mother's complexion. Every other feature was identical to Jack, especially her piercing light blue eyes. George blurted out, "Gosh, she is the spitting image of Jack!"

Alexander's mouth dropped open with a different thought, 'My gawd, she's gorgeous!'

🐈 🐈 🐈 🐈 🐈 🐈

"Maximilian, we are ready."

The chef entered the room, carrying four wooden bowls, announcing "Spinach salad with grape and almond dressing."

"Wonderful! Maximilian takes such good care of us." He was the same man who knocked on their doors and greeted George by the stairs.

As they finished the salad, he appeared again, rolling a cart, "Olive-and-almond roasted serrana estriado." He leaned over between the two men and whispered, "Black sea bass." He swirled to pick up plates while he stood up to continue his announcement, "With rice-and-mint stuffed grape leaves."

The cat came into the room and rubbed against Natania. "Mind your manners, now. I am sure Maximilian has a piece for you, Sweetie." The cat trotted off to the kitchen as if she fully understood.

Maximilian returned every few minutes to check on his guests, making sure their wine and water glasses were always full. He stooped again so only George and Alexander could hear his whisper, "The rosé wine is from Señora Natania's vineyard." He cleared his throat," ¡Salud!"

"Everything is delicious."

"Yes, he is a wonderful chef! I am so pleased to have him here. He and his wife live downstairs. She is a delightful

244

woman and it is nice to have a man around. Her name is Suzanne. But you won't see either of them much. They prepare meals and tend to themselves. Then, of course, there is always Ramón."

"Ramón?"

"Yes. You met him. When you first arrived." George gave her a puzzled look. "He greeted you with a rifle."

"Ahhhh."

"Yes. That is my brother. He was the foreman when Jack built this place and he makes sure I am safe."

That brought him back to the question he still hadn't heard answered. "You were about to tell me how Jack died."

Maximilian reappeared, "I have piña al ron for dessert!" He leaned over to whisper, "Pineapple and rum over cake. Coffee?"

Natania answered, "It is getting cool out here. We'll take it inside."

Even though they talked for two more hours, Natania never answered George's question.

"There was nobody after Jack. Who could follow Jack? He was a man's man! ¡Era un hombre de hombre! Oh, what a lover he was!"

Jacqueline blushed, "Oh, Mother!"

Natania swallowed more wine, "Well, it's true!"

There was a question George wanted to ask, but didn't know how to say gracefully. "How have you gotten on?"

Natania sensed his discomfort and eased it along, "Jack told me where he had buried his gold. As I have needed anything, I have sold a bar of it. My brother does it for me."

"Ramón?"

"Yes. He takes it far away, so nobody will know where it has come from. He backtracks on his way home to evade anyone that might follow."

"Have there been some?"

"He thinks so. But he has always lost them. I have only needed to sell a few bars. There will be a lot more for Jacqueline, even when I am gone."

"Aren't you worried about it being found and stolen?"

She raised her glass for another gulp, "No. Jack was very, very clever!" With that, she drained her glass. "It is late. ¡Buenas noches! George, I will see you in the morning. We will go to Jack's grave."

George and Alexander began to rise.

"Don't get up. Jacqueline, tell Alexander about yourself. It is a nice evening for a stroll along the beach. Take the lantern." She had seen the looks they had been giving each other. With that, she dashed from the room.

The following morning George came downstairs and saw Natania, already on the terrace, reading and drinking coffee.

"Buenos días."

"Buenos días, indeed! What a gorgeous day!"

"Coffee?"

"Please!"

"I have had Maximilian prepare breakfast just the way you like it?"

"Oh?"

"Yes. It was one of Jack's favorites, too; although it is not easy to get on short notice. When you first arrived I told Maximilian what he would need to do and he took the shotgun along the cliffs." She turned her head, "Maximilian, we are ready!"

He arrived with two large plates. "I'll bring coffee and juice next. Eggs. Toast with creamery butter. Potatoes sautéd in olive oil with garlic. Roast rabbit!" George's mouth watered and his eyes got big.

They enjoyed their breakfast.

"What time is it?"

"Almost eight."

"I slept like a rock."

"Good! So did I."

"Where are the kids?"

"Alexander and Jacqueline? I am not sure they came in last night." George frowned. She patted him on the forearm. "It is fine. They built a fire on the beach. They talked a long time. They are sailing now."

"Sailing?"

"Yes. They will probably fish and bring home dinner. Maybe they will swim later. I don't expect to see much of them today."

"Oh?"

"You don't mind them getting acquainted, do you?" She gave him a sheepish grin.

He shot one back, "Not at all!"

"Are you ready for a walk?"

"Yes," said George as his eyes lit up at the thought of stretching his legs. Natania placed her arm in George's and led him away.

"My parents were both killed in the war."

"I'm sorry."

"I don't know what happened to my other brothers. Ramón is all I have left."

George patted her arm. "And Jacqueline."

"Yes, of course. I meant those older than me. When Jack was--when Jack died, a part of me died. I knew I was--how do you say it?--'With child'. I was glad Jack had left me a part of himself."

"She does look like him."

"Yes! That is my blessing. I wonder if she had looked like me if she would have..." She trailed off. "She has always been my blessing and my constant reminder of Jack."

"When were you married?"

"We weren't. There wasn't time for that. He died shortly after he came here to live."

"How did he die?"

"We're here."

They had built a monument with large rocks. Granite stones were piled together eight feet long. It served as a wall. The monument attached to the stone wall was about seven feet high, shaped like a dome, hollow, with a narrow opening.

"I had his name engraved on this rock." It was at the entrance, etched in bold relief. "I don't think he was of my faith, but I built a shrine to the Virgin Mary for him anyway." They entered the simple alcove where a clay statue stood on a shelf--painted shiny blue, red, and tan. It was course and gaudy, he thought. Natania crossed herself.

He recognized candle holders and flowers in small vases. There was something else on the shelf he couldn't make out in the dim light. "What is this?"

"It is a picture frame. I'll bring it outside." She lifted the frame and placed something that had been draped over it on her arm.

It was a picture of the two of them--the only photo she had. He looked happy. He was looking at her. She was laughing, with her head thrown back. The frame was simple--light brass with a wooden inlay, which was now nearly worn away.

"What's this?" He pointed to what she had placed on her arm.

"A rope." She hesitated and tears welled up in her eyes. Quietly she said, "Jack was murdered. Strangled. I found this around his neck when I returned from the market. I couldn't throw it away. It took him away from me, yes, but it is also the last thing to touch him while he was alive."

She handed George the rope. He fingered and recognized it instantly--it was unique; rubber coated, double-braided sisal rope from Tanzania. Jack used it to outfit all his ships. He gently handed it all back to her.

Jacqueline and Alexander were inseparable. Sailing, swimming, hiking, and laughing together. They had to pry them away from each other for meals. After two weeks, George was not surprised when Alexander announced he had decided to stay.

"How long?"

"I'm not sure."

"But you will come home?"

"Yes. Well, I think so."

George smiled. "This can be part of your life. But it cannot be all of it. Do you understand?"

"Yes."

"I have always been proud of you, Son."

"I know, Dad."

"I'll be leaving soon."

"Alright."

George told Natania it was time he should be leaving.

"I understand."

He had to admit he had some kind of feelings for her. Maybe he had mixed up his feelings with his feelings for Jack. In any event, it was time to leave. Ramón drove him to Barcelona in a rumpled old Fiat. It was more rust than paint, but the motor purred. They didn't say one word the whole trip. When they arrived at a hotel near the docks, George opened the back and grabbed his suitcase. He extended his hand to Ramón.

Ramón didn't reach back; he smiled slightly with a kindly expression, put the car in first gear, and drove slowly away.

George grinned as he watched the Fiat disappear.

It was many days before George would sail, but he was happy to be going directly to Miami from Barcelona.
"You won't mind being on a small freighter, will you?"
"Not at all!"

As George returned from Europe without Alexander, he mulled over his future. He had made plenty of money during the war, but that cash cow was, for the most part, dead. Regional skirmishes were difficult to manage and high risk, even though they paid well. He had dismissed most of his crews at the end of the war. He still transported goods on his ships, but what he could charge was barely enough to cover expenses--not that he needed money. His only real hobby was reading war histories. He needed something else.

A few weeks later, he received a telephone call from Washington.
"Hello!"
"Is this George Cash?"
"Speaking."
"George, my name is Admiral Timothy Briscoe. We met when I was a very junior officer and adjunct to Admiral McCorley. Do you remember me?"
"I'm afraid I don't."
The Admiral laughed. *"I'm not surprised. My main responsibility was to make sure McCorley had coffee. I'd like to speak with you about a business opportunity."*
"Oh, you are not with the military anymore?"
"Well, that is difficult to explain. Could we meet next week?"
"That would be fine. Where?"
"I'll come get you."

At midnight before his appointment, as he was headed to bed, George noticed two men in a black sedan parked on the street in front of his house. He didn't pay it much mind and nodded off a few minutes later.

At first light, there was a knock at the front door. Rebecca, tending to the coffee pot in the kitchen, grasped her robe tightly around her as she answered the door.

"Yes?" She asked quizzically.

"Good morning, Ma'am. We are here to pick up Mr. George Cash." He had a file folder under his right arm.

"He is in the shower. I'll tell him you are here. Won't you come in?"

"I'll wait out here. Please close the door."

A few minutes later, George came to the front door with a steaming cup of coffee in his hand. He noticed the black sedan was now in his driveway.

"Good morning! My wife tells me you are here for me."

"Please step outside and close the door."

Without saying anything more, the man turned on a flashlight and placed it up to George's face. George winced and moaned involuntarily, but didn't say a word. The man turned the flashlight down to his papers and scanned the photograph attached by staples to the inside cover. Next he reached forward, as if to shake George's hand. Instinctively, George reached his hand out to grasp his, but the man jerked his hand up and grabbed George's right thumb. He started to pull his hand away at the greasy substance being applied to his thumb. "Sorry, Sir. This won't take but a second." He reached into his suit pocket for a 3-by-5 card and pressed it against the ink he had applied to George's right thumb. He matched the card to the thumbprint in the folder. It was identical. He handed George his handkerchief to wipe off the ink, took the coffee cup from George's other hand and placed it on the floor of the porch. "Let's go, Sir."

"Am I under arrest?"

George was locked into the backseat. The two men were quiet in the front; not answering any of George's questions, other than to assure him he was not under arrest. They drove to Point Clear, Alabama and parked off the road near the bay. "We're here." The driver jumped out of his seat and opened the door for George. They walked toward the beach where two 20-person Navy launches were on the shore and four marines were standing guard with submachine guns. He was escorted to the boat on the left. There was a sailor at the helm.

"Get in." George climbed aboard and was handed a life vest. The two men climbed into the other boat, as did the four marines. A few seconds later the two launches were traveling at full speed toward the gulf.

"If I'd only known, I would have brought my pole. I like trolling." The sailor, straining to hear over the noise of the full throttle motor, just smiled. The two launches continued at full speed through the mouth of Mobile Bay and into the Gulf of Mexico, with George's boat in the lead. The land disappeared behind them. In a few minutes George noticed a ship on the horizon. It was the USS Canberra (CAG-2), a Boston class guided missile cruiser, reportedly on 'training exercises' in the Caribbean.

"Welcome aboard the Canberra, Sir. Can I get you anything?"

"Coffee!"

"Have you had breakfast, Sir?"

George ate breakfast by himself in the empty Officer's Mess, while two Marines stood guard nearby. Soon a Navy Officer came to George's table. "How was the chow, Mr. Cash?"

"Excellent!"

"Let me lead you to the head, where you can wash up, and then upstairs."

"Mr. Cash? I'm Admiral Timothy Briscoe. Call me Tim." He reached out his hand.

Taking Tim's hand, he shook it hardily, saying in humor, "We meet again!" Tim got the joke and smiled--neither man remembered meeting the other before.

"This is Mr. Smith and Mr. Jones."

"Are those really their names?"

"They will suffice for now. Please be seated."

"George--May I call you George?"

"Please do."

"George, we have a unique opportunity for you. During the war, you were able to evade detection by us and the enemy. We have attempted to duplicate this, but our efforts keep falling short. We have identified five people or businesses, you included, who seemed to have certain skills we need."

"In what area?"

"I'll get to that."

"First, let me show you the map." He walked over to a large map of the United States mounted on the bulkhead, where five zones were identified.

"Each of you five showed an ability to evade detection while smuggling items in different areas of the country. Here is the Northwest Zone. Where Oregon and Washington meet the Pacific Coast." He pointed to a green line on the map. "And here is the Southwest Zone, where Arizona and New Mexico borders with Mexico." While Briscoe stepped to the other side of the map, George noticed all five green lines on the map. "Here is the Northeast Zone, where Maine and Massachusetts touch the Atlantic. And the Southeast Atlantic Zone. Georgia, South Carolina, North Carolina at the Coast." He stepped away from the map. "We want to offer you the Southeast Gulf Zone. Mississippi, Alabama, and Louisiana at the Gulf of Mexico. This is especially important to us right now, as the Communists are infiltrating our country from Cuba."

"Could I get a pencil and paper?"

"We would rather you not. By the time we are finished, you will have everything you need."

Throughout the day, George learned this was a joint military and CIA project. The job was to annually bring into the United States a 200 pound load, undetected. "We will give you one week to bring your load in." He looked at his notes. "It has to cross from the Gulf of Mexico into Mississippi, Alabama, or Louisiana. Your seven days are December 1-7. On December 7th, mail in where the load can be found. That should be easy for you to remember."

George mumbled, "Yes, a day that will live in infamy."

'Smith and Jones' discussed how to identify the load ahead and after the smuggling effort.

"Well, it has been a long morning. Let's have chow."

The men walked to the Officer's Mess. It was empty with a sign reading 'CLOSED' and two guards at the door. George's questions were met with wide eyes and terse, monosyllabic responses. Once lunch was over, they returned upstairs, "Has it ever occurred to you, that I don't have the skills for this?"

"You don't have it now. But you have shown the resourcefulness to develop it in the past."

"How do I let you know when I am starting to bring my load in?"

"You won't."

"What if I fail?"

"Depending on the nature of the failure, we may not continue on with you the following year. But you can make multiple attempts during your week."

"Do you know how expensive this is going to be?"

"We expect it will be quite expensive."

"How do I get paid?"

"You will send all your invoices to a post office box that will be on your postcard. Three days later you will receive a deposit in your checking account for 140% of the invoice, tax-free."

"Tax-free?"

"Yes, you will be exempt from filing both Federal and State tax returns."

"Including payroll?"

"Yes."

"Can I quit any time?"

"Yes."

"Do I send in a letter?"

"No. Just quit sending invoices. When you don't fulfill your annual transport, you will be taken out of the program."

"And if you discontinue the program?" Neither 'Smith' nor 'Jones' had an answer to this question.

"Will you be monitoring me during the year?"

"No," Smith lied, "only during your assigned week." (In fact, George's every step were monitored in great detail using multiple methods continuously. After the load had been transported, Briscoe would take that into consideration in evaluating the success of each of the five 'targets').

The Gulf was calm at sunset, as George got into the launch. "Here is your postcard. Don't lose it. On the back of the card was a photograph of Admiral Timothy Briscoe in shorts and a Hawaiian shirt on a dock in Key West, Florida with a 494-pound Blue Marlin hoisted next to him. Holding fishing poles on the other side of the Marlin were 'Smith' and 'Jones'. On the reverse side, there was a cancelled three cent

"Win the War" US stamp from 1942. The text in the body of the postcard read, "George, hope to see you December 7th. Wish you were here. All the best! Tim." The card was addressed to "George Cash" at a PO Box in Mobile, Alabama. The address was where he was to mail his invoices.

As the boat returned to Point Clear, George's mind was swirling--about property to buy, boats, balloons, submarines, and planes. The next day, he hired his first and only full-time employee.

🐈 🐈 🐈 🐈 🐈 🐈

Natania had given Jacqueline a well-rounded education; now she included Alexander.

"We will be spending Christmas in Rome this year. Start working on your Italian and Latin. You have two months. I will tutor you on your Italian; Ramón will try his hand at teaching you Latin."

For the next six weeks nothing but Italian was spoken in the home after noon each day.

"Alexander, I fear my brother is turning you into a monk."

Alexander looked at her sheepishly. He knew what she was getting at.

"Has he converted you to the Catholic faith? Are you a monk now? Have you taken a vow of silence each afternoon?"

"Jacqueline parla molto bene."

"Perché non è vero?"

"I don't know."

Soon Natania took a different approach with Alexander. He couldn't spend time with Jacqueline unless his Italian and Latin improved every day. Natania took long walks with Alexander, arm-in-arm, speaking nothing but Italian. With that change he made remarkable progress.

The young couple fell in love with the art and opera during their trip to Rome. Natania loved the pageantry of the Vatican. They all found Rome to be coarse and dirty--dusty, buildings crumbling, polluted, with heavy, noisy traffic, and especially loud, earthy people--and loved it.

The following year, Natania took them on trips throughout Europe, Western Asia, and North Africa. She insisted they learn the native languages and cultures. Then it was time for Natania to have a talk with them.

"Maximilian, please make us an extra pot of coffee." Alexander loved the robust, naturally sweet coffee Maximilian made. But it was unusual for Natania to have an extra serving, much less order up a full extra pot. "We have some important things to discuss this morning."

"What would that be, Mama?"

"Your futures."

Maximilian returned with a round, chrome coffee pot on a tray with three fresh cups and four saucers, one spoon, napkins, a small bowl with sugar, and a miniscule pitcher of cream (nobody used cream and it ended up in a saucer at Natania's feet, where Sweetie lapped it up).

Natania started, "It has been over a year, Alexander. What are your intentions?"

He had just taken a sip and nearly spewed his coffee. "Well, I, ah..."

"Yes?"

"We have been talking marriage."

Without smiling she said, "Of course. I have known you would marry since the first day you met."

"You have?"

"This comes as a surprise to you?"

Jacqueline shook her head 'no', while Alexander shook his 'yes'. The ladies laughed.

"No, that is not the future I was asking about."

"Oh."

"What career would you like to undertake?"

"I have been thinking about college."

"Where?"

"Back in the states. I had good grades in high school."

"In what field would you study?"

"I have really gotten to enjoy our travels. I was thinking perhaps foreign service."

"You would be good at that." She had been thinking of pushing the love birds out of the nest for quite some time. "Good. I would like you gone by the fall. If you decide to marry by then, Jacqueline may go with you." Alexander had grown used to the easy life. His head was racing at what he was hearing. "I do have a single request if you and Jacqueline marry. I would like you to take Jack's last name. Either hyphenated--Cash-Evans--or with an 'and' as we do here in Spain--Cash y Evans--or just Evans. I do wish that Jack would be remembered in that way."

That seemed odd, but his brother had changed his last name and George didn't seem to mind. "Let me think about it." In reality, he was okay with it but wanted to write to his father first.

"Fair enough."

When George received the brief letter from his son, he laughed. He figured his son was getting close to popping the question and wondered if they would be invited to the wedding. He jotted off a quick reply that he had no objection to the marriage or the name change, and that he loved the thought of honoring Jack in this way.

George and Rebecca attended the wedding--a small religious service by a padre on Natania's estate. White ribbons hung along the walls overlooking the sea. The seagulls sang a wedding march from the cliffs below. Ramón escorted his niece down the make-shift aisle, with tears streaming from his eyes.

The trip was a good break for George and Rebecca. When Penny's parents had sold the store and retired to Chattanooga, the old neighborhood wasn't the same. They sold their house and moved to a ranch east of Mobile, where George had plenty of property for his projects, privacy, and access to the waterways. Rebecca's large garden reminded her of Idaho.

Alexander had been writing Georgetown University concerning their requirements, and had been accepted for the fall semester for a course of study leading to work at the State Department.

The newlyweds descended the stairs of the TWA Lockheed L-749 Constellation in mid-August, 1959 at Washington National Airport during a heat wave. The oppressive humidity made the passengers sluggish and sticky with sweat before the last step. The flight arrived in the late afternoon, and the ground crew worked at a snail's pace getting luggage off the plane. After going through customs, the pair sat at a bar drinking what they hoped would be refreshing--lemonade--before walking to the taxi stand.

"Where to, Mack?" The taxi driver did not turn around or offer to help with the suitcases.

"Willard."

The newlyweds spent the next three days indoors. By the fourth day, the oppressive heat had broken and it was time to look for an apartment near school. They found what they wanted above a bookstore in Dupont Circle. Most days, Alexander walked the mile-and-a-half to and from campus, stopping for a cigarette and coffee at an open air bistro about mid-way. Jacqueline spent her spare time at the bookstore downstairs and shortly landed a job there. She missed the beach, sailing, swimming--and, of course, her mother. Surprisingly, she enjoyed the noises of the area--the creaks of the wooden floors, the automobiles, and the muffled sounds of people talking in the bookstore.

They spent Christmas and semester breaks in Alabama, and returned to Spain for summer vacations, paying rent for the room above the bookstore for the two months they were gone. It was small and intimate, but the newlyweds never seemed to mind. Alexander studied by the hour at their small kitchen table, with a coffee pot continually brewing. Late at night the couple wandered through the National Mall arm-in-arm looking at the lights of the White House, Lincoln Memorial, Washington Monument, and the Capitol Building. Jacqueline was always looking for new places to walk in the evening. The four years seemed to fly by and he accepted an internship at The White House where he met another intern, assigned to the State Department. They called her 'Meadow'.

"Hi, I'm Meadow. May I call you 'Alex?'" she said as she entered the conference room. She held out her hand. They were both early for the staff meeting. His boss had not gotten around to introducing him to most of the State Department liaisons, but she had heard of him.

"No." He held out his hand to meet hers.

"Why not?" Meadow softly joked.

Alexander was taken aback by the question, but not offended by her playfulness. "May I call you Med?"

They laughed and she patted his arm. "I like that. You know ninety-nine percent of guys would allow me to call them 'Alex.'"

"That is why I like standing firm for my full first name."

"Why do you go by 'Meadow?'"

"It comes from 'Meadowlark', which is a translation of my first name."

"I like it! It's peaceful, serene."

"That's exactly why I took it!"

"Tell me about your internship."

"This is my second. My first one was at the White House, for two years. I worked a great deal with the State Department, so now I am interning there."

"But you deal a lot with the White House?"

"Yes. It is easy to get pigeonholed, even at our level."

"Where would you like to be working?"

"Anywhere but the Bureau of Indian Affairs!"

"Why not?"

"Do you know why that Bureau exists? Do you know what they do there?"

"No.

"They can't answer those two questions either!" They laughed again.

Her birth name was He-dow Sacagawea Charbonneau Trujillo. He-dow means Meadowlark, from which she gave herself the nickname 'Meadow'. She had mesmerizing dark brown eyes with a round face and dimples in her cheeks. Her smile was wide and welcoming. Her teeth dazzling white and straight as could be. She wore her hair with a modest curl. She was tall and slender, her skin even, dark, and unblemished.

They made a point to get together for lunch at the White House cafeteria, whenever Meadow was available.

"How are things?"

"Fun. There is always something going on at the State Department!"

"Like?"

Meadow shrugged, "Some idiot starting World War Three!" Alexander smiled. "Our enemies this week. Democrats next week. Republicans the week after."

"When do we get our turn?"

"I'll see if I can get interns on the schedule!"

"Meat loaf again."

"I'm afraid so. You know, the All-American meal--the potatoes collect votes from Idaho; the corn collects votes from Iowa; the butter collects votes from Wisconsin. The meat," she punched it with her fork, "collects votes from somewhere, I'm sure, even if I can't rightly identify it."

"Maybe it is Buffalo!"

"Bison. And you guys killed that all off--for fun."

"I guess!"

"We should go over to the House Cafeteria soon."

"Why?"

"First off, you'll never see Eisenhower having lunch here. But over there, you do see REAL Congressman eating lunch." Her eyes glistened.

"Really?" Alexander feigned surprise.

"Of course, it is the lower rungs," in a mock serious tone.

"Oh."

"Yeah. The deal makers all have lunch with each other. Making deals, of course. The smart congressmen are busy collecting graft over their lunches. You can't do that at the House Cafeteria!"

"I suppose not!"

"So we'd be stuck with all the honest congressman--not taking graft, lining their pockets."

"The place is empty most of the time?"

"Yep. Never need a reservation."

Alexander liked her from the beginning and one evening in early November, invited her home to dinner. There was a chill in the air as Meadow briskly walked up the pavement and knocked on the door.

"I'll get it!" Alexander yelled. "Welcome! Come in."

Jacqueline strolled in from the kitchen, a bowl in the crook of her arm as she whipped cream by hand. "Hello! You must be Meadow. Welcome to our home. I'm Jacqueline."

"Thank you. Yes, I'm Meadow."

"Alexander, get us some wine!"

"That would be nice."

"I'm finishing my masters," Meadow said, then bit into her dessert.

"In what?" Jacqueline asked, taking a sip of coffee.

"International Relations. Emphasis on Political Economy."

"How did you decide to study that?"

Meadow took a long pause. "If you understand my cultural heritage, you will see my interests. That is not to be critical; few people do. I wasn't entirely kidding, Alexander, when I suggested I would want to work anywhere but the Bureau of Indian Affairs. Everyone has to deal with at least one layer of bureaucracy--local, state, or the federal government. The Bureau of Indian Affairs just adds one more for Native Americans. Treaties our forefathers signed have been ignored by states and feds. What is left is a bureaucracy which prevents Indians from escaping or upsetting the status quo."

"But you escaped."

"To some degree."

"How did you do it?"

"I have not taken from the hand that would enslave me. But I also haven't gotten very far."

"True. But you've gotten a good education. A college degree. Now finishing up your masters."

"Yes. In spite of the odds, I have done well. What I have achieved is not rare, but not common."

"Okay."

"I don't dress as an Indian. I don't flaunt it. I don't push it into anyone's face. But, I have little doubt, when push comes to shove, institutional prejudice will get me stuck."

"Institutional?"

"Yes. The very government programs that most whites expect to raise Indians up will in fact drag us down."

"How?"

"Because they exist as institutions, if for no other reason."

"Why?"

"Let me ask the questions. Name any other Federal agency that exists to handle the 'affairs' of any other racial or ethnic group."

"There isn't any that I can think of."

"So, why can't I deal with my own 'affairs', instead of the

government having to be involved?

"I'll show you my Certificate of Degree of Indian Blood, if you'll show me a certificate showing me whatever kind of blood you have. And why? So we can't intermarry without giving up 'alleged benefits'? Hah!

"Did you know the Bureau of Indian Affairs was in existence for a hundred years before we got the right to vote?

"Why is this agency under the Bureau of Land Management? That is very telling!

"Why do they manage the over 55 million acres of what they acknowledge to be our land on our behalf? Can't I manage that myself?

"Explain to me why we maintain nations within a nation? But those nations have few rights and only those 'granted' by Congress?

"The bureaucracy wants the Indians to provide leadership over their own community, while they really maintain authority and control? How long do we have to live with this model? Why can't the Indians attain authority and control over themselves? Or perhaps let's give Indians authority and control over the whole country for a while?"

"More wine?" Alexander had never seen her so worked up.

Meadow became a frequent visitor to their small apartment.

NINE

The staff meeting ended at ten twenty-five and Abraham returned to his office in the Pentagon. He was there on a six-month assignment to review curriculum across the military training schools. As he wandered down the hall, he was daydreaming about his upcoming trip--taking the family to Alabama for Christmas break. His secretary, spotting him coming through the door, smiled pleasantly as she asked, "Coffee, Sir?"

"Please." It was his fourth cup this morning, but he could drink it all day and still sleep like a baby at night. Coffee seemed to help with his headaches.

"Mail is on your desk. No calls."

"Thank you."

Abraham removed his coat and sat down at his desk. His secretary entered with his coffee and quietly placed it to his right. Steam rolled off the top; just the way he liked it--hot and black.

He scanned the envelopes. He could just about guess what each contained without opening them; the Army operated on routine. He arrived at one that did not have a return address. 'That's curious', he thought. He looked closer to see his address had been typed and the envelope marked 'Personal'. He felt the envelope and it contained some objects. They were heavy and lumpy. "Okay, what is this?" He carefully tore the envelope along the right edge, blew inside to fill it with air, and reached in with two fingers.

It's a ring! What is... Hey, it's a West Point ring. He gasped, "1950." He looked carefully as he slid it off its mounting. *No, this is MY ring. This is MY West Point ring!* Further down he saw another ring, Oh my gawd... "It's MY wedding band! How the hell..."

He looked back inside the envelope--no note. He looked again at the mounting, and did a double take. Dropping the rings on the green desk mat, he spun his chair around to the waste basket and projectile vomited.

The wrenching sound alarmed his secretary, who came through the door in a flash, "Are you alright, Sir?"

"I'm not sure. Must have been something I ate."

"Can I get you some water?"

"No, thank you. Let me just have a moment."

"Certainly, Sir. I'll be right outside if you need me." She closed his office door behind her.

A few minutes later he came out of his office. He was ashen.

"Are you alright, Sir?"

"I'm not sure. I am going to go home. Would you cancel all my appointments for the day?"

"Of course."

"And there is something I need you to do."

"Sir?"

He leaned closer. "Take this envelope." She reached up and grasped it, but he didn't let go, until she looked him in the eyes. "Don't look inside." His face was drained of blood and his hand was shaking. "Take it down to the incinerator--NOW. I'd do it myself, if I could, but--this needs to be done immediately!"

"Of course, Sir." She stood up, with a bewildered look on her face. She would obey her supervisor to the letter. But he did not go home until evening.

"I'd tried to call you yesterday. Where were you?" asked the General.

"I went home sick."

"Yes, that is what your secretary said. But when I called your wife answered and said you weren't there."

"I had something--" There was a long pause. "Are you asking as my boss or as my friend?"

"Abe, if there is anything I can do, let me know. Are you in some kind of trouble?"

"Yeah. I went A.W.O.L. yesterday!"

"Come on. I want to help."

"Okay. Did you remember me ever telling you about my rings?"

The General's brow furrowed. "I don't quite remember."

"I received these in the mail yesterday." He held out his hands to show the rings.

"What? Let me see. Ah, you lost them, no, they were..."

"These are the two rings I was wearing when I was captured in Korea."

The General's jaw opened. "What? How, the fu..."

"Yes, that is what I was wondering. But I also was thinking I may need to report a war crime."

"What?"

"Yes. Is it unlawful to mutilate the body of an enemy soldier?"

"Of course."

"I don't know the name of the enemy soldier. I don't know who mutilated him. I don't know whether he was dead before he was mutilated."

"But you know he was?"

"Yes. I can't be sure he was killed. But--would I need to report it?"

"Well, that is hard to say. You have so little information; you can't quite make a formal report."

"So, General, what do you suggest I do?"

He thought for a minute. "I'd write a 'memo to file'; detail what you received in the mail, and that you discussed it with your superior. But don't send me a copy. What did you do with the, eh, remains?"

"I had my secretary burn everything."

"That's good. Cremation is honorable. Alright. But, off the record, how did you know that there had been a mutilation?"

"The rings I received in the mail--"

"Yes?"

"--had been slid onto the rolled up right ear of the North Korean soldier who stole them from me!"

Lieutenant Colonel William Anderson ran two steps at a time up the stairs into Roosevelt Hall at Fort Lesley J. McNair. He knew his way around The National War College (NWC). A gorgeous view overlooked the Potomac with summer in full bloom. Anderson had urgent business.

Abraham was deep into his lecture.

"Armies have always been dependent on support and supply. During World War II, large Armies stalled multiple times to allow their supplies to catch up. The Battle of the Bulge was lost by the Germans when they simply out ran their fuel supply. Use of small helicopters in Korea for supply and medical demonstrated a new supply capability. Superior enemy numbers and difficult terrain could be overcome through the air. Air Mobility, Gentlemen, will decisively assure success in future conflicts."

Abraham noticed Anderson come into the lecture hall as he finished speaking. The students, all promising military and diplomatic personnel, exited the hall while Anderson stood at the rear returning salutes to many. Finally, he had a clear path to the front. "Abraham!"

"Andy, how have you been?" He saluted.

Returning his salute he barked, "Great! But you are in deep shit!"

"Me?"

"Yes, Abe! I am afraid your career is over! Lemnitzer told me to personally grab your ass and drag it to the Pentagon. The Joint Chiefs have split up--some are heating the tar; others are plucking the chicken feathers! Let's go."

"But my afternoon classes..."

"Taken care of."

On the ride over, Anderson told him the truth. "The President is sending a team over to Vietnam to look things over. In parallel he wants to get some support over there--equipment and troops--low level stuff until the team reports back. The French got their asses kicked there, but he wants to rough up the Communist guerrillas a little, coming from the north and China."

"So I will be leading the team into..."

"No, you'll be organizing stuff here."

"Why me?"

"Obviously, the Army's assessment of your inabilities to teach!"

In November 1961, Abraham Cash stood aboard the USNS Core, a refitted World War II "baby flattop" aviation transport (T-AKV-41). He watched the single file lines of over 400 personnel slowly snake over the deck of the carrier. They were U.S. Army Aviators and support personnel from the 57th Transportation Company in Fort Lewis, Washington and the 8th Transportation Company from Fort Bragg, North Carolina. Each carried their duffle bags aboard. In a few hours, most would be barfing their guts up from the time they sailed under the Golden Gate Bridge until they steamed up the Mekong River, docking in Saigon. On the heels of the Bay of Pigs invasion disaster the previous spring he knew how important it was to get this operation right.[52]

The day before he had watched 33 CH-21 Shawnee "Flying Banana" helicopters--with its distinctive bent hull shape and tandem rotor helicopters designed and built by Piasecki Helicopter--loaded and lashed down on deck. The previous morning, he had watched thousands of black 55 gallon drums of aviation fuel and hundreds of black with pink stripe drums loaded below deck--Agent Pink.

The first of his 'two babies' began before Christmas--Operation Chopper. It was almost anti-climactic as he sat for two days, while American Aviators transported more than a thousand Army of the Republic of Vietnam (ARVN) paratroopers into a suspected Viet Cong complex, 10 miles west of Saigon. The Viet Cong retreated after the initial, short, overwhelming skirmish. There were no combat stories, no heroism, no accidents--just quiet, quick 10 mile shuttle

---

[52] The Bay of Pigs (Spanish: Bahía de Cochinos) is a mistranslation. In this application, the word Cochinos is not the derisory slang word meaning "dirty pig", but the local name for the Balistidae family of Orangeside Triggerfish (Sufflamen verres) found in the shallow, coastal environs and coral reefs of the tropics. The fish are plentiful in the Gulf of Cazones (Spanish: Golfo de Cazones) on the coast of southern central Cuba.

trips back and forth. Twenty soldiers at a time--fly, land, unload, return, and repeat--all day long. Modest. Boring. Routine.

It wouldn't take long before the Viet Cong, National Liberation Front (NLF) began to expose the disadvantages of deploying forces by helicopter--flying into forests and jungles and vulnerability of hostile fire. Unlike with other aircraft, the Viet Cong learned not to lead helicopters as they shot (as one would do with a shotgun when hunting geese).

His 'second baby' was nearly as routine--Operation Ranch Hand. They cleared vegetation alongside highways to expose trails, supplies, and camps using a defoliant containing the deadly chemical Dioxin.[53]

After a month of watching the lumbering Chase Fairchild Aircraft UC-123B Providers he was ready to go home. He had spent his time since Korea at Fort Sill, West Point, the United States Army War College, and The National War College, mostly teaching and helping with strategy. He had not been in the field much. After Korea, he wondered how he would fare--and all had gone well. His brother was asking him to come down to Alabama for some 'R and R' and to discuss doing a 'family activity', whatever that meant. But first he would need to return to Washington and write endless reports on what was accomplished and give countless presentations to those who already had read the reports.

"Well, guys, I'll be heading back tomorrow." There were handshakes all around.

"Sir, I think we can handle it from here."

"I know you can. Get home soon."

---

[53] Agent Pink, the first "rainbow herbicide", was the code name for a powerful herbicide and defoliant used during the early days of the Vietnam War. It's only active ingredient was 2,4,5-Trichlorophenoxyacetic acid (2,4,5-T), a synthetic auxin, a chlorophenoxy acetic acid herbicide, broad-leafed plant defoliant. Developed after World War II, it was widely used in agricultural. The more infamous herbicide, Agent Orange, came later. Chase Fairchild Aircraft UC-123B Providers sprayed the liquid over wide swatches of the countryside, sometimes at rates twenty times higher than recommended. Nearly twenty million gallons of herbicides were dropped from US planes, frequently painted to look like Republic of Vietnam aircraft.

"We'll be tryin'!"

"Hey, what's this?"

"Poster we're doing."

"Nice." It showed a Fairchild Provider in the air with Pilot Smokey the Bear at the controls and mist coming out the back.

"I'll send you a copy when we get 'em printed up."

The poster was less than half done and Abraham couldn't make out the text that had been blocked out. "Great. What is this going to say?"

The artist swept his hand in the air, as if he was envisioning a billboard, "ONLY WE CAN PREVENT FORESTS!"

The whole family arrived in Alabama by the day before Christmas and stayed through New Year's Day. Meadow agreed to join Alexander and Jacqueline in Alabama with the rest of Alexander's family. Mel and the kids came early to spend extra time with Rebecca and George. Christmas and the day after were given over to a candlelight service, presents and feasting. The rest of their time was leisurely--snacking, napping, drinking, and talking. By the end of the week, everyone had caught up with everyone else. Frequently the post-Christmas discussions revolved around religion or politics.

The following spring, Thomas's sermon came from the Book of Isaiah, chapter 43. He concluded it by rereading from verse 2, "When you pass through the waters, I will be with you; And through the rivers, they shall not overflow you." He paused for effect. "Please bow your heads."

He looked out and spotted the United States Army full dress uniform creeping in the back door--dark-blue coat, light-blue trousers, white turndown-collar shirt, black four-in-hand necktie, and dark blue service cap tucked into the elbow. His polished brass buttons reflected the morning sun across the room. He chuckled to himself, thinking, 'Little bastard would show up at the end'. "Let us pray."

After the prayer, he saw that Abraham had seated himself in the last row. "Before I dismiss you, I would like to introduce you to the black sheep of my family." Everyone laughed. "In the back row, where he would not be as conspicuous nodding off, is my little brother, just back from the Far East, Lieutenant Colonel Abraham Cash, United States Army. If you would like to shake his hand--I'm not sure why anyone would--he will be joining Penny and me on the front steps." He raced down the aisle to hug his brother, with Penny close behind.

"You had to suck me into the receiving line?"

"You have to came late to my sermon! And you had to sit in back? Payback!"

"Sleeping's best in the back. Far away from all the bad noise--only place to be when you preach!"

"We weren't sure when you were getting in."

"I wasn't either. The train got in about 90 minutes ago."

"Penny is getting the kids and we'll go out for lunch."

The kids couldn't get enough hugging and touching their Uncle Abe. The waitress brought water and menus. "I'll be back to take your orders in a jiffy!"

"This is great!"

"Where were you, again?"

"Place called 'Viet Nam'. I ran two short projects and got out of Dodge."

"Great! Glad you are back safe."

"No sweat. One was to surprise the enemy and put a thousand South Vietnamese into a North Vietnamese position."

"How'd it go?"

"Great. We used helicopters to do the drop. The enemy wasn't expecting that at all. We had a brief firefight with the first coupla helicopters, but then they ran with the good guys chasing them into the jungle."

"What was the second project?"

"Putting down weed killer."

"Weed killer?"

"Yeah. The jungle is built up so much; the enemy hides snipers, camps, and supplies in the grass. We thin the grass out so our guys can hit'em."

"Our guys?"

"The South Vietnam Army."

"How many of our troops are there?"

"United States? Only advisors and pilots. About a grand."

"What is this thing we're doin' there?"

"We're just cleaning up where the French left off. They spent about twenty years there, but got tired of it. Left a vacuum when they headed home. So we're going in to train and help out."

"But what are WE doing there?"

"Sorry, that question is above my pay grade. It's for the generals to know, and me to find out when I read history books in a rockin' chair on a porch somewhere during my retirement."

Thomas laughed. "No really!"

"The politicians think we need to stop the Commies, or they will simply keep rolling up one country after another. We stopped them in Korea, now we are putting our finger in the dike here."

"How long will this take?"

"We learned a lot from Korea. I think we'll get to the checkmate pretty quick. Overwhelm the Soviets with force. Bloody their nose and negotiate peace."

"I thought you said it was North Vietnamese we were fighting? You just said the Soviets?"

"Well, the Soviets are behind it. Same as China."

"What? China? The Soviets AND China?"

"Yeah?"

Thomas took a big swig of ice water. "I remember seeing an old *Ripley's Believe It or Not* picture book somewhere. The caption said the Chinese could march past a point four abreast FOREVER, because the population would grow faster than the marchers could march."

"So?"

"Are you sure that's an enemy you want to fight?"

The waitress returned, "Are you ready to order?"

Abraham pushed back from the table, "I liked that dessert."

Penny said, "It is a specialty down this way. It is called chess and vinegar pie. Vanilla buttermilk pie with a cornmeal crust. They throw in a little vinegar to cut the sweet. Sometimes they serve it with pecans. You won't need sugar in your coffee for a week!"

"I loved it! But I gotta watch it." Thomas patted his

stomach. "There is one other thing I want to discuss with you."

"Shoot."

"Ever spend any time in Huntsville?"

"Sure. I trained some people there. Army base. RSA. Redstone Arsenal."

"Yeah."

"What about it?"

"The Vice-President asked Billy Graham to have a crusade there."

"What? Why?"

Thomas laughed. "Is that so outrageous that a vice-president would ask a preacher and evangelist to go to a military base to share the gospel of Christ? I guess it is! Johnson wanted help with negros in the South. He thinks it's time to expand voting rights. Get rid of the poll tax. This is his payback."

"Where is Johnson from?"

"Texas. So, maybe not quite as bigoted as the Deep South."

"Oh, really? I'm not so sure."

"So Lyndon was talking to Billy..."

"Oh, we're on a first name basis, I see."

"...and Johnson asked why he's always talking all over the world, and skipping the Deep South. Billy took him up on it--did 15 Crusades last year blanketing Florida. Now he has a handful more throughout the South, including Redstone Arsenal."

"So the 'VP' presses the Army to host a Crusade. But how are you involved?"

"My stand on civil rights is clear. I align with Johnson. So they asked local like-minded senior pastors to lend a hand."

"But shit, you must be a hundred miles away."

"Yes, they are helping out."

"What does this have to do with me?"

"I want you to come join us."

"Me?"

"Yeah. And if you come, Alexander will as well."

"Oh, blackmail!"

Thomas grinned. "The Graham organization said they could help get you stationed down here for a few months."

Abraham looked shocked. "You got all the bases covered?"

"Mel and your kids are all for it!"

"This is going to be a pretty big feather in your cap! Put you on the national stage, huh?"

"I don't know if I would put it that crassly." But he had to grin.

On the way home, Abraham asked if there was somewhere he could pick up medicine.

"What do you need?" piped in Penny.

Abraham answered, "Cough medicine and aspirin."

"We have aspirin at home. I don't know where we can get cough medicine on a Sunday."

Thomas said, "I haven't heard you coughing."

"That is because I took some earlier. Just ran out."

"We may have some at home. Otherwise, we'll have to wait until tomorrow to go to the pharmacy." Over the evening and next day, Abraham consumed an enormous amount of aspirin. His headaches had stayed bad since his injury in Korea. He kept his aspirin, alcohol, and cough medicine consumption secret from his family, friends, and the military. He was hooked on codeine and had been for years.

Thomas stood in the podium, watching the reaction of his audience as he concluded his sermon. He pulled a slip of paper out of his Bible and began to read,

"During the Nazi reign, a Lutheran pastor by the name of Niemöller wrote:

'First they came for the communists,
and I didn't speak out because I wasn't a communist.
Then they came for the trade unionists,
and I didn't speak out because I wasn't a trade unionist.
Then they came for the Jews,
and I didn't speak out because I wasn't a Jew.
Then they came for the Catholics,
and I didn't speak out because I was Protestant.
Then they came for me

and there was no one left to speak out for me.'"[54]

He slowly returned the paper to his Bible and took his time removing his reading glasses, letting the words soak in. "We live in a very fragile world. We need to be neighbors to one another. That means standing up to wrong. The Soviets terrorized their own people during their civil war, and in Mongolia, and in Poland. And what did we do? Nothing! The Chinese terrorized their people, and what did we do? Nothing! We appeased the Nazis and turned a blind eye. And millions died. Millions.

"We are no better. We terrorized our own natives. Declared it our destiny and pushed them off the land. We called it 'manifest destiny'--manifest means 'obvious'. Our 'obvious destiny' was the joint sins of first coveting, then stealing another's land! And why isn't it somebody else's destiny to take from us?"

There were audible groans and grumbles from the congregation.

"We have a family friend who is an American Indian. Meadow is her name. She has opened my eyes.

"We stand at a crossroads. I know this is not going to be popular, but the time has come to repent of our ways! It is time for us to speak out. This time we need to speak out for the lesser in our community, for the negro.

Two men had heard enough and walked out, but most people politely just sat.

"'Do unto others as you would have them do unto you!' comes straight from the mouth of our Lord. It should be a constant reminder to us.

"That is why this summer I will be joining Billy Graham in Huntsville. At the Redstone Arsenal. Will you join me in praying for this crusade? Bless the work of the Holy Spirit as he convicts us of our sin and redeems us anew!" He sat down. The nearly full church was eerily quiet. He thought, 'I may have just ended my career'.

Finally the church organ broke the awkward silence.

---

[54] Friedrich Gustav Emil Martin Niemöller (1892 - 1984) was an anti-Nazi, German theologian and Lutheran pastor.

The CIA agent looked intently at the radar detection screen and smiled. "We got the little weenie." The office was just off the main road onto the naval station. It looked like any other beat up warehouse.

"Of course you did. You cheated."

"Come on. How did we cheat?"

"You told him you wouldn't follow him during the year."

"So."

"If you hadn't known he was coming by boat, you wouldn't have caught him."

"Well--that is debatable."

An aide hurriedly walked through the door and came directly to the agent. "Sir, this came in the mail this morning."

The agent opened the letter and read it. "He did it!"

"He didn't have time to set another one up."

"Yes, another one."

"We nabbed it at the last moment. He didn't have time to set up another try."

"You're missing something. You interpreted another try as sequential."

"What do you mean?"

"You interpreted the instruction that he would try, fail, and then try again. He didn't. He tried multiple approaches at the same time. You were busy tracking the boat; you lost sight that he would use another method."

"So did he succeed?"

"If these coordinates are what I think they are, he succeeded." he held up the letter, "A trip to the airport will explain it."

The CIA dispatched two agents. In a storage shed at the airport they spotted something of interest.

"Look there!"

"Pull back the canvas."

"Shit!"

"A one-person plane."

"Doesn't prove squat."

"Bright Orange. Look, it's got his symbol."

"Circle with UJ2. What the hell does that mean, anyway?"

"I haven't a clue, but he always uses it."

"Still doesn't prove anything. He could have put it here ahead."

"True. Let's take a closer look inside. There! Look at the seat. What is that?"

"Curaçao newspaper *Amigoe. Shit!*"

"What?"

"Dated December 1."

"He made it."

"Do you think he flew this little thing from Curaçao?"

"Yes."

"Way too far."

"Probably Curaçao to Haiti to Southern Florida to Mobile."

"Yeah. That's three six hundred mile stretches."

"This thing is a flying gas can. Look at the tanks on this baby. Lucky he didn't blow himself up!"

"Let's tow it in and tear it apart."

"Well, he's got guts. I'll give him that."

"I'm guessing he did three legs over three days."

"How do we find out?"

"We will never know for sure, unless we ask him. Once we rip out the engine, we can figure how many hours it's been flown. I guess he did practice runs here, drove it down, and flew it back after picking up a newspaper on the first."

"Yes, he played by the rules. He is a go for next year. And next year, I'm not letting you track every step. It is going to be your job to find him in the days leading up to December 7."

It wasn't Christmas until the family got their fill of playing with George's toys. It was amazing the variety he had put together--sail and speed boats, canoes, airplanes, gliders, tractors, hot air balloons--all at the CIA and Military's expense, tax-free, and with a tidy profit! His family didn't know what George did for a living, but they knew his toys were part of it. While most of the target smugglers were predictable in the methods they used, George was not. As far as he was concerned, any method was fair game--no matter how unconventional. The first one to exit the program cheated and was easily found out. George was above that. The other four stuck to power boats and airplanes--and did not last more than a few years.

Abraham pulled strings to briefly get himself assigned to the Redstone Arsenal in northern Alabama. The base had been created just before World War Two to store chemical weapons; now they were busy developing ballistic missiles. The nearby wetlands of the Tennessee River, with abundant birds, mussels, and butterflies provided an idyllic setting which masked the serious business of the base.

Helping out with logistics for the Billy Graham Crusade was pretty easy after the work he had done in Vietnam. Meadow, Alexander, and Jacqueline were all there. Jimmy McManus Victory came to Huntsville one final time. Thomas and Penny moved to Northern Alabama and stayed with a couple who hosted them for two weeks. The crusades were jam packed every day and Graham was at the top of his game. Thomas had one opportunity to pray publically to an opening session; otherwise he sat and was introduced each night.

Jimmy McManus Victory shared sitting on the stage with Thomas and other dignitaries. Victory, now well-advanced in age, had an easy laugh. The years had dimmed his sight and his heart.

Thomas introduced him the evening it was Jimmy's turn to pray.

"Jimmy, about twenty-two years ago, I came to faith at one of your events."

"Well, where was that?"

"Mobile."

"I was there many times!"

Thomas laughed. "I imagine you were!"

"What do you remember?"

"Oreo cookies!" The crowd laughed.

"Yeah. Well, I never told anyone I had stock in NABISCO! Used to get the cookies fer free. I'll bet I ate a million of them!"

"And how do you eat them?"

"Slip off one side. Eat the frosting. Crush the outside biscuits. Of course, I sometimes eat'em, too." He demonstrated his technique, as laughter and applause filled the arena.

The few days they had together were fun and the family

was not looking forward to leaving.

"We didn't have much of a chance to let our hair down."

"Yeah, but it was good."

"What do you say we go down to see Mom and Dad?" asked Thomas.

Alexander looked away. "I can't get away that long right now." They had a doctor's appointment back in D.C. concerning why Jacqueline couldn't get pregnant.

"Yeah, I know. Just a thought."

TEN

"Hello. State Department."

"Meadow Trujillo."

The operator scanned her large chart. "One Moment, please."

The phone rang in Meadow's small office in Foggy Bottom. Her secretary answered, "Miss Trujillo's office. May I help you?

"Miss Trujillo, please."

"Miss Trujillo is not available. May I help you?"

"Yes. Please have her call Larry Lash with the Idaho Republican Party at 592-0923. Oh, area code 208. Tell her it's personal and urgent."

Meadow had spent a long day at the White House. Exhausted and upset, she thought of driving straight home but decided she better swing by her office. What she had been working on all day looked like the start of World War III.

She walked from the parking lot to the steps of the Harry S Truman Building. The building was dimly lit on the outside and work crews were busy polishing the terrazzo floors of the one-and-a-half-million square-foot limestone building. There were conspicuously more security guards than usual, but few people would know why. She did. She showed her identification and pressed on toward the bank of elevators, hoping to be in and out in minutes.

The office was locked and empty. She scrambled through her purse to find her key, wondering if she had ever used it before. She searched the wall to locate a light switch--'where is it?'--and flipped them up. There were two neat stacks her secretary had left her on the green blotter desk mat. She grabbed the taller stack and leafed through the day's mail looking carefully at each return address. 'Good', she thought--nothing urgent. There was also a stack of pink call back slips, the top one marked urgent and personal. She set that aside and scanned the rest, 'These all can wait'. She looked at the clock. 'They've gone home long ago. Two hour time difference to Idaho. Won't be there'. She dialed. 'What the heck! At least I can say I tried'.

He answered on the first ring. *"Larry speaking."*

"Is this Mr. Larry Lash?"

"Speaking."

"Hello, this is Meadow Trujillo from the State Department, returning your call. Uh, it was marked urgent and personal."

"Hello, Miss Trujillo. We have never met but I would be interested in meeting with you. I'm with the Republican Committee in Idaho. We have been hearing great things about you from our contacts at State."

"Well, I am extremely busy. To be honest, I am not sure when I would be able to meet."

"Your mother mentioned you were planning to come home to Idaho for Thanksgiving."

"My mother? You talked to my mother?"

"Yes. Only in finding the best way to contact you."

"I see. Yes, I am planning to come out. But that is at risk at this time."

"I understand. But if you did come out, would you be willing to invest an hour in talking about your future?"

She paused and thought. "If it didn't interfere with my family plans and the topic was sufficiently enticing, I would find the time."

"Excellent. We can speak further as we get closer to your trip. But for now, I'll leave you with one question to ponder: Have you ever considered running for Congress? Good night."

As she hung up she shook her head and smiled, thinking 'If we all live through the weekend, I'll consider it'. The numbers the CIA had been throwing around the last two days--'as many as a hundred intercontinental ballistic missiles'--were mind-boggling.[55]

She grabbed her purse, coat, and keys, flipped off the lights, locked the door and pulled it tight behind her, before dashing toward the elevator. It was nearly midnight on October 16. She had worked 41 hours straight and was longing for a good night's sleep.

Larry Lash wasn't smiling. He poured himself another two fingers. He knew contacting Miss Trujillo was a fishing expedition. The Democrat Congressman from the Idaho Second Congressional District was reeling--Mormons were up in arms over their fellow Mormon Congressman Ralph R. Harding's comments on the House floor calling Latter-Day Saints Apostle Ezra Taft Benson a "spokesman for the radical right of this nation." Enough were outraged to swing the election. Harding was a sponsor and great supporter of both civil rights legislation and equal pay for women. Who better to land the knockout punch than an American Indian woman? It was radical. It was a long shot, but Idaho was just 'pioneer enough' to go against the male-oriented, old boy network of Idaho Democrat party politics. Besides, he didn't have anyone in the stable gutsy enough to go after Harding. Lash thought, 'An unknown? An Indian? A woman? Yikes! What am I thinking?' He gulped down the booze.

---

[55] In what wouldn't be the last time intelligence estimates would lead political processes and foreign policy astray, some intelligence estimates in the early 1960s put Soviet intercontinental ballistic missiles (ICBM) at 75. There was rhetoric of a huge 'missile gap' during the Kennedy-Nixon election debates, with the Soviets leading and pulling away. Khrushchev claimed the Soviets were building missiles 'like sausages'. In fact, the USSR had four ICBMs to the US's 170 (range of 5,500 kilometers; 3,418 miles). The United States was also building at a faster pace.
What the USSR did have in quantity were 700 medium-range ballistic missiles (with a range of 1,000-3,000 kilometers; 621-1,864 nautical miles). In essence, they needed to be close to the United States to be any threat at all; Cuba became the only logical place in the Soviets sphere of influence. After the crisis, the United Stated removed Jupiter Intermediate Range missiles (with a range of 2,400 kilometers; 1,491 miles) that had been positioned in Turkey and Italy and were obsolete from the day they had been installed.

"What the hell did I do?" barked Alexander, as he threw down his napkin.

"Nothing!" barked back Meadow as she stood.

"What is it, then?"

"I wish I could tell you!" She slammed her fist on the table, splashing coffee over her untouched lunch. Leaving her tray for Alexander clean up, she stormed from the State Department cafeteria like a heat-seeking missile and headed to the elevator. Her associates thought, 'The rumors are true! A lover spat!'

She pushed people out of the way as she moved to the back of the elevator and crossed her arms. Three days ago she knew things even the President did not yet know. The next day she was pulling together photos, documents, Soviet statements, details that were going to be seen by the President, nine members of the National Security Council, and five senior advisors.[56]

Now she found herself on the heap pile of history and she didn't like it a bit. She was standing in the wings, excluded, waiting for the call that never came.

She returned to her office and routine tasks left unattended for too long. What more she would learn about the Cuban Missile Crisis she would read about in the Washington Post. Each subsequent step was handled upstairs or in the Oval Office. Everything took place just outside her reach. Tantalizingly close. Her mind was unrelenting--would they see this, would they understand that. I need to be there. I can help them. She felt her work was always incomplete--never any closure, never any finality. An immediate crisis may have been averted, but it felt like just the first of two shoes to drop. She waited in suspense for the next one. Always waiting.

Even the Surface-to-Air missile (SAM) that claimed the life of USAF Major Rudolf Anderson, Jr. in his U-2F over the skies of Cuba at noon on October 27, and the shelling of US

---

[56] The group would be formally named the Executive Committee of the National Security Council (EXCOMM) on October 22 by National Security Action Memorandum 196.

Navy RF-8A Crusader aircraft on low-level photoreconnaissance missions snapping pictures in western Cuba later the same day were handled at the highest level. As far as she and the world knew, nothing had happened.[57]

On October 28, 1962, cooler heads prevailed at the highest levels in the United States and Soviet Union. The 'quarantine' continued until November 20 when Worldwide US Forces DEFCON status level was reduced from three to four. Large numbers of flyovers continued through December, watching the Soviets dismantle 42 missiles and their support systems, pack them onto eight ships, and return them to Russian soil. A convoy of ships sailed on November 5th through the 9th. Subsequent negotiations resulted in removal of Soviet IL-28 bombers in early December.[58]

When October turned into November, Meadow made airline reservations. She called her family. Then she called Larry Lash.

The day after Thanksgiving, Lash landed his red-and-white 1960 Cessna 172A Skyhawk four-seat airplane at the Stanley Airport in Idaho. Consulting for the Republicans paid well and Larry enjoyed flying his airplane at every opportunity. It was a crisp, cool morning and a rusted out, fire-engine red 1948 Ford F-3 pickup truck drove out and stopped upon seeing the plane. It was unusual to have a plane land here this late in the year.

"Howdy!"

"Hello!"

"Engine trouble?"

"What? Uh, oh no, everything is fine. Do you know a Jerry or Jerry's?"

"Everyone knows Jerry's!"

"Can I get a lift?"

"Sure."

---

[57] It was later determined the decision to fire the SAM was made locally by a Soviet commander acting on his own authority.
[58] The United States was careful to call their actions a 'quarantine', not a naval blockade. By International Law, a blockade is an act of war. Unlike a blockade (where no goods pass), ships without military weapons were boarded, searched, and allowing to proceed.

Lash spent the balance of the morning drinking hot, black coffee up the road two miles on Highway 75 at Jerry's, looking out over white capped hills, and watching the Salmon River leisurely slide through the peaceful meadow. He read through his few notes on He-dow "Meadow" Sacagawea Charbonneau Trujillo—it didn't take long because he didn't have much. He got out his legal pad and ball-point pen, and waited.

He learned that the 1960 census counted 35 people living in Lower Stanley. Most seemed to have come through the restaurant today.

"Good morning!"

Larry stood. He didn't know exactly what he expected to see, but this wasn't it. "Meadow?"

"Yes, are you Larry?"

"You can't miss with the Rainbow Trout here."

"That sounds wonderful."

"Caught this morning. So fresh the fillets wiggle themselves over while cooking in the fry pan. Almond crusted."

He scanned the menu--Bull, Cutbow, Brook West Slope Cutthroat, and Lake Trout. Plus Mountain Whitefish and Chinook Salmon. "Quite an assortment."

"They don't have all of them every day, but generally a good selection. They know where the fish hide and never hibernate."

After Meadow and Larry enjoyed lunch, he put all his cards on the table. Meadow sipped her coffee before answering.

"I'm honored that you have thought of me. I will consider it and pray about it. But my first inclination is that I would consider it a future step and I'm not quite ready for it yet. I appreciate your candor and honesty."

"Well, think about it some more over the next few days and call me with a definitive answer after you get back to Washington."

"I will."

"And I do hope if you don't throw your hat in the ring this time, you will still consider it as a future step."

"I will."

"And I need a favor. Would you mind giving me a lift back to the airfield?"

"Of course."

They shook hands as she dropped him off near his plane. "Until we speak again."

She turned off the engine to wait as he checked his plane and started the engine. Taxiing to the end of the strip, he turned it around, and pressed the throttle forward. In a few seconds, he was banking his plane as he gained altitude, thinking 'rats!'

The low flyovers above Cuba continued daily while Meadow had been gone. She was invited to the daily CIA meetings where agents passed around pictures and described progress the Soviets were making in removing military hardware.

By mid-December, Meadow was thinking of Christmas in Mobile, Alabama.

In early December, a CIA agent threw down the newspaper on his partner's desk. "Balloon."

"Balloon?"

"In addition to the plane, he came in by hot air balloon."

"You telling me he got by us two ways?"

"Yeah. And I even saw it."

"What?"

"I saw his balloon. The color mentioned in the caption didn't even spark me. Look at the photograph. Bright orange, the newspaper said. I saw it in the sky when I drove home from work yesterday. You don't see many hot air balloons."

"Hey, but how do we know it met the two hundred pound requirement?"

"That's a good question."

"You have a magnifying glass in your desk drawer, don't you?"

"Yes."

"Look closely at the picture in the paper."

"Is that a circle with 'UJ2' inside it?"

"I can't be sure, but it could be."

"Delivery!" the man rolling in a package yelled.

"Huh?"

"I have a carton for you." The single carton was resting on a hand cart. "Where do you want it?"

"Right there."

"You sure? It's pretty heavy."

"Oh, well, cart it over against the wall." He did.

"Sign here." The delivery man ripped off the receipt and handed a copy to him.

"What the heck is that?"

He looked at the Bill-of-Lading, "Two hundred pounds of dumbbell weights."

"What?" The agent hadn't a clue how George figured out where to send it.

Pedro smiled as he took off the borrowed delivery man's hat, lifted the red hand cart into the bed of the pickup, raised the tailgate, and drove away.

The family came together at Christmastime to exchange presents, pass around chocolates, eat meals, laugh, play, drink, and take long walks with the dogs through the Alabama pines. There was a nip in the air, but not a cloud in the sky. Everyone had arrived, except Thomas and his family, who were due in the following afternoon. After too much wine, George walked with Meadow on one arm and Rebecca on the other when he observed, "Government is too concerned with their own affairs. If Government had their way, when you drove two miles over the speed limit, you'd get a ticket."

"True," Rebecca laughed.

"Why can't they mirror the other side of the coin and always let you slide?"

"I don't have an answer for that?" said Meadow.

"It can never do that. That requires the 'human spirit'. Governments don't have spirits--they serve their own interest first, THEN the interest of their constituents."

"Well, I've seen that dozens of times at the State Department."

"Sure. Make alotta money collecting traffic fines. A ticket is just another tax. If you didn't have fines, they'd have to pay the patrolman's wages some other way.

"And they like confusing things, when they spend our money. When you fill up your car, you pay a gasoline tax.

What's it for?"

"Taking care of roads?"

"But do they take care of roads?"

Meadow laughed, "No, we've got potholes everywhere."

"Right. So where did that money go?"

"I don't know."

"Neither do they. They're not looking out for us, because they see the world in their own way. When the potholes get big enough, they raise taxes to fix the roads. We pay twice and they don't blink an eye."

The Cash ranch had rolling hills that led to a grove of Longleaf Pine in the sandy soil, just up the beach from the Gulf of Mexico. The buildings were on the north end of the property. Ten years earlier, George had crews clear walking paths and lined them with Sweet Azalea. The mature plants brought pleasure to the nose and the eye, as Monarch butterflies soon invaded the area. The pine grove was filled with red-cockaded woodpeckers, brown-headed nuthatchs, salamanders, and frogs. Their walks took them in a large loop from the residence through the rolling hills to the grove and beach, then back through the rolling hills. On their way back, George observed, "Cycles of good and bad never end."

"What do you mean?" asked Meadow.

"There are seasons when things click. Luck goes your way. You can be walking down the street and a ten dollar bill crosses your path in the breeze. If you had been there five seconds later, it would appear to have been a slip of paper flying by--an advertisement, a coupon--whatever. If you had been at that point five seconds earlier it would have skirted by behind your heels. But two things occurred as they did: You reach down and grab it before it's gone.

"And we all go through seasons of bad times. The car needs repairs. Parking ticket. You get sick. You name it."

"Okay."

"They're all just cycles. Sometimes you can go down the same road you always drive, going the same speed you always go, but a patrolman had an argument with his wife, or his teeth are givin' him fits, and he gives you a ticket. It is simply your season to get the bad break. The next day he doesn't even notice you.

"Or like my business. I get paid to sneak stuff by the government. I happen to hit a good cycle. Any fool could do it!

Government convinces itself they can't do it for themselves and you're the right guy; so they hire me at an outrageous rate to make boats, planes, balloons--whatever toys I want. For me, it's just a good cycle. It's all unnecessary, if you think about it. But the government has a blind spot; some bureaucrat thinks they gotta do it. Cover his ass." Meadow and Rebecca looked at each other, trying to understand anything about his business.

"During good cycles you ride it for all it's worth. During bad cycles--like prohibition or smuggling--you hang on and ride it out."

After dinner, George told everyone to follow him as he scampered out the back door.

"Well, I'll be," said Alexander. He had followed on George's heels and as he came out the back door he realized he was in the shadow of a large, hot-air balloon. "Let me grab my camera!"

"I'll take everyone up. But it has to stay tethered. I may need it again." He spent the next four hours taking family members up and down, 300 feet into the sky over Mobile for a fabulous view of the city.

The family was assembled in the living room, waiting for Thomas and his family to arrive, while George was tinkering behind the house. The girls were mixing drinks. They were admiring the Christmas tree that Meadow and Benjamin had been decorating since lunch, when they thought they heard a car pull up out front.

Seeing Thomas swing the door open, Abraham said, "Father, forgive them, for they know not what they are doing."

Thomas answered, "I'm not a father! I'm a pastor. Got it? And what are they doing that requires forgiving?"

"They are trying to perfect the Vodka Manhattan. Trial and error. No--entirely error so far. Dreadful!"

He turned to Abraham who returned a sheepish grin then to the girls. "For the love of God! Mel! Jacqueline! Stop it this instant, do you hear me!" He whispered, "How was that?"

"Very assertive, Father. I mean Pastor! Good to see you!" Abraham hugged his brother.

"You too, General!"

"Yeah, right."

"Drink?"

"Not right now. But I don't think I'll wait for the perfect Vodka Manhattan either."

"Where is that beautiful bride of yours? There she is! Penny!"

Penny came through the door into the living room, with a large grin, "Hello, everyone!" She went from person to person, announcing their name and kissing them.

"Monsignor, may I kiss your ring?"

"No, but I do have something you can--"

"Now, be good!" warned Rebecca as she raised her index finger.

"Padre, I do have a deep theological question for you: If a Jew speaks pig latin, can he eat his words?" Everyone sneered and booed.

"Hey, Numbnuts! What is Dad working on these days?" asked Thomas. He hated his new nickname.

"Oh, it is all top secret!" replied Alexander.

"When do we get to see?"

"You mean, when do we get to play?"

"Alright! You know me too well."

"Tomorrow is Christmas, so he won't be working. He thinks Friday."

Alexander fumed when even his pastor brother called him Numbnuts. He and Jacqueline had seen doctor after doctor concerning their infertility. They heard a dozen times, "Just keep trying." Then they examined Alexander. He tried drinking no alcohol, they tried no sex, they tried frequent sex, he tried eating more fish, he tried boxer short, and he tried briefs. They had tried for five years! Nothing worked.

The urologist turned from his microscope and looked at the young couple at his desk. It was always the hardest part of his job. "I'm sorry. Have you considered adoption? This is very common; low sperm quality."

Alexander sat stunned and thought about the teasing he would receive from his brothers. They would be merciless.

Her hopeless feeling displayed on her face, Jacqueline asked, "Is there a medical term for it?"

Normally he would have said, 'Oligospermia'. Instead, he made up a term for Alexander which sounded more exotic, "Minimaspermaqualitas."

At breakfast the day after Christmas, Meadow was looking at her palm as she sat next to George.

"What do you have there?" George asked.

"This?" She showed him her brass medallion.

"It's beautiful!"

"Thank you."

"New?"

"No. It is very old."

"What a beautiful eagle. It really looks like it is soaring; not like other coins where it is holding arrows, or whatnot. Louis and Clark. 1806! Is it a replica?"

"No. Original."

"Original! My gosh! You must be proud."

"But that's not why I carry it."

"Oh?"

"Yes, look on the other side. Those are my people!" He looked carefully at the opposite side--crowded with a number of scenes, including Indians. He thought that was a wonderful sentiment--that she'd remind herself of her heritage, her Indian race, and culture by the coin she carried. "Those are my people. That is my grandfather, many times over, and his mother."

"Wonderful!" He handed back the coin, but didn't catch what she meant. She proudly looked at the coin and returned it to her pocket. Meadow knew a great deal about her family history--warts and all. She was proud her family played an important role in the formative years of the country.

Late that night, when everybody but she, Alexander, and Jacqueline had gone to bed, Meadow told stories of her family history as they had been passed down through the generations.

After chapel at Mission San Luis Rey de Francia, a

forty-one year old Battalion guide with the United States
Military took a native girl on a picnic near the ocean.
Margarita was fifteen and a servant, but they enjoyed each
other's company. Jean Baptiste had been born during the
winter of 1805 at Fort Mandan, North Dakota. His father was
a French-Canadian trapper named Toussaint Charbonneau.
As an infant, he had ridden on the back of his fifteen-year-old
Shoshone Indian mother during the first transcontinental
expedition across the United States. Her name was
Sacagawea.

Jean Baptiste had been taking Margarita to picnics on
Sunday afternoons all summer. He taught her smatterings of
French, English, German, Spanish, and Shoshone; he was
fluent in a number of native languages. She was a quick
learner and a good wit. They swam naked in the ocean in the
heat of the day and lay on blankets, listening to the waves
and talking. It was common for soldiers in the military
outpost in Alta California around the time of the
Mexican-American War to take up with Luiseño Indian girls.
They made love in the shade of the Peruvian Pepper Trees
(Schinus molle) at sunset. The beach below them was filled
with squawking seagulls. Jean Baptiste roasted a pair of
quail he had trapped over a fire on a crude spit and ground
bright red-pink peppercorns onto the birds. Smoke billowed
into the cloudless sky.

The following week, in the Battalion headquarters,
Colonel John D. Stevenson looked at Jean Baptiste carefully,
thinking 'He is the perfect man for this position'. "Jean
Baptiste, in consultation with Military Governor Richard
Barnes Mason, I am appointing you Alcalde."

"That is quite an honor, Sir." He was becoming the
civilian authority (combination mayor, sheriff, clerk, and
judge) for a territory covering 225 square miles. But it would
not last long.

When Jean Baptiste found out Margarita was with child,
he was pleased--and concerned. He had lost a son during
infancy twenty years earlier named Anton Fries; his mother,
Anastasia Katharina Fries, was a soldier's daughter. Of
course, he hadn't married her.

On May 4, 1848, Maria Cantarina Charguana was born.
Three weeks later she was baptized at Mission San Fernando
Rey de España by Father Blas Ordaz, under log entry #1884.
He listed her mother as 'Margarita Sobin'. "And the father?"

"Jean Baptiste Charbonneau." The priest smiled knowingly.

The restless Alcalde resigned the following August. Perhaps he saw the end of his position was coming when the United States won the war--certainly a civilian government would soon be established. He claimed "because of his Indian heritage others thought him biased when problems arose between the Indians and Whites in the district." Within a month, Jean Baptiste deserted his new family to seek his fortune on the American River panning for gold. His daughter was raised by her mother and an indian named Gregory Trujillo, in the La Jolla band of Luiseño Indians in the foothills of the Palomar Mountains.

The wild streak her father left her led his daughter eventually to the Lemhi River in Idaho. Each generation carried forward the history, stories and traditions of their elders right down to He-dow Sacagawea Charbonneau Trujillo, known among the family as 'Meadow'.

ELEVEN

Each year, George reviewed articles in scientific studies and frequently found items in *Popular Mechanics* which were simple and already partly developed. He'd contact a stranger, offering to fly him down to Alabama to learn more. On occasion, this led to a partnership where George provided resources (always the Government's money) in exchange for a 'joint experiment' in which his new partner was never brought in on what George was doing.

Even George's failures were spectacular.

"We captured something on SONAR last night."

"What was it?"

"We're not sure. Something going about 50 knots was identified--then it slammed into the beach near Fort Morgan."

"Think it is Cash?"

"We're sending SCUBA divers to have a look." It didn't take long to locate what they were looking for, but it took everyone by surprise.

"Ever heard of a 'Long Lance.'"

"Sounds familiar, but I don't remember."

"I'll give you a hint: Japan."

He looked worried. "A 93?"

"Yes."

"George shot a 93 at Mobile?"

"Yes."

"You can't be serious! Where the hell would he come up with a Japanese Torpedo from World War II?"

"Beats me. But what we found was 30 feet long and two feet wide. We estimate it weighs 3 to 4 tons. The explosives had been removed from the case, of course. It is painted bright orange. Nobody could spot his typical 'UJ2' with the circle, but we see less than half of it anyway."

"Oh, that's George alright! What should we do with it?"

"I guess we need to salvage it."

"How are we going to hide this from the press?"

At 0400 the next morning the Torpedo was towed into a secret dock in Mobile Bay.

"Will you look at that?"

"Amazing!"

"You don't see many World War II era torpedoes!"

"Much less one painted bright orange."

"Holy Christ, I have never seen one this long."

"Yes. I suspect that is what made it fail. Pretty complicated. No payload at the tip would have changed both the weight and the weight distribution. Plus the currents must have had an interesting effect."

"I doubt he was able to do testing."

"No, this was a one-shot deal, I'm sure."

"Kinda spooky though."

"What's that?"

"Shooting a Japanese torpedo into Mobile Bay on December 7th."

An agent ran into his boss's office without knocking. Out of breath he choked out, "You're not gonna believe this!"

Since this agent had never before broken this protocol, he put down his pen. Intrigued, he said "Try me."

"NORAD reported a gas explosion."

"Where?"

"Off the coast of Louisiana?"

"They scrambled AFNORTH?"

"Out of Tyndall Air Force Base? Must have been a slow day there!"

"Or a hellofanexplosion!"

"What did they find?"

"Look at these pictures! Two long barges placed end to end."

"Right."

"Look here."

"Hummm. Looks like twisted track."

"Right. Now look over here. Two hundred feet away."

"What is that?"

"Steam."

"Steam?"

"Well, mostly."

"Mostly? What else?"

"Spectral analysis said gasoline."

"Okay."

"The guys think the barge was used to shoot something. These pictures were taken forty-seven minutes after the explosion. Look at the water pattern."

"Okay, if they shot something off the barges, why aren't they trying to recover it? Or leave?"

"We don't think there's anybody on the barges."

"What? So what do your guru's think?"

"Better sit down."

"Why?"

"Do you know what the date is? They think George attempted to duplicate a V-1 attack from the tracks on the two barges off the coast in the Gulf of Mexico. And that he triggered it remotely."

"A V-1? Shit!"

"Yeah. German Flying Bomb that attacked London. Only he was trying to place his payload in some open cow field in Mississippi. If it hadn't crashed into the water and blown up, he probably would have gone through undetected."

"Got to give him credit. He's crazy. But maybe like a fox. He's not at all afraid to fail. Let's hope his next failure doesn't cost him his life."

It was May, 1963, when George and Pedro experimented with an unmanned, water-tight capsule launched from Mérida, Mexico. In a few weeks, hurricanes would begin developing in the Atlantic and some would create havoc for boating in the Gulf of Mexico. But here in May, when air and sea temperatures were nearly the same, the sea was calm.

George had to get this testing finished to have any hope of final testing in his manned submarine after hurricane season, before launching his live run after Thanksgiving.

George hoped the 'Cuban Vortex' would not propel him too far east, past Florida and into the Atlantic, and that he would land somewhere in his target field. But there was only one way to know how his submarine would respond---and that meant trial and error.

"Why do you want to try this?" They were sitting on the beach, a prototype capsule at their feet, drinking a dark, ice cold Mexican beer in the Mérida sun.

"Pedro, where is your sense of adventure?"

Pedro laughed, "Oh, I get plenty of adventure working for you!"

George grinned.

"Boss, this is pretty risky. There is not enough battery to take you all the way. You are relying on the currents, winds, and waves too much."

"I'm not sure why I'm attracted to it. I guess I want to prove it can be done."

"It would make more sense with a safety boat alongside."

"No. That would be too easy to spot. The capsule is buoyant on its own. I will have safety beacons aboard and a waterproof radio."

"Yes, I know you always use the best technology, but this has severe limitations."

"Did I tell you that Jeff devised a method for containing batteries in individual compartments that will drop to the bottom when exhausted, to reduce weight as I go."

Pedro shook his head. "You are taking a heck of a risk."

"What's the worst that could happen?"

"You could die?"

Five months later, George's crew and Pedro were anxious with Hurricane Flora fresh in their minds. A few weeks before, in early October, it had pounded Cuba with as much as an inch of rain per hour over four days, killing over seven thousand people in the Caribbean--the most in the Atlantic Basin since the 1900 Galveston Hurricane. It was such a bad hurricane, they would retire her name.

While his men fussed and fidgeted, George was not particularly concerned. The hurricane was two weeks past and on the other side of the gulf--might as well have been an eon ago and a million miles away for all he cared. He was only concerned with proving his submarine seaworthy during her final trial.

A boat dropped George and his submarine off before sunset. The weather in Mérida was warm as he sat on the beach drinking beer, cooking chicken and rice over a wood fire. He had minimal provisions aboard the personal submarine he named 'The Natania'. It was bright orange with a simple symbol painted near the back--a circle enclosing the letters 'UJ2'. He slept in the warm sand of the beach that night, with a duffel bag for a pillow and a light blanket covering his legs. Lazy waves pounded against the shore, rocking him to sleep. In the morning the sun rose on the water to the east, while the seagulls sailed over to see the strange sight of a man sleeping on the sand. It was a good thing he had used a long line to secure the submarine to a tree or it would have drifted off on its own.

He carried a compass, map, watch, and sextant to sail by. During trial runs, he had a boat assigned to keep tabs on his progress. They would come by, spot him, and radio in his position, but they had been instructed not to contact him unless he was in distress. What they seemed to have forgotten was that he was in a submarine and would be below surface most of the time.

"Well, I guess I better get going," George said out loud to nobody. He used the line to pull the submarine into deeper water and climbed aboard. "Damn." He had gotten more water into the submarine than he had in all the times of practice. He bailed with a paper cup, then turned on the electric and diesel motors, and pulled down and secured the clear plastic, water-tight Plexiglas top. He dipped just below the surface to check for leaks.

"Yeah. No leaks!"

The submarine was built with a closed-circuit rebreather and an ingenious system for dropping empty tanks and batteries when exhausted. He tested the device; it was working well. For most of the trip he would not use the rebreather as the submarine had two semi-rigid hoses off the top with a ball mechanism to trap water from entering. The rebreather would only be used when he dove.[59] A primitive SONAR system alerted him to approaching boats.

"There it is! Got the position," said one of George's support crew member as he reached out to shake another crew member's hand. The trailing boat was sixty feet behind George when he spotted him bob above the surface.

"Took us all day to find him, and we had the best available information."

"Yes. As he gets further along there will be more variables to deal with."

"What do you think if we ask George to come up at noon every day and stay up until we find him?"

"The boss was pretty explicit about not contacting him. 'Find me. Log the location and time. Disappear and do it again a few hours later.'"

"Okay. Let's back off and calculate where we expect him to be in two hours."

"Sounds good. Let's call this one in." It turned out to be the only time they found George's submarine.

The submarine hit the edge of the 'Loop Current' and

---

[59] The body consumes oxygen in air and produces carbon dioxide and nitrogen. A rebreather absorbs the carbon dioxide and nitrogen by a process called scrubbing, recycles unconsumed oxygen, and then adds oxygen to replace what has been consumed. The rebreather's circuit remains breathable on a fraction of the gas of SCUBA systems. Rebreather gas is warm and moist, making it comfortable without causing dehydration. When Dutch inventor Cornelis Jacobszoon Drebbel (1572 - 1633) built the first navigable submarine around 1620, he accidentally invented a crude rebreather when he heated potassium nitrate (saltpetre) in a metal pan--which emitted oxygen and absorbed carbon dioxide.

sprung to life. He had hoped to catch the loop, but didn't realize it would propel him through the water so fast. He took the submarine down to 20 feet and his speed picked up dramatically. He didn't want to stay down long as the rebreather would consume too much oxygen. He needed to save it for times he absolutely needed to be under the surface.

After four days and nights, George was exhausted. "Whose idea was this?" He laughed to himself, thinking 'I am crammed into this coffin, everything hurts, I'm tired, I'm freezing, the noise is driving me crazy, and I don't know where I am'. As it approached noon, it was time to take it to the surface, pop the hatch, and use his sextant to sight the sun and measure latitude. He smiled, "Better than half way!" He had been making 4 nautical miles per hour. It was 540 to New Orleans and 590 to Mobile. He started doing the math in his head; five and a half days...midnight tomorrow! Perfect.

He knew from his compass that he had been heading straight north the whole trip, which would take him to Louisiana. He expected he would begin drifting east soon, putting him in the middle of his target. That meant longer than five and a half, but it was close enough. "The end is in sight!" he said, as he pulled the Plexiglas top back down and latched it. He took the submarine just below the surface. "I've gotta get some sleep." He hadn't expected the submarine to be quite so noisy. The SONAR pinged away continually; as he began blocking out the noise mentally he dozed.

The emergency SONAR alarm awakened him. He was dazed and disoriented. He reached over to turn the alarm off, thinking 'Oh, shit, I gotta dive!' It was too late. Before he got his hands on the diving plane controls the hull of the fast moving fishing boat slammed onto the top of the submarine at the front and banged it down hard.

"Holy shit, what was that?" said a passenger of the 'for hire' fishing boat.

"It's all okay, folks" replied the captain nervously.

"What was that?"

"I'm not sure. Almost like we hit something. I didn't see anything. Maybe some debris from the hurricane? We see driftwood out this far often. Whale? Shark? Manatee? I don't know."

"Any problem?"

"Nah, we're fine. About another ten minutes and we can start fishing." If he had gone below he would notice his boat was taking on water. It was just a slight trickle. They made it home fine.

But when they got the boat out of the water, the hull had been punctured and was scraped orange. "What the hell do you suppose caused that?" rubbing his hand over the ruptured seam.

By the time George revived, the sun had gone down. He had a splitting headache and when he placed his hand to his forehead flakes of dry blood crumbled into his eyes. He blinked and tried to brush it away. He couldn't locate his compass. The motion of the submarine seemed different. The Plexiglas top was now fogged over and on closer inspection it was cracked. He lifted his head up to see how it had happened. "No wonder I have a headache."

'How long have I been out?' There was no telling. The small diesel engine still propelled him forward. He wondered whether or not he should try to lift the top and locate his trailing boat. 'No, don't throw in the towel yet' he told himself. His heart was pounding. 'I must settle down' he thought, 'Sit back, relax. Take a look at the top again in the morning'. He tried to remember where he packed aspirin. The boat was more unstable, but everything appeared to be operating properly. SONAR was still active. "THAT was a close call!"

He felt sleepy, unable to recognize hypoxia, caused by lack of oxygen pressure in the damaged rebreather.

Four days later the long orange capsule bobbed in the waves near shore. The submarine had run out of fuel and was drifting. Local farmers collected to watch the strange visitor from a ridge. Two farmers dropped their tools, ventured down the cliff to the water, and waded out for a closer look. One grabbed the waterlogged rope attached to the front while another peered inside the cracked top.

"Un hombre!"

He looked up to the men standing on the ridge. "Ven pronto!"

Soon they had the submarine pulled in. While some examined the damage to the front, others tried to figure out the latching mechanism for the top. Finally the Plexiglas sprung up and the men hinged it open. George was white and motionless. His eyes were open, with a blank stare. The tallest farmer reached into George's shirt to feel for a heartbeat. "Está vivo!"

He was still unconscious when they got him into town. They rushed him through the shabby waiting room and onto an examination table in the back. The doctor looked worried as he took his pulse, then ripped George's shirt at his throat.

It didn't take long for word to leap 115 miles from Rio del Medio in Punta, on the north shore of the Caribbean, to Havana. Soon a turquoise blue 1955 Ford Station wagon was on its way with three armed soldiers to collect the American Spy.

Penny was cutting up onions and sweet peppers for a tossed green salad when she heard the dog bark. She looked at the clock. Five-oh-eight--right on schedule. She listened for the rumble of his Chevy coming up the driveway and thought, 'Chicken casserole will be done at five-twenty-five; sit down to eat at five-thirty'.

She looked up from her cutting board next to the sink as she heard the door open. The dog had been slapping his tail against the trash basket and pawing the floor for a few minutes already when her husband walked in the door after work. Penny gave him a smile. "Hi, Honey. How was your day?"

"Interesting, if nothing else," replied Thomas. He reached down to pet the dog.

'That's an exciting reply', she thought as she said,

"Really?"

"Yes. I got a call from Mac this afternoon."

"Mac? Wow! How is he?"

"He's good."

"What did he call about?"

"Well, I...could we talk about this after dinner?"

Penny looked at Thomas warily, "Of course. Dinner is in twenty minutes."

Dinner came and went. Homework with the kids was next. Then it was helping Andrew with his Scout project. Getting Jesse down took all the energy Thomas could muster. Penny sat on the sofa, waiting for Thomas, when she heard water running in the shower. She checked on the kids, before quietly opening the door to their bedroom. The light from the hallway crept into the room enough for her to see Thomas was asleep. He was too still, she thought. Maybe he is faking it. She turned off the light and quietly opened the bedroom closet, felt for her nightgown, grabbed it, and returned to the bathroom to change, brush her teeth and hair. When she returned to their bed she whispered, "Thomas." He did not respond, so she lay next to him and quickly fell asleep.

The alarm clock went off at 6 a.m., and she quickly reached over Thomas to turn it off, while his hand was slowly creeping out of the covers.

"Good morning!"

"Good morning! How are you?" He yawned.

"Good. Weren't we going to talk about something last night?"

"Uh-huh." He fluffed his pillow and turned to face her. "I don't know if you are going to like this."

"Okay."

"Mac wants me to apply at his church for Senior Pastor."

"Oh, my gosh!"

"Yeah, that is what I thought, too."

"But you have always wanted that. We've been praying..."

"I know, but..."

"Yeah, leaving is always hard." She cuddled next to him. "So what do you think?"

"I think you're gifted. We have been blessed to have been here, but it's been four years."

"Five. It will mean a move."

"Yeah, just when a Pastor's wife gets the cupboards the way she wants them, it is time to pull up stakes!"

"Well, I don't have the job yet!" reminded Thomas.

"Yeah, but if I know Mac--"

"He wants me to get together with another guy for lunch."

"When?"

"Today."

She thought, 'Light blue suit, white-shirt, blue tie with yellow. Is his best white-shirt in the wash? Hummm', but didn't say anything.

Thomas asked, "But what do YOU think?"

"You know I'm always with you!" She kissed him lightly, sprung out of bed, went to the closet, coming out with the ironing board, electric iron, and water bottle.

It was shortly after seven in the morning when the Church secretary called out, "Pastor Thomas!" He peeked in from his office. "I have a Mr. MacKenzie for you."

"Thank you. Put it through."

He didn't know why he was bothering to shut the door. The walls were paper thin and Mrs. Granada listened in to every call as soon as he closed the door. 'Watch what you say', he thought to himself. 'If she figures out I may be leaving, it will be all over the county by evening. I hope Mac doesn't say anything awkward'.

The phone rang and Thomas answered, "Mac, how are you?"

"Good. Still on for lunch?"

"Sure, I set aside Fridays for polishing and practicing my sermons so my calendar is clear."

"Good. Gary will meet us at one thirty at Milo's Hamburger on Tenth North."

He looked at his watch. "Oh, I better get going. It's a long drive."

"Alright. See you soon."

"Bye." He began to put down the receiver, thinking Ol' Granada will not have a clue! Half-way down, he heard *"Oh, and Thomas, bring your resume!"*

"What would you like?" the waitress asked.

"I'm waiting for someone."

"Try the sweet tea!" He turned to see Mac's welcoming smile.

"Two sweet teas to start."

"Gary called to say he would be a few minutes late. Some personnel issue at the plant."

"Fine."

"Hey, you look good in that suit. You didn't have to dress up for us."

He had dressed up, but he didn't really want to admit it, "Well, I--"

"Hey, I know what pastor's make. If that is your everyday attire, I'm not sure we can afford you!" He laughed and grabbed him by the shoulder. "Good to see you!"

Gary came in three minutes late, "Hi, guys. Sorry I'm late. You must be Thomas!"

"Yes, Thomas Buck this is Gary Gene Knaus. Gary, Thomas. Gary is our board chairman."

"We should order. I don't have all afternoon."

"That's a pretty good hamburger."

"Thought you would like it. Almost as much as I like this!" Gary pulled out a 3M 1/4 x 3 inch magnetic audio reel from his coat pocket and rolled it on the table.

"What's this?"

"Pretty impressive sermon from last Easter."

"Where did you get that?"

"I got my sources!"

Thomas laughed, thinking about Gary--Elder Board Chairman, prosperous businessman, Rotary member, seemed like a 'wheeler-dealer'. "I'll bet you do!"

"Let's talk about your theology before we get too far along."

By the end of the meeting, all three men were grinning. "His retirement is scheduled for June, but he is not opposed to bringing you on early. So think about how soon you could get here and also about the salary I mentioned. Parsonage is on the property and is empty. Henry thought living there didn't give him and Marilyn enough privacy--not that they needed much! It's in good shape. We have been keeping visitors and guests there every so often. I've gotta talk to my board. So call me next week." Gary handed Thomas his business card.

He looked at it and slipped it into his pocket. "I've got to talk to my pastor, too."

Before Gary and Mac were out of the parking lot, Thomas had his coat and tie off. He already knew the decision he was going to make. He was smiling and dreaming as he pulled his white-over-green 1954 Chevrolet Two-Ten Deluxe Series, Model 2103 4-Door Sedan into traffic. The 235 cubic-inch 'Blue Flame Stovebolt Six', 125 horsepower motor purred with delight, as the Powerglide automatic transmission softly shifted and he settled back for his 250 mile drive home. She was past her prime, but he kept her in mint condition. He was king of the world and one happy man. He started dreaming of where to take his wife to celebrate! Dinner at a secluded spot, wine and candles, maybe even a little a little 'ooh-la-la'!

His talk with his pastor the next day went well ("Mrs. Granada already told me you were leaving!"), but Sunday was a disaster. Everyone was making a fuss, saying how sorry they were to see them leaving, and how much they had enjoyed the family.
"Well, it's not a done deal yet."

By mid-afternoon on Monday, he was making the call to Gary which would make him the next Senior Pastor of Birmingham Peace in Christ Church the following month. Immediately after the call, his phone rang.
"Hello, this is Pastor Thomas."
"Thomas! This is your mother. Your father is missing!"
On the phone line he heard Mrs. Granada gasp.

The following spring, Meadow entered the darkened briefing room in the headquarters of the Central Intelligence Agency, Langley, Virginia, to find Agent Douglas M. Taylor with a handful of photographs and a handheld magnifying glass.
"Good morning, Meadow."
"Hello, Doug." She sat next to him. They exchanging pleasantries and idle chit-chatted as a dozen others filled the conference room, carrying folders and coffee cups, waiting for

the meeting to begin. Doug, meanwhile, kept looking at his photographs in the magnifying glass, preoccupied. Meadow wondered if things had taken a turn for the worst.

Doug placed the photographs and magnifying glass on the table and began. "Good morning everyone." There were muffled replies. "This is our regularly scheduled, quarterly briefing to look at fly-over photos. Our objectives have been accomplished, I am passing along photographs from yesterday--there is little left to see." He handed four of the five photos to Meadow to review and pass around the table. There was nothing at all to see so the passing went quickly. "There has been no build up where the Cuba's previously placed missiles. There is one thing we still need to figure out, but it doesn't appear to be threatening. Just images we can't put a finger on. They may be left-over tools or camouflage, we don't know. If we see something of concern we will get this team back together. Please continue to pass the photos along so I can collect them. Thanks to each of you for your hard work and with that I will dismiss us!" Everyone applauded, while many stood to leave.

Doug said, "Thanks, Meadow!" and popped her on the knee with his one remaining photograph.

"Good job, Doug," she whispered in reply. As she got up to leave, he resumed looking at the photograph with his magnifying glass. He'd asked dozens of people about the image, off to the side, at the border of the field. They had made scores of trips over the thing at low level and this was the best image they had come up with. He would never know how close he came to finding out what it was that morning. While the balance of the photos made their way quickly around the table, he stared through the glass and thought, 'Thirty foot long tube, with 'U', a 'J', and a 'Z' or a '2' inside a circle'. "What the hell could that thing be?"

She carried in her purse a photograph of George, herself, Alexander, and Jacqueline standing in a wicker gondola with UJ2 in a circle silhouetted against the flame from a liquid propane burner of an orange hot air balloon.

Some days are light. Others are dark.

Some days are like every other: And some are like no other.

Some days are personal--like one's wedding day or the birth of a child. Days one will never forget.

Other days, never to be forgotten, are shared--a nation attacked, the death of a leader.

Every twenty years we seem to have such a day, which is so planted in our collective memory, that we can sense every detail even years later. The sights, the smells, the sounds are implanted in our collective memories. Generations upon generations can relate to the feelings we collectively carry.

In the future we would remember airplanes flying into buildings and buildings collapsing. Spaceships exploding in midair, killing brave pioneers.

We know each other will have something to share, so we want to know what plants the other person's feet to the cement. We seek to share the common experience, which will contain a different texture. We lean forward to ask one another, 'Where were you when you heard?'

Meadow, Alexander, and Jacqueline were together having a late lunch in the White House cafeteria. It was a rare treat--once in a blue moon, they would have a Friday lunch together or a picnic. The tweak to start a long weekend. Friday lunch, then final duties of the week--filing away reports, reading this tidbit and that, making the final phone calls of the week, chit chatting with co-workers, "What will you be doing this weekend?" Clear off the desk, maybe slip out a few minutes early. A quiet lunch; followed by a quiet afternoon with a quiet weekend ahead. Instead, during lunch they heard a woman shrieking, "The President! The President!"

Rebecca liked soap operas. She had been ironing, thinking maybe she would fix a tuna salad today after her show. The daily routine, frequently flooded with the thought 'I

miss George. When will he come home?' She looked at the
door. 'Today's show had been good. I like 'As The World
Turns'. They always seem to leave you in suspense on Friday.
Why do I like this show so much? I'll watch until it ends today.
Then I'll get up and make lunch. Come back to catch the news
while I eat. Maybe a toasted tuna sandwich instead? What's
this?' Rebecca looked at the graphic on the screen and heard
the words: "Here is a bulletin from CBS News."

At that same time in Birmingham, Alabama, Pastor
Thomas closed the door to his new office. 'Finally some peace
and quiet'. It was Friday afternoon. His sermon notes were
scattered over his desk. Rehearsal time. He began to run
through his material slowly--bit-by-bit and point-by-point.
'Pretty clever opening, if I do say so myself. Good joke this
week. If I change this little bit, I can make it about
myself--everyone loves self-depreciating humor. It brings the
pastor down to human level, even when everyone figures out
it's just a joke. My gosh, the phone is ringing off the hook out
there today'. "Get back to work," he told himself. 'That is a
good Scripture to use. A direct quote from Jesus would be
better, but you can't do much worse than the Apostle Paul.
Why is that phone ringing so much? I need peace and quiet to
concentrate--I am ready for my walk through!' There was a
knock on the door. 'How many times have I told her no
interruptions on Friday afternoon while I practice my sermon.
This damn well better be good!' Gently he said, "Come in." The
door flew open.

The phone rang as he raced into his office at the
Pentagon. "Cash, here! Oh, Hi Honey! No, I haven't heard
anything. Just got out of class. Last one for today, so I'll be
coming home--what? WHAT? HOW? When did you hear? Are
you sure? Walter Cronkite? Do they know how he was shot? In
a parade! They shot him in a parade? In Dallas? Jeezus! Do
they know WHO shot--Well, I guess I--I'll be home as soon as I
can, but it may be a while. Bye, Honey! Thank you for letting
me know. Yes, it is sad. Are you okay? I love you, Mel." He ran
out to find a television.

"Alexander, come into my office immediately!"

Alexander followed his boss into his office on the fourth floor of the State Department headquarters, thinking, 'What did I screw up now?'

"Did you hear?" He didn't wait for Alexander to confirm that he knew the President had been assassinated. "Until we find out what is going on in Dallas, there is nothing to do." He paced in front of his desk with his eyes on the floor. "We are going to have to reassure our friends, while carefully watching our enemies!"

"Why?"

He hadn't heard Alexanders question. You can't predict what an enemy might do. They might be behind this thing! They might think during the transition of power that it is the perfect time to attack. The DEFCON level is being taken to Full Alert!"

Alexander let out a sigh.

"What? This is no time to be sentimental. The safety of our country is at stake! We are the vanguard. Us, the military, and the CIA! I suppose they'll be flying the body back to Washington as soon as they can get it out of the hospital. I don't know how long that will take, but if they can't pull strings, who can? Alexander, I know this is a great shock and very sad, but we just have to muddle through this right now. Our country is depending on us!"

In Cuba that evening a soldier walked to George's cell with a rusty tin plate in his hand and a broad smile on his face. He had been drinking. Celebrating. "Here is your dinner. Enjoy it today. Well, we're winning. We got the bastard. One more capitalist bastard out of the way. He should have left us alone! You don't know what we are capable of doing. It's only a hundred miles to your coast. We get our agents through all the time. They did it this time! Didn't you know Fidel would find a way? They blew away his head today. He was in a parade and they blew his head off. Serves him right after what he did to us. Your President is dead. I knew he couldn't outlive the Revolution!" He set down the plate outside the cell where George could reach through the bars to slide it under the door. He wasn't hungry, absorbed by what he had heard.

The President's body lay in state in United States Capitol rotunda and the whole nation was numb. So much hope! So much encouragement! He was so young. What will happen now?

The bar should not have been open on Sunday morning. People who never went to a bar were there. A businessman had been sitting on a bar stool all night, no coat, his tie askew, watching the black and white television flicker. He hadn't said much. A steady stream of people came in and out to watch the coverage. The man was not inebriated, having nursed his drinks all night. He didn't want to be drunk and miss out, but he didn't want to be sober either. The crowd startled as the man began speaking loudly, with slurred speech, "That Commie bastard got what he deserved! I'd have done that myself, given the chance. Some nightclub owner? No wonder he got through the police line! They let him through! I'd let him through, if I knew he was gonna kill the bastard. It's better this way!" He looked around at the startled crowd before returning to his drink.

The bartender, concerned his patron might pick a fight, walked over to the businessman, "You alright, Buddy?"

"The Country can get over it quicker this way. It was justice, wasn't it? Some crimes don't deserve a jury trial. String'em up! Quicker, easier. Why drag us all through the lies, false claims, nasty details, appeal after appeal, Supreme Court ruling, the execution. Think what the family must be going through! The nation can't sleep at night. We're all on a knife edge. Get him buried. Get our President buried. With grace--dignity--honor--respect. Let us mourn. Now, we can carry on what he started. But I'll never forget this day!" He raised his glass to salute the dead President.

The bartender stood in front of the man determining whether he should throw him out. 'Hell, I feel the same way'. He poured him a freebee.

'Where were you when you heard?'

Life went on after JFK was assassinated. A great leader was dead, but the new President admonished the Nation to move on. He asked God's blessing and told the military to guard the Republic. Fall fell and winter cast a shadow on the already gloomy nation. Spring rains came early offering the promise of renewal as it washed away the vestiges of snow on West Point's extensive lawns.

Abraham's headache today was excruciating, but he had to press on. He rubbed his forehead, closed his eyes, and grimaced. Taking cough syrup with codeine at the rate of two bottles a day, he had vodka in his desk, his car, and hidden in his workshop in the garage. He drank bourbon at home and was taking aspirin at a staggering rate. His stomach continually upset, he could no longer sleep unless nearly drunk.

Mel was worried about him. She caught whiffs of the bourbon and couldn't keep enough aspirin in the house. She didn't know how serious the cough medicine problem had become, nor did she know about the vodka. Everyone in the military drank; it was a way of life--part of their culture. Her own father had. Abraham had been in pain ever since Korea. She understood. He was doing what he did to get by. He never complained. He wasn't going out by a disability discharge! He lied to his doctors about his pain and alcohol use and they accepted him at his word.

He kept moving to various Army educational institutions and his superiors thought him eccentric, moody, maybe unstable, but an excellent instructor. They rumored about his war wounds--that explained things.

He was concluding his lecture, thinking about another shot of cough medicine.

"September Eleventh was a day that will resonate through the ages. It will go down forever in American history. A great American city was ruthlessly attacked. That morning people were running for their very lives. All hell had broken loose. Terror reined.

"Ruthless. Barbaric. Mark my words, a black day in our history! But we would rise from the ashes. September.

Eleventh. Seventeen Seventy-seven. The Battle of Brandywine. Brandywine Creek. Thirty miles southwest of Philadelphia in Birmingham Township, Delaware County, Pennsylvania. Marie-Joseph Paul Yves Roch Gilbert du Motier, Marquis de La Fayette, often known simply as 'Lafayette', Major General of the Continental Army, under the command of General George Washington, organized a successful, orderly retreat which saved his men from being routed."

From that point, Abraham did not glance toward his notes. His hands sweeping in front of him. The battlefield right there in his classroom, as if he and his students had an eagle-eye view of the fifty-acre battleground. Painting a picture with his hands of the British and Continental Army columns, as he scampered from one column of desks to another. Abraham explained the exploits of the Hessian mercenary Wilhelm Reichsfreiherr zu Innhausen und Knyphausen on the right flank, even as he mocked his descriptive, elaborate name. He told of the bad intelligence given to Washington and his own stubborn assumptions. He made it sound as if he had been right there, an interloper onto the discussions of Washington and his senior officers. He told of the Battle of Cooch's Bridge and the second battle to take place there in eight days. He danced the American countercharge as he swept toward the podium, which turned into retreat as he scampered to the rear doors of the classroom. His students took it all in, unable to keep their eyes off this crazed professor bringing the lessons of war to their eyes.

Sweating profusely and out of breath, he returned to the podium. The hour was up. His hands pressed down on the podium as he leaned forward, "The national capital, Philadelphia, was abandoned to the British later that day. La Fayette was wounded--a bullet in his leg. Washington cited La Fayette's 'bravery and military ardour' and recommended he command a division! La Fayette returned shortly to exact vengeance for the lead they had to dig out near his knee.

"You are dismissed, Gentlemen."

After the soldiers exited his classroom, he collected his notes and placed them in his brown leather case. He returned to his office, dropped the well-worn case on the floor and closed the door. His headache was pounding. Abraham plopped down onto his chair and put his legs up on his desk.

His classes were done for the week. It was Friday--Valentine's Day. He should have gotten her a card or be taking her to dinner, but he had not made plans. She said she would make them a nice, quiet dinner at home.

He often graded essays or prepared for the next lecture on Friday afternoons, but today he was exhausted. He opened his desk drawer and, without looking pulled out a lowball glass followed next by the nearly empty quart vodka bottle. He poured the remaining clear liquid into the glass and tossed the bottle in the trash. Days of hiding his empties had long since passed.

The janitor opened the door and saw the Colonel sitting at his desk. "Excuse me!" He backed out as quickly as he had entered, thinking to himself he would swing back by later to dump trash and clean the floor. It happened often that he would need to return to finish somebodies office. No big deal. Just part of the job.

When he returned three hours later the phone was ringing, but the Colonel didn't answer. The janitor's shift was nearly over. The floor could wait, but he had strict instructions to empty trash cans every day. Ants. "Colonel? Colonel, could I just empty your trash. Sir?" He hated to disturb his sleep. "Sir? Colonel? Are you alright?" He grabbed his shoulder and shook him. "Sir!" He grabbed both shoulders and shook harder.

The autopsy read--'cerebrovascular thrombosis'. There was no need to mention the high level of alcohol in his blood on his paperwork. The Army doctor doing the autopsy noted the bleeding ulcer, evidence of high blood pressure, and excessive aspirin in his stomach. But not on the death certificate itself; no need bringing more pain. Leave the family with the memory of this courageous, heroic soldier who simply died of a stroke. If the technology had been better they would have observed a shard of steel in his bloodstream, which caused the clot to form behind it. The remnant of his steel helmet had poked into the side of a vein more than a decade and half earlier and a world away. It stayed there, undisturbed and undetected. During his lecture, while he acted out the Continental Army retreat, he jarred it loose. Its jagged edges began turning, tumbling, moving, catching, releasing as blood pounded it forward into Colonel Abraham Cash's troubled brain.

Abraham died on Valentine's Day 1964 and was laid to rest two weeks later. He was thirty-three. Melbourne was unsettled when the Army suggested he be buried at Arlington National Cemetery. When she called her mother-in-law, Rebecca replied, "Bring him home to me."

The train with Abraham's body picked up members of his Honor Guard, coming from Redstone Arsenal. Reserves from Mobile made up the Military complement. Thomas performed the service at his parent's ranch. Both Thomas and Alexander gave eulogies. Mr. Dodd, Abraham's high school science teacher said a few words as did Abraham's best friend at West Point, Colonel Tomas "Tom" Nolan.

"He became our classes first Centennial Man! He walked off over one hundred hours of indiscretions. I remember one of his first, when he should have been at attention on the parade grounds he was caught looking at the snow. Being from the South, I guess he'd never seen snow before. He didn't seem to mind walking off those hours. The graduates always respected Centennial Men, frequently admitting to themselves, "There, but for the grace of God, go I!"

He told of being best man in Melbourne and Abraham's wedding. He teared up as he thought of twice holding their wedding rings in his pocket, abruptly quit speaking and quietly slipped back to his seat.

The interment took place in an grave prepared on George and Rebecca's ranch. Melbourne Dawn continually hugged her three children--eleven-year-old Laura; Juliann, who would turn ten that summer; and their comic brother, Andrew, seven. The soldiers gave a twenty-one gun salute. A bugler played Taps, the notes breaking when he was overcome with emotion.

Colonel Nolan stepped forward to present the folded American flag to Melbourne. Nolan forgot exactly what he was to have said. "Mel, this comes from a grateful nation." She held it proudly to her breast.

The rest of the family returned to their homes the

following day. Mel put the kids to bed and joined her mother-in-law on the porch. "Nightcap?" she asked.

"Bourbon," Rebecca replied.

She prepared the drinks on the rocks, returned to the porch carrying the bottle and two glasses, and handed one to Rebecca. "I didn't know you drank bourbon."

"I don't. George did and when I get to missing him, I sip it in the evening. It reminds me of his breath. It helps me sleep." They sat quietly and drank. Rebecca poured another shot for Mel and refilled her own glass. "It's not right to have to bury your own child. Just not right. Not fair. So much life left unlived." Mel nodded. "So what's next for you?"

Mel stared into her glass. She didn't want to think about it.

Rebecca paused. "I know it is too early to be thinking of these things, but you are a young woman. You may want to remarry."

"Oh, Gawd!"

"I know it is hard to think about now."

"Hard? Impossible!"

"You could live another fifty years. You may want to have another man in your life."

"The last thirteen were not what I expected. He left for Korea so soon after our wedding. When he came home he was a shadow of himself." Rebecca nodded. "There will never be another man for me. Abraham--even as a shadow of himself--was the love of my life. I couldn't ask for another, better man."

Colonel Tomas Nolan thought about his secret as his limousine pulled into traffic on his way back to the airport. He and a grizzled, salty old sargent would carry it to their graves.

A few months after Abraham was deployed to Korea, Nolan followed him over. He had been assigned to investigate The Hill 303 Massacre which took place on August 17, 1950. He was interrogating a prisoner who had been found stripping American Army dead of souvenirs--watches, wallets, small flags, Bibles, rings, whatever he could find. Even through his nervousness the North Korean had a goofy smile. He knew enough English that he believed he could charm his way through the interrogation. His small eyes darted back and forth as he anxiously brushed his hair with his handcuffed hands. He was dark with large misshapen ears.

Nolan asked, "Where did you get these?" He held out two rings he had taken from the prisoner.

"I find on dead soldier."

Nolan sensed it was a lie. He examined the rings closely. He was wearing a matching West Point ring on his right hand. He recognized the wheat pattern on the shiny, new wedding ring. He looked inside the band; it was engraved 'Abraham and Melbourne - forever together - June 10, 1950'. He had held this ring once before. He hadn't heard Abraham Cash was dead. He unbuttoned his shirt pocket and slipped both rings inside. "In thanks for these, I am going to let you try to escape." He gave the prisoner a sad smile, "I know who they belong to." He unlocked the prisoner's shackles and handcuffs, grabbed him by the collar, and pulled him out of the interrogation room. A sargent was standing guard at the door.

"Sarge, are you a man of--justice?"

The sargent didn't know quite how to answer. "I guess so, Sir."

"So if you were to witness something you would need to give testimony of it--say in a court of law or at a court-martial?"

"I guess so, Sir."

"Even if the bad act was the right thing to do?"

Wondering where this was headed, he shifted his weight nervously. "I guess so, Sir."

"Hummm. Then you are not gonna wanta watch this." Nolan turned his head to the prisoner, "RUN!"

The prisoner was frozen for a second, unsure what he should do. Slowly and steadily, Nolan unbuttoned his holster and extracted his .45 M1911, single-action, semi-automatic handgun. The prisoners eyes got big and he turned and raced down the hall. Nolan pulled the gun up, chambered a round, flipped off the manual safety, looked down the barrel using the Patridge sight, and squeezed the trigger. The back of the prisoners head exploded. He stepped forward while extracting his knife, cut off the prisoner's ear, and returned to the Sargent. "Thank you for not watching. Could you clean up this

315

mess for me?"

"I'd be honored, Sir!"

TWELVE

Meadow's distress over her work carried into conversations at lunchtime for the next few weeks. Finally, Alexander and Jacqueline had her over for dinner one evening to talk things out. Meadow despised Secretary of State Dean Rusk. Kennedy had felt the State Department was "like a bowl of jelly." Johnson kept everybody on JFK's cabinet and couldn't seem to see the problems. It came up often during dinners or cocktails in Alexander's home.

"Bowl of Jelly!" she confided to Alexander and Jacqueline. "I hope somebody gives the man a backbone for Christmas!" Alexander laughed.

Jacqueline added, "Oh, it can't be that bad!"

"You don't work for the man! If they ask his opinion, he says, 'But I can't give you my opinion; you haven't told me what it is yet!'"

Alexander roared at her imitation.

"He is the one that came up with the brilliant idea to split Korea."

"Well, he is from the South! Probably thought the North should have let the South go during the Civil War!"

"Yeah, easy to make those decisions when it is not your country you're splitting up!"

"I understand Kennedy was going to can him!"

"That was the rumor. Then Johnson hung onto him."

"I'm afraid he's stuck now!"

"How so?"

"Well, how can you fire the guy who simply parrots everything you say?"

"Ouch!"

After dessert, they sat in the living room while she continued to let off steam like a tea kettle.

"Kennedy complained the State Department 'never comes up with any new ideas', but that wasn't true. It just all gets squashed at the top," Meadow whined.

Alexander said, "I guess I am not as close to it as you are."

"Two weeks ago there were a dozen of us pulled together to look at options to a problem. I can't talk about it, but we came up with seventeen different solutions! We ranked them by a criteria we developed and presented them to Rusk. A few were 'no brainers' and he rejected each one."

"Sounds like you need a vacation."

"I've been thinking something more drastic! Yeah! Come on, it's 1966 for God's sake. We have been there too long. Can't they see we are heading down the same path as the French? Only took them twenty years to figure out there was no winning this war! Now will it take us twenty more?"

"Well, nobody wants to be the first President to lose a war on their watch!"

"Right, so keep fighting an unwinnable war?"

"As long as you are still fighting, you haven't technically lost," said Alexander.

"Do we have to kill off fifty thousand men before they set their egos aside?"

"Shit, we're not even close to that. And we must have killed a quarter million gooks by now."

"The army estimate is 160-170,000."

"Including civilians?"

"Probably. Can't tell one from the other."

"So, what are you going to do?"

There was a long pause before Meadow quietly said, "I am not making any difference where I am. So I am going to take a vacation and see some people in Idaho."

The next week, Meadow spotted the red and white Cessna between the peaks as it descended toward the air strip. "Hello, Larry!" she yelled to the idling plane that had just pulled to a stop.

"Hi, Meadow. I'll get this plane buttoned down and be with you in a minute." Soon they were headed north on Highway 75 two miles to Jerry's. "I remember the awesome fish."

"Still the best!"

After dinner, they started reviewing options. "We've already got a Republican in the second Congressional district, George Vernon Hansen.

"We've got Len Jordan in the Senate and they've got Frank Church. I don't see changes there anytime soon.

"Of course, if you are willing to move over to the first Congressional district, Compton Ignatius White, Jr. is vulnerable. Jim McClure has already got a jump start on the primary, should go head-to-head well with White in the general next fall. You could test the waters against McClure. But you would have to move, of course, and become a Mormon."

"Become a Mormon?"

"Only if you want to win."

She pulled at her hair. "Any other options?"

"There is always the State legislature."

"That doesn't play well with my interest in working against the Vietnam war, nor my experience at State."

"True."

"You might want to meet with Jordon to see if he has anything for you--staff position? speech writer? spokesman?"

Meadow was discouraged. She hadn't yet resigned from the State Department, but she couldn't picture herself going back.

The next few days, she made the rounds in government offices throughout Boise, before continuing their discussion at Larry's home. Meadow never saw it coming. Even when Larry asked if she wanted him to light a fire in his bachelor apartment, she didn't see it.

When he brought her a glass of sherry, she didn't know the spider was playing the fly. Teasing. After he handed her the glass, he sat closer on the couch than he had.

When he sat down beside her, staring into her eyes, shifting his focus from one eye to the other; it still didn't click. When he gave her reassuring words, she thought his concern was for the difficult decision she had to make. And it was; in part.

When he reached over to reassure her, he cupping her chin with his hand. When she spoke with her hands, he lightly reached over to stroke them, as he reinforced her points. She didn't even notice. When she brushed the hair from her face, he reached over to gently smooth it and his eyes caressed her as if he were using his hand. But did she see it?

He gave her his soothing words and tender smile. She didn't realize he thirsted to taste her, when he coated his parched lips with his tongue.

It is amazing how the mind works. From the instant we are conceived, our minds guide us, steer us away from danger, protecting us from hurt. It blinds us in order to protect us; prevents us from seeing that which might hurt us. Then, in an instant, it stops. Instead of protecting us it casts us forward into the abyss. It does something counter to every instinct. We are shocked by it when it happens. Nothing could be further from our minds. It is so preposterous, it even has its own four-letter word: Love.

Even when she leaned over to kiss him, she wondered to herself, 'How is he making me do this?' When he kissed her back, it was not forceful, selfish, and demanding--it was passionate, but in the best way, a sharing way.

Meadow and Larry were each swollen, engorged. Leaking fluid. She writhed and grabbed and pulled him in and they made love by the dwindling fire. A million-and-a-half of her nerve endings sprung to life and she guiding him until he had stroked them all. She howled like a Banshee Indian.

After her trip to Idaho, Alexander and Jacqueline invited Meadow down to the family ranch; more than the usual number of the family were assembled there this year for

Easter. Being with the kids, walking, boating, napping, and talking would help her through her slump at the State Department. Curled up on the couch, having pre-dinner cocktails in the Alabama spring, Meadow looked at Alexander's face not believing what she heard.

"No, I'm serious!" replied Alexander.

Meadow laughed, turned her face away, and yelled, "Your brother has gone CRAZY!"

"What?"

"He is sounding like your Father! Alexander has gone crazy. We need to call the ambulance and cart him off to the loony bin--perhaps Republicans need Democrats, but Democrats need Republicans? Huh! That is insane."

"Hear me out then." The family gathered around Alexander and Meadow. "If you realistically look at the two political parties, you will not see much difference."

"How so? One sides with workers and the other with businesses."

"To some degree. But they are just two sides of the same coin. Without workers you have no businesses: Without businesses you have no workers. So, compromise offers the best solution."

"Compromise?"

"Yes, compromise. Valuing what the other side brings to the table. And not horse trading--I get my piece on this issue, you'll get yours on that--real compromise."

"Can you give an example?"

"Sure. Johnson got legislation passed for the biggest expansion of Social Security ever with the introduction of Medicare. Even Republicans saw a need for a larger safety net. Look at what Republican John William Byrnes did; he got enough Republicans on his side to pass it. He took what the Administration proposed and molded it into a viable, workable system. Medicare now has the necessary checks and balances the Democrats left out.

"Democrats will always drive to a more compassionate America; Republicans will always drive towards fiscal responsibility. Together, they make America great!

"With the changes for Democrats in the Old South we already see the old grudges and revenge plots disappearing. Ideological extremism, so prevalent in the 30's, will soon become a thing of the past.

"Those who have scorned compromise in the past will be

dumped on histories dust heap!

"Mark my words--Political conviction, not political calculation, will prevail."

Meadow looked him squarely in the eyes, "You're so full of shit, even your eyes are brown."

Jacqueline laughed hysterically.

Thomas said, "I was reading Genesis 17 the other day. That is where God creates a covenant with Abram. Okay, so God promises to bless Abram, to turn him into mighty nations, great wealth, with Kings and all. Only, there is one catch. Circumcision." Everyone laughed. "So Abram has to circumcise all the males over eight days old. This includes his slaves and hired men. I want to know how that went down! 'Okay, men, God is gonna bless me no end. Just made these big promises to me. Kings, wealth, land, the whole enchilada. But there is a catch, boys! It's gonna cost each of us a little skin!' How do you like that for compromise!"

After breakfast the next morning the family was sitting around the table, finishing their coffee. Thomas said, "Do you know why Abraham couldn't have sacrificed Isaac a year later than he did?" He made it sound as a great Biblical lesson for life was coming their way.

"No, why?"

"He was twelve. A year later, he would have been thirteen--making him a teenager."

"So?"

"Since when is killing a teenager a sacrifice?"

"Good one," replied Alexander.

The United flight from Mobile to Washington D.C. on a Douglas Aircraft DC-6 should have been smooth as silk. She was the ultimate piston-engine airliner of the 50's and 60's, powered by Pratt Whitney R-2800 Double Wasp radial piston engines--reliable and economical. The flight was scheduled to take three hours cruising 300 miles per hour at 20,000 feet over the spine of the Blue Ridge Mountains. Updrafts and downdrafts from hills and ridges below buffeted the plane most of the way. There were lingering odors from recently repainting the Capital Airlines plane after United acquired the carrier. The engines rumbled along. Jacqueline curled up next Alexander on the bench seat with her head on his lap and was asleep in an instant. Looking down, he thought 'Gawd, she's beautiful!'

He tried to lose himself in the fabulous vista below--but she was squeezing him out of his seat.

He lifted her head with one hand and swirled a blanket with the other to make her a pillow.

He squeezed into the dual bench seat across the aisle to listen to Meadow pick up from an earlier conversation.

"Diplomats rarely work in the sunlight. My boss can't tell me anything that would help, while I am expected to walk a tightrope! If we fail, everyone knows; if we succeed, nobody knows."

"What do you suggest?"

"Better coordination between the military and us would be a good start."

"Yes, you need them working together. Dad said, 'You need the military to end the fights and the diplomats to start them!'"

"Not funny." She thought about asking about progress in finding George, but couldn't find the words.

"Actually, there is an element of truth to it. When we want to get our point across, send in the State Department. If they respond incorrectly, fall back on the military."

"Negotiation works best, but it can't stop there. Consider the Berlin Airlift. Allies couldn't budge the Soviets so they negotiated with previous enemies to side step them. Talk is cheap. If you aren't ready to back up your stance with bold steps, you aren't going far. The Allies were rational, pragmatic, swift, and decisive--and delivered the goods. It went a long way in healing a wounded Germany and exposed and embarrassed the Soviets. Half a dozen countries who felt threatened joined NATO."[60]

---

[60] The Berlin Blockade (June 24, 1948 - May 12, 1949) was the first major crises of the Cold War. During the multinational occupation of post-World War II Germany, the Soviets blocked railway and road

Alexander remembered something he wanted to tell Meadow. "Did you know Patton, at the end of World War II, told the Secretary of War, 'I would have you tell the Red Army where their border is, and give them a limited time to get back across. Warn them that if they fail to do so, we will push them back across it.'"

"Yeah, he was a master of diplomacy!"

"He wanted to go from Berlin straight to Moscow. Said that was where the next war was gonna be; why not finish the job while we had all those men in Europe? Turned out to be right."[61]

"What amazes me is that the Allies couldn't keep the Soviets in the areas that they had agreed, what was it, six months earlier?"

"More like four. Potsdam."

"Now we have a Cold War."

"Nothing 'cold' about it."

Meadow looked out the window, "You got that right!

---

access to all sectors of Berlin, essentially giving them control over the entire city. Western Allies responded by organizing the Berlin Airlift to supply West Berlin. More than 200,000 flights, over nearly eleven months, provided an average of 4,700 tons of fuel and food each day. Three, twenty mile wide air corridors had previously been agreed to in writing, where roads and rails had not. It was expected that the airlift would only last a few weeks. By April 1949, they were delivering more cargo than had previously been transported into the city by rail. The success of the Berlin Airlift was embarrassing to the Soviets who had refused to believe it could be sustained. The air corridors into Berlin were maintained until 1990, after the fall of the Soviet Union.

[61] At the conclusion of World War II United States Army General George S. Patton, Jr. (1885 - 1945) said of the Soviets to Secretary of War Robert Porter Patterson, Sr. (1891 - 1952), "I understand the situation. Their supply system is inadequate to maintain them in a serious action such as I could put to them. They have chickens in the coop and cattle on the hoof -- That's their supply system. They could probably maintain themselves in the type of fighting I could give them for five days. After that it would make no difference how many million men they have, and if you wanted Moscow I could give it to you. They lived on the land coming down. There is insufficient left for them to maintain themselves going back. Let's not give them time to build up their supplies. If we do, then... we have had a victory over the Germans and disarmed them, but we have failed in the liberation of Europe; we have lost the war!"

Bombers and Fighters carrying nuclear bombs. Nuclear warheads on thousands of missiles on both sides. Tell me what's cold!"

"We're asking for an accident. Anything can give an excuse for the firing to begin."

"Oh, we've had our share of accidents. You just don't hear about them. Tell me what good comes from this--just one thing!"

"Well, there is one. War is great for the economy. Military bases feed whole towns. Aircraft companies. Port cities. Oil. Big steel. Communications. Electricity. Educational institutions. Then there is the softer side: food, housing, clothing. Yes, the military drives the economy!"

"Drives?"

"Well, not actually drives, but plays a big part. Don't forget--World War II spending took us out of the Depression to become, fifteen years later, an economic juggernaut!"

As for Thomas, after participating in the Billy Graham crusade he remained involved in evangelical events and later in civil rights campaigns. He liked the limelight of being a white preacher at negro crusades and protests. He refused to see minorities as different from anyone else; many times to the consternation of his new congregation. He was being called to be the 'salt and light' of the church. Being the light was easy--preaching to illuminate the path forward could be fun. But salt can be an irritant; like splashing seawater on one's face to wake him up, some might get into eyes. Both instructing and confronting was part of being a good pastor.

His most controversial step was to invite Reverend Howard Thurman to preach in his pulpit one Sunday. He left it as a surprise when he invited him up, after the doors had been closed. Earlier he had asked the ushers to block the exits while his guest was in the pulpit. Thurman spoke, not of the civil rights movement, but of Mohandas Karamchand Gandhi.

"Gandhi said, 'I like your Christ. I do not like your Christians. They are so unlike your Christ'. What an indictment to all those who call Jesus our King!

"Each one of us shares the blame that the world does not see Jesus when they look at us! We are without excuse.

"We can do better than we have. He called all to come unto Him. He was gracious and giving to everyone He met, even those who would reject Him! And what has He done for each of us who call ourselves Christians here today? 'Greater love hath no man than this, that a man lay down his life for his friends.'"

The new week carried grumbling and talk of removing Pastor Thomas, but it came to nothing. A few hateful letters. Eggs tossed from a passing car onto his garage. Thomas resolved not to let it bother him.

"We will not reverse a hundred years of hate, with twenty minutes of sermon," he told Penny. She hugged him tightly--proud, and yet, afraid. She pushed the anonymous threats out of her mind, even as she could see the egg smashing against the windshield of her car.

He met monthly with pastors of like mind, regardless of race, for lunch and to talk. Every time was behind the scenes at one of the church's kitchens, hidden from prying eyes. He didn't want to cause problems for them and they didn't for him. But they kept up the ongoing conversation they knew, maybe instinctively, would be needed to bring them together. "The time will come to step out of the shadows in some way, to be arm in arm with friends, but when and how, nobody can say."

On July 2, 1964, President Johnson signed the Civil Rights Act of 1964. Four days later John Lewis led 50 blacks to the Dallas County Curthouse to register to vote. Sheriff James "Jim" Gardner Clark, Jr. had his men beat and arrest them. One week later, Judge James Hare issued an injunction forbidding gatherings of three or more people under sponsorship of various organizations or leaders. The injunction allowed him to jail anyone he perceived violated his order. The Justice Department took over the oppositions legal maneuvering when the small civil rights organizations ran out of money. But the damage was done; voter registrations came to a standstill and organizations driven underground.

On April 16, 1965, the United States District Court for the Southern District of Alabama, Northern Division dissolved Hare's defiant, blatantly unconstitutional injunction.

Thomas fumed at every twist and turn of the court battles. He had raced home after leading worship services and flipping on the TV on the way by to let it warm up while he shot upstairs to the bedroom to change his clothes. Penny put down her purse and stood before the television for a moment before she would prepare lunch in the kitchen. She took off her earrings and kicked off her shoes while watching in stunning silence before calling out to Thomas.

"Honey, come here! Quick!"

"What is it, Penny?"

She stood in front of the television pointing, "Look!"

"Where is this?"

"Selma."

"My God! What have they done?" They stared at the grainy, black and white images of Alabama State Police beating marchers with night sticks while tear gas clouded the sky around the Edmund Pettus Bridge. They were speechless and later learned Dallas County Sheriff Jim Clark had ordered all white males in the county over twenty-one to report that morning to the courthouse to be deputized. It became known as 'Bloody Sunday'.

Thomas was ready to respond when Martin Luther King, Jr. called on clergy across the nation to join him in two days to continue the march. That plan was squashed by Federal Judge Frank Minis Johnson, Jr. who ordered the march suspended until he could hear from both sides later in the week. Instead of marching on Tuesday, they prayed and dispersed. There was no telling how this judge, born and raised in the Deep South, and a one-time classmate of Governor George Wallace might rule. On March 16, Judge Johnson ruled for the protestors, saying their First Amendment right to march in protest could not be abridged by the state of Alabama: "The law is clear that the right to petition one's government for the redress of grievances may be exercised in large groups. These rights may be exercised by marching, even along public highways."

Five days later, Pastor Thomas Buck began the march King had called for with eight thousand protestors being careful to observe Judge Johnson's restrictions not to block traffic on the two-lane portion of Highway 80. On Thursday, March 25, 1965, he was prominent among the 25,000 people marching from St. Jude Educational Institute, a private, Roman Catholic high school in Montgomery, to the steps of the Alabama State Capitol Building. His congregation could clearly see the tall white man holding a white cardboard placard in a sea of negros on their grainy television screens. Many were not happy.

The next Sunday, Thomas preached with exuberance of his experience of the previous week. He also talked about the Vietnam War and about disproportion numbers of negros being drafted into military service. A handful of men from his congregation had heard enough. They sat upright and eyed one another without saying word.

The following Tuesday was trash night and three aluminum cans were brimming full. In the late evening he wished Penny 'good night'.

"Are you coming up soon?" she asked flirtatiously.

"I am going to do a bit more reading. Then I need to take out the trash."

"I love you, Honey. Do you know how proud I am of you?"

"Oh, come here." They kissed and she did not want to let him go.

"This negro issue is going to take some time."

"You stood up for what is right. That's what counts."

"Thank you. Are you sleepy? I'll try to be quiet with the cans."

"No, not a bit. You will come to bed soon, won't you?"

Penny blew out the patchouli candle and set the holder down on the flat finial on the newel post at the base of the stairway. The scent filled the air, while dying beads of white smoke drafted up the stairs behind her.

After ten-thirty, he smelled something exciting. Jean

Naté fragrance waffled in from the bedroom. Instantly Thomas was aroused and engorged. His eyes lit up and he crimped the page and closed his book as he sprinted out to the garage and lifted the door. Jean Naté meant one thing and he wasn't about to pass up dessert! It had been her signal to him since their honeymoon. A fleeting thought told him to go upstairs; but he knew himself--the trash wouldn't make it out in the morning. One by one, he quickly dragged the cans around his car until all three were sitting at the top of the driveway. He pulled a small red hand cart from next to the wall and scooted it beneath the first can. Instantly he deposited it next to the curb. He could see himself running up the stairs, taking every third step. He turned and in a flash was back at the top of the driveway, scooting the metal flange of the cart under the trash can he was tipping slightly with his left hand. He dropped the can next to the curb. He could see her spreading her legs under the sheets and stretching as he dropped his clothing on the floor. Collecting the third can, he turned and was dropping it at the curb, when everything went dark.

Early the next morning the paperboy frantically beat on the front door. "Mrs. Buck, Mrs. Buck! Come quick. Something's the matter with your husband."

She came to the door in her robe, "What's the matter?"

The boy was running away from her, pointing. "Quick. It's your husband."

The first few days in the hospital it was unclear whether Thomas would survive. He'd lost a great deal of blood after seven hours on the driveway. Penny was beside herself. He would survive, but never speak nor walk again. A gray cloud hung over their household for weeks.

Thirty years later, three members of the congregation confessed to the assault. They had hidden next to the garage. One ran up from behind and hit him with a baseball bat. They just meant to scare him. No member of the family attended the court hearing--it wouldn't have helped to restore Thomas.

Alexander's mood was like the sky outside his office--slate gray. He had been pacing or looking out the windows of the floor office in the Harry S Truman State Department headquarters for nearly two hours, since he had received word from his boss that he had bad news--and to cancel his meetings and wait in his office until he could get back to him. In early 1967, Alexander was being assigned to the Embassy of the United States in Tel Aviv-Yafo, Israel. For years, he and Jacqueline had talked about which foreign embassy they wanted to be assigned to, if given the opportunity. Israel always came out at the top of their list. Now with their house sold and airline tickets purchased, he knew the news wouldn't be good.

"We are going to need to suspend your move for a bit."

"But, Roger..."

"Let's just say things are heating up behind the scenes. Staying here will reduce risk to your family."

"How long?"

Roger said, "I am guessing six-to-nine months," while he was thinking, 'maybe forever'.

"We just sold the house."

"I know. We'll help you find temporary quarters. You'll be here in Washington, but you'll still be working on Israel."

"How?"

"I am assigning you to Ambassador Eban. They have been hinting, and not too subtly I might add, at wanting greater access to the President."[62]

"Are we giving that to them?"

"They are going to make Rusk more available. After he has worn him down, they may let Johnson have a shot at him."

"What will our position be?"

---

[62] Aubrey Solomon Eban (1915 - 2002). Fluent in ten languages, he endeared himself to others with his dry wit. He commented, the Palestinians "never miss an opportunity to miss an opportunity." Eban was highly effective and ever the optimist, observing "history teaches us that men and nations only behave wisely once they have exhausted all other alternatives." He served as Israel's Ambassador to the United States from 1950-1959 and as Foreign Affairs Minister from 1966–1974.

"We won't provoke the Russians."

"How does that help Israel?"

"It doesn't."

"And it helps us by keeping us from fighting the Soviets on two fronts?"

"Correct. We have our hands full with them in Vietnam. Better a regional war in the Middle East than World War Three."

"Are we kidding ourselves?"

"Absolutely."

By Easter, the family was together at the ranch in Mobile. Alexander's move to Israel was still on hold and they were living in a cramped, dingy yellow apartment in Georgetown. Getting away from the apartment was turning out to be a favorite activity these days, with no end in sight.

Alexander and Jacqueline enjoyed talking with Thomas about the history of Israel, as well as current events since 1948.

"Is the Nation of Israel the fulfillment of prophecy, Thomas?" Jacqueline asked. She was excited that this could be taking place while they were there. It was the Bible coming alive! She reached over to squeeze her husband's hand.

"I'm not convinced it is. Truman was sure; I just don't know. Two thousand years later the nation reforms? Where have they been? More importantly, what have they become over the years? Are they the remaining remnant from so long ago? It's hard to tell."

Alexander looked at his brother closely, "But you do believe the land prophecies in the Old Testament about coming together of the Jews?"

"Of course. I'm just not sure whether that is a spiritual promise or a physical promise. Or a 'physical' promise in the New Jerusalem in heaven."

"But wasn't the promise to Abraham an unconditional promise. And God gave it to him on earth. And He did start its fulfillment on earth?"

"That's all true!"

"It doesn't rely on the Hebrews in any way?"

"Yes, it is a one-sided promise God made to Abraham."

"So, why do you have trouble with it?"

"It seems so far-fetched."

Alexander arranged three meetings between Eban and senior officials.

"How is it going?"

"Roger, I've got Rusk tonight and McNamara in the morning meeting with Eban."

"What about Johnson?"

"He's waffling."

"And?"

"I don't see how he can avoid him much longer. Eban is shrewd."

"Have you sized him up yourself?"

"I like him a lot. Straightforward. Smart. Witty. Hilarious as hell, actually. A guy we can trust. But--"

"What are you thinking?" He looked carefully at Alexander before adding "Off the record."

"I'm thinking, can he trust us?"

Johnson tried to reassure Eban as they sat with administration officials on leather couches in the Oval Office. Alexander watched the exchange with rapped attention. He head swiveled back and forth as if he were watching a tennis match.

"Time would not work against Israel, it would not lose by waiting for the Secretary General's report and Security Council consideration. During this period there would not be any deterioration in the Israeli military position. We know it is costly economically, but it is less costly than it would be if Israel acted precipitously and if the onus for initiation of hostilities rested on Israel rather than on Nasser."

"Mr. President, with all due respect, how can we be sure time will not work against us?"

"Your best stance is working through the United Nations."

"I can appreciate that from a political standpoint, but not militarily."

"Listen, our best intelligence says no attack from Egypt is imminent," Johnson lied.

"That is easy for you to say, my friend; the gun isn't

pointed at you."[63] Slowly and precisely, Eban went on, "Is there a disposition on the part of the US to take action?" There was no immediate reply, so Eban continued, "Time is extremely important. I intend to respond to my Cabinet that there is such a disposition on the part of the US to act."

Johnson nodded.

"When Nasser sees a US Navy escort ship, he'll think twice about closing off international waters."

Johnson nodded again.

"I would not be wrong if I told the Prime Minister that your disposition is to make every possible effort to assure that the Strait and the Gulf will remain open to free and innocent passage?"

Alexander could feel the tension in the pit of his stomach.

Johnson replied, "Yes."

Eban had seen the intelligence on the Egyptians, who called themselves the 'United Arab Republic' (UAR). "Our intelligence leads us to conclude an attack on Israel by the UAR is imminent. I don't understand why we have come to different conclusions. Perhaps if we put our intelligence people with your intelligence, we could come to a consensus?"

Secretary McNamara intervened, "We have had three separate intelligence groups look into the matter in the last twenty-four hours and our judgment is that the Egyptian deployments are defensive."

"I hope you are right."

"Besides, you'll deal the UAR a set-back," snapped McNamara.

"You'll whip hell out of them!" Johnson added.

Under Secretary Eugene V. Rostow said, "And, of course, you know we have conveyed to the Egyptians your concerns in the strongest possible terms."

Eban ignored the cheer leading and posturing. "Might we link at the military level?"

The President leaned forward and pounded a fist into his open hand, "All of our intelligence people are unanimous regarding the assessment; that an attack is not imminent;

---

[63] Central Intelligence Agency report prepared on the day of this meeting (May 26, 1967) contradicts what Johnson told Eban. Either an alternate report was prepared or the CIA report was creatively redacted to align with the story Johnson wanted to tell—'attack is not imminent, wait for the United Nations'.

and that if the UAR attacks you will prevail."

Eban calmly replied, "I am confident we will, if it comes to that. But at the moment we don't have any military group to plan with, and we need to be planning for all contingencies. If our Intelligence units cannot come together, could our military planners?"

He couldn't move the Americans off their stance.

Johnson held up his open hands. "Mr. Ambassador, if Israel will not start military operations, I promise you we will provide Israel with all the oil it needs."

Eban thought to himself, 'Oil is the last of my worries', but he said, "If a preemptive attack is in our best interest, we will have no choice but to attack."

Soon Washington announced that it would only intervene on Israel's behalf if the Soviets intervened first.

Alexander felt sick when he recognized the United States wasn't interested in preventing a war between Israel and Egypt. They would play chummy with a 'friend' and lie to them as long as it did not endanger American interests. Peace wasn't a priority at all.

THIRTEEN

As George recovered from his injuries, he worried about his family. "Do you think it would be possible to notify my family that I am alive?"

His interrogator just laughed.

He found he could push his worries out of his mind by concentrating on other things. George had a vast collection of books in his library at home. His appetite for World War Two books had been voracious during the last fifteen years. He loved to read anything he could get his hands on, but especially his war histories. He asked his guards to bring him newspapers. Generally they ignored his requests, but on occasion he would find a copy of *El Habanero* when he returned to his cot after exercise. He soon tired of the predictable, repetitious propaganda. Once he identified his benefactor, as asked the guard to get him a specific book: *The Rise and Fall of The Third Reich*.

The guard shook his head.

When George was asked to write out his confession, he was given paper and pencil. He wrote down, 'La subida y la caída del Tercer Reich - Shirer'. He crumpled up the sheet as if he were going to throw it away, but later slipped it into his shirt pocket. When the guard came by again, he handed him the paper. Once more the guard shook his head, but placed the crumpled paper in his pocket. On his day off, he took the page to a bookstore. The clerk looked at the wrinkled sheet, laughed, shook his head, and returned the paper to the guard without saying a word.

The guard walked in a library carrying his panama hat with a unlit cigar between his lips. He wore blue slacks and an embroidered, open-collar, white, short-sleeve shirt. He saw a sign hanging by a wire from the ceiling light fixture: Información. The woman sitting at the desk reminded him of his grandmother. She smiled and he returned a nervous grin.

"¿Puedo ayudarle?"

He removed the paper from his shirt pocket, unfolded it, and slipped it onto her desk. She placed her hands on the paper and smoothed it, glanced at him, then turned and picked up her reading glasses. She pondered what was written. Frowning, she looked the guard over carefully. This could be a trap. The Communists had spies everywhere.

"¿Por qué? "

"Es para un amigo."

¿Dónde trabajas?

He thought, 'why would she want to know where I work?' "Prisión."

She pushed the paper back to him. "¿Estás tratando de hacer que nos maten? "

'Am I trying to get us killed?' "Non!"

¡Fuera!

His books on the shelves back home would not leave him alone. He could feel their smooth pages. He knew the texture of the dull, red cloth covers. He would run his finger along the top of the dust covers, and nearly give himself a paper cut; in his mind. He would open a new book and feel the tension as it resisted and tried to close. He would open it fully and feel the strain as the spine contorted to the breaking point. Then he would do something he had rarely ever done. He would continue to press open the spine until it cracked.

He would dream he was back at Chet's library. Rebecca would be there, curled up on a couch, reading, with a cup of tea on a nearby table. George would wander around looking at the books that filled the shelves. He could hear Chet speaking to him, "They contain much of the world's knowledge." He looked up to see him, but Chet wasn't there. "A man who can read is never alone or without the means to find an answer."

George had nightmares that he was in Chet's library. He would pick a book off the shelf and open it. But the words were distorted, elongated. The letters were sliding down the page. He could smell the solvent they had used to clean the ink from the printing presses. They had used too much! They had gotten it on his book! The ink was washing off the pages. He could see the letters sliding off the pages. He looked on the ground and there were black lines on the floor in the shape of single chevrons. The chevrons were all along the floor. But they were not made up of lines. He bend down for a closer look, they were the ink letters fallen off the pages onto the floor, piled like lumps of goo--dissolving black gooey letters, becoming liquid and leaking, disappearing into the floor. Over time, the black chevrons would fade away into the oak floor.

Other times, George would reach for a book on the shelf and it would instantly disappear, leaving a puff of smoke, and a musty smell. He moved his hand down to a row of books on the shelf below and as he ran his index finger across their spines the volumes vanished, one-by-one. He tried it again with the next row down; like running a finger across the keys of a piano. When he got to the end of the row, he turned his palm up and watched the dust settle on his skin. Dust got into his nose and he'd woke up sneezing.

Each time he would dream, he noticed there were fewer and fewer books in the library. Some had slipped away; others he had destroyed himself. He awoke in a cold sweat.

In his dreams, he would open one of his World War Two books and read in great detail for a while. But soon there were missing parts. 'Oh, no, they are not missing! They are fading.' He would try to make out the missing word, usually just adjectives: "Starts with an 'H'. Is that an 'o' or an 'e'? What is that word?"

During the day, he tried to recall every detail of what he had read in the distant past. He would march across his cell, terrorized by a missing word, someone's name, or a foggy, vague minute detail. His guards thought he was going mad. Sleep brought him no relief.

And then it would happen--like a movie in Dolby Stereo

70mm and Technicolor, with every detail remembered vividly—he would peacefully dream.

Franklin removed his reading glasses to watch gardeners tend the roses. The springtime sun beat through the office windows, warming him. Bone weary from war and interminable stress, he was looking forward to his two-week vacation. The war was going well, but an uneasy peace was on the horizon. With a small smile on his face, he lit another cigarette. He wanted to be alone--to finish off what couldn't wait. Soon enough he'd be on a speeding train, with mountain and ocean views creating a barrier to the world. Time with his family and friends would be refreshing—drinks, meals, naps, small talk, and swimming.

When the phone rang he decided against answering it--Grace would take care of it. She came in without knocking a minute later and handed him a slip of paper. Looking at it he thought to himself, 'I should have taken it'.

Noticing his ashen-gray complexion and baggy eyes, she thought, 'A vacation will do him good'. "Is there anything you need, Sir?"

He thought of having her fix him a martini--'Ah, too early'. "No, thank you Grace." She began to close the door. "Oh, Grace."

"Sir?"

"I hope you will be able to enjoy the next two weeks. Just think--tomorrow night we'll be in Georgia! You deserve a rest. Are you packed?"

"Thank you. Just about, Sir."

"I couldn't do it without you!" He grinned as he exhaled a cloud of smoke. It meant a lot to her when he expressed his personal thanks, which he did often. It helped to keep going during long hours and trying times. She nodded and closed the door, as he picked up the phone and began to dial.

After two weeks in Georgia, the trip had been somewhat restful; as refreshing for him as anyone could expect. He didn't feel up to swimming, which wasn't like him at all.

There were hourly updates, progress reports, the critical numbers, and advice to give (or reserve for later). The experiments out west were going well. That was a decision he wish he didn't had to make, but there was no choice--for better or worse, it could change the world forever.

The cottage was considered ramshackle by some, but he loved it. Five rooms, not counting the entrance hall and deck, surrounded by pine trees and water.

"That soup was wonderful. Shall we move to the living room?"

He sipped his coffee; the conversation was lively and congenial. He thought 'there is nothing more refreshing than my friends!' Then reality intervened, "What time is it getting to be?"

"About one."

"Thursday today, isn't it?"

"Yes, the twelfth. Sir, there are papers you need to sign before Madame Shoumatoff arrives. Documents and letters."

"Oh, right, Hassett. Bring them here. She won't be long today, will she? We need to be working on my speech."

"I told her she could have you from one-fifteen to one-forty-five." He made a mental note to remind her at one-thirty that she only had fifteen more minutes, or the whole afternoon would slip away again.

He sat in his chair in the mid-afternoon. The Georgia-pine paneling in the living room gave a warm glow in the afternoon sun. His feet were cold and he was bundled in a blanket. He had removed his tie. His eyes looked tired and he couldn't muster a smile for long. His friends still chatted away on the couches nearby, while the artist continued the portrait. He would add a quip or two, darting his eyes over in their direction, flashing a sly grin, then quickly return his attention to the artist.

"Fifteen more, Elizabeth." She nodded and continued on.

His head tilted forward and he grabbed the back of his neck with his right hand, "I have a terrific pain in the back of my head." He slumped forward, unconscious.

Arthur Prettyman sprang into action, yelling "Isaac, help me!" The two men lifted the limp body onto the bed in the next room. Prettyman picked up the phone and called the doctors. Next he called Grace.

Drs. Bruenn and Fox where there immediately.

"McIntire? It's Hacky. I have Bruenn here; he needs to talk with you."

There were low voices and tortured gasps, while in the next room, cousins were wandering in and out, weeping.

"Hacky, get Paullin!" Dr. James E. Paullin, a heart specialist, was soon driving southwest at breakneck speed from Atlanta, eighty miles away.

As Paullin's tires skidded to a stop on the unpaved, gravel driveway, the telephone rang and the clock chimed three-thirty.

"Hacky."

"Mac here. Has Paullin arrived?"

"He just pulled in."

The door swung open, as both doctors in the bedroom yelled, "Quick!" Hacky held out the phone and Paullin took hold of it only long enough to set it down on the table, before running into the bedroom.

He slowly came back two minutes later. His slumped shoulders told the story. He picked up the telephone receiver. There were tears in his eyes. "The President is dead."

The movies he would play back in his mind give him some semblance of relief. He would not fret about the details again; instead, he would play the movie in his mind. He could pick up the story at any time and begin at any spot.

The smoke from FDR's cigarette went up his nostrils. He could feel the texture of the heavily starched, white table cloths. He could taste the coffee with rich cream and not quite enough sugar. He could see the bright splashes of color from the oil paints on the artist's palette. The smell of linseed oil would permeate his clothing for days afterward. He could feel the rocking of the train. He would open the window and the mist from the breakers collected on his face as the railcar clicked along the tracks against the Atlantic coast.

A year earlier, FDR had had a physical. They identified chronic high blood pressure, systemic atherosclerosis, coronary artery disease with angina pectoris, and myopathic hypertensive heart disease with congestive heart failure. At 3:35 p.m. on Thursday, April 12, 1945, a massive cerebral hemorrhage (stroke) ended his life. He was sixty-three.

FDR's biographer James M. Burns likened his efforts to simulate the economy during the Great Depression to "the general of a guerilla army, fighting blindly through a jungle." With a parade of presidential advisors coming and going, contradictory policies were formulated and execution was haphazard. Everything was tried; many policies failed and were reversed. Others were of questionable success. FDR kept pitching. His economic policies probably extended the Depression; World War II lifted the United States from the lowest depths to economic super stardom.

Like his predecessor, he believed the Great Depression was caused in part by people not spending or investing. But unlike his predecessor, he had great confidence in the American people and that together they would 'right the ship'. What FDR brought to the nation was spectacularly successful and rare in politics--a believable hope. He made America believe in herself again.

'Why am I dreaming about this grinning, yellow-toothed, chain-smoking, old cripple as he works himself to death?'

There was no reply to answer his question. But his mind would move on to the next chapter. The torment would begin again.

🐺🐺🐺🐺🐺🐺

The Speaker had his feet up on his desk when his visitor nodded, passed by his secretary, and came through the door to his private office unannounced.

"Long day, Harry."

"Damn, I'm dry."

"I'll take care of that." Speaker of the House Samuel Taliaferro Rayburn pulled a bottle of I. W. Harper bourbon from his desk, poured three ounces into two classes already filled with ice, and handed one to the Vice-President. It was an afternoon ritual the two shared every day Congress was in session.

"Thanks, Sam. Did you see the roses outside?"

"Nope. Haven't been outside all day."

"Sam, ya gotta take time for yourself. Get outside. Take a walk."

"Harry, I don't know how you do it!"

"Do what?"

"Get away from those Secret Service agents."

"It's easy. Most of those bastards are so out of shape..." Rayburn laughed. "When I really want to stretch my legs, I head down to see the Marines."

"Shit! That must be..."

"Five miles round trip."

"How long does that take you?"

"A little over an hour. I have always been a walker. Cleans the mind."

"What's your secret?"

"I do it early in the day. When I'm the most fresh. After my breakfast drink."

"Your what?" He lifted up his glass. Rayburn laughed. "I got the Education Bill loaded up for the end of next week."

There was a knock on the door. Rayburn's secretary leaned into the room, "Sorry for the interruption. Mr. Truman is needed at the White House immediately."

"Thank you."

Truman took another swig, "FDR must be back in town."

"I didn't think he was coming back so soon. He loves it in Georgia, I hear."

"Hope he got some rest. Looked like hell last time I saw him. I never know what he's doing. They don't tell me shit about anything."

"Really?"

"Yeah, I talk to the President about once a month. When he needs a favor!" Truman gulped down the rest of the bourbon.

"Well, I don't have anything that can't wait."

"Me either. You keep those bastard Republicans from

342

stealing the stationary supplies, and I'll see ya tomorrow." Rayburn lifted his glass and smiled. "Thanks for the Harper's, Sam."

Escorted to Eleanor Roosevelt's second-floor study, she informed him the president was dead. Truman's first concern was for her and he asked if there was anything he could do, to which she responded, "Is there anything we can do for you? You are the one in trouble now!"

Shortly after seven that evening, Harlan Stone, Chief Justice of the Supreme Court administered the oath of office to Harry S Truman in front of the cabinet, senior war administration officials, the leadership of Congress, and his family. The press was led in by Press Secretary Steve Early for photographs. Truman said to the reporters, "Boys, if you ever pray, pray for me now. I don't know if you fellas ever had a load of hay fall on you, but when they told me what happened yesterday, I felt like the moon, the stars, and all the planets had fallen on me."

"Mr. President, the press was asking about the San Francisco Conference later this month. Have you made a decision?"

"Yes, Steve. You can announce I plan to attend and give the opening address. Secretary Stettinius briefed me on the plans."

"Very good, Sir." He escorted the reporters from the room.[64]

"Thank you, Gentlemen and Miss Perkins. I know this has been an exhausting day for each of us and I will not keep you long. I can tell you that I need each and every one of you. I will carry on to the best of my ability and I can assure you I am completely aligned with FDR's goals of winning both the war and the peace. I don't know what your individual plans had been, but I need each of you to give me the same support you have been rendering. To that end, I request that each of you remain at your posts for the immediate future.

"Tomorrow morning will be given over to preparing for the funeral. After that I will meet with each of you individually as quickly as I can. I will need you to brief me with the understanding it will take me some time to absorb

---

[64] The United Nations Conference on International Organization (UNCIO), which brought together fifty Allied nations from April 25, 1945 to June 26, 1945 in San Francisco, California, resulted in the creation of the United Nations Charter.

everything necessary. I am a different leader than Franklin was, and will need your advice, council, and patience.

"Thank you for the wonderful service you have given to our Country. God bless us, every one. Good night."

Silently, the cabinet members left the room, except Secretary of War Henry Lewis Stimson. "Mr. President, I need to speak to you about a most urgent matter."

"Very well."

"We have an immense project underway, developing a new explosive with unbelievable destructive power. I have personal control of the entire project. It will be the most terrible weapon ever known in human history. It is ultra-secret and we must bring you up to speed on it as quickly as possible. It's called Manhattan."

"Manhattan?"

"Yes, Mr. President. The Manhattan Project. I will have Jimmy see you tomorrow to give an overview and set a time to run through the details. That's all I am free to tell you right now." Truman looked at him quizzically and didn't say a word.

"Bess, how about an old-fashioned?"

"I'd love one. Did you see those men outside?"

"Yes, they are reporters. Are they bothering you?"

"Well, no. I guess I'll get used to it."

"We'll be living in a fishbowl now." Truman fixed her drink and poured three fingers of I. W. Harper for himself. He leaned over and smelled the white tulips.

"Well, Harry, you are in for it now!"

"Yes, I am afraid I am."

"You have a lot of good people working for you."

"I'll need them all."

"You know the Democrat leadership was figuring Roosevelt wouldn't survive this term."

"I didn't after I saw him last time, but not this soon."

"Yes, it is quite a shock. He seemed like he would go on forever."

"I feel so ill prepared."

"You are."

"That son-of-a-bitch didn't tell me anything. I just learned we are developing the most powerful weapon in the world. Ain't that hell?"[65]

---

[65] On April 24, Stimson and Leslie Groves delivered to Truman reports and details on the Manhattan Project. They told Truman that

🐺🐺🐺🐺🐺🐺

Once again George felt some relief. But now there were two movies which didn't make sense.

George could taste the Harpers and feel the glass, cold from ice cubes. He smiled at the Speakers easy manner and gentle laugh. George laughed at Truman's cuss words. His legs ached and he was winded from trying to keep up, stride-for-stride, with the little man in the white suit. He could smell the wax on the heavily-polished office paneling. The banister on the stairs felt slick as he climbed to meet the First Lady. He could smell Eleanor Roosevelt's perfume and see her big teeth as she joked with Truman even in these, most trying circumstances. He pushed his nose deeply into the tulips to get any scent, even though what little he got

---

Germany couldn't develop the atomic bomb, but the Soviets could in as little as four years. "…within four months we shall in all probability have completed the most terrible weapon ever known in human history." Truman authorized the continuation of the project. President Truman issued a statement announcing the bombing of Hiroshima using a new weapon. The press release in part read: "It was to spare the Japanese people from utter destruction that the ultimatum of July 26 was issued at Potsdam. Their leaders promptly rejected that ultimatum. If they do not now accept our terms they may expect a rain of ruin from the air, the like of which has never been seen on this earth. Behind this air attack will follow sea and land forces in such numbers and power as they have not yet seen and with the fighting skill of which they are already well aware." Three days later he announced an atomic bomb had been dropped on Nagasaki.

"I realize the tragic significance of the atomic bomb. Its production and its use were not lightly undertaken. But we knew that our enemies were on the search for it. We know now how close they were to finding it. And we know the disaster which would come to this nation, to all civilizations, if they had found it first.

"Having found the bomb we have used it. We have used it against those who attacked us without warning at Pearl Harbor, against those who have starved and beaten and executed American prisoners of war, against those who have abandoned the pretense of obeying international laws of warfare. We have used it in order to shorten the agony of war, in order to save the lives of thousands and thousands of young Americans."

was bitter. George smelled the hay and jumped up to help pull the bale off the President. The flash bulb in the Cabinet Room blinded his eyes and he thought of another flash a few days away over the skies of Japan.

Roosevelt had been imperious as President, personally controlling major decisions and not seeking advice or counsel from any of his vice-presidents. None had been prepared in the least to succeed him. Truman came to be FDR's running mate for his fourth term in what was known as the "Missouri Compromise"--political maneuvering at the Democrat Convention in 1944 to find the most acceptable option. Roosevelt rarely contacted Truman, didn't inform him of decisions, and met infrequently with him during his 82 day vice-presidency. The day Truman took office, Joseph Stalin, Premier of the Soviet Union, knew more about the ultra-secret Manhattan Project developing nuclear weapons than he did.

George thought of this country bumpkin, so different from his predecessor, thrust onto the world stage. A vaudeville act, to be sure. White suit, straw hat, and cane. A rim shot from the drummer. He watched for a hook to drag him away.

But why? What do these dreams have to do with each other? 'Am I supposta know something here?' Again, there was no reply to answer his question. Soon his mind would move to the next chapter. The torment would begin again.

Eva wore his ring and proudly displayed it to everyone she met. He thought it best this way. "Tonight, my dear?"

"Yes, at midnight." He had been buoyed by hearing of the death of FDR seventeen days earlier but recent events had turned his mood sour. He still was hopeful the change of leader would bode well for him in negotiating peace with the Americans.

As Joseph escorted him downstairs, the judge's eyes were large. A minor official authorized to perform civil wedding ceremonies, he'd been shaken from his bed for the occasion. In a rumpled black suit, he weakly asked, "May I trouble you for a glass of water?"

"Certainly. Wait here." Joseph opened the conference room door and introduced him to the happy couple; the groom was in a military suit, the bride wore a black silk dress. "Guten Abend!"

"Welcome to our home. We've lived here since January."

"Thank you for coming."

The judge eyed Joseph, not knowing what to say. Joseph patted him on the arm, "I'll get you that water." As he entered the hallway, Joseph loudly announced, "It is time to come to the wedding, everyone! We are in the conference room."

The judge took the water and threw it down his throat, as if it were a brandy. Composing himself, he pulled a black leather book with a silver cross place marker attached by rosary beads from his pocket. He opened it to the section titled 'Wedding' and scanned the preliminary questions.

"Do you both assert you have been baptized in the one holy and universal Church?"

They both said, "Yes."

"Are you each free of inherited diseases and is your blood pure Ar..."

Joseph laughed nervously and interrupted, "I think we know the answers already; you may proceed with the wedding."

"Of course. I was only following..."

"I understand." He motioned with his hand to move forward.

"...I pronounce you husband and wife. You may kiss the bride." The groom stepped forward sharply, took his bride into his arms, and kissed her passionately. There was applause around the room.

"Please sign our guest book! We will have champagne and breakfast in my study." He pointed to an adjoining door. "Thank you, Judge. That was a wonderful service. Will you be joining us for our celebration? You already have met Joseph. This is his wife, Magda. Martin Bormann, Gerda Christian, Traudl Junge, Major Bernd Freytag von Loringhoven, General..."

Before the judge could answer, Joseph handed him off, "Otto, please see the good judge out. Auf Wiedersehen!"

Moët et Chandon 1937 Champagne flowed into monogrammed, gold-rimmed champagne glasses with swastikas and eagles, and breakfast was served on gold-rimmed Colditz porcelain dishware decorated with butterflies crafted from the initials, E. B.

"This sausage is wonderful! My complements to the chef!"

"Have you tried the egg dish?"

"It is delicious."

"Strudel?"

"Please."

The groom snuggled with his bride, "That was a wonderful wedding! I hope you are as happy as I am."

"Yes, my love." She lit a cigarette.

"I guess I will never cure you of those."

She raised her champagne glass, "This either!"

He smiled. "There are a few things I need attend to, my dear. For one, now we are married I need to change my will. You will excuse me."

"Yes, Dear."

"All of you please continue to enjoy our celebration. Unfortunately, there are important matters I need attend to at this moment. Traudl, are you ready?"

"Yes, Sir."

They went into his adjoining office. At four o'clock, they returned. "Thank you, Traudl."

At eleven in the morning, the groom reappeared, looking tired and dejected. "Otto, have Dr. Haase join me at once."

"Yes, Sir!"

"I need to be absolutely positive these work." He opened his palm.

"There is only one way to know--test them."

"How do we do that?"

"Either a person or animal."

"Would a large shepherd work?"

"Certainly."

"How long would it take?"

"Ten, fifteen minutes."

"Painful?"

"Not at all--like going to sleep."

He didn't speak for a minute. "Alright. Use them on Blondi and her puppies."

"Blondi? Your dog?"

"Yes, they'd do unspeakable things to her if they knew she belonged to me."

"Very well."

The phone rang and Otto answered it. "Yes, he is here." Otto held out the phone, "General Keitel."

"General, what is the situation? I see. No, they must stay where they are. No. Absolutely not."

As soon as the phone was hung up, it rang again. "Yes, he is here." Otto held out the phone again, "Wolff from Italy."

"Hallo Karl, what have you to report?...When?...How?...By the ankles?...In public?...How barbaric!...Thank you for calling...Yes, it is distressing news...I know you are doing your best...Yes, keep us posted, Wolff." He hung up.

He looked tired, like a man completely resigned to his fate. He spoke with Otto and his assistants. "Do you understand--what happened in Italy cannot happen here!" He gave them further instructions.

Dr. Haase returned, "It worked as expected."

The phone rang and Otto answered it. "Yes, he is here." He held out the phone, "General Keitel."

"The whole city?...Twenty-four...I see...I understand...I am disappointed in you, Keitel...No, they must remain." He hung up the phone. "Dear, let us go to bed."

Near one o'clock the next day, General Keitel was calling again.

"Encircled?...Defensive?...All of them?...Go ahead and try to break through...Goodbye, General."

After lunch, each said their farewell. Even Joseph and Madga's children were led in to say 'goodbye'. By two-thirty it was time. He led her by the hand to the study and closed the door. They sat on the couch talking for the next hour about his dreams and disappointments. "If only my generals had not let me down."

He pulled off his swastika ring, admired the square ruby

in the center, and placed it on a nearby table. "It is time, my love."

It was like taking communion; he handed her one tablet and held the other in his fingers. He raised it to her lips as she did the same for him--they fed each other this last time. She sat back.

He reached into his pants to locate the opening to the specially-sewn pocket and felt for the cold steel the pocket hid. Finding it, he pulled it out. He looked at the exquisite engraving on the handle of the Walther PPK 7.65 mm, admiring the excellent workmanship. He abruptly reached over with his left hand, pulled back the slide, raised the pistol to his temple, and pulled the trigger.

🐺🐺🐺🐺🐺🐺

Another movie! This time in German!

George began to fear the night.

He could smell the dank concrete and feel the clammy, soggy walls of the bunker. It carried a vague urine smell. He could hear the sausage sizzle as he watched grease spatter from the copper skillet. The sweet fragrance of large, dark plum-red, firm Bulgarian bing cherries in the savory strudel. The sound of snapping heels. Blond dog hair on Hilter's heavy wool coat. Brylcreem pomade on the Führer's dark brown hair. Clinking glasses and china. The loud ringing from the incessant telephone calls. Champagne bubbles bursting in George's nose. Grease on the pistol.

There were eighteen days between the deaths of Franklin Delano Roosevelt and Adolf Hitler; both had seen the inevitable fall of Nazi Germany. Roosevelt died of a massive stroke while vacationing: Hitler killed himself while imprisoned, rather than face vengeful reprisals at the hands of the Soviets. Hitler had secluded himself in his Führerbunker ("Leader's shelter") fifty feet beneath a garden at the Reichskanzlei (Reich Chancellery) in Berlin since January. Two days after Hitler died the Soviets took Berlin;

six days after that the War in Europe was over.[66]

Hitler's will expelled Reichsmarschall Hermann Göring and Reichsführer-SS and Interior Minister Heinrich Himmler from the Nationalsozialistische Deutsche Arbeiterpartei (Nazi Party) for their indiscretions at the end of the war. Having blamed his military leadership for losing the war, he named Großadmiral Karl Dönitz as Reichspräsident of Germany; the last President of the Third Reich. He was the logical choice--the Navy had done the least damage. Dönitz held office for three weeks, encouraging the German military and people to struggle on. Dönitz was equally ill-prepared to take the reins of state as was the new President of the United States Harry S Truman, FDRs third vice-president.[67]

"God, why do you haunt me with this lunatic? Whatever it is you want me to see, I'm not getting it!"

Nine weeks after accepting Nazi Germany's unconditional surrender, Allied leaders met in occupied Germany at the Potsdam Conference (July 16-August 2, 1945). During the Yalta Conference, five months earlier, the Allies had designed how Axis surrendered territory would be split up and administered. In attacking Germany, the Soviets

---

[66] The French prevented the Soviets from taking Berlin on May 1, a day that had been expropriated by the Soviets for political demonstrations and celebrations (May Day or International Workers' Day). Stalin told Eisenhower that he wasn't interested in Berlin, and then raced to be there by May Day, causing staggering Soviet losses to mount during the campaign.

[67] During the 1936 election, Truman's predecessor Vice-President Garner said things which fairly characterized the situation: "Our firm has two members. The senior member does all the talking and I do all the work." He also said, "When I switched from speaker to vice-president, it was the only demotion I ever had." But Garner retained his candidness and salt in his most famous quote about his dissatisfaction with the vice-presidency, describing it as "not worth a bucket of warm spit." That is what the newspapers reported: It is highly likely 'Cactus Jack' mentioned a different four-letter body fluid.

exceeded the territory they were to occupy and were not about to give it up, regardless of what they had agreed upon previously. There was much war treasure to be stripped away. During the Potsdam Conference, the Allies came together to determine the path forward. A rookie President and the man termed FDR's 'Assistant President', Southern politician James Francis Byrnes, would move all parties toward a pragmatic approach with far reaching consequences. Europe was split between east and west blocs of nations; the Japanese were given an ultimatum calling for unconditional surrender; and Korea--contrary to the wishes of all Koreans--was split north and south.

Four days following the conclusion of the Potsdam Conference, at the Broadcasting Corporation of Japan headquarters in Tokyo, a control operator was checking his equipment.
"Hiroshima station is off the air."
"Try another telephone line."
"I already have."
"Keep trying. It could be anything. I'll tell the boss."

Twenty minutes later the Tokyo railroad telegraph center was checking stations.
"Telegraph is out."
"Where?"
"North of Hiroshima."
"Keep trying it."

A few minutes later, telegrams began coming in with confusing reports; something about an explosion in Hiroshima.
"Telegraph still out?"
"Yes, Hiroshima and north. Everywhere else is fine."
"Could be anything. Better let General Staff know."

Headquarters of the Imperial Japanese Army General Staff repeatedly called Army Control Station in Hiroshima. The reports from the radio station and telegraph center indicated a glitch.
"Looks like all communications have gone out in Hiroshima."
"Yes, complete silence." He scratched his head. "There is not much in the way of explosives there."

"Raids?"

"None. We picked up three planes earlier. Probably reconnaissance aircraft."

"Doesn't make sense. Probably nothing."

"We should send someone down there to get reliable information."

"What do you make of the telegrams about bombing in Hiroshima?"

"Just rumors, like usual. Nothing serious."

A young officer of the Japanese General Staff was pulled in: "Fly out to Hiroshima, land, survey the damage or communications glitch, and report back. We need reliable information. Do you understand?"

"Yes, Sir!"

The staff officer drove to the airport immediately. After flying for three hours, the pilot said, "Look at that! Looks like a cloud. Or smoke."

"How far to Hiroshima?"

"A hundred kilometers."

"What happened?"

"I'm not sure. Keep circling."

"Everything is burning."

"I've never seen anything like this."

"Is there a place we can land?"

"I'll see what I can find to the south."

"Tokyo's not going to believe this."

"I'm not sure I believe it myself." The staff officer asked for massive, immediate relief measures.

Radio Tokyo described the scene: "Practically all living things, human and animal, were literally seared to death."

The clatter of the teletype pounded in George's head. A flurry of soldiers mindlessly running to-and-fro. Sharp salutes, orders, and bows. The aircraft buzzing as it streaked across the empty sky. Bouncing. He could see the massive gray cloud on the horizon. The blare of the sirens deafened him. Acrid smoke curling off burning flesh. George lurched to grab a handkerchief from his pocket to press against the nose. But still the smoke advanced through the weave of the cloth, up through his nostrils, and into his brain.

He woke with the start. His heart was pounding. "Oh God, thank you it wasn't real!"
'But it was real'.

He screamed, "I don't get it, God! Find somebody smarter! Quit tormenting me! Why would you want me to know this, if there is nothing I can do about it?"

'Why these dreams? What do they have in common? Leadership? Human folie?'

At last, the dreams stopped.

🐺🐺🐺🐺🐺🐺

Since 1966, George pretty much had full run of anywhere the Cubans placed him on their little oasis in the Caribbean. His guards didn't bothering to wear sidearms any longer; to where could George possibly escape? They gave him cigars and listened for long hours to his stories of smuggling across the Atlantic and chasing rabbits in Northern Idaho. He taught them English and they taught him Spanish, though he never let on that he actually spoke Spanish quite well. During severe storms, a guard took him with his family to find shelter in caves near the foothills. He played with the children and joked with the guard's wife until the storms passed.

George was moved repeatedly. Everywhere he was jailed he asked if anyone had seen his submarine. None had. The equipment on the sub couldn't possibly be used to collect, record, or transmit information to the Americans. He was again back at Bahía Honda, Pinar del Río Province, Cuba--43 miles west of Fidel Castro's prying eyes. Its sheltered bay at the eastern extent of the Colorados Archipelago and due south of the Florida Straits would provide an ideal launch location.

The following summer a sailboat was found adrift in Cuban waters. Soldiers hauled it onto shore and inspected it. There was no evidence of foul play. It was a mystery. The guards joked that a sailor had gone for a swim, lost his bearings, and the boat drifted away, leaving him to drown 40 miles from Miami. Others talked about it being used for an escape and that it had once been filled with American dollars. This led to extensive searches, but nothing was ever found. Not knowing what to do with the boat, some of the soldiers repaired the rigging and took it out into the Caribbean. One tried to sell it, but the others objected--it was theirs as much as his. During the winter, it ended up tied to a buoy in Bahía Honda harbor.

"You told us you sail, George. Is that really true or just one of your stories?"

"All my stories are true."

The guards laughed. They took George out to the boat that nobody owned and everybody owned. "Take us out!"

George carefully looked over the boat, checking lines and hardware, sails and winches. Satisfied with what he saw he replied, "Okay."

After twenty minutes of tacking across the bay, he headed north through the mouth of the bay and into the Caribbean. His guards sat at the stern watching George scampering around making adjustments. He close hauled just off the eye of the wind along the coast for an hour in the light airs. The water was translucent and inviting. He stripped naked in the glorious sunshine. His guards followed suit. George was once again free. He ducked close to shore, dropped the sails, peered down into the clear water, and checked his drift. 'Perfect' he thought. He dove from the bow and swam under the boat, surfacing ten feet beyond the stern. Timidly, one of his guards joined him in the water, while the other remained aboard, afraid the boat would drift away.

After swimming for a long time, George had an idea. He returned to the boat, looked through the cabin, pulling out drawers, until he found fish hooks and line. They had brought a little cheese and bread to eat, and he took a small chunk, placed it on the hook, and dangled cheese in the water. After fifteen minutes, he had caught a fish--just large enough to be bait. During the afternoon, he caught six fish--mostly, Emperor Fish. In the late afternoon, he landed a barracuda between his two guards. He laughed and yelled, "Take care of him. I'll head back." The long fish with fang-like teeth and large jaw thrashed around snapping at the men. They yelled and nearly jumped into the water to get away, before climbing over to the cabin, disappearing inside, and closing the door.

As George raised the sails he thought what a glorious day this had been. The water was refreshing; the salt air inspiring. Fish for dinner would be a rare treat. He thought he would cook them over a wood fire. The barracuda he would cut up, salt, and dry. He had one other thought as he tended the lines--America is a hundred miles away. If he wasn't tired from this day of play he might have turned the boat north. If he wasn't so out of shape he would have the endurance. Ah, he thought 'what might have been', as the sails popped and filled and pulled him back to where he had begun. Now, escape was never far from his mind. 'What do I need?' What he did have was a ready supply of fruit in groves and orchards, no matter the condition of make-shift shanties where he was hidden. His favorite was the Cavendish "Cuban Red" banana. He began to walk with purpose in his confined area. Thankfully he wasn't held in cells any longer. He stretched his muscles. As he physically prepared, the change in him was apparent to the guards. His muscles tightened, there was a change in his step, he laughed more, and his eyes held a hopeful gaze. For him, it was as if all his senses sharpened.

By 1968, the Cubans were ready to be rid of George Cash. They dutifully filled out the reports of his treatment (beatings), interrogations, and confessions; but more than six years had proven to even the most hard-hearted Communist that this guy was a tourist--lost on his toy submarine. Contrary to official reports the beatings had let up years earlier, because everyone liked George.

Through other nations, Castro had dangled George before the Americans a few times, but they never took the bait. They didn't know who George was and thought perhaps it was one of Castro's tricks. Castro had given up on George years earlier. He was left to rot with inadequate food and shelter, with no medical or dental care.

Each day thereafter, a different pair of soldiers from Bahía Honda came to George to sail in 'their' boat. He was only too pleased to grant their requests. They brought lunch, sometimes beer or wine, and always cigars. George fished and swam and the day would end back at the bay, barbecuing fish. He received a present of swim trucks, a blue baseball cap, and a fishing rod and reel.

Soon, the soldiers constructed a rough brick fireplace on the beach. George laughed to himself, 'Aren't you supposta have the prisoners do that?' Then a picnic bench arrived; stolen from a nearby park. Each day, George entertained his guests, but never lost the dream of sailing home.

He would see the Cuban patrol boat every day, but they never stopped or searched his vessel. Sometimes the soldiers waved, and George assumed they all knew about the daily sailing arrangements with their friends. He wondered if he would have trouble with them when he made his mad dash for freedom and he also wondered if he would be blown out of the water by the United States Coast Guard.[68]

He began thinking it would be helpful to take a pair of guards with him. They could wave off the patrol boats, as if it were just another pleasure trip. Certainly he could find a pair

---

[68] A steady stream of refugees make passage to Florida in small boats and unseaworthy craft (including at least one crafted from a lawn mower). US Coast Guard rescued the first refugees in July 1959 when nine were picked up off Dry Tortugas near Key West. They have rescued thousands over the years.

In September 1965, Fidel Castro announced beginning on October 10, 1965, the Port of Camarioca, Cuba would be opened for Cubans desiring to leave for "the Yankee paradise." Cuban exiles would be permitted into Camarioca to collect relatives. An application to the Ministry of the Interior was required, forfeiting land and other property left behind. The port remained open until mid-November, with 2,979 Cubans leaving their homeland. Thousands left by passenger vessels and soon commercial aircraft made 'Freedom Flights'. More 'boat lifts' occurred over the years. In the 1980s, Castro regularly exported the contents of his jails, prisons, and mental health facilities to Florida.

who were willing to escape with him. It was just a matter of asking the right questions. Abruptly, the sailing trips stopped.

George was tortured by the thought that he had let his opportunity slip through his fingers--'somehow, they read my mind', 'I gave away my plan', and 'I'm being moved again'. He couldn't sleep.

"George, es hora de irse!"

Shocked, George rose from the floor, thinking 'Damn, I'm being moved'. His head down and tears welling up in his eyes, he came outside his shack. He saw two soldiers with towels, swim trucks, a bucket of beer, and cigars. He brightened as he walked to the rowboat used to get to the sailboat buoyed in the harbor.

When he got to the rowboat he saw two new, one-gallon cans and two bags, one was marked rice and the other beans. "What's this?" The soldiers didn't answer so George unscrewed the can and dipped his finger inside, "Water?"

"The men talked about the boat. Maybe we could sell it. But we figure it doesn't belong to us. It never has. It belongs to you. We have enjoyed sailing with you, but it is time to set you free. The water should get you to America. The beans and rice are what remains of your rations." He fished money out of his shirt pocket, "We collected some greenbacks. Not much. We'll help you get all this onto your boat." Pedro grinned and looked at his friend, Juan, "If you invite us aboard we might have a final beer and cigar with you, and then you can leave."

"Well, you might as well have a second beer with me. I'm not going anywhere."

Pedro gave him as look like he had bitten into a lemon.

George pointed up. "No wind."

Pedro smiled, reached through the ice in the bucket, and yanked out another bottle. As they finished their second, a breeze was gathering from the west, as if God was telling George it was time to go.

By guess and by God, he sailed north, passing Fort Jefferson, Dry Tortugas, Florida on his port side. He sailed without stopping until he pulled into Tarpon Bay, north of Marcos Island. It was the beginning of the rainy season, but George was thankful there was not a cloud in the sky. He had sailed over 200 nautical miles. He had made it back.

Before dawn each day, Rebecca made tea, sat on the front deck, watched the sunrise, thought about George, and prayed.

After Abraham's death, Mel and her three children moved into Rebecca's mostly empty house. Andrew, who had turned twelve the previous March, was the spitting image of George. It caught Rebecca by surprise many times to see it and she would gasp. Then just about when Rebecca had adjusted to Abraham passing away, Thomas had his accident.

"What are they going to do?" Mel asked. "Penny's parents are gone. She wouldn't think of handing him over to a caregiver. How will she manage? Thomas needs nearly full-time care and so do their kids. How ..."

"We'll help. This will be their home!" said Rebecca. Her eyes glistened as she thought of how they would do it.

"But--"

Thomas, Penny, Andrew and Dodie moved in. Well, it would be more accurate to say Mel moved Thomas and the three of them in. Rebecca expected the adjustment to more active kids would have been the hard part. Or that having a third woman in the house might upset the apple cart. But the real drain had been Thomas. He wasn't demanding. He could sit on the porch or in front of the television for hours. He could feed himself, though he often choked. But he couldn't speak. He grunted and groaned for things--salt, pepper, napkin, to be taken to the bathroom. He would try to hide the frustration he felt. He often got cold in his wheelchair and needed to have his legs covered.

Mel, Penny, and Rebecca would eye each other, without saying much. They could see it in each other's eyes and feel it in their own. They tried not to let it come across to Thomas. But they all felt it--gnawing at them. The drain from having witnessed a vital, active man--who made his living through his mind and his voice--converted to this and silenced forever in one senseless moment. They helplessly watched him be helpless. He expressed himself through his facial gestures, seemingly positive about his condition.

The ladies called what had happen to Thomas an 'accident', primarily in an attempt to protect the children. It was a little white lie they told themselves to protect the children. But the children knew better; they understood who it really protected.

Early one morning, the first day of July, Rebecca walked out to the deck in her pink robe and matching slippers, with Lipton tea brewing in her mug. She was extra early this morning--the stars were beginning to disappear in the east and the birds had not yet begun to sing their daily greeting to the sun. She sat on a wooden chair facing the road in front of her property. There was no traffic. She could make out the table more by imagination than either sight or feel. She heard the reassuring click of her mug as she set it down on the glass table top. It was cool and quiet as she began her daily ritual of asking for God's grace, mercy, and provision for George, and that he would come home to her soon. She had prayed this prayer two thousand times since he had been gone. She had long ago reconciled herself that God may never answer, but she could never give up hope.

In her mind's eye, she could see his plaid red shirt and jeans as he worked on her Uncle's farm. She would ride by on her horse, glancing in his direction to see if he was looking back. Most of the time she sensed him hoping not to be caught looking, but happy to see her. She heard his soothing words, softly spoken, as he comforted her after Uncle Chet's untimely death. His touch was gentle; reassuring her he would never leave her. In her mind, she could smell the wood from the barbeque on his clothes, the musty odor of rabbit's fir, the scent of clover and green hay. When he kissed her in her dreams at night, she tasted the Dr. Beeman's Clove Chewing gum, and during the day the licorice sticks he kept stashed in his back pocket.

She daydreamed of nights when she lay next to him and had pulled back the covers to see him lying on his side, facing away. Peaceful and quiet. She looked at his back and muscled shoulders. She listened to his relaxed, rhythmic breathing. She would sometimes touch him to see if he would stir. Some mornings she could see herself get up quietly to use the bathroom, brush her teeth, and put on a dab of his favorite perfume. Returning to bed, she cast off her nightgown and cuddled close, pressing her breasts against his back. Sometimes, in her daydreams, they remained motionless, their heartbeats synchronized; other times he turned to take her in his arms. They kissed--a mixture of toothpaste and clove.

Some mornings her day dreams would be of passionate love making. Recently her daughter-in-law had caught her on the porch while she dreamt.

"Are you alright?"

Through the haze she was ripped away, "What?"

"Are you alright? I thought you were hurt and crying!"

"No, no. I must have been dreaming."

"Of what?"

She thought to herself, 'dare a sixty-six year-old-woman have these dreams? How should I answer? Should I say I don't know? Should I say I don't remember? Should I try to lie?' "Of George."

In the place between wake and sleep, while the steam of hot tea floated to her nostrils, she barely heard the sound of boots crushing gravel. 'Probably a workman. Early today'. The boots slowly came up the steps, creaking boards beneath his feet. 'I'll make him breakfast if he asks'. A cracking, weak voice whispered "Rebecca, Rebecca." He placed his hands on her arms and she smelled his hot, stale breath, mixed with sweat and the sea. She opened her eyes, to see a hunched-over old man in the dim, red streaks of the dawn light. It came to her then; I'm not dreaming.

Penny came to the front deck to say 'good morning' to Rebecca. She noticed her mug was cold and more than half-full, 'That's odd'. As she carefully placed the mug in the sink, she heard noises from Rebecca's bedroom. Thinking she might be sick, she opened the door a crack, and closed it quickly. Wide-eyed she returned to the kitchen, embarrassed. 'My God, Rebecca's taken a lover!'

She sat down; stunned. Her imagination reeling. 'How am I going to explain this to the kids? Who is he? How long

361

has this been going on? I can't blame her; it's been over six years! Oh, Dear Lord!'

An hour later she heard Rebecca stirring and thought 'how am I going to raise this with my mother-in-law?' when she heard Rebecca's voice, "Guess who finally decided to come home?"

She turned her head and her jaw dropped, "George!" She ran to give him a hug. He was dirty and unshaven. He looked gaunt in his baggy clothing. One by one, as all the children woke up, Rebecca gave them the good news and reintroduced them to their much-changed Grandfather.

Thomas's eyes lit up as Penny rolled his wheelchair into the room. "Son!" George exclaimed. He hugged and kissed Thomas. Later that morning, Rebecca walked arm-in-arm with George out to Abraham's grave, beyond the rolling hills, near the grove of Longleaf Pine that stood before the banks of the Gulf. Six months before they ordered his headstone; it read--

ABRAHAM GEORGE CASH
SOLDIER, HUSBAND, FATHER
9/7/1930 - 2/14/1964

"Tell me about it."

"He had been having headaches since Korea. They had gotten worse. They found him late at night in his office, sitting at his desk. He had taught class that day. It was a stroke. He went fast. Didn't suffer. Penny had been frantically calling all that evening."

He stared at the headstone and did the math: "Thirty-three. Too short."

"You can say that--" The words caught and her hand reached for her throat.

Alexander and Jacqueline flew down from Washington the following weekend and stayed for a week. The first Thanksgiving and Christmas together were magical. After Christmas the family lingered for a few days and George was able to talk to everyone at length, one-on-one.

Jacqueline looked at Alexander before telling Meadow. An unspoken conversation passed between them. Alexander blinked his reply. "Did Alexander tell you? I fainted yesterday. We were at the adoption agency."

"Oh, my gosh!"

"They rushed me to the hospital emergency room. Asked me endless questions. Poked and prodded. Took tests. Meadow, I am afraid it's serious."

Meadow's jaw dropped.

"It's a terminal condition. I'll have it the rest of my life. There is nothing they can do. Alexander and I are just going to have to live with it. It will be hard, but we'll adjust." She reached over to grab Alexander's hands.

"I'm so sorry. What is it?"

"There's a medical term for it. Maybe you'll know it--'motherhood.'"

Penny told George, "It was when Thomas started preaching against Vietnam, that he ran into trouble."

"How?" asked George.

"He had been active against racial prejudice for years. Marchs. Sermons. Lots of people didn't like what he had to say, but they listened. Then the whole Vietnam thing stuck in his craw. It really started from the civil rights standpoint."

"How?"

"Well, a disproportionate number of black kids got called up--"

"Called up?"

"Yeah, drafted." George's eyebrows rose. "Whites could find ways out where blacks couldn't. Medical deferments. College deferments."

"I see."

"So Thomas started talking more about the war and the poor in his sermons. We'd had threats before after he had taken on an unpopular issue. Lots of preacher would 'sing along to get along'--tickle the church member's ears. Fire them up agreeing with their prejudiced point of view. But if Thomas couldn't see Jesus doing that, he never would. Sometimes they'd throw eggs at the car and garage after some sermon. Nasty phone calls. They would rant and rave and call us 'nigger lover', threaten us, but nothing ever came of it. It shook me up a bit, but Thomas kept calm.

Then one night--I'd gone to bed--they ambushed him. Cops figured it was a baseball bat. Thought it might have been three from the footprints. No witnesses. They never caught them." She thought of lying in bed waiting for him. Her anticipation. The perfume she had worn and the signal she thought he never received. How she missed making love to him, even now. She began to cry and George held her.

"What do the doctors say?"

"Severed spinal cord. He'll never walk. They can't figure out why he can't talk."

Late that evening, George smiled as he looked for his youngest son, "Alexander!"

"Sir!"

George grinned. "Sir? You're mighty formal these days!"

Alexander grinned back. George handed him his glass. "Refill this for me. Then come back. I want to hear about Vietnam."

George had lost thirty pounds and his old clothing sagged from his frame. In preparing to sail, he had been walking and stretching and felt good for the first time in years as his muscles and mind tightened and firmed. He and Rebecca took trips to the dentist and to buy new clothing. She helped him pick out a new suit as if they were getting ready to go to the prom and they took it to a tailor for the final touches. She picked out a narrow gray and red necktie and pressed it again the white cotton shirt.

Arm-in-arm they took long walks down to the beach and cuddled on the swing on their back porch. They often slipped away for a nap together in the late afternoon, before it was time to prepare dinner.

"What's that squeaking sound?" Little Andy said with a grin. "Are they playing trampoline in there?"

Mel dropped her dishtowel on the table and came over. "It's not nice to listen in on others." She shooed him away from his grandparent's bedroom door, but had to giggle to herself. She had heard stories about how the kitchen ladies made fun of them when George and Rebecca were newlyweds.

A few days later, George teased Rebecca that her breasts where what he missed most.

"It would take a hellofalot more commies than they got to keep me away from these! This is all I thought about!" He held them and kissed them, while Rebecca laughed. With age they sagged and wobbled, but he told her that just made them more interesting. She pressed his head between them, while she bent down to kiss the top of his balding head.

When George turned the doorknob to leave their room,

he heard something drop. Whatever it was that had fallen off the doorknob clanked onto the oak floor. He could smell machine and citronella oil and it reminded him of bicycles. He reached down to pick up the small, black, red and white tin can from the floor: 3-in-One Oil. He mumbled, "How doya suppose that got there?"

Mel would laugh at George and Rebecca. But it was a stinging laugh. They ran around like teenagers having an illicit love affair--sneaking off to bed when they thought nobody was listening or fondled each other when they thought prying eyes wouldn't see. But the only eyes and ears that didn't notice were their own. 'Oh, gawd, could I do that? Could I ever be with a man again? There are some cute guys at church'.

The unthinkable would happen. It would take a few more years, but love would find its way back into her life. She would marry again and they would live at the ranch.

Life settled down. By spring there was a garden to put in and odd jobs around the house that George could do, rather than always calling in help. George spent long hours sitting in the morning sun, looking south at the pine trees in the distance. He had more time to think about his experience. He would come into the house, quiet and introspective.

He couldn't help but think about the dreams he had had in Cuba. What did they mean? George swirled the ice cubes in his glass in the darkened room and thought, everything has changed and nothing changed. Major leaders in the war were dead and replaced--the replacements hadn't been prepared for the reigns of state in either war or peace. And the war dragged on. The end of war in Europe signaled the start of the next war. Just as the 'war to end all war' hadn't brought peace, the next world war hadn't either.

The Second World War did not go out with a whimper. It drew to a close with two of the largest explosions mankind had ever heard--150,000 immediately dead and tens of thousands more to die from the torturing, painful effects within a year. In the days afterward, few faulted Truman for his decision to drop Atomic Bombs--it saved American soldiers and brought an end to war. A long, painful war had come to a shocking conclusion.

'Or had it?' George wondered. He thought about another weapon so horrible that nobody would ever consider using again--the Gatling gun. Instead it proliferated into various types of machine guns and became ubiquitous during this war. George had read one of John Steinbeck's war correspondences from a battlefield in Italy were he had written, "All war is a symptom of man's failure as a thinking animal."

The cost in ravaged lands, roads, businesses, and infrastructure was staggering; not to mentions lives, minds, and limbs. As many as 79,184,700 people were dead from the war; four of every 100 people on earth.

American soldiers and sailors walked off ships into American ports on the Pacific and Atlantic coasts. While people were cheering the returning troops and the promise of peace, the oasis on the horizon turned out to be a mirage. The expectation that defeating the Axis would lead to peace was false. As people tried to put their lives back together, a potentially more deadly future loomed ahead. An ally one day became an enemy the next.

More than boredom was taking a toll, and Rebecca could sense George was turning moody and ill-tempered. Rebecca let it go for a while, then asked, "George, what's the matter?"
"War has cost me two sons and a daughter. "

"Rebecca, we need to do something different. I had a lot of time to think while I was held. I want us to pull the family together this summer. No, no, that won't work. I want Alexander and my first born grandsons from each of my sons to spend July and August with me."
Rebecca looked surprised. "What do you want to do?"
"I need to teach them the ways of war."

FOURTEEN

On July 1, 1969, George began his first family retreat. He had cleared off the oak dining room table, except for one glass of water on a coaster. He sat at the head of the table in a captain's chair with two chairs close by at each side. George was sixty-eight. Alexander was almost twenty-nine. Andrew Buck was thirteen; the oldest son of Thomas and Penny, he went by Andy. With brown hair, and black frame glasses, he was serious and studious. Ulysses was eleven and the oldest son of Abraham and Melbourne Dawn. With sandy hair and a ready smile, Ule loved being with his grandfather. Benjamin, the oldest son of Alexander and Jacqueline Evans was one.

"Dad, I am not sure having Ben here is a good idea," said Alexander.

"Why?"

"He's just a baby."

"He will grow into it. If you can't manage, hand him over to me. Alright?"

It seemed preposterous to Alexander, but he obliged his father.

George cleared his throat. "My son and my three grandsons. You have been invited here for the next two months--"

"What?" exclaimed Alexander.

George continued without skipping a beat, "--to do something no family has ever done before. We, together as a family, are going to become the stewards of world peace!"

Alexander's jaw dropped. He looked at his father and

wondered if he was going to need to have him institutionalized.

"Each day while I was a prisoner in Cuba, I thought how we are approaching peace in the wrong way.

"I listened to my sons talk about their experiences. I have my own from World War One and Two, from the wars we had over Prohibition, and Cuba.

"Can a War College teach peace? Can it teach both war and peace and not slant one direction or another? Of course it can't.

"As countries we make some of the most important decisions under the stress and strain of imminent danger, when we are least likely to be able to apply the lessons of history. Thus, we keep repeating the same mistakes. When I returned from Cuba, I learned about Vietnam from Alexander, Meadow, and others. I discovered we were not applying the things we had seen and learned in Korea or World War Two.

"Everywhere I look, I see the world failing to learn the lessons of the past."

The only person following George was Alexander. He shifted uncomfortably, thinking 'Where is Dad going with this?'

"I believe we need to change the model. Instead, we need to become people of peace, by learning and teaching the lessons to ourselves and the world. We will be having one lesson per day. I will teach these and you may ask questions. Then we will discuss what we have all learned. Each day for the next two months, will follow the same pattern of teaching, discussing, and memorizing; followed by intense play the remainder of the day. Doesn't that sound fun?"

Nobody answered.

"Instead of trying to learn something, I intend for us to become something different. So our lesson for today is—

1. War should always be the last resort; except when it should be the first resort."

"I can't believe what I am hearing. Dad, I don't understand what you are trying to accomplish."

"You'll have to trust me."

"You have an infant, two pre-teenagers, and me--and you are discussing your learnings from war?"

"Yes."

"And you are expecting what?"

"World peace."

"Dad, I don 't..."

"I don't know any other way. But we need to instill what we have learned into our young. Traditional methods continually have failed us."

"How can this possibly work?"

"I haven't the faintest idea. But we are no worse off for trying a different approach."

"And you think in two months--"

"Oh, no. I don't think we will be anywhere in two months. Or two years. And maybe not in two decades." Andy and Ule stared at Grandpa and Uncle Alexander. "I intend we will be doing this every summer."

"Every summer?"

"Absolutely. Two months every summer. Until we have become people of peace."

"People of peace? I don't know what the hell that means!"

"Watch your tongue. And I don't know what it means to be people of peace either. But I'll learn. And so will you."

"But how can you expect these boys--" He waved his hand over Andy and Ule. They sat quietly watching, their eyes big. "--and how do you expect Ben?" Benjamin had fallen asleep in his arms.

George took Benjamin from Alexander. "Oh, I have the highest hopes for Ben. He has the best prospects of benefiting from what we have to teach. He has nothing to unlearn at all. These other two will be able to apply what they learn to their lives."

"But--"

"Don't you see that every squabble they have in the schoolyard will be an opportunity to learn? They have the most to gain. They, and their children, and their children's children."

"You are serious about this, aren't you?"

"Yes, I am. I believe they will just enjoy the sports and play the first few years--maybe five--but over time they will absorb the lessons and be able to apply them."

"What if I don't want to do this? Or have my son do this?"

"Oh, I believe you will. I believe that by the end of this first summer, you will become our strongest advocate. I believe you will extend what we are doing to areas you cannot imagine. But you have to give this a try. Give it until the end of summer, to get the vision for what it could be. If you decide you cannot buy into it, then you are free to go."

Alexander shifted back in his chair and it creaked, but he didn't answer. He rubbed his forehead with the palm of his hand, while he bit his tongue.

"Alright, where was I. Oh, yes--
"1. War should always be the last resort; except when it should be the first resort.
"We will memorize that phrase after today's lesson. We should endeavor that war would always be our last resort. You would think that from the sheer terror we see in war, the ever-more destructive weapons, the after-effects, and the economic destruction, we would be loath to use war. But we aren't."

He concluded with: "There are times when war should be used immediately. Think if we had stamped out Hitler in 1935, instead of 1945! The problem lies in knowing which case applies--first or last. Alright, let's memorize our first phrase."
Alexander rolled his eyes.

The first weeks only George and Alexander memorized the phrases, but in short order, through repetition, Ule and Andy came along nicely. The first day the group, including Benjamin, went boating together all afternoon and ended up having a barbeque near the house for dinner.
All of them were exhausted, and Alexander excused himself and took the boys off to bed early.
"Thanks, Dad. That was a fun afternoon."
"How about the morning?"
Alexander didn't reply.
"Quite alright. Goodnight." George thought to himself, 'I don't know either'.

Rebecca brought coffee out to George. "So how did Day One go?"
He sighed. "I'm not sure. But we just have to try this."
Rebecca rubbed his shoulders.
"Alexander thinks I'm crazy. Maybe I am. But he said he would give it a while. That is all I can ask."
"How did the boys do?"
"Andy and Ule were wonderful. I think it is all just so new to them. They loved sailing, just the five of us. The baby was great. Of course he slept in the carrier and ate a good deal."

"What did Jacqueline say about all this?"

"I don't know. I'd love to be a fly on Alexander and Jacqueline's wall when he tells her I am planning on doing this for sixty days!"

As he finished his coffee, George reached over to hold Rebecca's hand. "There is a nautical term--'By Guess and by God'.

"You can make a guess. It can be a lucky guess, or an educated guess. By, in any event, it is just a guess. That is what I want to do.

"Now, God can take that guess, and turn it into pulp. But I don't think God will. I think God wants us to find peace. He can take a bad guess and make it a success, in spite of ourselves. Or take a good, educated guess and bring forth fruit.

"We think that peace has to be this humungous, unwieldy effort across nations. But why would that be the case? It has never worked in the past. Why can't one family become the standard-bearers for peace? I don't know if what we try will come to anything. I am hopeful that God will honor our humble attempt."

By the end of August 1969, what his father had been doing and saying had grown on Alexander. He had memorized 45 phrases. Surprisingly, Andy and Ule had learned more than 30. Whether they caught the insights behind them was another question, but Alexander was willing to try it again the following summer.

As the Vietnam War dragged on, unrest, anger, and bitterness spread. The Presidency had gone from one party to another; the players changed, but the war raged on. Nobody seemed to be able to stop it. There was talk of a different path, but never a different path.

By 1973 the talk around the annual conference was of a phrase the Nixon Administration was using--'peace with honor'. George lectured as sunlight beamed into the conference center though the Georgia pines, "Nixon's talk of 'peace with honor' is reminiscent of 1938, when Sir Neville Chamberlain, British prime minister, upon returning from meeting Hitler in Munich was seen waiving a piece of paper and saying, 'My good friends, for the second time in our history, a British Prime Minister has returned from Germany bringing peace with honour. I believe it is peace for our time. Go home and get a nice quiet sleep'. Once again, the world saw neither peace nor honor."[69]

Each Christmas, while relaxing in Alabama, George and Alexander told Meadow about the conference. She seemed interested. 'Aunt' Meadow loved the children and spoiled them. She played with them and continually grabbed one to hug as they ran by. They loved her mint chocolate chip cookies with creme de menthe frosting. The parents were sure the kids were getting a buzz.

She was brushing crumbs from Timothy's face when he asked, "Where is Uncle Jim?"

"He didn't come with me this time?"

"Why?"

She didn't know how to answer him. "Uncle Jim and I decided--we decided not to be together anymore."

"Why?"

"Well--sometimes people just grow apart."

"Why?"

Rebecca decided it was time to intervene. "Timmy, come give Grammee a big hug!" Meadow forced a smile as he ran to his Grandmother.

George said, "Meadow, can I get you a cocktail?"

Meadow was startled back to reality. "Oh, no, I have hot tea going somewhere here." She looked around to find her mug. "We injuns don't do well with alcohol!"

Everyone, except Timmy, could see Jim was not right for Meadow. Timmy was the second miracle birth for Jacqueline and Alexander.

Jim wasn't right because nobody could replace Larry

---

[69] The phrase goes back to Marcus Tullius Cicero's (106 b.c. - 43 b.c.) *Letters To Atticus* (written in 49 b.c.), "Until we know whether we are to have peace without honour or war with its calamities, I have thought it best for them to stay at my house in Formiae and the boys too."

Lash. Larry always was and always would be the love of Meadow's life. After resigning from the State Department, Meadow left for Idaho and moved in with Larry. His mother was gracious and charming after Larry announced, "Meadow has moved in with me!"

Small, with a twinkle in her eye, she took joy in looking for men for Meadow and young Mormon girls for her son.

"Meadow is living with me."

Each time and in every way they tried to tell her she failed to see what they meant, insisting in her mind that Larry was now a landlord and Meadow was his renter.

"I keep sending Larry nice young girls, but he never calls any of them for a date. I'm worried." A frown developed on her face. "You don't think he's a fairy, do you?"

Meadow burst out laughing. She thought of three hours earlier when he rode her like a bucking bronco! Yee-haw! "I'm pretty sure you have nothing to worry about."

Even when they hugged, kissed, and were 'arm-in-arm', his mother couldn't see it. The rest of the family understood. When Larry pressed the issue, and she still wasn't getting it, Meadow pulled him away. "Let's not hurt her."

"What?"

"Does it matter to you?"

"Well, I..."

"Listen, I know a couple who went off on their own together and asked God to marry them. What do you think?"

Larry calmed and thought for a minute. "That's the corniest thing I've ever heard!" The engagement ring in his pocket that day was the closest they came to marriage.

Years' later, Meadow saw it turned out for the best. She had been working in the Governor's Office for six months, when Larry got the call to move to Washington.

"I don't know what to say."

They both knew they were at the pinnacle of their aspirations. He had always dreamed of being on the big stage, and at last it had come. She recognized their paths were meant to cross, but not to run together. She gave him the greatest gift of love she could; she let him go.

"But I want you to..." He stopped. It was too much for him to ask her to give up her career for him. He couldn't bring himself to take her back to Washington. She hugged him tightly. Whenever anyone told her she had made the wrong choice, she would say, "And you are a hopeless romantic!"

Three months after Larry left, Meadow contacted one of the men Larry's mother tried to set up with her. There was something special about him.

"Hello."

"Hi. Is this Meadow?"

"Yes."

"Meadow, you don't know me. My name in Jim Stockland. Alice Lash suggested I give you a call and..."

Meadow broke out laughing.

"What is it?"

I'm sorry, Jim. I know Alice means well, but I'm already in a relationship..."

"Oh!"

"..with her son!"

"What?"

"Yes, it's something she either can't see or accept. We've tried to tell her. We have been living together for nine months."

Now it was Jim's turn to laugh. *"Well, I'll..."* He drifted off.

"No, you don't have to do anything."

"Oh, yes I do. It's okay. I'm her mailman. I see her every day, so she is bound to ask. I'll tell her we went to dinner and that you're just not my type. It was a fun dinner and all..."

"Where?"

"Uh, dinner at Mario's. But there just wasn't any spark. Although, I'm sure it would have been fun!"

Something about his 'playing along' grabbed her attention. So she just happened to visit Alice's house one day around the time her mail was delivered. They walked, talked, and had some romance. He even attended retreats in Mobile with her. But it was more of a friendship, than a romance. A way to move beyond Larry, that quickly had run its course.

Jacqueline later came to Meadow to apologize. "I'm sorry for what Benjamin said--"

"Oh, it's nothing."

"--and I'm sorry about Jim."

She looked down at her hands. They had been together for two years. "It's better this way. The white men just want to notch their guns by bedding an Indian squaw and the red men find me threatening, I guess."

"I'm sorry."

"Just the way it is. Someday women will be able to play a bigger role in American politics. Until then the same traits that are attractive for male politicians--confidence, assertiveness--are viewed as pushy in women."

"Ah."

"We'll get beyond it eventually. Until then--"

"Yes."

"I just have to listen to the rumors and keep chasing your husband!"

Jacqueline laughed and hugged Meadow. They each remembered when she had used that line five years earlier.

There had been open rumors about an affair between Alexander and Meadow, when he nervously decided to get them together to discuss what was being said. He was concerned hurtful words may have gotten to Jacqueline and wanted to set the record straight. Jacqueline knew they had a special bond and deep friendship and that if it turned sexual, it would be a short-term mistake that neither could sustain. She reached into her purse and opened her checkbook to the calendar page.

"Okay. You can have him Monday, Wednesday, and Thursday, except for nights of PTA meetings."

Meadow played right along. "Right. But I also need him on Saturday nights!"

"And how would that look, us two coming to church in separate cars!"

"I suppose that won't look right. Gotta keep up appearances. Besides, who said I would want him?"

"Good point. Steals the covers. Snores. Puts his cold feet all over me."

"Disgusting!"

"Come to think of it, I'm not sure I want him either! Come on, you gotta help me out her, sister! Take him off my hands. Just a couple nights a week. I need the rest!"

Meadow folded her arms and pouted, "I don't think so!"

Jacqueline sat next to her, folded her arms, and pushed out her lower lip, "Well, if you are going to be that way about it!"

By the spring of 1976, George and Alexander thought it was time to expand their circle. Andy was now twenty years

old and attended Gordon College, intent on following his
father's steps in the ministry. Ule was eighteen. He wasn't sure
what he wanted to do with his life, but he enjoyed what he
learned from Meadow and Alexander. Both boys relished
summers with their grandfather. They didn't see anything
unusual in what they did for two months each summer, as they
didn't have anything to compare it with. Ben was seven. He
loved to mirror what his big cousins were doing and could
rattle off each day's phrase as if singing words to a song. They
were meaningless to him, but George knew he would grow into
it. The sing-song words and their deep, underlying
significance would one day attach.

"It is time to ask friends to join us."
"I agree, but where do we start?"
"Let's start with Meadow and maybe one or two of your
associates at the State Department. People who would benefit.
Hey, and let's invite Natania! She lost four family members in
the war."
"It is going to be awkward."
"I would think so. Join us for two months. We will talk
about issues of war and peace in the morning and play all
afternoon."
Meadow agreed to attend for the summer of 1977. It was a
start.

George began constructing a main building, chapel, and
cabins for one hundred guests and twenty support staff on
their ranch, away from the house.
His vision was that attenders each year would incur no
costs, other than transportation to and from the retreat. He'd
feed and entertain them for two months and start sharing
more and more of the teaching with Alexander, and have Andy
and Ule leading discussion sessions. In the next few years he
wanted them to take on the lion's share of the work.

When Meadow reluctantly agreed to attend it was
because of her relationship with Alexander and Jacqueline,
and the years she had spent with the whole family in Mobile. It
seemed to her to be an odd activity; a retreat to discuss peace
for two months. She knew they spent plenty of time outdoors,
so the summer would not be an entire loss. She had resigned
from the State Department and spent time in Congressional

and State offices throughout Idaho. She was now writing speeches for the Governor of Idaho and making herself known throughout the state. But the request for a two-month unpaid sabbatical was most unusual.

"Meadow, why do you think this two-month period away will benefit the people of Idaho?"

"The retreat is about 'peace', I think that is applicable to everyone."

"But why in particular to Idaho?"

"I don't know."

If the Governor hadn't been planning a long fishing vacation in August, the sabbatical would have been ruled out.

Once the conference began, she offered resistance to some of George's initial thoughts. On Day Three, George began with the phrase "World War One taught us to respect the defeated, or pay the price of more war."

"Respect the defeated? Doesn't that play into their hands?"

But as the retreat went on, she began to put the pieces together. She understood how these things needed to become 'embedded in our thinking and in our lives'. She soon started a tradition that became a hallmark of retreats to the current day. She came to lunch on July 15, after everyone else had arrived and were waiting for her to begin eating. She ran up, pushed her chair under the table, and stood behind it--

"1. War should always be the last resort; except when it should be the first resort.

"2. There is a lot of money to be made in war; therein lies a great danger."

She continued on through to the current day--

"...14. Khrushchev taught us public pronouncements are not intended for our ears; ignore them.

"15. The Cuban Missile Crisis taught us Intelligence can be both spectacularly good and spectacularly bad at the same time."

George beamed and everyone applauded. At dinner time, everyone listed off the first fifteen phrases in unison.

Toward the end of the retreat, Meadow observed, "Someday politicians will say it can't be done this way." Her enthusiasm for what this could become peaked as the retreat drew to a close. "Adding me has broken the barrier."

"How so?"

"I am the first person outside the immediate family to attend. In addition, I am a woman, a minority, and an Indian. That should tell you anyone is free to come and give their thoughts and learn the lessons."

"So, how do we enlarge the circle?"

"Alexander, you need to get your boss here next year. I know a few others at the State Department and in the military to call. The hard part is that it is a two-month commitment during the summer. This is not going to be easy."

The 1978 retreat included Meadow and two others from outside the family. It was slow, but they hoped to get Alexander's boss to come the following year.

By the 1980 retreat, there were sixteen attenders on cushioned folding chairs in the main building. They kidded George that every attender could have five bedrooms to themselves! They were now nearly filling two of the guest cabins and the meals were prepared by four staff people. This was the first year a microphone was being used as George's voice was beginning to fade.

George took a long drink from his glass of water and cleared his throat. "My son, three grandsons, and our assembled guests--welcome! You have been invited here for the next two months to do something that has never been done before. Together we can become the stewards of world peace.

"For those of you who don't yet know me, my name is George Cash. I was born on June 6, 1901. George Cash was not my birth name. My last name was Montague; like his father before him, my father couldn't resist naming me...Romeo. I ran away when I was fifteen; I couldn't stand the beatings and hunger any longer. I never saw my brothers or sisters again. I hope my leaving gave them courage to escape. Otherwise, they probably died young. My adopted family raised rabbits for the United States Army during World War One. It was a seemingly innocuous introduction to the ways of war. We were on the periphery, making a good living on the modest war industry of those days. As that ended, I was introduced to another type of war--prohibition. It was as vicious a war as you will ever see, even though it was on a modest scale. But war it was nonetheless. I saw men die and I killed. My own infant daughter was a casualty of that war, murdered while she slept peacefully in her crib. We did not deserve her death, but it was the price we paid for the war we conducted. And what was the purpose of that war? That I cannot answer. Many have said you cannot legislate morality, but that doesn't hit the heart of the problem. The problem is that we wage war too easily when we use guns and rifles to try to enforce the things we cannot otherwise convince men to do on their own.

"I became more engaged in war when I smuggled during World War Two. We had quite an operation, I'll tell you. Somewhere in the world, somebody needed or wanted something, and I supplied it. And I made money. A great deal of money. But I lost men and it nearly cost me my marriage. I lost my best friend. It was dangerous and exciting at the same time. Our government encouraged my illicit activities, granting me waivers to trade freely with our enemies. Do you believe that they would do that? How many American soldiers did I kill indirectly? I sold the Nazi's essential war materials to make bombs, guns, harden armor, and manufacturer tools of war. I traded with all sides, made tons of money, and my government encouraged my efforts, even as they benefited themselves. And I looked the other way from the slaughter I enabled.

"Which led me to working with the military and CIA directly. I devised methods of bringing things over our borders. I was handsomely paid. The CIA used this to develop methods of tracking, I guess. I really don't know. Then I had an accident which led to me becoming a prisoner in Cuba for six years. During that time my middle son died. It was probably from his severe Korean War injuries, but they won't say. And my oldest son was injured fighting another kind of war. Another victim of another senseless war.

"But some good came from Cuba. Each day while I was a prisoner, I thought how we approach peace in the wrong way. Everywhere I look, I see the world failing to learn the lessons of the past.

"I see us trusting whether we go to war to politicians, who make some of our countries most important decisions under the stress and strain of imminent danger, when they are least likely to be able to apply the lessons of history. If they err in their judgments, we toss them onto the dust heap of history; if they lead us to victory, we call them statesman. But the damage is done, either way. They leave in their path death and destruction that is astounding. And, we keep repeating the same mistakes.

"So we are trying to change the model. We are trying to become people of peace, and I think we are beginning to succeed. Those fruits may still be far off. Thank you for joining us this year. I trust it will be time well-spent.

"We will be having one lesson per day. I, or my son, will teach these and you may ask questions. Then we will discuss what we have all learned. Each day for the next two months, will follow the same pattern of teaching, discussing, memorizing. At meals, those of us who have been here before will assemble to repeat out loud the sixty phrases we need to remember. Then the rest of you will be let in to repeat the phrases you have learned thus far.

"And we will follow that by playing the remainder of the day. We have added speed boats, a baseball field, and basketball hoops to our simple complex this year. You will see and play with some of my toys; including many I developed to evade the CIA. And, no, contrary to rumor, I do not have a submarine. Well, I don't have it back yet, anyway.

"Instead of trying to learn something, let us become something different.

"So our lesson for today is—
1.   War should always be the last resort; except when it should be the first resort."

The conference fell into the same pattern that had developed during the 70's. Arrival on July 1. The first lesson of "The Sixty" on July 2, consecutively through lesson number sixty on August 30. Departure on the last day of August.

As the peace retreats continued, they needed to institute a new rule. Other than family members, Natania, Meadow, and Larry Lash, an attender could only come twice--once when they had been invited for their first time, and one time when they escorted a family member or friend for their first. But soon that rule went by the wayside for anyone who wanted to teach.

Natania would attend each year; at least for a few days. The first year she met a gentleman and they spent all their spare time together. After that, she would spend a few days before retreats visiting with the family, and afterward visiting her newfound friend. Soon he was spending his winters in Spain and romance found them.

At the 1988 retreat, George gave the concluding lesson for the year. His voice was weak and it cracked as he stood close to the microphone, "...stripping away the corruptions, complexities and indulgences that have grown up over the years. Be patient; soon we will have our opportunity."

There was a standing ovation. It was remarkable that at eighty-seven years, he had been able to, once again, host the retreat and teach a handful of lessons. He talked about the twisting that was now taking place, as we attempted to shift "from 'in crisis' to 'every day' thinking" and changing the context from war to peace. "There is a long way to go--we will have our 'starts and fits'--and do not become discouraged with our steps backward."

Alexander had taken the lion's share of the teaching, with Andy, now a pastor and religious leader in Fairfax, Virginia; Ulysses Cash, on the staff of the Joint Chiefs; and Ben, working as a middle manager in the State Department, each teaching many sessions. At the 1989 session George welcomed the participants and shared in social events, then listened in on his son and grandsons. He was proud of each of them.

In the last decade there had been repeated requests for press interviews, photographs, and magazine articles--all of which had been denied. George was also asked by the media to give them printed copies of their materials. "We don't hand out any printed materials. And we never write down 'The Sixty' phrases."

While the 'Sixty' were often quoted individually (usually without their corresponding number or reference to where they had originated), they had never been written down for the retreat attenders. They had probably been in George's personal notes, but no other eyes had seen the list.

He told retreat attenders as early as 1975, "Don't ever write down the list. That defeats the purpose. If you need help remembering, jot down those with the first word or two, and perhaps a key word. Here is why we do this: it needs to be in your brain, not on paper. If it is on paper, you can always refer to it--but you won't. In times of crisis, when you need to react quickly it can't be on a slip of paper back at your desk, at home, in your car, in your bedroom, or who knows where. No, it needs to be firmly planted in your head. Nowhere else will do. In your head is the only place for the list."

Many repeated 'The Sixty' on their own, either out loud or to themselves daily. That is how they kept it fresh in their minds until the time they would be needed. Some got together with others privately to run through the list periodically.

Meadow concluded her lecture as the kitchen crew prepared to serve lunch. They were especially noisy today, but other than Meadow nobody noticed. Everyone else was mesmerized by what she had to say. It came straight from her heart. She started from the early days of the conference and her initial reluctance to come, followed by what she had learned, and what had been reinforced each year. "There were no short courses on peace. No weekend abbreviated session. No yellow and black 'Cliff's Notes' to getting there. There was only a single, focused, effort-filled, full-commitment to the process of becoming a Peacemaker."

Some of the 'Sixty' were eye-opening,
"21. The Korean War taught us a stalemate can be a victory; but you have to know what a win is."

They had always thought of the Korean War as a disaster, a stalemate, until George opened their eyes to what the war had achieved. Whether or not you believed the Korean War had actually been won was secondary to the truth that lay behind it--a war is a success if it leads to peace, even an uneasy peace, such as the Cold War. Our conventional measures were not helpful.

There were some things to which all could agree--

"28. Nazi Germany taught us some enemies are beyond redemption; eradicate them as early as possible."

George had the attenders look within themselves when he talked about all the lives lost in the Holocaust. "If the world had stepped forward in 1934, instead of 1942, how many lives could have been saved? Of course, the hard part is in the recognition of whether or not an enemy is beyond redemption--that requires something difficult to come by and uncommon to man--it requires 'thinking.'"

and "29. Neutrality is a false peace."

"Neutrality never has worked. It has just put off the inevitable, allowing things to fester and become worse. Fast and small wars are better than allowing the enemy to get big. The root cause of neutrality is inward thinking--thinking only about yourself and your own people--and not considering the implications for others."

One theme that played through many phrases was to think beyond yourself. "You need to consider things in the full context of what is good for all parties, including (and maybe especially) your enemies. It is difficult to think about the enemy's needs. But Kennedy got through the Cuban Missile Crisis without all-out war by doing exactly that."

The most controversial topic was religion--
"30. The only real peace we find is in our faith. All peace extends from that. Those without faith cannot find peace.

31. Beware of a god so small that man has to do his dirty work for him."

In later years, Pastor Andy taught these in a masterful way. "For me, personally, it all starts with the Prince of Peace, Jesus Christ. For you it may be different. Peace is a continuum, with the personal and spiritual on one end, and the general, societal, World War on the other. We can see the outlets for our personal relationships in the 'Sixty' if we look carefully. It does not matter whether you follow my faith or not. But faith has consequences, both good and bad. It helps me to find what is good in and for my fellow man and teaches me that there are consequences if I ignore or forget that."

Pastor Andy gave the conference an image that would be repeatedly used, from Isaiah 40: 31, "'But they that wait upon the LORD shall renew *their* strength; they shall mount up with wings as eagles; they shall run, and not be weary; *and* they shall walk, and not faint.' Let that be God's promise to us! We can soar in His strength!"

The last decade had seen things added--a Luau and paragliding. The 'Thomas Buck Worship Center' had been opened for Sunday services and was used as a Church year round. The original cabins had been replaced, giving each attender a modern single bedroom with a private bathroom.

George had not set up a foundation to fund the retreats. He had always used his personal funds. A not-for-profit foundation was established in 1988, and regularly received gifts of $10,000 or more. The retreats could continue on for the foreseeable future.

Each meal began with the attenders rattling off the sixty they had learned thus far. The final dinner each year with a hundred voices--

"...59. By holding the balance between peace and war gently in our hands, we will become the one's the world turns to in a crisis. War will never be eliminated, but it can be used only when necessary. We will know how to assess 'necessary': We will be the guardians.
"60. Be patient; soon we will have our opportunity to change the world."
Alexander stepped to the microphone. "Andy, please come forward for our Invocation, followed by dinner."

From that conference on, they steadily received requests for more than one hundred to attend. They developed a criteria that selected those most likely to net results soon, and placed the balance on top of the list for the next year.

The last night of the 1989 Conference, they presented the 'UJ2 Copper Pin' to George.

He was eighty-eight. Then they handed pins out to all attenders. The following week, the staff sent pins to all previous attenders. That night was the last retreat for George, he died the next December.

After George passed away, they upgraded microphones, speakers, and podiums. Over the years, they began using PowerPoint presentations, movies, slide projectors, videos, screens, electronic white boards, computers and HDTV monitors. While the technology advanced, the core material remained unchanged. The lecture was of the heart and soul of what they presented; that the sixty must be deeply imbedded in the brain remained unchanged. What George brought forth was carefully preserved. His grandson's held it as preciously and tenderly as their Grandfather had held baby rabbits on the deck to show them off in their youth.

Alexander stood and his shoulders slumped as he looked out the window into his pitch-black backyard while his knuckles turned white from tightly gripping the phone receiver. This three-minute phone call was certainly one he had expected, just not this soon.

"Alexander, if you want to see your mother one final time, you better get down here now!" Penny's voice cracked under the strain of calling her brother-in-law. She had carried the burden of doctor's appointments, ever-changing medications, and frequent lab tests. She shared the news among the family, but saw Rebecca's decline first hand.

"I thought they were giving her six months, and that was only--when?"

"A month ago. It's progressed quickly. Let me know your flight plans."

He hung up the phone while Jacqueline stood next to Alexander. Her armed were clinched and fists tight, afraid of the answer to the question she had to ask, "Do you want me to go with you?"

"If you would like, Jacqueline. But Mom is in a coma." They had planned to come down in a month to get things started for the annual summer retreat. Jacqueline sensed he wanted to make this trip alone. Relieved, she said, "I think I'll wait."

It was a Sunday night, but they couldn't find a flight out of Washington until early Tuesday.

As it turned out, Rebecca passed away the day Alexander arrived and saw her in the convalescent hospital. She had not been the same since George died in December of 1989, followed a month later by Thomas. Thomas's body had been dead since he had been assaulted. He hid his frustrations well and accepted his lot in life, not wanting to be a bother to his wife, children, or the balance of his family. He'd write comments on a notepad, but if he desired to write something more extensive, nobody knew. The man who spoke for a living was quiet; the man who marched for great causes, stilled after over twenty years in a wheelchair.

Rebecca was unresponsive when Alexander last saw her. There was a musty, sour odor to the room. It was clean, but the light through the shades gave everything a sepia tone. Her sheets looked like heavy, vintage velour. He hardly recognized her. She shuddered as she breathed. Her brow furrowed, her hair gone to gray and balding. Gone was the beautiful, vibrant woman he had always known; left was a shell, worn beyond recognition, awaiting the heart to give up. He stood at her side, holding her limp hand, and prayed.

Melbourne had followed three years later. Breast cancer--too far along when it was caught; too late to help with anything but the pain. She invested her energy in her new husband, her children, their spouses, and her grandchildren. She helped out each year with the annual retreat, as did every family member.

Alexander died of natural causes quietly in his sleep in June of 2016, at 76. He had retired from the State Department sixteen years earlier and devoted full time since to his family's pursuit. The whole family came to Alexander's memorial service at their church; interment was private. In a long row, away from the cabins, retreat center and house, the family rested: George, Rebecca, Abraham, Melbourne, and Thomas. A spot for Penny. The ground torn up to receive Alexander today. A spot for Jacqueline and room for one more. That place had been offered to Meadow, but she hadn't yet decided if that was where she wished to be buried.

Now it was up to the grandsons to carry it forward on their own.

Three Republicans had already announced their candidacy for the Idaho Governorship, when Meadow threw her hat into the ring. She had worked all over Idaho as the Governor's speech writer, senior advisor, legislative assistant, and confidante. She and Benjamin had twisted and tugged at the decision between them from every angle. They mapped the 'pro and cons' in great detail. Having not run for office before turned out to be a great asset--she had all the experience she needed, but little baggage clung to her. She was well-respected among her colleagues, but less known by the public. She was in the middle of the pack in a four-person race, when the Democrat party threw the Governorship at Meadow's feet.

When she had announced her candidacy for the Republican primary, she used slogans such as 'Let Meadow Lead The Way' with images depicting Sacagawea facing the future with her son, Jean Baptiste Charbonneau, on her back--right off the dollar coin. Instead of concentrating on their own primary, the Democrats accused her of pandering to ancient history and of trying to steal an Indian heritage that did not belong to her. It propelled her above her fellow Republicans.

She ignored it all and focused on the issues most basic to Idaho voters. When she won the Republican nomination, the Democrats made her out to be a cheap imitation of a national hero, a liar, and a hanger-on. She persevered in ignoring it all, until her Democrat rival basically told her to "put up or shut up" during a nationally televised debate.

"Fine," she said while rolling up her sleeve. "Take my

blood and match it to Sacagawea. We will see who is lying and who has been slinging mud." Her campaign manager, having seen this coming through comments on social media, had the foresight to have a nurse standing by in uniform complete with American Red Cross badges, who drew blood and handed the vials to the Ada County, Idaho Chief Medical Examiner--all on live television. It was instantly plastered everywhere.

The Democrats were stunned. They had never considered she actually could be a descendent of the great American Indian pioneer. "How will they ever find Sacagawea's DNA?" they cried. Soon dozens of libraries, museums, and private collectors claimed they could help. The Republicans put pressure on The Smithsonian Institution to provide what they considered the best source--snippets of her hair that had been received with artifacts sent to President Thomas Jefferson.

During the whole time the Democrats were distracted, Meadow focused clearly, coherently on key local issues. Her only comment about the whole affair came after the blood results showed conclusively her bloodline. "Now that it is known that I have been telling the truth about my descendency, and that the Democrats have made repeated false accusations, they are saying, 'Well, it really doesn't matter!' I have one question in response, 'If it really doesn't matter, why did YOU bring it up?'"

The Idaho voters, always open to change and forever pioneers, elected the first Native American Governor in a landslide.

A few days after Thanksgiving in 2016, the Governor sat in pajamas, barefoot in her first floor sitting room, next to her bedroom in the 7,370-square-foot mansion she temporarily called home. She was 76 years old, but most people thought she was in her early sixties. Her kitten, Sugar Bear, slept on her lap.

The modern, elegant, red-tile roof and beige stucco exterior were not to her tastes, but she loved the location, the arched windows, and dramatic 360-degree vista. It had been built on a hillock with a commanding view, now covered in lush Kentucky bluegrass. The balance of the house was used for meetings, events, and official functions--most of which she did not need to attend. Occasionally she made surprise visits to charity events that rented the facility. The living quarters were on the first floor, and most of it was closed off. The bedroom was much too large for a single lady with modest needs; so she had it split, to make a smaller bedroom with this adjoining sitting room. She had to admit that when she left office, she would miss the place.

She was alone tonight, drinking a Coeur d'Alene Cellars Chardonnay and reflecting on three things in particular she would miss about this room--the 30-by-50 foot American flag she could hear snapping in the breeze day and night; the screams and laughter of the children playing at nearby Highlands Elementary School; and the beautiful view, especially in the evenings, of the Idaho Statehouse and downtown Boise.

Meadow had had dozens of conversations with the President-elect over the last three months of 2016. There had been interviews with his transition staff and with the FBI, who searched under every rock to find dirt on Meadow. Benjamin served as her advisor and confidante as she made the most important decision of her life. She had turned over reams of records, speeches, policy memos, and tax returns. Tonight she was expecting the call for which she had been waiting. She had kept it secret, except for her immediate staff. She had already inquired about their interest in moving to Washington to be on her staff there.

Her private telephone rang and she placed her wine glass on the table to answer it, without awaking the kitten.

"Hello, this is Meadow."

"Meadow, how are you?"

"Good evening, Mr. President."

"Oh, let's not get ahead of ourselves! Mr. President-elect."

She laughed at his correction, given lightheartedly, "Okay, Mr. President-elect."

"Well, you know as well as I do what we have been doing here. Everything checks out, as I knew it would, so I would like to move forward with your nomination. Of course,

it won't be official until after the Senate has a shot at you! Just have fun with it, and don't give them anything more than they ask for. We are all solidly behind you. You'll do a great job!"

"That is excellent news, Sir."

"So, one last chance to back out! What do you say?"

"I am pleased and honored to accept your offer to be nominated for Secretary of State!"

They had small talk about other nominations. One alumni member was being appointed to the Joint Chiefs of Staff. She also followed up on a recommendation she had made--Ulysses Cash becoming an Undersecretary of Defense.

As she hung up the telephone, the kitten awoke, yawned, and shook her head. Meadow petted her and placed her on the couch.

The ringing telephone awoke Benjamin from a deep sleep. He reached over to the alarm before realizing the noise was the phone, then scooted his hand over to the receiver. His mouth was bone dry from sleeping with it open. He let it ring one more time while he scrunched his mouth to collect saliva and swallowed to coat this throat. *"Hell-o,"* his voiced cracked.

"60. Be patient; soon we will have our opportunity to change the world."

Recognizing Meadows voice, Benjamin smiled.

--The End—